THE LONELY ONES

Håkan Nesser is one of Sweden's most popular crime writers, receiving numerous awards for his novels featuring Inspector Van Veeteren, including the European Crime Fiction Star Award (Ripper Award), the Swedish Crime Writers' Academy Prize (three times) and Scandinavia's Glass Key Award. His Van Veeteren series is published in over twenty-five countries and has sold over 15 million copies worldwide. In addition to the popular Van Veeteren series, his other books include the psychological thriller *The Living and the Dead in Winsford* and the Barbarotti series. Håkan Nesser lives in Gotland with his wife, and visits the UK regularly.

HÅKAN NESSER

THE LONELY ONES

Translated from the Swedish by
Sarah Death

MANTLE

First published in the UK 2021 by Mantle
an imprint of Pan Macmillan
The Smithson, 6 Briset Street, London EC1M 5NR
EU representative: Macmillan Publishers Ireland Ltd, 1st Floor, The Liffey Trust Centre,
117–126 Sheriff Street Upper, Dublin 1, D01 YC43
Associated companies throughout the world
www.panmacmillan.com

ISBN 978-1-5098-9229-7

Originally published in 2010 as *De ensamma*
by Albert Bonniers Förlag, Stockholm

'Aubade' extract from *The Complete Poems* © Philip Larkin, courtesy of Faber and Faber, Ltd.

1 3 5 7 9 8 6 4 2

A CIP catalogue record for this book is available from the British Library.

Typeset in Dante MT by Palimpsest Book Production Limited, Falkirk, Stirlingshire
Printed and bound by CPI Group (UK) Ltd, Croydon, CR0 4YY

MIX
Paper from
responsible sources
FSC® C116313

Visit **www.panmacmillan.com** to read more about all our books
and to buy them. You will also find features, author interviews and
news of any author events, and you can sign up for e-newsletters
so that you're always first to hear about our new releases.

The town of Kymlinge and its environs do not exist on the map and certain military and academic circumstances have been changed to fulfil the requirements of decency. That aside, this book is in many other respects a truthful story.

'Can we speak of a human being's innermost core?' asked Regener. 'Is there any point?'

'I don't know,' replied Marr. 'Perhaps.'

Erik Steinbeck, *The Gardener's Horizons*

Prologue, September 1958

He awoke to the sound of voices arguing.

It wasn't Mother or Father. They never argued. You don't get arguments in the Holy Family, do you now? Father would say and laugh in that serious way that left you not knowing if he was joking or really meant it.

It wasn't Vivianne arguing, either, or any other living person. No, the voices were inside his own head.

Do it, said one. It would serve them right. They're not fair on you.

Don't do it, said the other. You'll get a thrashing. He's bound to notice.

It was odd that you could be woken by voices that didn't really exist, he thought. He looked at the clock. It was only half past six. Twenty minutes before he normally got up. That was odd, too. He hardly ever woke of his own accord. Mother generally had to wake him, and sometimes twice.

It was because it was a special morning, of course.

Yes, that was it. And because of what he'd been thinking last night. Before he went to sleep, that thing the voices were arguing about. He had no doubt dreamt about it, too – he must have, though he couldn't remember having done so. He lay there for a while and tried to get back into the same sleep, but it didn't work.

He sat up and swung his legs over the side of the bed. I'll do it, he thought. It's quite possible nothing at all will happen, but I'm so angry. It isn't fair and, when something isn't fair, you've got to do something about it, just as Father says.

Don't do it, that other voice told him. He's bound to notice, and how on earth will you be able to explain it then?

He won't notice, said the first voice. Don't be such a bloody coward. You'll regret it and feel ashamed that you were too scared, if you don't. It's such a little thing, after all.

Far from it, said the other voice. You'll regret it if you do it. And it's not a little thing.

But it wasn't so clearly audible any more, the voice that wanted to stop him. Not much more than a whisper, really. He got up and went over to the chair where his clothes were hanging. He put his hand in the pocket of the light-blue cardigan to check.

Yes, the box of pastilles was still there. As easy as pie, he thought. It would be as easy as pie, and the likelihood of him getting caught was less than a fart in a storm. That was another thing Father used to say. Other people said a needle in a haystack, but Father always said a fart in a storm.

The other voice tried to whimper something but it was so faint that he couldn't hear it any longer. No more than you could hear – well, yes, and he couldn't resist a giggle about it – a fart in a storm.

He went into the bathroom and realized his whole body was tingling. The decision felt like a warm ball inside his head.

ONE

1

Rickard Berglund was in many respects a rational young man, but he had an unusual aversion to Tuesdays.

This hadn't always been the case. The rationality had always been there, certainly, but in the closing years of the 1950s – before he had taken the step up from Stava School to junior secondary in Töreboda – Tuesdays had been just the opposite. They used to have a certain glow about them, at least in the late winter and the spring. The reason was a simple one, or a dual one really: Tuesday was the day his *Donald Duck & Co.* comic plopped into the mailbox, and it was also the day his mother served Shrove Tuesday buns in hot milk when he came home for his lunch break.

This combination, sitting down to a big bun, freshly dusted with icing sugar and just keeping afloat in a big bowl of milk with sugar and cinnamon, and with a still-unread comic – it seemed virtually untouched by human hand – placed to the left of his bowl on the red-and-white-checked oilcloth . . . well, the simple awareness of this impending delight often made him run the 400 metres between school and the white house in Fimbulgatan.

It was only later that Tuesdays assumed a different complexion. Above all in the years 1963 and 1964, when he had changed schools and grown out of Donald Duck, and his father Josef was in the sanatorium at Adolfshyttan before he died.

Because that was the day of the week he and his mum Ethel took the bus and went to visit him. The bus was blue, had worn seats and four times out of five it was driven by the vastly overweight father of Benny Persson – his tormentor at Stava School. It was dark by the time they got back to Fimbulgatan, he hadn't done his homework and his mother's eyes were red with the tears she had surreptitiously shed on the journey home.

But his father didn't die on a Tuesday, it happened in the night between a Friday and a Saturday. The funeral was held quietly, about a week later. It was November 1964 and it rained all day long.

Perhaps it wasn't even those sanatorium visits that lay at the heart of his antipathy to Tuesdays, but it was hard to know. From an early age Rickard Berglund had a very definite conception of how the various days of the week appeared. Their colours, for example, and their temperaments – even though it would take a number of years for him to understand what the word 'temperament' meant. So Saturdays were black but warm, Sundays red of course, just like on the calendar, Mondays were dark blue and safe . . . while Tuesdays always presented a hard surface, greyish-white, cold and dismissive, and working your way into them sometimes felt pretty much like biting down on the porcelain of a handbasin.

Then came Wednesday, a dark, dark blue, which especially towards evening often contained a promise of both prosperity and warmth, Thursday with its sky-blue sense of freedom and then white Friday – but the whiteness of Friday was of a completely different kind from the icy chill of Tuesdays.

He didn't know where he had got this clear image of the week's wheel – or how he could even know it was a wheel – and he had sometimes wondered if other people perceived it in the same way as he did. But he had never, at least not until his twentieth year, discussed the matter with anyone. Possibly for fear it would be interpreted as some defect in his own head.

The Tuesday phobia had persisted, at any event. In his years at upper secondary it was always with a sense of gloom that he awoke in his lodgings on Östra Järnvägsgatan on that day of the week, well aware that he could expect nothing good to come out of the next fifteen to sixteen hours. Neither in his school work nor in relations with his classmates. The nature of Tuesdays was hostile and as hard as enamel, and all you could do was try to get through it. Steel yourself and survive.

Perhaps in the long run it would prove useful in some way.

But today wasn't Tuesday. It was Monday. The date was 9 June 1969 and the railbus from Enköping stopped with an extended screech and a jolt at platform four at Uppsala Central. It was twenty past eleven in the morning. Rickard Berglund picked up his green canvas bag and stepped out into the sunshine on the platform.

He stood stock still for a few seconds, as if trying to preserve the moment and imprint it on his mind – this long-anticipated moment when his feet first touched the ground of this oft-serenaded seat of learning. The student duets, the folk songs, the male-voice choir. It was all so grand.

Although, as he stared down at those feet and their immediate surroundings, he could unfortunately not detect anything particularly special. They could have been any old feet on a platform in Herrljunga or Eslöv or some other godforsaken backwater in the kingdom of Sweden. He gave a reluctant sigh. Then he shrugged, joined the flow of people heading straight through the station building and took possession of the city.

At least that was how he expressed it to himself. *Here I am, taking possession of the city.* It was a way of keeping his anxiety at bay; thinking in italics meant taking charge of reality. He knew it was something he'd got from a book he'd read sometime in upper secondary, but he couldn't remember the title or the author's name. But anyway, it was a simple and effective trick: *thoughts in italics overcome the hostility of your surroundings.*

Out on the station forecourt he stopped again. He looked at the overblown and slightly garish sculpture in the centre of the paved circle and thought it was probably famous. There were so many famous things in a university town like Uppsala. Buildings, monuments, historic places, and in good time he would discover them all, calmly and purposefully; there was no hurry.

He walked on, straight ahead, crossed one big, busy street and a couple of smaller ones, and a few minutes later he was down by the river. The Fyris. He crossed it via a wooden bridge, saw the cathedral reaching into the sky from the heart of the old town, rising away to his right, nodded happily to himself and set off towards them.

Everyone needs a big plan and a little one. The big one is for how you intend getting through life, the other one is for getting you through the day.

This wasn't his own italicized phrase, unfortunately, but came from Dr Grundenius. Of all the teachers of varying degrees of oddity that Rickard Berglund had encountered in his three years at Vadsbog upper secondary, Grundenius was the one who had made the strongest impression on him. Domineering and unpredictable, he was sometimes downright moody, but always interesting to listen to. Often both surprising and keen-sighted in his observations and questions. Religion and philosophy. A reputation for being stingy with his marks, but Rickard had got a very good final grade in both subjects; it was hard to know if he had really been worth it. Hard to judge your own worth.

At any rate, he had a big plan and a little one. As he tramped along by the river towards the cathedral, its pointed spires appearing to brush the cloud-tufted sky, the big plan surfaced for inspection in his head. *Life*. Rickard Emmanuel Berglund's time on earth, as envisaged and calculated.

Theology.

That was the foundation stone. The land he had been set to till, or something along those lines. It wasn't a decision he had taken at any specific moment; it was more as if the conclusion had gradually seeped into him, inexorably and as if decreed by fate, over a long succession of years. Perhaps even with his mother's milk; because there was a God, he had known that fact all his conscious life, but with the death of his father Josef he had also realized it wasn't just a question of the safe and benevolent bedtime-prayer God of his childhood, but more complicated than that. Considerably more complicated.

Worth enquiring into.

Josef Berglund had been a pastor in the branch of the free church known as Aaron's Brothers. It was an early offshoot of the Missionary Society, but the collective prayers of its parishioners in their shepherd's last difficult days had not lessened his suffering one jot, nor that of his wife and son, and this was what had prompted Rickard Berglund's reappraisal of his less-than-nuanced image of God.

Why doesn't He hear our prayers?

Or if He does hear them, why doesn't He grant our humble wishes? Why does He let the faithful suffer?

On the rare occasions when he had raised these points with his mother Ethel, she had unerringly declared that it was not for mortals to have any conception of *His* deeper purposes and motivations. Not at all. For mortals' simplistic interpretations of good and evil were always doomed to come to naught in the broader perspective of the hereafter. Not even such an eventuality as the suffering and death of a simple, God-fearing free-church pastor are we able to weigh and evaluate with any certainty.

Something like that, and more in the same vein. But Rickard Berglund *wanted* to have some conception. He demanded comprehension, even as his mother insisted that such an ambition amounted to spiritual arrogance, and this was generally where their conversations ended. He couldn't challenge her on that point; if what was needed was a battle and a wrestling match with God, then that was an enterprise he would have to undertake on his own. Rickard and Our Lord? The meaning of his life?

He came up in front of the dark doorway. The open space before the cathedral was liberally bathed in sunshine, but the heavy doors into the sanctuary were carefully closed and lay in shadow. He decided not to go in – or, rather, had already decided on the train, when he was drawing up his plan for the day. It was too early; he wanted to study the exterior first, its majestic, slightly threatening architecture, and locate the Deanery that apparently housed the Faculty of Theology – it must be that big square building to the south of the cathedral . . . or was it west? He was already unsure of the points of the compass . . . and the much more unassuming church building beyond it must be Holy Trinity, of course. The 'peasants' church', as the local people once named it. Rickard Berglund had studied the most important landmarks of the city in the illustrated volume *Uppsala Then and Now*, which his mother had given him for his twentieth birthday in April. She was as keen on his plan for life as he was, and he sometimes started to wonder about the way these future prospects were accepted unopposed, as a matter of course. Was it really that simple? Oughtn't there to have been some alternatives available for him to discount, at least?

He went on past the Deanery, round the peasants' church and took a short flight of steps down to Drottninggatan. Up to his right he could see the imposing university library, and higher up on the ridge there were glimpses of the castle between the leafy trees. On the slope up to the castle the bird-cherry and lilac were still in bloom after a late and hesitant spring, and he thought how lovely it looked. He crossed Drottninggatan, continued along a lower road, Nedre Slottsgatan, and ended up at a cafe that looked out over a rectangular artificial pond. Mallards, a pair of swans and a few other indeterminate water fowl were floating around in languid, early-summer mood, or that was the impression they conveyed, anyway. You couldn't really tell, of course. He ordered a pot of coffee and a cheese-and-salami sandwich – this, too, was part of the plan, he remembered, and felt a sense of satisfaction at having completed these opening steps so simply and elegantly. He hadn't needed to ask the way even once, and he'd managed to incorporate almost everything he had set himself: the River Fyris. The cathedral and the Faculty of Theology. The old university building Gustavianum, and its successor. The university library, Carolina Rediviva, the castle from a distance, and a cafe with outdoor seating. *Incorporated.*

It was still only a quarter past twelve. He had a bite of sandwich, savoured his coffee and fished his call-up papers out of the inner pocket of his bag. He hesitated for a second before pulling out the thick book, too, and setting it gently on the table, once he had carefully checked the surface was clean. *Selected Works. Søren Kierkegaard.* He had read about forty pages on the train, and found himself engaging in the same reflective process as at the bus stop back home in Hova. He assumed that in Hova there was not a single person who had read Kierkegaard; in Uppsala how many could there be? A hundred? A thousand?

And the rest of them? Schopenhauer. Nietzsche. Kant. Not forgetting those new philosophers . . . Althusser, Marcuse and those other names that escaped him. It was a pleasing thought that in this city it could very well happen that someone at a neighbouring table in a cafe just like this one, or in the queue at the grocer's, would be familiar with both Hegel and Sartre.

Rickard Berglund had a canon, a reading list of all the authors he was intending to acquaint himself with over the coming year, before devoting himself to theology in earnest. Maybe he would even dip into Marx and Lenin, just to orientate himself a little. Nothing human should be alien to you, Grundenius had tried to impress on him . . . *nor a good deal that is inhuman, either.* If you don't study your opponent, you'll never be able to defeat him.

Rickard didn't believe in communism. America's war in Vietnam was no doubt unjust in many ways, but that wasn't the whole truth of it. Stalin had more lives on his conscience than Hitler, you only had to look in the history books; and Rickard had an almost physical aversion to protest marches. Frenzied crowds, slogans and simplistic demagoguery. It was the same with the hippie movement and pop music and all the long-haired freedom fighters. All this somehow wasn't his concern. Rickard Berglund hoped, or rather presumed, that he would find the antidote to this scourge of the age, in an environment that lived and breathed classical education and tradition. *Alma Mater, jerum jerum jerum, o quae mutatio rerum* . . . All in good time, he thought, all in good time I shall get a foothold in this town.

He read the curt command on his call-up papers for the hundredth time.

Location: ACNO. Army College for Non-Commissioned Officers. Dag Hammarskjölds väg 36, report to the duty guard.

Time: Monday 9 June 1969 between 13.00 and 21.00.

Duration of training: Fifteen months. Discharge date: 28 August 1970.

When Rickard Berglund tried to imagine all this time, all these days of totally unknown content and unknown conditions, something started to constrict his throat. If he didn't concentrate on fighting it down, he could very well give way – that was how it felt.

Perhaps he wouldn't be able to stick it?

Perhaps he would be sent home to Hova with an exemption warrant after a few weeks? How could you know if you'd be up to it?

Or would he be transferred to some entirely different posting with some entirely different regiment somewhere else in the country? That would be even more ignominious. It said in the accompanying information he'd received that this could happen. This was the fate that awaited 10–15 per cent of those who'd been selected for General Staff training. What if he ended up in Boden? Or Karlsborg? Uppsala had been his winning ticket in the enlistment lottery, and it was vital not to squander it . . . He sighed, and realized these were just the kind of sombre strains he had promised himself not to heed.

Because his plan was firmly in place. Fifteen months' military service at the Staff and Liaison College, then four years studying theology, maybe five, he'd have to see how it went. Then ordination and out into Sweden to preach the Word.

Simply that.

And if you'd been able to get through eleven months at Lapidus Concrete Co. Ltd, you could probably cope with most things. It was his uncle Torsten who had arranged the job for him in the reinforcing-steel section, starting three days after his university matriculation exams, and you could say what you liked about education levels in the rest of Hova-Gullspång, but he was certainly the only one who read Hjalmar Bergman and Bunyan in the coffee breaks at Lapidus.

It had earnt him a jibe or two, but that was all in the past now. He had left the concrete industry and his home on Fimbulgatan behind him. And the boyhood bedroom that had been his for as long as he could remember. His mother Ethel had done her best to fight back her tears in the kitchen that morning but hadn't really succeeded.

You're leaving me alone, she had sobbed. But that's how it

has to be, and do remember there's always a way back to home's door.

This was something she had thought out in advance, of course, and it had sounded like an old motto on an embroidered wall hanging above a rib-backed settee. She had started talking like that more and more, after the pastor's death, and deep inside he felt ashamed of the feeling of freedom that bubbled up in him as soon as he was out of the door.

A feeling of freedom when you were about to embark on your military service? That definitely wasn't something you could say out loud, but it was exactly the sensation he was experiencing. Life started in earnest today, that was the truth. He had been looking forward to this date all spring, and as he sat watching those unfamiliar ducks and unfamiliar swans, and those unfamiliar people strolling along the footpath, he thought that he – whatever happened in his life, however his big plan turned out – would never forget this moment. Cafe Fågelsången in Uppsala in the middle of the day on 9 June 1969. It occurred to him that he could return to this spot on this date every year, just to sit and philosophize a little, think back and think forward and—

But his train of thought was abruptly cut off by a shadow falling across the table, and its owner announcing his presence with a discreet cough.

'Kierkegaard, eh? Not bad.'

Rickard Berglund looked up. A tall young man in jeans, T-shirt and an open flannel shirt stood there watching him. A dark, uneven fringe of hair flopping over half his face, and a broad smile. He gestured to the empty chair by the wall.

'Sorry. But there are a few things I can't stop myself commenting on. OK if I sit down?'

Rickard nodded and put away his call-up letter.

'I saw that, too.'

'What? My call-up . . .?'

'Exactly. And I'm guessing you're not on your way to S1?'

He pulled out the chair and sat down, crossing one leg over the other before he took a packet of cigarettes out of his breast pocket.

'Want one?'

'No, thanks. I don't smoke.'

'Sensible.'

Rickard ventured a smile. 'What made you guess I wouldn't be going to S1.'

His new acquaintance lit a cigarette with a Zippo lighter and blew out a cloud of smoke. 'You don't look like a cable monkey.'

'Cable monkey?'

'That's what they call them. The seventh company of S1. Cable layers. Not many Nobel Prize-winners there. No, I'm assuming you're in for ACNO or Gen Staff?'

'Gen Staff,' said Rickard, and swallowed.

'Same here. Oh, sorry, I haven't introduced myself. Tomas Winckler.'

He held out his hand across the table and Rickard took it.

'Rickard Berglund.'

'Good to meet you. I hope we end up together. I thrive on a bit of educated company.'

He indicated the book and Rickard felt himself blush.

'So you . . . I mean, are you reporting for military service today as well?'

Tomas Winckler nodded. 'Sure am. We can trot along there together if you like. Or maybe you've other plans?'

Rickard nodded and shook his head in a single, confused movement. A waitress came up and put a cup of coffee and a cinnamon bun in front of Tomas Winckler. He stubbed out his cigarette and laughed.

'I saw you through the window when I was ordering,' he explained. 'And your book and call-up paper. And since they don't read Danish philosophers in the seventh, I assumed we might well end up as comrades in arms. Where are you from? Not Uppsala, I take it?'

'No.'

As ever, Rickard found it hard to admit he'd lived all his life in Hova, but he realized this was no time for easily uncovered lies. 'Hova, if you know where that is. And Mariestad. I was at upper secondary in Mariestad.'

Tomas Winckler nodded. 'I'd have guessed as much from your accent. And where would you place me in our long, thin country?'

Rickard considered this. 'Somewhere up north?'

'Correct.'

'But not way, way up?'

'Depends how you look at it.'

'Sundsvall?'

'Bloody hell. Now I'm impressed. There I am, trying out my best standard Swedish, and you pin me down to exactly the right spot. Bloody hell, like I said.'

Rickard laughed and gave an apologetic shrug.

'Just luck,' he assured him. 'Have you been to Uppsala before?'

'A few times. My family has a flat here in town. And you?'

'No,' Rickard admitted. 'I set foot here for the very first time today in fact. But I expect I shall stay on for the university . . . afterwards. It's a good place, isn't it?'

17

'It's brilliant,' confirmed Tomas Winckler, pushing his fringe out of his eyes. 'At least it is as long as you're still under thirty. Which we definitely are. What are you hoping to study?'

'Haven't decided.'

'Is that right? Well, nor have I, really. But I'm sure I'll be here for a good few more years.'

My God, thought Rickard with a sudden flash of insight. Here I am, chatting to someone I shall know for the rest of my life. Though I barely say 'Hi' to my schoolmates any more, only a year after we finished.

Tomas Winckler picked up the book and studied the blurb on the back. 'I've only read excerpts from his work,' he declared, 'but he's pretty damn sharp, this Dane.'

'I've just started it,' admitted Rickard. 'What are you reading at the moment?'

Tomas Winckler avoided the question. He leant back in his seat instead, re-lighting his half-smoked cigarette. 'If I asked you to describe yourself in just one sentence,' he said, 'what would you say?'

'One sentence?'

'Yes.'

Rickard Berglund thought for a second. 'I'm a young man with an aversion to Tuesdays,' he said.

Tomas Winckler gave him a look of surprise. And they both burst out laughing.

2

Damn dog, thought Elis Bengtsson.

Then he cupped his hands to his mouth like a megaphone and shouted at the top of his voice:

'Luther!'

He repeated the operation. To all four points of the compass.

Then he sat down on a tree stump and waited. No point wandering about looking for that wretched cur, he thought. Better to sit still and let the cur do the looking.

He had learnt that over the years. Dogs have a sharper sense of smell than humans and, if they want to, they can always find their way back to their master.

Luther was his ninth dog, no more and no less, and he had named them all after famous people: Galileo, Napoleon, Madame Curie, Stalin, Voltaire, Dr Crippen, Nebuchadnezzar and all-round champion sportsman Putte Kock.

And now Luther. Four years old, half German pointer, half scent hound and normally a very intelligent creature. But he had clearly picked up a trail, even though Elis Bengtsson had never used him for hunting. Sometimes even the best training didn't work, that was the plain fact of the matter.

He had run off somewhere in the boggy bit at Alkärret and now, half an hour later, up on the crag at Gåsaklinten where they usually stopped for a breather and a little treat, there was still no sign of him.

Elis Bengtsson checked his watch. Five to two. He'd promised to be home by half past two to drive Märta to the health centre.

Damn woman, he thought. Why couldn't she take the car herself?

But, on second thoughts, it would be much safer for her not to get behind the wheel. She'd passed her test back in 1955, but hadn't driven any kind of motor vehicle since 1969, when she backed into a litter bin in Nora torg square in Kymlinge town centre. Elis himself had been between the bin and the rear bumper until the very last instant and he'd made sure she didn't forget it in a hurry.

For his own part, he had fifty-seven years behind him without a single point on his licence and, health permitting, he planned to carry on driving until his own funeral.

There was no reason to fear that his own health wouldn't permit it, either; Märta was the one with multiple ailments, not him. Osteoporosis, angina, dizzy spells and Lord knows what else. He had already forgotten what today's appointment at the doctor's was about. If he'd ever known, that was.

He sighed, hauled himself up from the tree stump and tried to focus. He went a little way up the slope before he called out again.

'Luther!'

Round the four points of the compass again, that was the plan, but he had only reached the second when he heard barking from down in Gåsaklyftan.

He called in that direction once more, and again received an answer.

Gåsaklyftan, he thought. What the hell is going on?

*

Talking about it afterwards – with Märta, with nosy, one-legged Olle Märdback from the house next door and with the police – he was keen to claim he'd had a premonition.

He said that as soon as he'd heard Luther barking the first time, he'd realized what was waiting for him down at the bottom of the sheer drop.

Gåsaklyftan – Goose Gorge. He wasn't even sure it was really called that, but it was the name they'd given it last time. Goose Hill and Goose Drop were well-established local names, but Goose Gorge? He didn't know.

Last time. How many years ago was it? 1975.

Thirty-five years, in other words. A generation, you might say.

But he probably hadn't had a premonition, not really. It wasn't until he was up on the hill at the edge of the drop, staring down at Luther and at the body lying there – both of them a good twenty-five metres below him – that the previous experience resurfaced.

But once it did, Elis Bengtsson's mind was in a whirl. I must be dreaming, he thought. It's just not possible for the same thing to happen again.

He felt suddenly light-headed, and it was a good job there was a little birch sapling growing right on the edge, because if Elis Bengtsson hadn't been able to grab hold of that, he could easily have ended his days in Gåsaklyftan, too.

'What did you say?'

'I said, you've got to ring the police. There's a dead body in Gåsaklyftan.'

'Another one?' said Märta.

'Another one,' said Elis. 'But the other time was thirty-five years ago.'

'Oh my God,' said Märta.

'Ring the police and get them out here,' said Elis. 'And hurry up. Luther and I will stay here and stand guard. You'll have to forget the medical centre for today.'

'But, Elis, my appointment's tomorrow. It's Sunday today.'

'Sunday?'

'Yes.'

'Well, it doesn't bloody matter what day it is. Do as I say, for once, and ring the police.'

'Yes, yes,' said Märta. 'But tell me one thing: if it's so urgent, why didn't you ring the police yourself?'

'Because I've only got this mobile phone,' said Elis angrily. 'You can't talk to the police on a mobile phone.'

'Oh. I see,' said Märta, and then he cut her off.

Women, he thought.

'Shut up, Luther!' he shouted the next moment. 'I'm coming down.'

And, for whatever reason, the dog stopped barking.

3

Once she had covered the first twenty kilometres on the E18 between Örebro and Karlstad, Gunilla Rysth pulled into a parking area and sat there behind the wheel for a long time. It was absolutely necessary.

If she had gone on, it would have ended in disaster; it simply wasn't possible to drive and be convulsed with tears at the same time.

Not unless you wanted to crash the car and kill yourself, and she didn't actually want to go that far.

In spite of everything.

Though until she found this little lay-by – just short of Kristinehamn, it was – she had been toying with the thought, she couldn't deny it. But only toying, in some sort of desperate effort to escape her conscience and the dreadful sense of guilt that comes from crushing another human being.

For Lennart had been crushed – there was no other way of describing it. In the last five minutes of their conversation he hadn't uttered a word, just sat there looking at her with an expression in his eyes that put her in mind of a dying animal. An animal she had just shot, which, as its life bled into the ground, stared at its executioner with an unspoken *Why?* in its gaze.

That was the way he'd looked, wasn't it? she thought. Yes, exactly like that.

Why? What harm have I done you?

I love you, you know that. We love each other. We two were going to live together.

Just over four years. They had been together for almost exactly fifty months; for the first twenty – or was it thirty? – he had given her a rose to mark each month. They had started in the second year of upper secondary, so that was one-fifth of her life, and one-fifth of his.

He was the first one she had kissed, the first one she had been to bed with. But not the only one. And she was the first and only he had kissed and loved. There was no doubt about that. No doubt at all.

He's going to kill himself.

That was the thought thudding away beneath all those tears. He's not going to get through this.

He'll opt for death.

And there she sat in the parking place outside Kristinehamn, crying and crying.

She'd been putting off the decision for three months.

Ever since Easter. That was when she'd met Tomas, at that fateful choir camp in Östersund. Blithely unsuspecting, she had gone up there with her friend Kristina, whom she'd known since childhood. By the evening of the second day Tomas had kissed her and said they had no choice. They were made for each other. It was written in stone and he had never been as sure of anything in all his life.

It was like some cheesy story. If she'd come across it in *Women's Weekly* or *Teen Dreams*, instead of in real life, she would have snorted with derision, turned the page and not read another line.

The following night they'd broken into a summer cottage nearby and made love for four hours.

What's happening to me? she'd thought.

What the hell is happening?

That was just like a teen magazine, too. I'm behaving like a total featherbrain, she'd told herself. An infatuated bimbo. In the first days after getting back from the camp, she hoped it would prove to be just a fling with a charming bastard. Hoped he wouldn't call, and she'd be able to bury what had happened deep in her heart and go back to Lennart. Safety and Lennart. Friday-evening beer and pizza at The Stork with the rest of the gang. Kids and a nice little property in Sommarvägen in three years' time.

But she only had a couple of days' grace. He rang on the third evening, just as he'd said he would. She lay in bed in her pathetic rented room and they talked half the night; a romantic, whispering rain pattered its constant accompaniment on the windowpanes and sill, and by the time she put down the receiver in the light of the early dawn, she knew. Goodbye, Lennart Martinsson, she thought. Thanks for the four years.

Then she had put it off and put it off, until today. How cowardly can anyone be? How cruel? How much hurt can they inflict on another person?

She emerged from the parking area twenty minutes later. The well of tears was not bottomless after all, but although her weeping had abated, she felt no better. Not a bit.

Because this wasn't only about Lennart. It was about life, and all sorts of other people. Her parents: her father the staff sergeant, and her mother the office clerk. Her sister. Lennart's family: her future father-in-law the major, and her future mother-in-law the handicraft teacher. She and Lennart were engaged and the expectation was that they would shortly be married. Get a house, have children and do all the other usual things; become proper grown-ups, in other words. Martin, Kristina, Sigge and Naomi – everybody they knew was counting on it all happening. Lennart Martinsson and Gunilla Rysth had been . . . what was the phrase? Rock-solid.

What would they say? Why hadn't she come out with it sooner? Why wait until the very last second before she went to Uppsala to visit Birgitta? And then just drive off without sorting out the mess she'd created.

Was there somebody else?

No, she'd said dismissively. Of course there wasn't. What did he think? It was just that it wasn't working any more; there was no one else involved. She had to follow her heart.

Only Birgitta knew about it. Knew about the choir camp and knew about Tomas. She'd said the shit was bound to splash her, too, when it hit the fan, but she didn't care. She'd already been studying in Uppsala for a year and had developed a broader outlook on life. And when people rang her from home she'd say yes, Gunilla was staying with her, in her student room in Rackarberget, sleeping on a mattress on the floor. And yes, she'd just found out how things stood with Lennart. They were both very sad about it. But that was life, feelings weren't always something you could control, time's a great healer . . . blah-blah-blah.

She realized thinking about Birgitta helped a bit, and perhaps it really was the case, she noted in slight surprise, that the further she went from Karlstad, and the closer she got to Uppsala, the easier it felt to be alive. Between Örebro and Arboga she even switched on the car radio, but felt suddenly ashamed of her own frivolity and the tears started again.

Swimming, perhaps drowning, in a sea of emotions: that was an expression she'd come across somewhere and it was a pretty fair description of the state she was in. But she wasn't planning to drown. The hell I will, she told herself, and blew her nose fiercely on the last paper tissue in the packet. She was going to start living, wasn't she, not stop?

It seemed a safe bet, at any event, that it would be some time before she made the trip in the other direction. Months, or even years, if it was up to her. Staff sergeant and office clerk and sister could say what they liked.

At least I have my Sigurd, she thought when she stopped to fill up in Hummelsta. That was his name – the Volkswagen she had bought from Lennart's cousin last summer. Red and a bit the worse for wear, with more than 100,000 kilometres on the clock. But as reliable as a grandfather clock, touch wood.

There actually was a mattress waiting on the floor in Birgitta Enander's student room, but only for a few nights. From 1 July, on Tuesday, something completely different lay ahead. Gunilla hardly dared think the thought, but it wasn't easy to keep at bay: a two-room flat on Sibyllegatan in Luthagen. She had found the district and the street on a map in the library in Karlstad, but it hadn't given her any clear picture of the surroundings. Naturally not.

The flat belonged to an aunt of Tomas's but seemed to be a sort of general family perk. When it was clear that Tomas would be doing his military service in Uppsala, it went without saying that he was offered the chance to rent it. Because wasn't he going to stay on afterwards and study? Of course, and family always came first. The aunt herself lived in Spain all year round; Sibyllegatan was just an insurance policy in case her third marriage hit the rocks.

That was how Tomas put it, anyway. Gunilla had seen pictures of the flat; he'd sent her a set of photos and whenever she looked at them, or even just thought of them, she could feel her body tingle. Once she got so turned on that she had to find relief in masturbating in the shower. She was going to live there with Tomas! They had met three times altogether (apart from the days in Östersund; once in a borrowed room in Sundsvall, and once – when they'd met halfway – at a motorway hotel outside Västerås), and now they were going to live together. She and Lennart had never moved in together in the four years of their relationship.

If I'd told Mum she would have had a fainting fit, thought Gunilla. She didn't care to imagine what her father would have said and done, and she knew this was her best means of self-preservation. Whoever she told the truth to, or asked for advice, they would have told her she was out of her mind. Her sister. All her friends. Everyone.

So don't think about it. Silence is golden. Breaking it off was one thing. But breaking it off and moving in with another guy was simply unthinkable. They would have condemned her actions.

They were *going to condemn her actions*.

Everyone except Birgitta. I'm not saying you're doing the right thing, she'd told her. But I'm pretty sure I'd have done the same. If that's any comfort.

And then she'd roared with laughter in that typical way of hers.

★

The key was in a plastic bag under her bike saddle, just as they'd arranged. Birgitta was working all summer in a restaurant outside town and wouldn't be home until after nine.

It was now two-thirty. Gunilla dragged her heavy luggage upstairs, one bag at a time, and unlocked the front door of the student flat. Five rooms and a shared kitchen, Birgitta had explained, but over the summer it's just me and Jukka there.

Perhaps Jukka had a job to go to, as well. He wasn't home anyway, and Gunilla was left to look round in peace. Not only Birgitta's room, but also the shared areas. Kitchen, WC and bathroom. It looked pretty untidy, despite three-fifths of the tenants not being in residence, and she was struck again by how fortunate she was to be moving into a flat of her own with the prince of her dreams before the start of her very first term. She remembered Birgitta had had to take a room with a family for the first few months and was over the moon when she got a flat share in the student quarter at Rackarberget.

Prince of her dreams? Wherever had that come from? It had an ironic undertone that Gunilla didn't like the sound of. The prince of your dreams inevitably proved a fraud when you got to the heart of the matter, and Tomas Winckler wasn't a fraud.

She would have found it hard to explain to anyone else how she could be so completely sure about that, but then she didn't plan to try. To repeat: silence is golden.

I could marry him, she thought. Just like that, he'd only have to ask.

Jesus Christ, she thought immediately. Calm down, don't be such an idiot, and don't forget your pills! You're twenty years old; weren't you going to get that degree first?

She opened the fridge door and decided she needed to get some shopping in. There were a shelf and a section in the door marked with Birgitta's name, but all the fridge had to offer was a litre of milk, a tube of salted cod roe and three yellow onions. Birgitta had told her she got meals at the restaurant, breakfast, lunch and dinner, but if Gunilla was ravenous, all she had to do was go to the shops and stock up. There was no need for either of them to worry about what Jukka ate.

On the 'Birgitta' shelf in the cupboard she found a box of cornflakes, a packet of crispbread and a bottle of ketchup. Oh well, Gunilla thought, I'm only going to be here for three days. By Saturday I shall have a kitchen of my own, and it won't look like this one.

She checked her watch. It was three hours until she would be meeting Tomas on Nybron bridge. Her body sang at the thought of him, but she stuck firmly to her resolve to go food shopping rather than taking another shower.

She was ten minutes early. She'd been worried about not finding the way, but it was just as he'd said. The bridge really was right in the middle of town.

It was a warm evening but the streets were pretty quiet. He had told her it would be like that. Before the students came back at the end of August, Uppsala was a typical example of small-town Sweden, dozing away the summer. Attractively green, to be sure, especially west of the river, but the majority of its population was elsewhere.

She didn't mind that. Quite the opposite; slowly growing into the place, absorbing all those new impressions for a couple of months before getting down to serious work in the English department – wherever it was – what could be better than that?

Well, maybe Tomas having as much free time as she did, but you couldn't have everything. He was doing his military service over at a place they called Polackbacken, and would be tied up with that until next autumn, but he was off most evenings. Saturdays and Sundays, too, and in mid-July – that was only two weeks away – he had a week's so-called harvest leave.

She leant her elbows on the stone balustrade of the bridge and looked down to watch the turbid water swirling rapidly past. My life, she thought, my life can't get any better than it is right now.

And how a thought like that could come into her mind so soon after she had wept uncontrollably at her own wretchedness in a Värmland car park was a matter she decided not to examine too closely.

Certainly not right now, because she spotted him striding towards her from under the big trees on the west side of the river.

He had a bunch of flowers in one hand, and a bottle of wine in the other, and half an hour later they were on a rug behind a protective screen of bushes on the slope at the base of the castle. She laughed out loud when he told her he had pinched it from a military store and laid it out ready on his way down to Nybron. He hoped she wouldn't find it too itchy.

4

The distance between the house and the flat was exactly 1,100 metres, but only if you took the direct route.

Eva Backman shunned the direct route. She made a detour that took her round the whole town, more or less: Oktober Park, straight through Rocksta and the woods, past the new fire station, past the cemetery, the sports ground and Hessle school, and as she came in through the front door, she realized it had taken her an hour and a half.

That was roughly what she needed, she'd come to understand. The detached house in Haga, where she'd lived with Ville and their three boys for fourteen years, and the flat on the top floor of one of the newly built blocks in Pampas were two different worlds. Eleven hundred metres, a fifteen-minute walk, it was way too short. She needed some kind of transitional space, and that was why she went the long way round on Sundays.

But only every other time. Only in this direction. On the Sundays when she went the other way – from life as a single person to being a mother of three – no such transition was needed, for whatever reason.

She also wondered whether this arrangement was as brilliant as she had first thought. It was two years since the divorce, eighteen months since she moved into Grimsgatan.

All five people involved had thought it an excellent solution, especially the boys, who hadn't had to move or be subjected to too much upheaval. They had a dad one week, and a mum the next. Changeover on Sunday, and variety is the spice of life.

Well, it wouldn't go on forever, Eva Backman was in the habit of consoling herself. Jörgen would be twenty in January; in two or three years he and Kalle would both have flown the nest, so they could sell the house and get their finances on a better footing.

A five-year waiting room, she thought, registering that the fridge was as empty as when she left it, a week before. Is this any way to be living, with the menopause just around the corner?

She was forty-six. What was the alternative? Find a new man? And if so, how? How the hell would she set about it?

Go back to Ville?

Not on your life, she thought. She took a cup of coffee with her and went out to sit on the balcony. She knew he would leap at the chance, if she so much as hinted at it. That was almost the worst thing. He wanted her back; he had stopped saying it out loud every time they met, but she could see it in him. It was that sort of feeble, pleading look he had – he sounded that way on the phone, too, and she was finding it harder and harder to bear. Pull yourself together! She wanted to say. Do something – find yourself another woman at least, there must be loads of them in the sports club, sighing for you. But for you and me it's all over, *finito*.

Yes, anything at all but getting back into the old rut. Though why she was sitting in the afternoon sun on the balcony of her own property and thinking about her former husband was a valid question, of course. Weren't the ninety minutes of transition enough?

Fuck it, thought Eva Backman. Life sucks.

But as she sat in front of her laptop paying bills, she thought back to the previous evening. That was considerably more pleasant.

She had been for dinner at Barbarotti and Marianne's, at Villa Pickford. It wasn't the first time, far from it, but it was the first time there had been ten of them round the table.

Three adults, seven teenagers. Marianne had said that this must surely be absolutely unique, and perhaps she was right. Three typical products of the 1960s, who'd had kids with three others of the same vintage but not currently present, she had pointed out, spurring on Barbarotti to propose a toast.

Sweden's youth is its future!

He'd told them that was the motto on the medals you were awarded for sports at school in his day. Nobody had believed him. He had even left the table to go and rummage in drawers and shoeboxes so he could prove it to them, but returned empty-handed. He'd claimed his first wife must have purloined his medal stash and taken it to be melted down for sordid financial gain. They would have made her a very decent profit, if he did say so himself. But in a quick informal survey of those round the table, he lost the credibility match 9–1.

That was the first time Jörgen, Kalle and Viktor had spent time with Gunnar and Marianne's children, and she'd felt a few butterflies in her stomach as they got into the car for the drive out to Kymlingenäs.

You're nervous, Mum, I can tell, Kalle had said. You don't

need to be, you know, we can come up with the goods when we have to.

And he was right. There hadn't even been that much effort required; there were moments round the big table when she'd had to dab at the corner of her eye. Why did life so seldom look like this? A big group of people eating together round a table. Kids and parents. Conversation and laughter. Why did it have to be so bloody difficult? Why have we forgotten the time-honoured social function of sharing meals in this country?

Or maybe it was the long intervals – the very fact that it happened so rarely – that made it so special? Would she tire of it if it happened every day?

She interrupted her own train of thought. Clicked to make her payment and looked at the clock.

Half past five. Time to pop out and get some food in for breakfast. Tomorrow was Monday.

She was at the cheese counter when Barbarotti rang.

'Thanks for yesterday,' she said. 'Everyone on our team had a great time.'

'Ours, too,' said Gunnar Barbarotti. 'We'll definitely be doing that again.'

'Is that why you're ringing?' asked Backman, 'to invite us to breakfast tomorrow? If so, I won't bother with this shopping. I'm in ICA Express, laying in supplies.'

'No, it isn't a breakfast invitation,' said Barbarotti, 'though if you're really keen, you'd certainly be welcome. I'm out in Rönninge. In the forest, that is.'

'In the forest?'

'Yes. There's been an incident. Asunander called me, and

now he's decided it would be just as well for the two of us to look at it together. You and me, that is.'

'What's happened?' asked Backman.

'A death,' said Barbarotti.

'A death?'

'Yup. Well, more of a death plummet, to be precise; a fatal fall.'

'What are you raving about?'

'A body, found at the bottom of a sheer drop,' Barbarotti elaborated. 'A fall of twenty to twenty-five metres, I'd say. Most things seem to point to it being an accident, but there are certain aspects.'

'Oh, and what are they?' asked Backman.

'Well, only one really,' said Barbarotti. 'Hang on a minute.'

He was gone for a few seconds; she could hear him talking to someone else. Then he came back on the line.

'Sorry, yes, just the one strange aspect, to be precise. Thirty-five years ago they found another body in exactly the same place.'

'Thirty-five years?'

'Yes. On 28 September 1975.'

Eva Backman accepted the half kilo of Gruyère that was being passed across the counter as she processed the information.

'An accident?' she asked. 'That other time, too?'

'Well, that was how they classified it in the end,' said Barbarotti. 'But it took them a while to decide.'

'You sound as if you've been briefed,' said Backman.

'I've been here for three hours,' admitted Gunnar Barbarotti. 'And I think it sounds a bit fishy.'

'Fishy?'

'Yes.'

'Has the body got a name? Today's, I mean.'

'Not yet,' said Barbarotti. 'He didn't have any form of ID on him.'

'He?'

'Male of about sixty.'

Eva Backman moved off towards the dairy section, thinking as she went. 'Is there anything else that seems fishy?' she asked. 'Apart from the fact that he's in exactly the same place?'

'It just feels that way.'

'Is that a fact?' said Eva Backman.

'I know you haven't got my razor-sharp instincts for these things,' said Barbarotti. 'We can hardly expect that.'

'Don't talk crap,' said Eva Backman.

'All right,' said Barbarotti. 'I only called for a bit of a chat, really. I've got Wennergren-Olofsson here with me.'

'Ah,' said Backman. 'I see. So this is something we'll be tackling tomorrow morning in fact?'

'Exactly,' said Barbarotti.

'Death by plummet.'

'You've got it,' said Barbarotti. 'Right, I'll let you get on. But we liked your kids. See you tomorrow.'

'Liked yours, too,' said Backman. 'Sweden's youth is its future. And thanks for the briefing.'

'Don't mention it,' said Barbarotti.

5

I am Maria, also known as the sparrow.

I'm Super Tomas's little sister and people think I'm mental.

I've got no problem with them thinking that. Just the opposite. For me it's ideal to have them under that impression. Because I know that this is nothing to do with mental illness. It's to do with evil.

Or if not evil, then certainly egoism. I think of myself. Other people will have to mind themselves.

I'm no Hamlet, not by any means. People don't think you can be evil nowadays. Particularly not if you're a young woman, nineteen and pretty. One might even say stunning.

And clever. It surprises them that I'm so clever, with matriculation grades that are actually just as good as the ones Super Tomas left school with, two years ahead of me. Although they changed the grading system from letters to numbers in the interim. The teachers were surprised, at any event, as indeed were my parents. I wasn't; I know my own worth.

I was pretty when I was eight, too. That was when I fell off a swing, landed on my head and underwent a personality change. I don't relate to other people the way you're meant to. That's what my psychiatrist says anyway. His name is Douglas Dinesen, I've had the same shrink the whole way through. My dad and mum trust him, everyone trusts him except me. I know he's starting to get the hots for me and I'm not going to see him any more.

Because I'm off to Uppsala now. As I say, I'm clever but I have a personality disorder. I'm going to read French, initially. They assumed I'd be sharing Auntie Becka's flat with Tomas, started going on about it back in the spring, but I said no thanks. Having grown up in the shadow of that golden boy, I know it's high time to move out into the sunlight.

I might go for law eventually, but I'm starting with French. It sounds suitably irresponsible and I have no set plans for my life. I'm going to take a room in a house in Norrtäljegatan. I've put a cross on the map; it's only ten minutes' walk from the station. I'm taking the train tomorrow, so this is my last evening up here. My bags are packed. Dad wanted to drive me the whole way, but I said not on your life. I'm leaving the nest and I'm going to do it on my own wings. Don't they get it?

Mum's been crying all evening. Well, maybe not the whole time but the tears well up at regular intervals. They won't know what to do with that big house, she says. Once Tomas and I have both gone. Didn't they think we'd ever grow up? Sell the damn thing, I think to myself, and if she doesn't stop blubbing I shall say it out loud, too.

Sell the damn thing and move to Spain like Auntie Becka. And like those fucking Friesmans you're always going on about. Nobody rolling in money like you two has any reason to stay in Sundsvall, do they? In Spain you can play golf and lie by the pool, drinking sweet wine from morning till night.

I couldn't care less about them. And that's my problem. I couldn't care less about other people. Especially boys. If I'm ever going to meet anybody, something that goes beyond a one-night stand, it'll have to be somebody as twisted as I am. As twisted and as clever, then we could really make it work.

I can't stand all that wimpy, positive stuff. Hopeful, enthusiastic drivel. Life is an arsehole. I am evil.

I am nineteen years old and stunning and I think only of myself – keep that in mind, people. Tomorrow I shall write a few words from my new life on Norrtäljegatan in Uppsala. Maybe.

I am Maria, also known as the sparrow.

6

'Who was it who realized the same thing had happened in the same place thirty-five years ago?'

'Elis Bengtsson.'

'Elis Bengtsson?'

'The chap who found him. He was here last time, too.'

'Wha-at? The same guy who . . .'

Barbarotti's phone rang and Eva Backman stopped. Barbarotti dismissed the call.

'Sorry. Yes, he was in the vicinity last time. This time he found the body. He lives near there and was out with his dog . . . both times.'

Backman eyed him sceptically.

'How likely does that sound, do you reckon?' she said. 'For the same person to happen to be – how did you put it? – in the vicinity? On two different occasions, I mean.'

'Not particularly likely,' said Barbarotti, with a glance at his watch. 'But we'll be seeing him in ten minutes, so perhaps we can reserve judgement until then.'

'And we still don't know the name of the new corpse?'

Barbarotti shook his head. 'Afraid not.'

'What was its name in 1975?'

Barbarotti consulted a piece of paper on the desk. 'Maria Winckler,' he told her. 'Aged twenty-five. On a short-term teaching contract at Kymlingevik School. English and French, and she'd only been working there just over a month when it happened.'

'Was she local? Did she live in Kymlinge?'

'She'd moved here,' said Barbarotti. 'And only a short time beforehand.'

'I see,' said Eva Backman, wondering what it was she saw.

'There was a group of people out in the forest looking for mushrooms, apparently,' Barbarotti elaborated. 'Or lingonberries. She fell down a sheer drop; there's a fault scarp out there. A fall of at least twenty metres. It's known locally as Gåsastupan – Goose Drop.'

'Goose Drop?'

'Yes. It's supposedly one of those clifftops that old folk were meant to have thrown themselves off in the old days, so they wouldn't be a burden.'

'That's just a legend,' said Eva Backman. 'That sort of thing never really happened.'

'Is that right?' said Gunnar Barbarotti. 'Well, be that as it may, it's now happened twice within a space of thirty-five years.'

'But they decided to classify it as an accident in the end?'

'Yes.'

'Could she have jumped?'

'I assume so.'

'Could she have been pushed?'

'I assume so.'

Eva Backman thought for a moment. 'Do you remember this?' she asked. 'Or weren't you living in Kymlinge at the time?'

'I arrived the year after,' said Barbarotti. 'When I started at upper secondary. No, I hadn't heard anything about it. Not until now. Shall we go and talk to Mr Bengtsson, then?'

'I'll say,' said Eva Backman.

Mr Bengtsson had a white shirt and a tie. According to their information he was seventy-seven but Eva Backman would have guessed at sixty-seven. He seemed full of vim and vigour, and she imagined it must be the dog-walking that kept him in good shape. His choice of outfit pointed to the fact that he viewed a visit to the police station as a delicate operation.

Barbarotti switched on the tape recorder and went through the formalities.

'I think we'll take things chronologically,' he said, once this was completed. 'If you don't mind. Can you tell us what happened in 1975, as far as you can remember it?'

'It's in your files,' said Elis Bengtsson.

'I know that,' said Gunnar Barbarotti. 'We're busy going through them. But perhaps you could give us a potted version, even so. Neither I nor Inspector Backman was here back then.'

'It was thirty-five years ago,' said Elis Bengtsson.

'Almost to the day,' said Barbarotti. 'A young woman had died. How did you come to be involved?'

Elis Bengtsson shrugged. 'I was out with the dog. Just like this time.'

'Go on,' Barbarotti instructed him.

'Though it was a different dog.'

'I had a feeling it must have been,' said Barbarotti.

'Madame Curie. A scent hound.'

Younger in body than in mind, thought Eva Backman.

'Go on,' said Barbarotti.

'I got there earlier last time.' He slid two fingers between his neck and his shirt collar and tried to create some space; perhaps the shirt was new and digging into him. Perhaps his brain wasn't getting enough oxygen. 'Just after it had happened. This body definitely looked as if it had been lying there longer.'

'How do you know?'

'You could kind of tell by looking. I think the doctor confirmed it, too. The one who came out.'

'Was it you who found the body in 1975, too?'

'No,' said Elis Bengtsson. 'There was already a group of people staring at it when I arrived. I got there last. It had just happened.'

'How many people were there?'

'Including the one who died, there were seven of them.'

'Seven?'

'Yes. They'd been out looking for mushrooms. They hadn't found a single one, as far as I could see. And it was hardly surprising; there aren't any, not just round here. You have to go to the damper places, over towards Rödmyren.'

'What had happened?'

'Well, she'd fallen. Twenty-five metres, straight down into Gåsaklyftan. Died instantly, poor little thing.'

Eva Backman cleared her throat.

'Why was there a police investigation, do you know?'

Elis Bengtsson stretched his neck. 'Because they suspected someone had pushed her.'

'And why was that?' said Barbarotti. 'What gave rise to those suspicions?'

Elis Bengtsson pursed his lips and kept his answer to himself for a few moments. 'I suppose it was because of what she cried out,' he said.

'She cried out?' said Backman.

'Oh yes,' said Elis Bengtsson. 'She shouted something before she hit the ground and died. Some of the others heard it, and I heard it, too. I was a fair distance away but I had good ears in those days.'

'What did she shout?' asked Barbarotti. 'I mean to say, isn't it pretty natural for someone to cry out, if they're falling off a cliff?'

'That was the point,' said Elis Bengtsson.

'What was?' asked Backman.

'What she shouted,' said Elis Bengtsson. 'Some people thought it was some kind of message.'

'Message?' said Barbarotti with a frown. 'So what did she shout . . . or cry?'

Something with a long aahh or uuhh sound,' said Elis Bengtsson. 'I heard that much, I was about a hundred metres away. Those who were closer had their own ideas.'

'Like what?' asked Backman.

Elis Bengtsson allowed himself another pause for effect.

'Some of them thought it was just one long syllable, an aahh, a kind of groan.'

'Right?'

'But a couple of them claimed she'd cried out "Murderer!" or "Murderers!"'

'Murderer?' said Barbarotti.

'Murderer, yes,' said Elis Bengtsson, and ran his tongue over his lips to moisten them. 'They thought she'd shouted it to let people know she'd been murdered. The last thing she did.'

Barbarotti and Backman exchanged looks and said nothing for a moment. Elis Bengtsson managed to undo his top shirt button.

'But she didn't shout the murderer's name?' asked Barbarotti.

Elis Bengtsson shook his head. 'No, she didn't. That would have been more sensible, but I don't suppose you think about being sensible in a situation like that.'

'Presumably not,' said Barbarotti. 'Do you know if there was anything else to indicate she'd been pushed?'

'Not that I know of,' said Elis Bengtsson. 'You'll have to look in your files. There was a Detective Inspector Sandlin; I talked to him several times . . . we both had the same breed of dog, as well. Scent hounds.'

'We'll be going through every word,' Barbarotti assured him. 'I'm afraid Sandlin has passed away.'

'I know. His pooch was called Birger, I remember. What a stupid name for a dog. Mine was called Madame Curie. I always name them after famous people.'

'Not a bad idea,' said Eva Backman. 'Right, shall we move on to what happened yesterday?'

It took Elis Bengtsson ten minutes to give an account of his macabre find in Gåsaklyftan.

He had been out on his daily circuit with Luther. They'd set out from home – Källviksgård farmhouse in Rönninge – after lunch and the radio news, at around five past one. Luther had disappeared after twenty minutes, when they were level with the power lines, and he heard him barking about half an hour later, while he, Elis, was sitting down for a few minutes' rest on the way to the top of Gåsaklinten. The dog turned out to be standing at the bottom of the sheer drop, guarding the dead body but not touching it. Elis Bengtsson had immediately called home to his wife, who had alerted the police. He, mean-while, had climbed down and stayed there until the police – in the form of a patrol car containing Olsén and Widerberg – plus a doctor and the ambulance staff arrived, just after three. It had taken a while to get them to the right location, and without a mobile phone it would have taken even longer. After he'd spoken to the police and the doctor, Dr Rislund, Elis Bengtsson had left Gåsaklyftan. By then it was around a quarter past four.

'Have you anything else to add, for the time being?' Barbarotti had asked when they had listened to his account. 'I'm sure we'll need to contact you again in due course.'

'Well, there is, in fact,' Elis Bengtsson had replied. 'This isn't only the second time things have happened in that place, you know. A hundred and fifty years ago a mother and child lost their lives up there. And further back still, the old folk threw themselves off that crag to help their families. Gåsaklyftan is a grim place, you all need to know that.'

'Thank you for that insight, too,' said Barbarotti, and switched off the tape recorder. 'And now Inspector Backman will show you out.'

'No need,' said Elis Bengtsson. 'I know the way.'

7

Rickard Berglund stopped at the florist's in Kyrkogårdsgatan and bought three yellow roses.

'Bit nervous?' asked the sales assistant as Rickard fumbled his change and dropped a couple of coins on the floor.

He picked them up and felt himself blush. The insinuation was obvious. The assistant assumed the roses were for a girl. And why shouldn't he? It was Saturday afternoon and Rickard was dressed up – or looking a bit smarter than usual, at any rate; he'd even splashed on a bit of aftershave, which was far from usual for him.

'Yes, just a touch.' He laughed, trying to play along. 'You never know.'

'First date?'

'Sort of.'

He nodded goodbye and beat a hasty retreat from the shop. *Sort of?* he thought. What on earth was that supposed to mean?

He looked at his watch and registered that he was early. He decided to take a stroll round the English Park and through the cemetery first. Five, Tomas had said. Come at about five. We thought we'd start off outside, sit in the garden for a couple of hours.

It was only 4.30. Rickard had paid one brief visit to

Sibyllegatan previously and knew the way; it wouldn't take him more than fifteen minutes to get there, twenty at most. Arriving too early was simply wet; Rickard's foremost priority was not to come across as a drip. Not today, and not any other day, either.

He set off diagonally across the park towards the building that housed the philology department. The grass beneath the old elms and larches had grown almost half a metre tall; presumably they didn't bother cutting it over the summer. A lot of things came to a standstill in Uppsala over the summer months, he'd come to realize. It was still two weeks until the students would be back to take over the place; today was 16 August, a beautiful, warm Saturday in late summer, and as he opened the old iron gate into the cemetery he felt as if life couldn't get much better than this. At least not if you were happy to make do with the more superficial aspects.

Twenty years old, on your way to a crayfish party in the company of good friends. Three roses in your hand. What else could you wish for?

But they weren't red, and the assistant had doubtless noted the fact. If they'd been flowers for a meeting with a girl, they wouldn't have been yellow. Would they? thought Rickard Berglund. Yellow roses had nothing to do with romance.

He sighed. The girl problem waxed and waned. There were times when he didn't care, and other times when it felt suffocating. Still being a virgin at twenty wasn't normal; two months at the Army College for Non-Commissioned Officers had taught him all sorts of things, including this. Of course there were a few others among the new intake who were in the same predicament as he was, he knew that. But they were in a minority, a glaringly small, covert and embarrassing minority.

Most of his comrades had girlfriends back home, others had met new young women in Uppsala – at the nurses' home on the other side of Dag Hammarsköldsväg, for example; it offered a smooth and convenient solution for all parties. Some did a bit of both. And they all seemed to be looking forward to the day when 10,000 female students would hit town.

Girls? Women? Ten thousand!

Temptations?

Sweden, the country of free love. Staffan, one of the boys at the barracks, had been in London for a month before the call-up, and claimed that was what they called good old Sweden out in the wider world of Europe. The country of free love? My God, thought Rickard Berglund, who hadn't seen any of those notorious Swedish sex films of recent years. Am I part of reality or not?

He pushed these gnawing doubts aside, stopped in front of an unassuming little grave and read the inscription on the stone.

Henrik Aurelius
Born 1851
Died 1874

That was all.

Twenty-three, thought Rickard. A young man who died nearly a hundred years ago. He was only three years older than I am right now.

He stood there trying to interpret the minimal information. A name and two dates, nothing more. Who were you, Henrik Aurelius? Why didn't you get beyond twenty-three?

And more: What did you die of? Did you get the chance to

be with a woman before your time ran out? Did you have a God?

Did you have a God?

If I knew I was going to die in three years' time, thought Rickard Berglund, would I dare to make an approach to a girl? When it clearly wouldn't really matter, and the Reaper's scythe would slash away any responsibility?

Conceivably, but he wasn't at all sure.

Or should he make a virtue of his ambivalence? Behave the way they used to in the old days: study for ordination first, like an old-fashioned cleric, then get married, and then tackle the matter? Wasn't that what he really wished, in fact: that his future wife would be untouched? A virgin, just as he was? Was he that unmodern at heart? Wasn't it just extreme cowardice – making a virtue of necessity, as he'd put it – and a shameful way of evading the actual problem?

What ought I to do, as a Christian?

Maybe the question was justified after all? Was there – in this closing year of the overwhelming and revolutionary Sixties – a moral stance for young people with a Christian faith? Hand on heart?

Rickard Berglund didn't think so. He had read Camus and Sartre, which presumably wasn't the best choice of literature to put in the hands of a future priest. Though Dostoevsky was classed as an existentialist. Existentialist *and* Christian.

Somewhere inside himself he also understood that the route to women didn't go via books and thinking. Neither Dostoevsky nor Kierkegaard, nor any of the rest. There was no help to be had from literature, only distractions and prevarications, when it came to this particular matter. *The delectable itch*, that's how he had seen it described somewhere; it was an expression he couldn't really push away, however hard he tried, and when he sought advice from Our Lord, he didn't feel any clear guidance was forthcoming. Almost as if it wasn't His subject. And it was true, wasn't it, thought Rickard Berglund glumly, it was true that the only thing Christianity had concerned itself with, these past 200 years, was injecting a sense of guilt into the itch?

So, what to do? Get a skinful and let it happen in an intoxicated blur? While the sense of shame and disgrace was deactivated? Wouldn't that be a radical way of getting to grips with the problem?

How did you approach it, Henrik Aurelius?

But there was no answer from the rough moss-encrusted stone, either. Sterile questions, he concluded. Thoughts running on empty. I'm a total moral coward. He left the cemetery and carried on in the direction of Luthagen.

But that last thought stayed with him. *Get drunk and let it happen.* There were no guarantees even with that method, of course. *Hope it would happen* was presumably closer to the truth. Rickard had been drunk twice in his life. The first time was over a year ago, a couple of weeks before his matriculation exams in Mariestad, and that was the night he twigged that the world presents itself in a different way, in another guise, to those in that much-lauded state. Seductive and irresponsible. Tempting?

Henrietta, a girl in his year at upper secondary, had kissed him, and he had somehow managed to kiss her back. He had held her in his arms, too, clasped her to him; the whole thing hadn't lasted more than a minute, but the memory of it, of the way her tongue had played with his, the feel of her body against his, well, that was precisely what this was all about, of course. The ecstasy. The giddiness in the blood.

The second time he'd been rather less than sober was this summer, on a week's manoeuvres in Marma, in the north of Uppsala county. Accommodation was in tents in the forest, he'd drunk five or six strong beers with his comrades and there hadn't been a girl for miles around. No ecstasy, no giddiness, just light-heartedness and a very full bladder.

He went past the cathedral school and totted it up in his head. Ten weeks, they'd made it through ten weeks now. It was three weeks since the harvest leave and it struck him that, personally speaking, he could have managed very well without those days off. He'd spent them at home in Hova with his mother, lying in bed in his old room upstairs, reading Freud and Jung while she stayed down in the kitchen, cooking him meals. In some paradoxical way, the gulf between them had felt twice as wide when they were both under the same roof. It was duty, nothing more than duty. And, deep inside, he was afraid she felt the same.

So he avoided going home at weekends. Apart from that harvest week, he had only been back once since his call-up. There were a few of them who stayed in the barracks over the weekends instead of going home to their mates, girlfriends and so on. Rickard enjoyed those free Saturdays and Sundays. Three meals a day, no duties or clock-watching, no uniforms; they provided the ideal opportunity for discovering the town.

In the company of Helge, a shy and reserved boy from Gäddede – a place in such a distant part of Norrland province that he literally couldn't get up there and back in a weekend – Rickard would take leisurely strolls around the town, map in hand, acquainting himself with the landmarks. The marketplace. The big Lundequist bookshop. The city park and the surging waters of the Islandsfallet weir on the river.

The old heart of the town, of course: the cathedral, the little square at St Erik's torg, the indoor market and the Dom- trappskällaren restaurant on the steps winding down from the cathedral. The canonry Skytteaneum with its arch over the road beneath, the Gustavianum and the individual build- ings of the student clubs: Norrlands, Söderman-Nerikes, V-dala, Gothenburg, Småland and little Västgöta. All the bridges over the River Fyris, and a cup of coffee with a slice of cake at Ofvandahls or Güntherska.

Sometimes he went to church, but never with Helge. He tried a variety of them: the cathedral, of course, and Holy Trinity, but also the smaller ones like Johannes, the mission church, the Baptists and even the good old Salvation Army on St Persgatan, hard up against the railway tracks. But no matter where he went, no matter which congregation he joined, he always came away dissatisfied. Unrelieved of his burden, somehow. He would think of his mother at such times, wondering what sort of life she was actually living and whether she really was simply waiting to be reunited with her pastor up in Heaven. She was only fifty-two, and had worked at the post office in Mariestad for the past twelve years, and sometimes – well aware that she could quite easily get to seventy or eighty – Rickard would feel a great heaviness of heart descend on him.

Was there any meaning to her life? Widow of a free-church pastor in Hova?

And what about my own? He would inevitably go on to ask himself. What is it about my own life that makes it any more meaningful?

They were dismal and difficult questions, and he had got in the habit of referring them on to God when he prayed.

Sometimes he thought he could detect some dim and vaguely consoling answer, but usually not. Usually it was just silence. There was something deeply unsettling about the fact that he scarcely ever registered anything but silence from that quarter. However hard he strained to listen.

Because these were exactly the things – these weighty and vital questions – that he would have to get to grips with, after his military service. A year from now, basically.

When the serious stuff started. The big plan. There was no immediate hurry about it.

No, there was no hurry about anything. He turned left into Geijersgatan and saw it was just after five. Time to shake off all those gloomy thoughts. Time to *carpe diem* and banish all those cares!

Time for a crayfish party at Tomas and Gunilla's.

'Here's Rickard, the brightest brain in the barracks!'
'Rubbish.'

It wasn't clear whether anyone registered Rickard's protest, because he was being gathered into a bear hug by Tomas as he said it.

A long table was laid on the grass between the flats, which were a couple of brown-plastered three-storey blocks, vintage thirties or forties. There were blocks of exactly the same design in Mariestad and Töreboda, too; it seemed to Rickard that there was something prototypically Swedish about these small-scale housing developments. Something decent and honest, but at the same time slightly depressing. Like a little Co-op store in the rain, say.

It wasn't raining, though, and the table was decked out in style: a paper tablecloth and paper plates, of course, and two loaded platters of red crayfish. Cans of beer and bottles of wine, a generous array. Brightly coloured serviettes; cheeses, baguettes and a big bowl of salad. Half a dozen people were already sitting down and the table was laid for at least as many again. We'll pick up the bill for the shopping and you can all pay your share afterwards, Tomas had told him. Rickard had no idea what the party would cost, but it was all the same to him. He still had plenty of savings from his year at Lapidus Concrete. Maybe he wouldn't have quite enough cash in his pocket right now, which would be tiresome, but it didn't really matter. If we're all going to chip in the same amount, I might as well make sure to have a few drinks, he decided at the same moment as Gunilla handed him a plastic cup of something bubbly.

'Hello, Rickard. *Skål* and welcome!'

'*Skål*,' responded Rickard. 'Good to see you again. You're looking lovelier than ever.'

This was bold and he had no idea how he'd dared say it, when she belonged to Tomas. There was no way it could lead anywhere. They had met twice before, and Rickard thought that if he could ever be together with a girl who came anywhere near Gunilla, he could ask for nothing better in this world.

And it wasn't only her, for that matter. Tomas Winckler was an enviable young man in every way. Rickard felt sure he wasn't the only one to think so. And yet he never felt the envy, somehow, that was the great and remarkable thing. Ever since their first encounter at the outdoor cafe table there had been a sort of bond between them; between Berglund and Winckler – it was hard to get out of the military habit of only using surnames – but Tomas got on with everyone else in such an easy, uncomplicated way, too. Even with his commanding officers. More than once Rickard had thanked his lucky stars that they had run into each other; if you were a good friend of Winckler's, no one questioned your worth or your right to exist.

For some reason. Rickard would reflect on this sometimes, but rarely came to any conclusion beyond the fact that general optimism and friendliness are good, practical tools in any social context.

Talent and humour did no harm, either, and Tomas had both of those. He'd read a bit of Kierkegaard, too, Rickard had checked. So even that; and maybe there was an arena where only they, Berglund and Winckler, came together. Rickard liked to imagine so, anyway. A slightly higher plane, or something along those lines.

'You could give Tomas a lesson or two in compliments,' Gunilla observed. 'But aren't those flowers for me?'

He handed them over and gave an embarrassed laugh. 'Of course. What a drip I am.'

'This is Maria,' said Gunilla, introducing a thin girl with dark hair, cut short. 'She's Tomas's sister.'

They shook hands and said hello. Tomas had told him his sister was coming, though he hadn't said much more. Clever but complicated was the way he described her.

'Why did he say you've got the brightest brain?' she asked with a little smile that was hard to read. 'He generally claims that honour for himself.'

'No idea,' Rickard defended himself. 'Must be a misapprehension.'

'That's a word I never trust myself to say,' put in a long-haired young man with a Småland accent and John Lennon glasses. 'It always comes out wrong.'

'How do you mean?' asked a girl in a straw hat who was strumming cautiously on a guitar. 'You've lost me again.'

'Oh, you know, messuprehension,' said Mr Lennon Glasses.

He laughed and took a swig of beer. All the others laughed too, except Maria, who contented herself with a slight twitch of the mouth. She's heard it before, thought Rickard. She's smart.

Tomas went round the table introducing the rest of them. The Lennon boy was called Bertil, the guitar girl with the hat was Susanna, and her boyfriend, tall and stringy as a beanpole and boasting a full, bushy beard, answered to the name of Boff.

'Well?' persisted Maria, once Rickard had sat down on a folding chair beside her. 'What makes you so clever then?'

Tomas came to the rescue before he could reply. 'It's possible I'm wrong,' he said, 'but he's streets ahead in our Army College chess tournament. And they don't let just any idiot enter that, I assure you, Sister dear.'

This was in fact the truth. Rickard laughed and swigged his bubbly. 'It'll pass,' he said. 'Your brother's in a sulk because I checkmated him the other day, that's all.'

'Anyone who puts him in his place deserves a medal,' said Maria. 'It's exactly what he needs.'

She lit a cigarette and smiled at them both and Rickard had a sudden glimpse of Tomas in her smile. The idea of a chess tournament had been mooted on the Monday after they returned from their harvest leave. They'd swiftly assembled sixteen players and drawn up the basic rules. Everyone would play everyone and they'd know the winner by Christmas. Five-kronor entry fee, and the prize would be a bottle of whisky.

Rickard had played four matches since then and, to his

surprise, had scraped together three wins and a draw. Three and a half points; it was absolutely true that he was currently in the lead. He had never thought of himself as particularly good at chess. He really only had the one tactic, something his father had taught him when he introduced him to the noble game: be cautious! Wait for your opponent to make mistakes, rather than making your own. But in any case, there was no way he would retain the lead all the way through the tournament, he was convinced of that, and nothing could have worried him less.

Other people turned up, and he chatted some more to Maria, who had just come to Uppsala to start a degree in French, and to Boff, who was an old friend of Tomas's who happened to be visiting. By just after half past five all the seats at the table were taken, the hosts handed out duplicated sheets with the words of the first song and, after the rendition, it was finally time to attack the red beauties.

This is going really well, thought Rickard Berglund.

Six hours later the party was still in full swing indoors. It was almost midnight but the supply of beer and wine seemed inexhaustible. Rickard didn't know how much he'd had to drink, but he was pretty sure it must be a personal record. His perceptions were blunted, to say the least, and it wasn't at all easy to work out what people were saying, although of course the volume of the music might be partly to blame. The Doors, the Rolling Stones and Creedence Clearwater Revival, he recognized those. Beyond that, it was all unfamiliar to him. Pop music had never really grabbed him; it was . . . it was as if this particular period was not the era in which Rickard Berglund belonged. He had thought about this before: he ought to have come into the world a hundred years earlier. Or later maybe, you never knew. But at this moment he didn't have much to complain of. He was squeezed onto a sofa between Susanna and a boy called Germund. Susanna was pretty clearly drunker than he was himself, and alternated between helpless giggles and falling asleep. Rickard hadn't been properly introduced to the boy, but if he'd understood correctly, Germund had been in Uppsala for a few years, reading theoretical physics or something like that – or was he about to start? He gave a slightly mournful impression, had a black suit and a short haircut and didn't look as though he really belonged in the Sixties, either. For the past half hour, or it could have been an hour, he had been deep in conversation with Maria, Tomas's younger sister. Their heads were together, only a few centimetres apart, and their expressions were permanently earnest.

No one else was taking anything very seriously; people sat around drinking, smoking and talking. Vietnam, apartheid, Martin Luther King and the state of the Swedish monarchy. A few of the guests had gone home but most were still there; Gunilla and Tomas were dancing, or at any rate were propped against one another in the middle of the room, swaying together. There was a small group out on the balcony; Rickard could hear them laughing and chatting because the door was open to let out the tobacco smoke. Everyone was smoking, and more or less continually. He himself had a cigarette between his fingers and was wondering how many he'd smoked that night. Probably more than in all the rest of his life put together, but he didn't inhale and what the heck did it matter anyway? From time to time another sort of smoky smell pervaded the room, sort of sweetish, and he wondered if it could possibly be hash or marijuana.

He drank some more wine and felt his head swim. Oh God, he thought, I oughtn't to . . . I really oughtn't . . . My mother would die if she saw me right now.

The realization that he was going to be sick came very suddenly, and it was only by sheer good luck that he avoided disgracing himself. He managed to stand up and get out to the hall and, incredibly, the bathroom wasn't occupied. He staggered in, closed the door behind him and lifted the lid at the last second. He stayed in there for some time, throwing up three times, though by the end it was mostly just bile. He drank some cold water, washed his face and hands, sat on the closed toilet lid to compose himself and by the time he emerged into the din, he had taken the mature decision to go home.

Or, rather, to the barracks, which was the only home currently available to him. But that was good enough. He located Gunilla out in the kitchen, gave her a quick thank-you hug and said he was well fed and happy and would be on his way now.

'How are you, Rickard?' she asked, and he detected a hint of maternal concern in her voice. 'Are you going to walk the whole way?'

'A bit of fresh air ishn't going to do me any harm,' replied Rickard Berglund, realizing to his horror that his voice was slurred. 'Thanksho much. Shay goodbye to Tomash for me!'

He slunk out of the flat, made his way as fast as he could down the three flights of stairs and came out into the warm August night. Lord God, help me to at least stay upright, he prayed as he noticed, to his dismay, that his mind and his body seemed to be speaking different languages. I'm drunk, but I really didn't mean to get that way.

He started walking in the direction that seemed right. No hurry, he thought, I've got all night. All of this long, lovely night. Maybe I'll meet a naked woman on the way.

A while later, it could have been an hour or perhaps a good deal less, he found himself back in the English Park, and as the grass was long and inviting, he decided to allow himself a nap. An impressive full moon had sailed up into the sky above the philology department, and he was filled with a sense, in spite of everything, of the wondrously multifaceted nature of life.

He was asleep within five minutes and did not stir until ten hours later, when he was woken by the sun shining in his face and a sensation something like his brain trying to crawl out through his skull.

8

'Right. What do we make of this, then?'

'I don't know. What's *your* take?'

They were on their way back into town. Barbarotti was at the wheel and Backman in the passenger seat beside him. An hour's inspection of Gåsastupan was more than sufficient, they both felt. Barbarotti had been at the site on Sunday, too, of course, and two younger colleagues, Torstensson and Svendén, were still out there, carrying out a search. They had orders to stay until darkness fell, but there wasn't much to indicate they would find anything, of course.

Or that anyone would bother continuing the search the next day.

'Pure chance,' said Backman.

'Tell me more,' said Barbarotti.

Backman shrugged. 'There's nothing pointing to any other explanation. Two accidents in the same place, with thirty-five years between them . . . Slightly unusual, I grant you, but such things happen. Or do you think otherwise? You tend to be the cussed one, after all.'

'Cussed, me?' said Barbarotti. 'What rubbish! I think you're right.'

Eva Backman studied a sheet of paper she was holding. 'Seven of them,' she said. 'That other time there were seven of them. Three men, four women. I'm surprised they felt the need for an investigation at all. It must surely have been more than just her crying out?'

'There are two files,' said Barbarotti. 'That Sandlin was a persistent devil evidently. I've heard about his methods before. He wanted to get to the bottom of everything, even if it was only someone throwing a bike in the river.'

'Yes, I've heard about him, too,' said Eva Backman. 'He carried on as a private investigator even after his police career was over, didn't he?'

'Yep,' said Barbarotti. 'He even had a go at the Olof Palme murder case, but he didn't get anywhere with it. There is one odd thing about this new death.'

'And what's that?'

'The wallet.'

'The wallet?'

'Yes. He had a watch, a set of keys, a comb, a loose hundred-kronor banknote in his back pocket . . . why didn't he have a wallet?'

'Maybe Elis Bengtsson nicked it.'

'You reckon?'

'No,' admitted Backman. 'It doesn't seem particularly likely. Though he didn't have a mobile phone, either.'

'There's no law obliging people to,' said Barbarotti.

'Really?' said Backman. 'Oh well, I'm sure they'll pass one soon. There's another odd thing, too, by the way.'

'Oh, yes?' said Barbarotti.

'You're right about the keys. But there was no car key. And no car. How did he get there?'

Gunnar Barbarotti scratched his head exaggeratedly. 'A long walk?' he suggested. 'Or maybe he lived locally?'

'Elis Bengtsson didn't recognize him.'

'You're right there,' said Barbarotti. 'I'm sure he keeps tabs on who's who round here. Could he have come by bus? Perhaps there's a stop somewhere nearby?'

'Don't know,' said Backman. 'But it was only three or four hundred metres out to the road from there, so it's not impossible, I suppose.'

'Someone could have given him a lift?' suggested Barbarotti.

'Someone who dropped him off and drove on, you mean?'

'I don't know what I mean. But I agree, it's a bit weird that there was no car parked anywhere nearby. Though he could have left a bike or moped out of sight . . . in a ditch or something.'

'Unlocked?' asked Backman. 'There was no bike key in the set.'

'Combination lock,' said Gunnar Barbarotti. 'Stop asking so many questions. This'll all be cleared up within a few days, either way.'

'How do you mean?'

'I mean he'll be identified. It's only a question of time, isn't it?'

'Yes,' said Eva Backman, turning her attention back to the sheet of paper. 'It's pretty likely, I suppose. They were almost all around the same age . . . the people who were here thirty-five years ago, I mean. Between twenty-five and thirty.'

Barbarotti pondered this silently.

'They were a group of people who knew each other quite well,' he said. 'It must have been quite traumatic for them, don't you think? The decision to hold the investigation and everything. Maybe they suspected each other . . . I wonder if they still keep in touch.'

'You'll be reading Sandlin's files, won't you?'

Barbarotti pulled a face. 'I might be,' he said. 'If Asunander lets me. But he might well see it as a waste of resources.'

'You'll do it anyway,' said Eva Backman. 'I know you. You'll take those files home with you tonight, no matter what Asunander says.'

'No need,' said Barbarotti with a grin.

'No need?'

'I took them home yesterday.'

'Good,' said Eva Backman with a yawn. 'I thought as much.'

'Yes, because if I hadn't got in there, you'd have taken them.'

'I don't give a toss for that old case.'

'You're such a bad liar that it's really embarrassing,' said Barbarotti.

'Haven't we got anything else to talk about?' Backman asked irritably.

'We could talk about our children?' suggested Barbarotti. 'I thought it was great seeing them all together on Saturday.'

'Yes,' said Backman. 'Sweden's youth is its future, it does give one a bit of hope actually. Don't you think?'

'Couldn't agree more,' said Barbarotti. 'There's only one really good way to measure the quality of a society. How we look after our children.'

'Wise words,' said Eva Backman. 'Did you come up with them yourself?'

'I'm quoting,' said Gunnar Barbarotti. 'I can't remember who.'

They'd just gone round the Rocksta roundabout when Backman's mobile rang.

She answered and listened for two minutes, interjecting no

more than a 'Yes', a 'No' and an 'I see'. She thanked the caller, said the news was 'Extremely interesting' and rang off.

'What was that?' asked Barbarotti.

Eva Backman held up her list of seven names from 1975. 'I don't think Asunander will have any objection to you going through those files,' she said.

'Oh?' said Barbarotti.

'That was Torstensson. They've just found a wallet.'

'Well, well,' said Barbarotti. 'And?'

'It had slipped down between two stones, apparently. There was a whole cairn of them out there . . . That was a stroke of luck – it could easily have lain undiscovered forever.'

'Right, I'm with you now,' said Barbarotti. 'So we've got his name then? What did you mean when you said Asunander would have no—'

'He's one of the seven,' said Backman.

'What?' said Barbarotti.

'The deceased was one of those present thirty-five years ago.'

'Bloody hell,' exclaimed Gunnar Barbarotti, going straight through a red light at the intersection between Fabriksgatan and Ringvägen.

9

It was on a Tuesday evening at the end of October that Gunilla heard Lennart Martinsson had crashed his car and been killed. Her staff-sergeant father rang to give the sparse details, like a newsflash on the radio. Lennart had been on the road from Kil to Arvika. He drove straight into a solid concrete pillar, no sign of braking, so death must have been instantaneous. No one could think of any reason for him to be going to Arvika, but everyone knew he'd been depressed recently. The accident had happened at a quarter past four in the afternoon. Visibility had been good. He had taken a day off work.

The call only lasted two minutes. Gunilla could hear her office-clerk mother in the background. She must have been standing there at her husband's shoulder to make sure he didn't start hurling accusations at his daughter. It had both worked and not worked; the accusations did not need to be put into words, when silence and the driest of statements were doing such an excellent job. Once Gunilla had hung up, she stood there at the window, staring out into the darkness and thinking that she might as well take the same way out.

He had done it deliberately.

Of course that's what had happened. Lennart had knowingly engineered the fatal crash because he couldn't see any point in going on without her. He had tried, done his best, endured it for a few months, but found he could no longer bear it.

He had taken his life and thereby burdened her with a sense of guilt she could never overcome. That was the brutal truth and there was nothing to mitigate it.

After her move to Uppsala she had only once been home to Karlstad, for her mum's fiftieth birthday at the beginning of September. She had only stayed one night, giving the excuse that she had to get back to her studies, and she had taken care not to be left alone in a room with any of them. Not her mother, or her father. Or her sister Barbro. Making sure always to be one of at least three afforded some sort of protection from attack; that was how it seemed to work, for whatever reason.

She hadn't seen Lennart since she broke up with him in June. He had phoned her twice over the summer – it wasn't hard to work out that her mother must have given him her number. The first time he broke down and started crying almost immediately; she spent quite some time trying to persuade him to stop, then she hung up. The next time, about a week later, he apologized, claiming he was feeling fine and had got over her. He suggested they could meet up as good friends. It was such an obvious lie and sounded so pathetic that she ended the call as soon as she could, apologizing in a firm but friendly way for having to dash off to a lecture.

And now he was dead.

A three-pronged sensation of regret, anger and powerlessness overwhelmed her as she stared out into the dense autumn darkness.

Regret at having caused the death of another person; there was no escaping that this was a fact.

Anger that he had behaved with such thoughtless egoism; taking your own life always amounted to laying blame on those you left behind. You skewered them with a debt they would never be able to repay.

Powerlessness in that there wasn't a single rational action she could take. Nothing she could think or say or do would in any way relieve what had happened, the definitive and terrible fact of it. Not now, not ever.

Tomas wasn't at home. He was always on duty on Tuesday evenings, and would very likely opt to sleep at the barracks afterwards. There was no point getting home at a quarter to eleven if you would have to be up before six. Particularly as they got to spend every other night of the week together. Back in July, Tomas had managed to wangle permanent overnight leave of absence; some psychiatrist at Ulleråker hospital gave him some kind of medical certificate that did the trick. Gunilla didn't know what it said, but she didn't care; all was fair in love and war, Tomas had been very careful to emphasize.

But tonight she really needed him; it was typical, of course, for this to happen on a Tuesday evening. She momentarily thought of Rickard Berglund and the Tuesday phobia he had told her about. Maybe it wasn't such nonsense, when it came right down to it? Maybe it was wise to approach that particular day of the week with caution?

What a load of bullshit, she thought, and left her place at the dark window. Lennart was dead. He would be just as dead tomorrow as well . . . on Thursday and Friday and all the other days of the week, forever and ever. He only got to twenty-two, and it was me who robbed him of his life.

It was a quarter to ten. Oh God, please let Tomas call, she thought. I don't want to be alone tonight. He hadn't promised to ring, but there was always a chance. And if he did, he would realize she needed him more than ever right now; he would come back home and lie close behind her and hold her tight, so tight. Perhaps they'd make love; that was a cure for everything, at least temporarily, and her period had just finished. Yes, I want to make love to him tonight, she thought. I want his baby.

It was a thought she had never had before, and she wondered why it had come into her mind in such a situation as this. For balance, maybe? A death and a new life?

Absurd, she thought, with a shake of her head. Not even God is allowed to think like that. I'm losing control here.

But if Tomas didn't call, what should she do? Who could she turn to?

Her friends? She paced the flat nervously, running through her circle of acquaintances in her head. And concluded that none of them fitted the bill. Birgitta, of course, she should have been an obvious choice, but they had grown apart since she moved in with Tomas. And Birgitta had known Lennart, which was somehow an obstacle.

She wondered about the other students on her course, but there was no one she knew well enough – and Maria, Tomas's younger sister, but she was out of the question. Tomas claimed she wasn't right in the head; he was only joking, of course, but she couldn't help sensing a grain of truth in it. There was something about Maria, an element of unpleasantness that she couldn't really describe. It wasn't there all the time, but it came through occasionally . . . a kind of hardness, or rigidity, that meant you couldn't really reach her. Maybe even something scary, she had thought a few times; sudden fleeting reflections that had instantly vanished back into the forbidden landscape where they belonged. What on earth did she mean: scary?

She stopped pacing and sank down at the kitchen table in the company of another thought: what would she say, even if she had someone to talk to? It was a good question.

Hi, my former boyfriend just crashed his car and killed himself. Do you fancy coming round for a cup of tea?

Well, yes, maybe that would work. Who wouldn't want to help in those circumstances, but that wasn't what this was all about. She didn't need just anybody. And why . . . why try to push death away by talking about it? Why imagine you could cure your sense of desperation with silly little sticking plasters of chatter? With tea? Why even try? Cheer yourself up by talking about other things . . . Why the hell should you *think of other things*?

Why not look the thing straight in the eye instead? Accept the pain without anaesthetic. The only sure thing in life was death, and now it had come to call. Death was the one she needed to talk to, that was the fact of the matter.

She decided not to phone anybody. Perhaps Lennart was looking down on her from his suicides' heaven, and she ought to show him some respect by not letting anyone else get mixed up in her sorrow. Not for these first few hours, this first night, anyway. Why not pour herself a glass of wine – but only one – and sit here at the kitchen table with a lighted candle, simply remembering him? Yes, why not?

And the moment she swallowed her first mouthful of wine, it hit her that she would have to go to the funeral.

It wasn't as unbearable as she had anticipated. It was worse.

Lennart Leopold Martinsson's funeral service took place on the Saturday eleven days after his life had ended in collision with a solid concrete pillar on a stretch of route 61 to the west of

Kil, and Hammarö church was completely full. Gunilla had her sister Barbro for company, but her mother and father had elected to stay at home. Barbro would have done the same if Gunilla hadn't pleaded with her to come.

I've got to have someone, she begged. If you don't help me now, I shall never ask you for anything ever again. I can't go to the church alone; they'll murder me with their eyes. Are you my sister or not?

Don't talk such crap, Barbro retorted. You've only yourself to blame. But OK, I'll come.

Tomas was out of the question, of course. They drove up from Uppsala together, but taking him to the church would have been a step too far. Did you see? They would have said. Lennart's scarcely in his grave and she's already got a new one.

Tomas hadn't acquiesced meekly, but in the end she persuaded him. For the duration of the funeral he sat in Wermelin's cafe and read Hesse. He'd also planned to take a walk and look at the town and the River Klarälv, but it rained non-stop.

She remained riveted to her pew. By people's looks, but also by her thoughts – that was how it felt. Lennart Martinsson certainly played the main role at his own funeral, but the female lead was without doubt Gunilla Rysth. She perceived this with a clarity that virtually deafened her, and it was the one time in her life that gave her some inkling of how it must have felt to be burnt at the stake as a witch in the seventeenth century.

Towards the end of the service all the friends Lennart – and Gunilla – had grown up with filed past the coffin at the front of the church, singly or in small groups, but when it was her turn, she suddenly found herself unable to move. She felt paralysed, nailed to the hard pew, and she knew that if she lived to be a hundred, she would never experience a worse moment.

Outcast.

Pariah.

Witch.

And she deployed the witch metaphor again in the car with Tomas on the way back to Uppsala an hour later. He laughed at first, but then grew grave.

'How the hell could they do that to you?' he said.

'My thoughts exactly,' she replied.

'I'm sorry,' he said. 'You're never going to have to go through anything like that ever again. You have my word.'

'Thank you,' said Gunilla. 'Do you know what one of his sisters said to me when we we'd come out of the church afterwards? "Thanks for killing my brother, you fucking whore." That was the only remark anyone made to me the entire time. There were three hundred people there, and I knew almost every single one of them.'

Tomas clenched his jaw audibly and she could see his knuckles turning white as they gripped the steering wheel.

'Never again, Gunilla, I swear it. What a bunch of pricks.'

'Ordinary people, Tomas,' she said. 'They're just ordinary people.'

When her mother rang a couple of weeks later to ask if she was planning to come home for Christmas, she said she wasn't.

No, she wasn't planning to do that, and her mother didn't ask for any explanation, either. She seemed to approve of the decision; the gulf that had opened up between them with Lennart's death was too wide to bridge. For now, at least.

She tried to find some kind of sound emotional logic in this paralysis of family relations, but the more she thought about it, the more barren and hopeless it seemed.

It must have been like that all along, she thought. It just hasn't been clearly visible until now. I knew it all along, but I preferred to close my eyes.

She wasn't sure if this was true or not, and she didn't want to brood on it any longer.

'It's medieval,' was Tomas's opinion. 'This way of thinking is totally out of place in the twentieth century. It's barbaric!'

Talking about her family sometimes made him furious, and she was secretly glad of his violent reaction.

'You broke off an engagement, that's all you did,' he went on. 'Is forced marriage the fucking norm in Värmland, then?'

'Shall we go to your parents in Sundsvall for Christmas?' she asked.

'No way,' answered Tomas. 'We'll spend it in Sibyllegatan in Uppsala. And on Christmas morning I shall get you pregnant.'

And so it was.

They spent a simple Christmas together in their little flat. Tomas had a whole week's leave, and she thought no one could wish for better days than this. Two people who loved each other. Enclosed in a shell that protected them from the whole world, from everything old and tainted and unjust, that was how it felt – and from the persistent rain and slushy snow outside.

Instead, candles and red wine and Leonard Cohen. *Songs from a Room.*

And lovemaking. Lots and lots of lovemaking.

When Gunilla got the confirmation in early February, it

seemed the most natural thing in the world. With the baby expected at the end of September, the simplest thing was for her to arrange a break in her studies for the autumn term. Her degree would take six months longer than she'd planned, but it need cost no more than that.

'You don't think we could fit in another one before you go back?' asked Tomas and she thought: well, yes, why not?

Then she wondered if it wasn't a bit presumptuous to plan your second child before the first one had even been born. But she found it hard to imagine anything could go seriously wrong.

10

'Germund Grooth,' said Eva Backman, passing Barbarotti a cup of coffee. 'Interesting name.'

Gunnar Barbarotti, having been on the receiving end of roughly a hundred thousand queries about his own name over the years, made no comment. He took the coffee and started to scrutinize the list of those involved in 1975.

On Sunday 28 September 1975, to be exact, when seven friends had gone out on a mushrooming expedition and only six had returned:

Rickard Berglund

b. 1949. Vicar of the parish of Rödåkra–Hemleby.

Anna Berglund

b. 1951. Wife of RB. Maiden name Jonsson. Journalist at the *Swedish Church Times*.

Tomas Winckler

b. 1948. Marketing expert at Handelsbanken in Gothenburg.

Gunilla Winckler-Rysth

b. 1949. Wife of TW. Bachelor of Arts. Translator.

Maria Winckler

b. 1950, d. 1975. Sister of TW. Living with GG. Teacher of French and English at Kymlingevik School.

Germund Grooth

b. 1948. Living with MW. Teacher of physics and maths at Kymlingevik School.

Elisabeth Martinsson

b. 1947. Teacher of art at Kymlingevik School. Single.

'Virtually the same age,' he remarked once he had gone through the names. 'You're right. Only four years between the eldest and the youngest.'

'Yep,' said Backman. 'They were all around twenty-five then. Now they're around sixty. Who drew up the list? Sandlin?'

Barbarotti nodded. 'I assume so. There's another one just the same in the folders, at any rate.'

He added a cross and the year 2010 after Germund Grooth's name. 'Two out of the seven,' he said. 'What do we make of this?'

Eva Backman didn't answer.

'If someone's got a plan to kill them all,' Barbarotti went on, 'he doesn't seem to be in much of a hurry about it. If he gives himself thirty-five years between each one, he won't be done for – well, what would it come to – a hundred and fifty years at least?'

'They were a couple,' said Eva Backman.

'Who were?' asked Barbarotti.

'Germund Grooth and Maria Winckler. They were living together in 1975. They weren't married, but being married was pretty much out of fashion in the 1970s.'

'Is that a fact?' said Barbarotti. 'Well, we're dealing with three couples and one loose horse here. And both the other couples seem to have made it up the aisle.'

'Or to the town hall,' said Eva Backman. 'Though one of them's a clergyman, and I'm guessing they don't go for registry office weddings.'

'What does it matter if, and how, they got married?' asked Barbarotti, tapping the list irritably with his pen. 'Three couples and one single person, that's the important part. And one of the couples no longer exists, because they died at precisely the same spot, thirty-five years apart. You still haven't told me what you make of a story like that.'

'My spontaneous guess?' said Eva Backman. 'Is that what you're angling for?'

'Yes,' said Barbarotti. 'Based on . . . on your twenty years of experience as a successful police officer, with a clear-up rate way above the national average percentage.'

'Nineteen,' said Backman. 'Years, I mean, not per cent. You're forgetting I had all those kids as well. But since you keep badgering, I suppose I'll let you have my suggestion. She slipped and he jumped.'

'What?' said Barbarotti. 'Hang on, let me think.'

He tried his coffee. Pulled a face and changed the subject. 'Does this foul brew really come from the new machine? It tastes even worse than it used to.'

'It's still running in,' Eva Backman informed him. 'Give it five or six months and it'll taste divine.'

'Great,' said Barbarotti. 'I'll look forward to that. But what did you mean when you said one slipped and one jumped?'

Eva Backman gave a shrug. 'Just a possibility,' she said. 'But pretty plausible, as far as I can see. If Maria Winckler, for instance, accidentally fell to her death in 1975, it could well happen that the man – this Germund, that is – wanted to be united with her in some way. If he'd decided to take his own life . . . for some reason.'

'United with a woman who died thirty-five years ago?' said Barbarotti.

'Inscrutable are the ways of the human mind,' said Eva Backman.

'Hmm,' said Barbarotti, staring down into his coffee cup. 'And they can be simpler than we think sometimes, too, don't forget. We've got three variants to play with, to be precise . . . times two, that is.'

'Yes, I know,' sighed Backman. 'The same old thing. Accident, suicide, murder . . . the last of which also includes manslaughter. Times two, as you say, Inspector. So, what's your own view of the matter?'

'I haven't got one,' said Gunnar Barbarotti. 'But I know which double I wouldn't bet on.'

'Which is?'

'Double accident. The idea that he would go and lose his footing in exactly the same place as his partner did, all that time ago – completely unintentionally – no, it just wouldn't happen.'

'Presumably not,' said Backman, picking up the list of names. 'Do we know which of the rest are still alive? All five or . . .?'

'We don't know a darned thing,' Inspector Barbarotti said. 'But it's time to rectify that ignorance now. Asunander wants a detailed report in' – he checked the time – 'almost exactly twenty-four hours from now.'

'OK then,' said Backman. 'Where do we start?'

'In different places,' said Barbarotti. 'I suggest I take the past. I do have slightly more experience, after all, and I've already appropriated Sandlin's files. You can poke around in the present. Find out where—'

'Where the five of them are today,' Backman interrupted. 'Yes, despite my youth, I agree with you. I imagine a few interviews will be required in due course. How long had Mr Grooth been lying there when Elis Bengtsson found him, by the way? Do we know that at least?'

'Not precisely,' said Barbarotti. 'But we should get the report this evening. I heard something about two days and nights. Or more than one, at any event.'

'Wouldn't Bengtsson have found him on Saturday in that case?' queried Backman. 'Rather than Sunday? I thought he did that circuit every day?'

'Maybe he's got other walks as well,' said Barbarotti. 'We'll have to check that.'

'I'll do it now,' said Eva Backman. 'I'll go back to my room and start ringing round. See you tomorrow then?'

'Yes,' said Barbarotti. 'I'm off home now.'

Eva Backman looked at her watch. 'It's half past three.'

'I know what the time is,' Barbarotti told her, 'but I left those files on my bedside table.'

'Absent-mindedness and old age go hand-in-hand,' said Eva Backman. 'Regards to Marianne.'

A good hour's work later, she had compiled a new list. A feeling of gloom had gradually descended on her. There was something about this jump forward in time; a group of twenty-somethings so suddenly transformed into sixty-year-olds – of course they had lived for many years in the meantime, had children and built houses perhaps, entered into new relationships, seen foreign continents and carved out careers, but the two isolated incidents out at Gåsaklyftan had an unpleasant shrinking effect on the time interval.

As if thirty-five years were no more than an hour, in fact. The hour it had taken her to chart the circumstances of each one of them on this very day: 27 September 2010.

And, of course, the sensation applied to her, too. Today twenty-five, tomorrow sixty. Or, worse still, what was the title of that old crime novel? *Today Red, Tomorrow Dead.*

She had four years to go to her fiftieth birthday. Barbarotti only had a few months, and didn't seem particularly bothered by the prospect. This, naturally, was of no particular relevance to the current investigation, but it wasn't always easy to separate work and private life in your head. Thoughts tended to wander, especially in the afternoons when your blood-sugar levels were hovering just above zero.

She sighed and went to the kitchenette to fetch a cup of the dubious coffee. She returned to her room and sat down to attempt a broad-brush analysis of the current state of play.

For those who had not plunged down into Gåsaklyftan, that was. If you wanted to be a bit dystopian about it.

So, there were five of them. None had had their lives cut

short in the period between September 1975 and September 2010, it turned out, and all five still lived in the kingdom of Sweden.

That was a good start. It meant she could get hold of them. Each and every one would be interviewed, if it were thought necessary. Eva Backman was pretty sure it *would* be thought necessary, nor did she disagree with that conclusion herself.

Both the married couples were still married. That had to be seen as unusual, she thought; if you married young in the early seventies, the chances that you would be celebrating, say, your silver wedding were pretty slim. She remembered she'd read an article on the subject, a while back. A decade later the odds were rather better, but still demonstrably below 50 per cent. Both she and Barbarotti fell into the latter category, as it happened, and neither of them had been able (or had wanted?) to keep their families together until the children had at least grown up. Things were as they were, and they did nothing to chase away the feeling of gloom. Life certainly did suck.

But Rickard and Anna Berglund were still married. So were Tomas Winckler and Gunilla Winckler-Rysth. The vicar and his wife (though Rickard Berglund didn't work in the church any more) lived in Kymlinge; they had left the vicarage out at Rödåkra and, since 2005, had lived at an address in Rosengatan. He had a job at Linderholm's, the funeral directors, and his wife had been too ill to work for some time. Before that she was a freelance journalist. Predominantly for the *Swedish Church Times*.

The Wincklers lived in Lindås, outside Gothenburg. They were both registered as self-employed, he in the travel business, she running some kind of consultancy.

Elisabeth Martinsson – the loose horse, as Barbarotti had put it – was now living in Strömstad and was an illustrator by profession. She was still a loose horse, but had been married for a while (seven years) in the eighties, and had a daughter, born in 1983.

The Berglunds had no children. The Wincklers had three.

The children were of no significance for her purposes, thought Eva Backman, pushing away her notes. But that was the sort of extra information you found yourself with, when you engaged in this kind of ferreting.

None of them had a criminal record, anyway. They all seemed financially stable, in the case of the Wincklers more than stable, but whether they still met socially at all, or whether there was – or had been – any unfinished business between them, was not something any of the databases could tell her.

But that was always the way, thought Eva Backman. If you wanted to put any meat on people's bones – or find the skeletons in their cupboards – you had to meet them face-to-face.

If not to interview them formally, then at least for a little chat.

About Gåsaklinten, for instance. Then and now.

That was what detective work was about, or an important part of it, at any rate. Asking people questions and weighing their answers wisely. That was what it basically came down to. Quite simple, really.

As regards Germund Grooth, who had shuffled off this mortal coil in Gåsaklyftan a few days earlier, Inspector Sorrysen had already dug out the basic details. She sorted through her sheets of paper to find the relevant one and studied it for a few minutes.

He was registered as living in Lund, where he also worked. *Had worked.* Senior lecturer in theoretical physics, awarded a doctorate in 1983. *Gradient Fragmentation Processes within Density Functional Theory.* He'd have been thirty-five at the time, she calculated. Well, she guessed that was quite a standard age for completing a PhD. He was single, had never been married, and had lived at the same address in Prennegatan for the past twenty years. He had published various other things in his area of expertise; he'd presumably made his mark in academic circles.

But no professorship, she noted. Ah well, not everyone could be a professor; it was pretty common knowledge that a lot of intrigue and scheming went on in the university world.

As for what could have brought a solitary senior lecturer in physics to the forests around Kymlinge on a weekend in September, she would leave that for tomorrow.

Unless it really was as simple as she had suggested to Barbarotti. That Germund Grooth wanted to end his days in the same place as his partner had done, three and a half decades earlier.

Like hell he did, muttered DI Backman to herself. Then she yawned and realized the time had reached five.

Sufficient unto the day, she thought. She switched off her desk lamp, left her room and started thinking about what she might make for dinner.

Dinner for one. It felt like a contradiction in terms, somehow.

11

Maria the sparrow here.

A week ago it was my twentieth birthday. I spent it very quietly.

Mum and Dad wanted to come down but I put them off. I told them I was going to the Stockholm archipelago with some friends.

The archipelago? In March? Mum queried, and I said they were stinking rich and the house was well insulated. They fell for it, especially Mum.

Tomas and Gunilla wanted to organize a birthday dinner at their flat, but I told them the same lie.

Friends? He must have thought. Have you got friends, little sparrow sister?

But he didn't say it. And he didn't ask the friends' names or which island their house was on.

When I say I spent my twentieth birthday very quietly, it's not the whole truth. I spent the evening with Germund in his flat in Tunabackar. We drank vodka and made love. He's the best lover I've ever had and, before we fell asleep that night, I told him it had been my birthday. He took it exactly the way I would have done. Said it was a good thing I hadn't said anything in advance, because buying presents had never really been his thing.

We must have fucked for four hours; I never get tired of him, even though it's one orgasm after another. Maybe it's because he doesn't go all ecstatic like other boys do.

Ecstatic and weak. I don't like that. Germund keeps his cool. He says the only things that really interest him are pure mathematics and physical love.

I know exactly what he means. *Pure mathematics and physical love.* All that emotional outpouring that sloshes around between those two poles – no, it disgusts me. Its tackiness and lack of rigour make me feel physically sick. I demand precision in life.

This is the only way Germund and I socialize. He phones or I do, to ask if we can meet up.

He comes to my place or I go to his. Usually the latter; my room is so small and the walls are thin, and even though I know how to keep my orgasms silent, I've no wish to share my love life with the Holmberg family, who live in the rest of the house. Though I bet Mr Holmberg, whose first name is Arne, would find it rather stimulating. He's given me a look or two, and Mrs Holmberg, whose other name I don't actually know, seems more interested in her loom down in the basement than she is in her husband. When Germund and I fucked for the first time in my narrow bed we gradually got into the same rhythm as her, or she matched herself to ours, I don't know which. Germund and I both thought it added extra zest.

But usually, as I say, we're at Sköldungagatan in his little flat. We drink a bit of vodka, sometimes we eat something with it, like crackers or gherkins or cheesy snacks, but never much because you don't make love so well on a full stomach. Then we do it. Smoke, and drink a bit more vodka. Do it again. When I say vodka, I mean either neat or with a touch of lime. Germund sometimes wants orange juice, but I never do.

87

We don't have breakfast together the next morning. Just shower and say bye, that's all. Since we met, we've been together ten or eleven evenings and nights, but we haven't been to the cinema once, or gone out for a coffee in town. What would be the point of just sitting in a cafe? says Germund. If you want that sort of cuteness from a guy, I'm sure you can find other willing volunteers.

Have I ever asked you to sit in a cafe in town with me? I ask.

Fair enough, says Germund. Sorry.

But one night he screamed.

It woke me, but not him. It was half past four, he must have had a nightmare and he was in a cold sweat. When I asked him the next morning, he said yes, he must have done; he did sometimes dream about his parents and younger sister.

They all died in a car crash. Germund was ten years old when he lost his whole family in a second. No, wrong, it must have taken longer than that, because the car went into a big river and they drowned. We've never talked about it, and in fact we avoid talking about our childhoods or our lives at all. We gave each other a brief account of our backgrounds, but no more than that.

I don't know how Germund took it when he suddenly found himself all alone in the world, but I've thought about how I would have reacted.

It's hard to say, of course, but I don't think it would have bothered me, deep down.

There are very few things that bother me deep down. I don't know if that's because I'm evil, but I like to stick to the truth.

*

Germund sees other women, of course he does.

He's an extremely attractive man. He also looks rather sad most of the time, and they generally fall for that. He arouses their maternal feelings; he can't help it. Sometimes we tell each other about our various conquests and find it very funny. When I told him about how things went between me and this boy Bengt Åke on my course, who I went with after the St Lucia student party in December, Germund had a laughing fit and could scarcely stop.

I know I'm attractive, too, and I raised the subject with Germund. That perhaps there's a third absolute, apart from pure maths and physical love – beauty.

He thought it over for a while and then agreed with me. I wouldn't want to be blind when you're riding me, Maria, he said. You've got a point there.

I know I've got a point. We always leave the light on when we're doing it.

I haven't been home to Sundsvall since Christmas, and I doubt I shall go up again before August. I've applied for a job for the whole of June and July at that pub called The Prophet in the town centre. I don't definitely know if I'll get it, of course, but the man who interviewed me seemed positive. Nearly all the other girls, and it is almost all girls reading French, will be going to France for the summer, naturally. It's seen as important to spend some time in an entirely French-speaking environment, but I don't care. I don't know whether I shall really take the next stage of the course this autumn or not.

I've no plans for my life; I've always had this feeling I shall die young, so there's not much point. But I shall spend a couple more years here in Uppsala, I'm sure of that. I like this town.

There's something about the atmosphere. And the anonymity; I can be myself and nobody interferes in what I do. There are so many students, they kind of can't keep track of what everyone gets up to. You can drift into one of the student clubs you don't belong to, say your name's Clarissa von Platen, you come from some little place on the west coast and you're reading art history. Not a soul will protest. It does amuse me.

Germund will be staying on here too, and that can't do any harm, either, of course. He's reading theoretical physics in parallel with the maths, so he's studying at twice the rate of everybody else. I might decide to do the same thing, in due course. Take two subjects instead of just one. The French really doesn't involve much effort, apart from the length of time I devote to reading all those books. Balzac, Stendhal and Zola, though Maupassant's the only one I like. I think Maupassant would have shared our thinking on pure maths and physical love.

Perhaps on beauty, as well.

Tomas and Gunilla are expecting a baby. They revealed this last week, when they invited me round for some home-made pizza and to sample their home-made wine. I pretended to be enthusiastic, but Tomas saw through it anyway. When we were on our own for a minute, I asked him if they were out of their minds; hadn't they heard of contraception? He just shook his head and gave me that usual big-brother look of his. Superior and pitying. And it wasn't the baby he felt sorry for, it was me. His crazy little sister who hasn't a single human feeling in her body.

Well, do as you like, I said. Just don't count on me for babysitting, that's all.

Wouldn't dream of it, said Tomas.

OK, I said. Congratulations then. Everyone has to be allowed to find happiness in their own way.

Even you, my sparrow sister? he said, trying to sound like someone in an Astrid Lindgren story.

Especially me, I replied, and I could see he wasn't happy with that response. He finds me disturbing and I've nothing against that. Just the opposite. And I think Gunilla's a bit scared of me, actually. That doesn't worry me, either.

The baby's expected in the autumn, anyway. There's plenty that can go wrong before then.

12

It was half past nine in the evening before Barbarotti got a chance to sit down for a concerted look at Sandlin's files.

When he was on his way home in the car, Marianne rang to say she had to stay at the hospital and take on a late-evening shift. One of her colleagues had gone home sick, and they had no fewer than six women in the queue to give birth.

He'd just have to cope, because who was he to stand in the way of women giving birth? To repeat: Sweden's youth is its future. With Jenny and Martin's help, he cooked dinner; with Johan's help, he did a running repair on the malfunctioning washing machine, and then spent an hour testing Lars on the French Revolution. It was reassuring to know that schools were still teaching the French Revolution and, if he wasn't much mistaken, in exactly the same way as they had done when he'd had to plough through it in his teens.

But after all this activity, he wished the kids goodnight. He told them he needed some peace and quiet for a detailed bit of police work, closed the door to the upstairs office that he and Marianne shared and laid out all the material from back in 1975.

He had only glanced at the files so far, not been through them thoroughly, as Backman possibly imagined. He had leafed unsystematically back and forth while sitting with some of the family, watching an old Michael Caine spy film on TV. In view of what had come to light in the course of the day, it seemed high time to tackle the task a little more seriously.

High time indeed. At least forty-eight hours had passed, probably more, since Germund Grooth met his death out at Gåsaklinten, and just as he had told DI Backman, Barbarotti found it hard to believe it had been a mere accident. Truth to tell, he wasn't inclined to accept the suicide theory, either, even though he couldn't give any real reasons for this intuitive judgement.

But perhaps there were leads to be found in what had happened thirty-five years before: the sudden death of the young and – by all accounts – beautiful Maria Winckler at the old clifftop leap. If such leaps had ever existed, but that matter evidently remained open for discussion.

She had been living with Grooth at the time, that much was not a matter for conjecture. And it also seemed indisputable that there must be some way to link them – the old and the new. It was only a matter of establishing how.

Only? thought Barbarotti. What the hell do I mean by *only?*

At any event, Asunander was expecting a report the following day, and a report was what he would get.

Sandlin was a scrupulously thorough devil, that was the least you could say about him, and Barbarotti was already well aware of the fact. The files were green and had tables of contents listing no fewer than sixteen transcriptions of interviews (the six surviving participants in the ill-starred mushroom hunt, plus ten other individuals, as yet unknown to Barbarotti), an autopsy report, a report from the search at the scene, plus assorted other bits and bobs. Sandlin's own running commentaries on the case, for example. There were eight of these, the first dated 29 September 1975 (the day after the death), the last 22 December the same year.

Two days before Christmas Eve, thought Barbarotti. Sandlin spent three months on this.

Before he gave up and concluded that it had in all likelihood been an accident, that is. Or that he had not been able to find anything to substantiate a contrary view, at any rate.

But he must have had his suspicions, Barbarotti realized. Even if you were a scrupulously thorough devil, you didn't spend three months on someone who happened to slip and fall off a cliff. That just didn't seem reasonable. What was more, some of the interviews had been conducted as late as November and December, so things hadn't simply run out into the sand, as they sometimes did. Sandlin had been actively working on the case the whole time, right up to Christmas. The decision to close the investigation, the final sheet of paper in the file, was dated 9 January 1976.

Moreover, noted Barbarotti, Sandlin had carried out all the interviews himself, in the presence of a colleague of course, as the regulations prescribed, but he had clearly liked to be in full control. He left very little to chance, as far as one could judge, and hardly anything in others' hands. Plainly not particularly enjoyable to work for, Barbarotti could see. One of those old-fashioned, stubborn miseries, presumably, who only trusted himself – and barely that.

He leant back in the desk chair for a while, considering his own behaviour. How many years did he have left before he, too, reached the misery stage? And which of his colleagues did he trust, when something really serious was at stake?

He shelved the first question. As for the trust question, he decided there were two: Backman and Asunander. Admittedly Asunander was both a misery and a pig-headed mule – and generally a bad caricature of how a boss ought to behave – but he had a subtle sense of intuition that was seldom wrong. You had to give him the credit for that, Barbarotti thought. And he had identified the man from Mousterlin, three years before. That alone was impressive.

And Backman? Well, obviously. All comment superfluous.

Inspector Borgsen, nicknamed Sorrysen because of his melancholy demeanour, was always dutiful, correct and, moreover, willing to work round the clock – or had been, before becoming a father – but he lacked precisely the thing Asunander had. The intuition. The flair.

He could, however, track down a runaway shoplifter in a desert, if he needed to.

Though why on earth would he ever need to do that? Gunnar Barbarotti sighed, bent his head to the desk again and returned to Sandlin's files. Might just as well start with the interviews, he thought, then turned the page and began.

Interview with Germund Grooth. Kymlinge police station. 29 Sept. 1975. Time: 13.30. Present: Detective Inspector Evert Sandlin, Detective Constable Sigvard Malmberg.

ES: I'd like you to give your name and address.

GG: Germund Grooth. Söderbyvägen 32C.

ES: Thank you. Is that here in Kymlinge?

GG: Yes.

ES: Allow me to express my condolences. But as I'm sure

you understand, we've got to look into the circumstances of this tragic death. Do you agree?

GG: I agree.

ES: OK. You and the deceased, Maria Winckler, were living together. Is that right?

GG: That's right.

ES: How long had you been together?

GG: Four or five years. It depends how you count.

ES: Really? How long had you been living under the same roof?

GG: About three years.

ES: Where do you work?

GG: Kymlingevik School.

ES: And Maria, where did she work?

GG: At the same school.

ES: So, two teachers?

GG: Temporarily, yes.

ES: What do you mean by temporarily?

GG: That we didn't intend it to be forever.

ES: Of course. Tell me more.

GG: We found those two jobs at the same school. She taught English and French. I taught maths and physics.

But neither of us has . . . had . . . a teaching qualification.

ES: So you haven't been living in Kymlinge for very long?

GG: We moved into Söderbyvägen on 1 August.

ES: I see. As I say, I'm very sorry about this tragic turn of events, but now I'd like us to talk a bit about what actually happened on Sunday.

GG: That's all right by me. As I've already told you.

ES: Good. OK, so the two of you went on an outing with some friends. Perhaps you could fill me in on some background?

GG: What do you want to know?

ES: Who you all were. How you know each other. Whose idea it was.

GG: There were seven of us. Three couples who've done things together over the years. Plus one other woman, another teacher at the school.

ES: Go on. Can you give me some names?

GG: Maria and me. Maria's brother Tomas and his wife Gunilla, they live in Gothenburg. And then Rickard and Anna Berglund. He's a vicar, out at Rödåkra. We were all together on Saturday night at the vicarage, where they live.

ES: That only makes six. Who was the seventh?

GG: Elisabeth Martinsson. The one from school.

ES: Was she with you all on Saturday night, too?

GG: No. And I don't know why any of this is important. My partner slipped, and fell to her death. What are you trying to get at?

ES: I want to rule out various possibilities.

GG: What possibilities?

ES: That it might have been something other than an accident. You know, don't you, that some of the group heard her cry out as she fell?

GG: Yes, I know that. I heard her cry out, too.

ES: Can you describe her cry?

GG: It was just some inarticulate sound.

ES: No words?

GG: Not that I could make out. I was quite far away from her.

ES: How far?

GG: I don't know.

ES: Can you make an estimate?

GG: A hundred and fifty or two hundred metres, I'd say. Not close to the edge of the drop.

ES: You couldn't see her?

GG: No.

ES: Could you see any of the others at the precise moment it happened?

GG: No.

ES: Why not?

GG: Because the trees were pretty thick where I was. Young spruces, mainly, and I couldn't really see in any direction. I was looking for mushrooms . . . like everybody else. I think we were quite spread out.

ES: You were quite spread out?

GG: Yes. If you're looking for mushrooms, there's not much point all looking in the same place.

ES: How long had you all been looking when the incident happened?

GG: A good hour. We'd talked about going back for coffee, and so on, at one. It was a few minutes after twelve that it happened.

ES: Did you find any mushrooms yourself?

GG: No. But I was really only looking for chanterelles.

ES: Do you know if any of the others found anything?

GG: I think Anna found some. Maybe Elisabeth as well, but I'm not sure.

ES: Did you and your partner see much of each other in the hour when you were all in the forest?

GG: Not really. We both set off in the same direction, but then we made for different areas.

ES: Did you talk to her much?

GG: Hardly at all, only in the car on the way out.

ES: So you and Maria went out there together?

GG: Yes, we met the others at the Rute Stones. There's a car park there and we'd arranged to start from there.

ES: Did you make any firm plans before you all set off into the trees?

GG: No, just said we'd have our packed lunch at one o'clock. We left the things in a particular place and said we'd all meet back there.

ES: But it didn't turn out that way?

GG: No.

ES: Roughly how far from the car park would you say you all went?

GG: Not very far. A kilometre, maybe.

ES: Yet you couldn't see any of the others when it happened?

GG: No. I've already told you that.

ES: What did you and your partner talk about in the car?

GG: Nothing in particular.

ES: Can you be more specific?

GG: No.

ES: Noted. Which of the others did you talk to as you were wandering about looking for mushrooms?

GG: None of them.

ES: None?

GG: We may have exchanged a word or two right at the start.

ES: And?

GG: Then we fanned out. That's only natural, isn't it?

ES: Perhaps. When the incident happencd, how long was it since you'd seen any of the others?

GG: I can't remember.

ES: Think about it for a moment, please.

GG: I think I saw Maria and Elisabeth five or ten minutes before.

ES: Were they together?

GG: No, apart.

ES: But you didn't talk to either of them?

GG: No.

ES: And it was twelve noon when you heard your partner cry out?

GG: A couple of minutes after, yes.

ES: What did you do?

GG: Well, naturally, I went in that direction.

ES: And?

GG: We all made for the same place, of course.

ES: Who was already there when you arrived, can you remember?

GG: Only Elisabeth. Rickard and I got there about the same time, though from different directions. Elisabeth was in a state, so I realized something had happened.

ES: What did you do?

GG: I ran over to Elisabeth, and she pointed down to the bottom.

ES: Go on.

GG: I looked down and saw her lying there. Do we really have to go through this, I told you all about it yesterday.

ES: I realize it's painful for you. If you need a break, do say so.

GG: I don't want a break. I want to get this done as fast as possible.

ES: All right. If we can just go back a little: you said you were all at the Berglunds' house on the Saturday evening. Was that when the idea for the outing first came up?

GG: No, it was suggested well before that.

ES: Elaborate.

GG: I don't get what it is you want me to elaborate on.

ES: I think you do.

GG: I don't know what you're talking about. We'd decided to spend the weekend together. Rickard and Anna had moved here, to Kymlinge, and so had we. We're old friends from our Uppsala days. We were all studying at the same time. And the Wincklers, Tomas and Gunilla, came up from Gothenburg. Like I told you.

ES: And the programme was a get-together on the Saturday evening, followed by an excursion on the Sunday?

GG: Yes, it was. Do you see anything odd in that?

ES: Not at all. I'm just trying to get all the details clear in my mind.

GG: In order to exclude certain possibilities?

ES: Just so. And this seventh member of the group, Elisabeth Martinsson, how does she come into the picture?

GG: She's only a colleague from school. Maria told her we were going out to the forest, and I think she asked if she could come along. She's new, too, and she hasn't got a car.

ES: So how did she get out to the Rute Stones?

GG: She came with the others. I think she lives somewhere along the way, so I suppose they picked her up.

ES: I see. And to return to the Saturday night, how did it go?

GG: It was uneventful.

ES: Could you be more specific?

GG: There's nothing to be specific about. We had dinner, then sat and talked. Tomas and Gunilla were staying over at the vicarage. Maria and I went home about twelve, I suppose.

ES: Which of you was driving?

GG: Why do you ask?

ES: Could I ask you just to answer the question, please, rather than firing back questions of your own? We'll get on all the faster that way.

GG: We took a taxi. We'd both had some wine.

ES: I see. And what was the mood like, that evening?

GG: The mood was good.

ES: Nothing out of the ordinary?

GG: Nothing out of the ordinary.

ES: What do you think happened out at Gåsaklinten?

GG: Me? I think she missed her footing and fell, of course. There's no point you trying to convince me of anything else.

ES: I see. When did you realize she was dead?

GG: As soon as I saw her.

ES: How could you be sure?

GG: She'd fallen twenty-five metres, straight down onto some rocks. Of course she was dead.

ES: But you didn't see her fall?

GG: No.

ES: Do you know if anyone else did?

GG: See her fall, you mean?

ES: Yes.

GG: No, no one saw it.

ES: And how do you know that?

GG: We talked about it, obviously. We had plenty of time to talk before the police arrived.

ES: How long, approximately?

GG: An hour, I'd say. Tomas got himself to a house nearby and called them from there. The rest of us waited where we were.

ES: And you discussed what had happened?

GG: What else would you expect us to discuss? Politics?

ES: And what conclusion did you reach between you?

GG: That she must have slipped, of course.

ES: No one was of a different opinion?

GG: No.

ES: Where were you while you were waiting and talking?

GG: We were down there. Right by the body.

ES: Wasn't it difficult to get down?

GG: Not in the least. There was a path to climb down, it took about thirty seconds.

ES: OK. But some of you had heard her cry out, isn't that right?

GG: Yes.

ES: And did anyone actually make out what she was shouting?

GG: I don't think so. They all heard it. Anna and Elisabeth had the idea it was a sort of long 'uuh' sound and then a couple of short syllables.

ES: An 'uuh'?

GG: Yes.

ES: As in 'murderer', say?

GG: Possibly, yes. Look, can't we stop this now? It doesn't feel particularly worthwhile. My girlfriend's just lost her life. I don't like being subjected to this.

ES: I completely understand that this isn't very pleasant for you. But unfortunately I have no choice. How was the relationship between you and your girlfriend?

GG: What exactly do you mean?

ES: Was it harmonious or did you have rows?

GG: Maria and I haven't had a single row since we met.

ES: You seriously expect me to believe that?

GG: You can believe what you like.

ES: And relations in the group as a whole, were they impeccable, too?

GG: You'll have to ask the others about that. Maria and I didn't feel we had any scores to settle with any of them, that's all I can say.

ES: And they had none with you?

GG: I'm not the one to ask about that.

ES: Elisabeth Martinsson, how well do you know her?

GG: I don't know her at all. It was Maria who asked her to come along.

ES: Was she afraid of heights?

GG: Eh?

ES: Maria, your partner. I'm asking if she was afraid of heights.

GG: No, not especially.

ES: No tendency to giddiness?

GG: No.

ES: Have you any explanation of why she fell, out there at Gåsaklyftan?

GG: No. You've already asked me that.

ES: Has she been feeling depressed?

GG: No, she hasn't been feeling depressed. I'm sorry, but I'm not prepared to carry on with this any longer. If you're going to ask me questions like that, I'd like a solicitor present.

ES: A solicitor? Why on earth would you want that?

GG: [*No answer*]

ES: Just one more thing. Could you mark on this map where you were when it happened?

[*GG does so. Time taken: less than ten seconds*]

ES: All right, you're free to go. Interview terminated at 13.48.

That was eighteen minutes, noted Barbarotti after flicking back through the pages to check. The interview had lasted no longer than that.

But reading it had not taken him even that long. A mere ten to eleven minutes. Perhaps Sandlin had deliberately left out some of the questions and answers. He had made the transcription himself, and the three people present had all signed it.

But had Germund Grooth really bothered to read through it? Very likely not. And that detective constable . . . Malmberg . . . No, in all probability he hadn't, either. To do so would have shown mistrust of a superior, and Sandlin was presumably not the sort of man you wanted to get on the wrong side of.

Why am I thinking about this? wondered Barbarotti. Why am I trying to see an old colleague, now deceased, in a bad light?

Maybe because the interview was so hard-boiled. It had a tone that he couldn't really get his head round. Grooth had just lost his partner and there should have been no reason to go in so hard. It was as if Sandlin genuinely suspected him. Grooth's reaction was justifiable; Barbarotti tried to imagine how he would have conducted an interview in those circumstances, and even though he still hadn't mastered all the finer points of the case, he felt pretty sure he would have gone about it in a different way. A bit less aggressively – surely that would have felt more natural? A little more gently?

Unless, of course, Sandlin had been damn sure he could smell a rat and was convinced there was something amiss where Maria Winckler's death was concerned.

And he had suspected it from the word go. Sandlin had been dead for twelve years. Pity, thought Barbarotti. I wouldn't have minded a little chat with him. Maybe that Malmberg was still in the land of the living? It would certainly be worth looking into.

He saw that the time was just past 10.30. All right, he thought. A cup of coffee and two more interviews.

13

If Anna Jonsson had opted for the shoes with the lower heels, everything would have been different.

However you looked at it – whatever fatalistic or political complexions you tried to put on it – that was the plain fact of the matter. In their early days together, in the summer of 1970, they both liked discussing this remarkable truth; it was a piece of private history, hard not to cherish and keep coming back to. Particularly on certain evenings, in the bleaker hours when there wasn't much else to talk about. When everything that ought to be simple and natural, and usually was, suddenly felt difficult and complicated. And there were such times, as Rickard discovered even in the early stages of their relationship, but he knew, too, that it was the way things had to be.

Because they were different, Rickard Berglund and Anna Jonsson, nobody could claim otherwise, and for the first time in his life Rickard understood the rule that opposites attract. Maybe she did, as well; he assumed she did, but they were both amateurs in the field of love, and it wasn't easy to tell.

It was one Tuesday evening at the end of April that the courses of their lives happened to intersect. There was no evening duty for once, and Rickard had gone into town with Helge. He couldn't remember if they'd gone with any particular purpose in view, or simply fancied a coffee at Güntherska or a hot dog from the Nybro Grill. Maybe they'd planned to take a stroll around and pop in to see if there were any interesting books in the sale at Lundequist's or in any of the second-hand bookshops; that was one of their regular ploys.

Anyway, they'd slipped into Viktor's Books on Drottninggatan. It was after closing time, but the legendary Viktor Persson wasn't the sort to shoo his customers out with a meaningful look at the clock – and it was as they emerged from the chaotic second-hand bookshop that they found there was a protest march coming their way from up at the base of the castle. Heading for the square at Vaksala torg, probably. That was the usual route. The banners were the usual ones, too, as were the slogans. As far as Rickard could judge, anyway. They were about Vietnam, about South Africa and something called PRO-K that neither Helge nor Rickard had heard of.

They stopped on the pavement and watched the left-wing crowd pass by. Those young people with their unshakeable beliefs. Rickard had read about Professor Hedenius and his attempts to equate Marxism with Christianity – he rejected them both, and on the same grounds, if Rickard had understood correctly – and Rickard wondered if he should try to get hold of the book. Could there be Christian believers among these ranks, marching in time and chanting their relentless slogans? That was a good question. Unshakeable beliefs came in a variety of forms. How did that sort of mental landscape function, if so? And Marxist priests in Latin America, he'd read about them, too. How did that work? What with opium of the people, and one thing and another.

He was deep in thought about such matters when it happened. A girl on the march tottered, gave a cry of pain and fell.

Or would have fallen, if Rickard hadn't smartly caught her.

Or did she fall straight into his arms, in fact? They would come back to that very detail from time to time that summer: had he in fact intervened at all, or had she just imposed herself upon him, so to speak? There was a certain difference, of course, at least in their private world of symbolism. In any event, he helped her to sit down on the kerb and sat down beside her.

'Are you all right?'

She groaned, rubbing her left ankle.

'Ow! Ow!'

'Does it hurt?'

'It hurts like hell! I must have sprained it! Oww!'

The marchers continued to stream heedlessly by. She attempted to scramble to her feet, but sank back down.

'Damn. I can't carry on.'

He stole a look at her. Her hair was a darkish brown, and cut rather short. She was thin-faced, with big eyes currently bright with tears. He could see that her foot was really hurting.

She was quite small and slight, and was wearing one of those Mah-Jong jackets, with a Yasser Arafat scarf round her neck, classic protest-march gear. Red cord trousers. No make-up.

But, yes, shoes with a little heel. Maybe to make her seem a bit taller, thought Rickard. And it was the heel that had made her lose her footing, he realized. She said nothing, just sat there looking at her foot. She ran her hands over it cautiously and gave a faint groan. Rickard became aware that Helge was standing just behind them, too shy to step in and help.

No one else stepped in to help, either. It was just Rickard, sitting there on the edge of the pavement with this stranger and her sprained foot, attempting to find something to say.

'Do you want to try standing up? You're welcome to hang on to me, if you like.'

'Thank you. I think I'll need to rest a bit longer before I try.'

'The demo? Do you want . . .?'

'I couldn't care less about them. Were you on the demo as well or . . .?'

'No, I was just watching.'

'I see. No, I can't walk to the rally at Vaksala torg with this foot.'

She had taken off her shoe, and he could see that the ankle was already starting to swell up quite badly. As the final cluster of marchers went by, she dabbed her eyes with the corner of her black-and-white-checked scarf and leant against him.

'Sorry about this, but I think I shall have to ask you to help me up.'

He did so. She tried to put some weight on the foot, but she couldn't. She grimaced with the pain of it and moaned.

'I'll come to the hospital with you. We can take a taxi.'

He started trying to tell Helge to go and get hold of a taxi, but she immediately protested. 'No, no, there's no need. It's only a sprain, for goodness' sake. But I . . . it would be good if . . .'

'Yes?'

'If you could stay and help me a bit of the way.'

'Of course,' said Rickard. 'Where do you live?'

'Glimmervägen.'

'Glimmervägen? I don't really know . . .?'

'Eriksberg. No, you're a student of course, and students don't know where Eriksberg is.'

'I'm not a student,' said Rickard. 'I'm doing my military service.'

'Oh? Sorry. But if you just help me up the hill, I can get my bus outside Carolina.'

'OK.'

He tried to provide some support by holding her under the elbow, but it didn't work very well. 'I think you might have to . . .'

'Yes?'

'It'd work so much better if you put your arm round my neck.'

She took off her other shoe as well, stuffed one in each jacket pocket and put her left arm round his shoulders. They began limping slowly along the pavement towards the slope. She barefoot, he in a pair of black clogs. After a few steps he put his arm round her waist, too, and as he did so, he felt something start to vibrate inside him. He didn't know what it was, but he couldn't deny it was vibrating.

'What's your name?' he asked.

'Anna. What's yours?'

'Rickard.'

'Rickard. Where's your friend gone?'

Rickard looked around for Helge, but he had vanished.

'I don't know. He probably went back to barracks. Were you with friends on the march?'

She pulled a face. 'Oh yes. There were a few of us.'

He waited for her to elaborate, but she didn't. It seemed a bit odd to him that none of the other demonstrators had stopped to help her. They had just let her fall. And yet the word 'Solidarity' had been on one of the banners, in white lettering on a black background. He wondered if he should ask her about it, but thought she might possibly take it as a provocation. And he didn't want to provoke her. On the contrary, he wanted to hang on to that warm, vibrating feeling and he wondered how to make sure it wouldn't all end igno-miniously at the bus stop.

She didn't say much, just held on to him and limped along; it clearly wasn't hurting quite as much any more, as long as she didn't put too much weight on that foot. It took them a few minutes to get up to the bus stop, and she studied the timetable and said she'd have fifteen minutes to wait for the next bus.

They sat down on the bench.

'I'll be fine now. You don't have to look after me any longer.'

'I'll come with you on the bus.'

'You really needn't.'

'I've nothing else to do.'

'Of course you have.'

'Yes, but nothing better.'

She gave a laugh. 'You're quite the gentleman, I must say.'

He laughed, too. 'Is there anything wrong with that?'

'No. But I . . . I'm used to managing on my own.'

'Couldn't you make an exception, just for once?'

She hesitated for a moment. Then she nodded. 'If you're absolutely sure I'm not keeping you from anything important?'

'I'm sure.'

'God, look at it!' She pointed to her foot. 'It's as big as a balloon.'

'We'll have to put some ice on it when we get you home. Or run it under cold water, at the very least.'

She nodded. 'You seem to know about this kind of thing.'

'They give us a bit of basic medical training in the army.'

'You don't learn how to kill people?'

'I shall never bear arms for real.'

'Oh? So why are you doing military service then? If you don't plan to fight for real?'

He shrugged. 'I don't know, quite. It's an experience, I suppose. But killing someone would be unthinkable.'

'All right. Well then, I hope you never have to.'

'Mm.'

They sat in silence for a while, contemplating her swollen foot.

'Rickard, I'm really grateful to you for doing this. You'll have a fair way to drag me in Eriksberg, too, just so you're prepared. It's at least two hundred metres from the bus stop to my place.'

'No problem. We do plenty of physical-fitness training in the army. I could carry you, if you wanted.'

She laughed again.

I like her, thought Rickard Berglund. And I'm sensing she doesn't think I'm too much of an idiot. To think it can happen this fast.

If only it doesn't end just as fast.

He stayed at Glimmervägen all evening. Anna Jonsson had a bedsit with a balcony that faced out over the city forest park. He helped her to cool the foot and bandage it up. Then she sat on the sofa with it well propped up and instructed him while he made tea and toasted sandwiches. Ham, cheese and tomato, nothing out of the ordinary; it was an unusually warm evening for so early in the year, and they ate on the little balcony. It was past eleven when he left.

She thanked him for helping her and gave him a hug. She was standing on one leg in her cramped little hall as she did so, and he couldn't help feeling she held him a little longer than she strictly needed to. A couple of seconds like that might mean something, but they might just as well mean nothing at all.

She'd given him her phone number, though, and he'd promised to ring the following evening to find out how she was getting on.

Whether she'd gone to work, for instance. She worked as a nursing assistant at the Akademiska hospital and it probably wasn't realistic for her foot to improve so much overnight that she'd be able to look after all those patients. Better for her to be a patient herself; she promised him that, if need be, she would get herself down to the local medical centre on Västertorg. It could turn out to be something more serious than a sprain, after all.

He took the path through the trees to get back to barracks and realized he was walking with a spring in his step. He was bursting with what had happened, even though he was well aware it hadn't been much. Not in that way, but if any of his mates at the barracks asked how he had spent the evening, he could answer that he'd been round at a girl's flat in Eriksberg. And it wouldn't be a lie.

He hoped somebody *would* ask. Somebody else apart from Helge, who'd naturally be wondering how the evening had unfolded.

She'd told him a fair amount about herself, actually. Unlike most of the other young people he'd met in Uppsala, Anna was born in the town. Her parents' house was in Salabackar, on the other side of Tycho Hedéns väg. She was now nineteen and had moved out after her first year in upper secondary, where she was on the two-year social-studies course. After that she took the job at Akademiska, where she'd been working for nearly a year, but eventually she hoped to become a journalist. She was currently writing articles for various left-wing magazines: the *Vietnam Bulletin*, *Clarté* and several others; it was a boyfriend of hers who was the main political activist, and her main role was really helping him with material . . . Or a former boyfriend, she hadn't really spelt it out, but Rickard interpreted her as meaning they weren't together any more. Or they weren't getting on particularly well with each other, at any rate.

'Was he on the march this evening?' he'd asked, and she'd nodded but made no further comment.

She hadn't said what he was called, and Rickard had interpreted that as a good sign. If she'd had a current boyfriend, she'd surely have mentioned him by name, wouldn't she? She'd talked about all sorts of other things: her parents, her two brothers, the dreary, heavy work at the big hospital. But she only had a few months of that to go now. In the autumn she was off to the college of journalism in Stockholm. She hadn't heard if she'd definitely got the place yet, admittedly, but her chances were evidently good.

Rickard had hesitated over whether to let on that he was planning to read theology; he assumed his choice of subject would not be particularly popular in lefty circles – the aforementioned opium of the people – but she accepted the information without mocking him. She told him her parents were both atheists, or at least she thought so, but they never discussed such things. Typical nose-to-the-ground socialists with no sense of vision, she claimed, and although her father had once been active in his trade union, he'd got fed up with it. Both her parents were old, anyway, and her father had retired; her two brothers were ten and twelve years older than she was.

'An afterthought,' she'd called herself. 'I don't think they wanted me, and I certainly wasn't planned.'

'And you've never had any sort of religious faith yourself?'

'Maybe when I was little,' she said. 'I went to Sunday school, even though Dad thought it was petit bourgeois and ridiculous. I even started the preparation course for confirmation, but I decided not to carry on.'

'Why was that?'

'I'm not really sure. Something didn't feel right. Maybe it was the priest who was teaching us, he never got through to me somehow, and I . . . well, if I'd had any faith before, I lost it then.'

'Most people who get confirmed have never had any faith at all,' said Rickard.

It was then that she put a hand on his arm for a moment. 'You're absolutely right there,' she said. 'Most people don't believe in anything.'

'What do you believe in?' he asked, and she took her time replying.

'Just at the moment, not very much,' she said finally, sounding rueful. 'Just at the moment I'm exactly the same myself, but sometimes it's more important to be able to ask questions than to hunt for the answers. Well, perhaps that sounds a bit odd, but I can't help it.'

'I don't think it sounds odd at all,' he assured her, and then they talked about the Vietnam War for a while, and the state of the world generally.

They talked about the injustices, about poverty, about socialism. He could tell she'd read up on such topics; she threw in plenty of acronyms for freedom movements and parties he'd never heard of, yet her political convictions didn't seem particularly fervently held. She didn't seem to be trying to win him over to her side. He supposed it must be like she'd said: it was the nameless former boyfriend who'd been the driving force.

But if you break it off with the boyfriend, maybe the political ideas go the same way? He didn't know, but assumed this was probably a simplistic way of looking at it. And she did have both Mao and Che Guevara on her wall.

He got back to barracks just before midnight. He and his comrades had now advanced in rank to the point where they were allowed to stay out all night if they wanted. As long as they were lined up for inspection at seven in the morning like everyone else, nobody said a thing. When he got up to the sleeping quarters he ran into Helge, who had just come out of the washroom on his way to bed.

'How did it go?' he asked.

'It went splendidly,' Rickard said. 'Where did you get to?'

'You rogue,' said Helge.

Rickard had to smile. To think there were young people still using the word *rogue* in this year of Our Lord 1970.

One, anyway. Helge from Gäddede.

14

Interview with Tomas Winckler. Kymlinge police station. 29 Sept. 1975. Time: 15.35. Present: Detective Inspector Evert Sandlin, Detective Constable Sigvard Malmberg.

ES: Your name and address, please.

TW: Tomas Winckler. 17 Annebergsgatan, Gothenburg.

ES: My condolences. No one regrets what has happened more than I do, but I hope you understand that we're obliged to ask some questions.

TW: Yes, I understand.

ES: It was your sister who died at Gåsaklyftan yesterday. Maria Winckler. Can you tell me in your own words what happened?

TW: I'm not sure what happened. I can't take it in.

ES: I can understand that you're in a slight state of shock. I'd really just like you to describe what happened out there, as you saw it.

TW: All right, I can try. But there isn't much to tell. She lost her balance and slipped, that must have been what happened.

ES: Must?

TW: Maybe she went too close to the edge and lost her footing on some loose stones, I don't know. I didn't see how it happened and none of the others did, either.

ES: Why were the group of you out in the forest?

TW: It was just an ordinary sort of outing. We'd brought a picnic lunch and we were hoping to find some mushrooms. We'd been together the night before at Rickard and Anna's; they and my sister and her partner have just moved to Kymlinge.

ES: Yes, we know. Whose idea was the outing?

TW: I don't know. We'd decided we'd meet up that weekend, and we must have made that arrangement about a month ago. Saturday evening at the vicarage, and so on. At Rickard and Anna's invitation, of course.

ES: And the mushroom hunt? Whose idea was that?

TW: I don't see why it matters whose idea it was.

ES: But you understand why I'm asking you these questions?

TW: Yes. Well, no, not really.

ES: Because I'm investigating the circumstances surrounding your sister's death. It's my job.

TW: I get that it's your job. But I wonder what these circumstances are that you're talking about. Or looking for.

ES: It's part of routine police duties to look into anything that isn't clear, when there's been a fatality.

TW: Yes, I get that, too. But what isn't clear about Maria's death?

ES: A healthy young woman falls from the top of a cliff. In broad daylight. Of course it could be an accident, but there are also other plausible alternatives.

TW: [*No answer*]

ES: You understand the alternatives I'm thinking of?

TW: Of course I do. I'm not stupid.

ES: Excellent. And what's your view of those alternatives?

TW: [*No answer*]

ES: I appreciate you might be finding this difficult. Perhaps it would be easier if we went through the alternatives one at a time. So, do you think there could be any possibility that your sister took her own life?

TW: [*Shakes his head but says nothing*]

ES: It would be helpful if you could give a verbal answer to my questions. We're recording this interview, as you know.

TW: I don't think my sister took her own life.

ES: Can you give me any reasons why you believe that?

TW: What do you mean? Why should she have taken her own life?'

ES: A lot of people do. How was your sister feeling? Was she depressed?

TW: Maria wasn't depressed.

ES: Were the two of you close?

TW: She was my sister.

ES: What does that mean?

TW: It means I knew her pretty well.

ES: So you all met at the Berglunds' home on Saturday evening. How long was it since you had seen your sister, prior to that?

TW: I don't know exactly.

ES: Think about it.

TW: It must have been in June I saw her. She and Germund were in Gothenburg then.

ES: When in June?

TW: Early on. Around the tenth, I'd say.

ES: So that was three and a half months ago?

TW: It's possible.

ES: And before that?

TW: What?

ES: When did you last see your sister before that time in June?

TW: I can't remember. And I don't see why this matters. Six months ago, maybe. But I don't think my sister was suicidal. I would have . . .

ES: Yes?

TW: I would have seen it on the Saturday evening.

ES: And you didn't?

TW: No.

ES: What was the mood like, that evening?

TW: The mood? It was good.

ES: All evening?

TW: Yes, the mood was good, all evening. I'm sorry, but I don't see what you're driving at here. I find your questions rather insinuating. What are you trying to get out of me?

ES: I'm trying to rule out those two alternatives we talked about.

TW: Suicide and . . .?

ES: Murder, yes. Is there anyone in the group who might have had a reason to kill Maria?

TW: My God! What the hell are you trying to say?

ES: I'm not trying to say anything. Do you really not see that I have to work this way? Don't you think it's important for us to investigate the circumstances surrounding your sister's death?

TW: Yes, of course I do. But the idea that one of . . . of us . . . could have . . . no, it's out of the question. Completely out of the question.

ES: Where were you when it happened?

TW: Pardon?

ES: Where were you when Maria fell into the cleft?

TW: I was some way off. A couple of hundred metres, maybe. I don't know.

ES: Were you on your own?

TW: Yes. I was looking for mushrooms.

ES: Were any of the others in sight from where you were?

TW: No. No, they weren't in fact.

ES: Tell me what happened.

TW: I heard someone cry out. I couldn't hear that it was her.

ES: What did the cry sound like?

TW: Sound like? It just sounded like a cry.

ES: And what did she cry out?

TW: I couldn't hear any words.

ES: You know some of the others think it could have been a message?

TW: I don't follow.

ES: She was trying to say something before she died.

TW: No. What could she possibly have been trying to say?

ES: You really haven't spoken to the others about this?

TW: No.

ES: What did you, personally, do after you'd all discovered Maria?

TW: The others stayed where they were. I went back to a house and phoned for help.

ES: Who took the decision?

TW: What decision?

ES: That you'd be the one to go for help.

TW: I can't remember. I might have done it myself. What does it matter?

ES: It was your sister who was dead. And yet you decided to leave her.

TW: Christ almighty. Somebody had to go and make the call, didn't they?

ES: I assume so. Didn't any of the others offer to do it?

TW: I don't remember. No, I don't think so.

ES: And you decided to go on your own?

TW: Yes, but it wasn't something we discussed. For God's sake, she'd just fallen to her death. Naturally we were all upset and in a state of shock.

ES: Naturally. If we go back to the Saturday evening, how did Maria seem then? Did you notice anything in particular?

TW: No.

ES: Anything she did or said that you've wondered about, looking back on it?

TW: No.

ES: There weren't any arguments or anything like that?

TW: No, nothing like that.

ES: How well do you know the others in the group?

TW: I know them very well. The Berglunds and Maria and Germund are good friends of ours.

ES: How did you all get acquainted?

TW: It was when we were at university in Uppsala. Rickard Berglund and I did our military service together, as well.

ES: An old gang of friends, you might say?

TW: Yes.

ES: And roughly how long have you known each other?

TW: About five years. Nearer six, actually.

ES: And Elisabeth Martinsson?

TW: I don't know her at all. She teaches at the same school as Germund and Maria.

ES: And she wasn't with you that evening?

TW: No.

ES: How did Maria get on with the others in the group?

TW: What do you mean?

ES: There must have been antagonism from time to time? Things must have happened occasionally. Try to think back.

TW: I don't know what sort of things you mean.

ES: If you've been in each other's company so often over a period of six years, surely there must have been conflicts?

TW: Of course there've been conflicts. But nothing that could have any bearing on my sister's death.

ES: How can you be so sure?

TW: Because I know these people.

ES: Really? If you think about how your sister seemed on Saturday evening, you can't recall her behaving un-usually in any way?

TW: No, she didn't behave unusually. Nobody did. We had a nice evening. There's no point carrying on with this line of questioning.

ES: None of the others did anything unexpected in any way?

TW: No.

ES: How did you spend the evening?

TS: How? We had dinner and chatted, and so on, of course.

ES: Did you drink much?

TW: No, not much at all. Just wine with the meal.

ES: What did you talk about?

TW: All sorts of things. We hadn't seen each other for a while.

ES: Can you give me any examples of what you talked about?

TW: What it was like living in Kymlinge, for example. That was only natural, wasn't it, seeing as all four of them had just moved here?

ES: You and your wife stayed the night?

TW: Yes, I told you, we live in Gothenburg.

ES: And your sister and her partner?

TW: What about them?

ES: How long did they stay?

TW: Until around midnight.

ES: How did they get home?

TW: I think they took a taxi.

ES: You think?

TW: They took a taxi.

ES: What time did you and your wife go to bed?

TW: Straight after Maria and Germund left. My wife's pregnant, she gets tired easily.

ES: I see. Have you any other children?

TW: No.

ES: And none of the others have any children?

TW: No.

ES: Or are expecting?

TW: Not as far as I know. I have to say, this all feels pretty pointless. Do you even know yourself why you're asking these questions?

ES: Let me worry about that.

TW: It feels like a waste of time, anyway.

ES: Do you know if Maria had any enemies?

TW: Enemies? No, she didn't have any enemies.

ES: Did you see anyone else out in the forest, apart from your group, that is?

TW: No. Well, yes, actually. A man with a dog came along just after it happened.

ES: Did you speak to him?

TW: No, I was already on my way to fetch help. I think the others spoke to him. He was there when I got back.

ES: Which other members of the group did you talk to while you were all out in the forest?

TW: None of them, basically. I was going round on my own, and so were the others.

ES: Which of them were closest to you when it happened?

TW: I think Gunilla was quite close by. Maybe Anna, too, but I don't remember.

ES: I've got a map of the area here. Could you put a cross where you were when you heard your sister's cry?

[*TW does so. Time taken: 15 seconds*]

ES: Thank you. How well do you know Germund Grooth, Maria's partner?

TW: I know him well.

ES: You seem a little hesitant.

TW: No, I'm not. I know him well.

ES: What's your opinion of him?

TW: Good.

ES: And their relationship, what have you got to say about that?

TW: I've no wish to say anything about their relationship. Nor about any other relationships, either. There really doesn't seem any point to this any more.

ES: That's your judgement. I shall make mine.

TW: Naturally. But I've nothing more to add, in any case.

ES: All right then, we'll finish here. But I may have reason to get back to you at a later stage. Interview terminated at 15.50.

15

The foetal heartbeat stopped on the last day of April and the baby was removed in two stages at the Akademiska hospital on 1 and 2 May.

When they got back home to Sibyllegatan, Gunilla noticed that the leaves were unfurling on the birch trees. They got out of the taxi and it struck her that she hadn't said a single word since they left the hospital. Almost all day, in fact – not during the procedure, or afterwards. It had been the same yesterday, in point of fact. Tomas had been trying to talk to her pretty much the whole time, but she couldn't remember a word he had said.

What's happening to me? she thought. Am I going to have a breakdown? Have I already had one? I feel as though I'm somebody else.

'The birch leaves are coming out,' she said, just to show him she hadn't fallen silent forever.

'Yes,' said Tomas. 'They're beautiful. Life goes on.'

Does it? she thought. How the hell can you know that?

He didn't mean any harm by it, of course, but to her it felt like a kind of mockery. To claim that everything carried on. It was exactly the opposite: everything had just stopped. The moment seemed precisely chosen, too; the moment at which April turned into May was undoubtedly the hub of the whole

Uppsala year. The child had died on the last day of April, the day they all said farewell to winter and welcomed the return of spring and life. The day they all partied from morning to night: open-air breakfast, traditional pickled-herring lunch, mass donning of white student caps at the foot of the castle, the race to student clubs for champagne, the whole carry-on . . . Thank goodness, she thought, thank goodness they hadn't gone in for much of a celebration themselves. Tomas was on duty until twelve, then they had a simple herring lunch at Sibyllegatan with Rickard, Maria and Germund. The others went to join the crowds below the castle around three, but she felt slightly unwell and stayed at home. Tomas wasn't away more than a couple of hours, though a slight whiff of cigar smoke hung around him as he came through the door.

Towards evening she'd started feeling worse, and at ten they went to the hospital, but by then it was already too late.

It would have made no difference even if they'd come in earlier, the doctor told them straight away. What had happened would have happened anyway.

They shouldn't blame themselves. He didn't say it, but she could see by looking at him that it was what he meant.

Blame? she thought. No, it wasn't about that. She wasn't sure what it was, but blame didn't come into it. Did the doctor think she'd been drinking beer and wine at breakfast and needed comforting, so she wouldn't reproach herself? She hadn't touched a drop.

Tomas helped her up the stairs. There was a bouquet of flowers hanging from the door handle. She wondered if it might be from Maria and Germund, but it wasn't. Of course not; Tomas had organized that, too.

'Are you tired?'

She nodded. Just as well to pretend she needed sleep. They wouldn't find their way back to each other today, whatever they did. She would just upset him. Drag him down into her own hopelessness. Better to lie there in bed and pull the quilt over it all.

Life's so damn fragile, she thought. Not just Lucy, but everything and everyone.

They'd called her Lucy, as if they'd known from the start that the baby was a girl. She didn't really know where the name had popped up from, but now Lucy was dead and there was no need to worry about her. She had never existed and consequently did not have to be called anything.

Punishment? That was what sprang to mind, once Tomas had tucked her up and gone out for some juice and fruit and anything else he thought she might want. Or perhaps simply because he needed to be on his own for a while. Was this about *punishment*?

Why not? Less than a year had passed since she broke it off with Lennart Martinsson, and now she had two lives on her conscience. His and Lucy's.

It wasn't a thought she could share with anyone else. Especially not with Tomas; he was far too rational and sane for anything like that. But she knew, deep inside, that some such dark connection did exist.

Between what you did and what befell you.

And there was no one to turn to. No one to talk to, and no mercy.

It was like sinking into deep mud.

This is the end for me, she thought. I won't get through this.

★

A week later, she saw a psychiatrist. His name was Werngren, he was in his sixties and he wore a yellow polo-necked jumper. She assumed it was meant to cheer up his patients.

This sort of thing is more common than you might think, he told her. Both losing a child in pregnancy and reacting the way you are.

And what do you know about it? she thought. The fact that it's common doesn't help in the slightest. How many times have you been pregnant?

Even so, he was probably the one who put her thoughts on the right track. Eventually. She saw him once a week right through to mid-July, and when she and Tomas went on holiday to Ibiza after his army discharge in August – in the brief window before term started – it felt as if they were embarking on something new.

As if thoughts of punishment, mud and misery really had decided to leave her in peace.

'I'm sorry,' she said as they were sitting on the balcony with a jug of sangria that first evening. 'And thank you for putting up with me.'

'Just say the word when you're ready for another go,' he said.

She didn't understand what he meant at first, and when she realized he was talking about another baby, she asked him kindly but firmly to shut up.

She had two catch-up exams to sit in early September; there were other things to focus on, apart from reproduction. She didn't tell him she'd gone back on the pill, and he didn't ask.

But something had happened to her. Even though Dr Werngren had put her back on her feet in a very general sense, and she could think back on Lucy, whom she had carried under her heart for eighteen weeks, without tears or anxiety attacks, she was not the same person she had been a year ago.

She knew it and Tomas knew it. It was like a weight, or so it seemed to her in the mornings. She always used to wake early and get up, if not with a spring in her step, then certainly with ease, relishing the prospect of a new day. With a sense of expectation. She wasn't entirely clear how she felt nowadays about whatever lay ahead, but it was definitely different. You had to stay vigilant; relaxing, or imagining that life was a laden table just waiting for you to help yourself, would be a mistake. A naive act of folly.

Caution is a virtue, is that what I've learnt? she asked herself. That it's better to be a bit pessimistic to avoid disappointment?

In September, Tomas started his economics course, and she passed both her catch-up exams and carried on with her German. In the middle of the month her staff-sergeant father back in Karlstad suffered a stroke, even though he was only fifty-seven and had never smoked – but it was only a mild one, and both her mother and her sister Barbro told her she didn't need to come home. She hadn't seen them for six months, and she quietly wondered if it would take a funeral to get her into the car for the 280-kilometre trip.

They had met up with Tomas's parents, though. A couple of times, in fact: in Sundsvall, and in Uppsala. They'd come to Uppsala in early June, on their way to Fuengirola in Spain, where they had just bought a house. They were thinking of selling their house in Sundsvall and moving down there for good, but they hadn't quite decided. They wanted to get used to the idea first.

And while they were doing that – getting used to the idea – the house down on the sunshine coast stood empty for long periods. It was an opportunity not to be missed. Tomas and Gunilla booked themselves in for a week in January, in the break between the autumn and spring terms. It wasn't the best time of year for southern Spain admittedly, but swimming in the sea surely wouldn't be the only activity available?

It was still only autumn, however. There were social events at the student clubs and choir singing and prelim exams and dinners; Tomas and Gunilla were both members of the Norrland club, and even those who had lost a child discovered that the city of eternal youth presented temptations hard to resist in the long run. In November they decided to throw a seasonal dinner party at Sibyllegatan: elk casserole with funnel chanterelles and glazed onions. Rickard Berglund had acquired a girlfriend, Germund and Maria were always on the list for obvious family reasons, and Tomas proposed inviting a couple of fellow economics students and their other halves, who he said were worth getting to know. Ten of them, so it was going to be a tight squeeze, but the elk meat they'd got hold of, from up in the forests around the River Indal, would serve twice the number. And they'd ask people to bring their own drinks.

Gunilla had no objections. Tomas seemed to feel an almost physical need to arrange this sort of social gathering, and what he'd said was true, of course: life went on.

16

Eva Backman had intended to start with the Berglunds, as they lived in Kymlinge, but it turned out to be an inconvenient time.

And that was putting it mildly. She already knew Anna Berglund was on sick leave, but what she didn't know was that Anna was in the final stages of cancer.

They *did* know that, however, at Linderholm's funeral directors, where Rickard Berglund had worked since abandoning his career in the church in 2005. Backman had already been pondering this peculiar change of profession. Or maybe it wasn't that remarkable? How were clergymen to earn a living if, for some reason, they no longer wanted to stand up in church and preach? What would be most suitable? The property business? Healing? Maybe it was quite natural to switch to the flock of funeral providers, so you still had a bit of contact with your old job? A funeral was a funeral, thought Eva Backman. Why not?

In any event, Holger Linderholm, who had owned and run the firm since the autumn of 1978, when his father died, informed her that Mrs Berglund had been diagnosed with cancer a few years before and hadn't got long left. She was up at the hospice, waiting to die, not to put too fine a point on it. Her husband was spending as much time with her as he could, and from the following week he would be on compassionate leave. For as long as he needed it.

But it could only be a matter of weeks, Linderholm told her. Possibly days; they were keeping her alive, but wouldn't extend her suffering unnecessarily. She was having morphine for the pain; it was a terrible way to go, really, but that was the way it turned out for some people. There was nothing anyone could do about it, and it wasn't fair.

Eva Backman asked if he was in touch with Rickard Berglund, and Linderholm said he was. As well as being work colleagues, they had also become good friends over the years. Even though Linderholm was more than ten years older. They had got to know each other when Berglund was still a clergyman; naturally they'd had quite a lot in common, even back then.

And Anna Berglund and his own wife had been friends, too. Ellen Linderholm had died three years before, but in earlier times the two couples had often invited each other over for dinner. And they would sometimes find themselves playing whist and Trivial Pursuit as well, he couldn't deny it.

Eva Backman gave him a brief outline of what had happened and why she wanted to get in touch with Rickard Berglund – but of course there was no rush, in the present circumstances – and Linderholm promised to pass on the message as soon as he got the chance.

Backman thanked him and went out to the car, where she sat studying her list before she rang the number of the Winckler-Rysth family in Lindås. The wife answered straight away; her husband was in London on business, she said, but yes, she had a moment to talk. What was this about?

Inspector Backman told her, and it went very quiet on the line for a few seconds.

'Hello,' said Backman. 'Are you still there?'

'I'm here,' Gunilla Winckler-Rysth confirmed. 'It just knocked me sideways, that's all. Him as well? What . . . what does this mean?'

'That's what I'd like to talk to you about,' said Backman. 'Have you got time this afternoon?'

'Yes . . . yes, that should be all right,' said Gunilla Winckler-Rysth with some hesitation in her voice. 'But we live in Lindås, and you must be ringing from . . .?'

'From Kymlinge, yes,' said Eva Backman. 'But I can be there in a couple of hours. It's no problem. Shall we say one o'clock?'

Gunilla Winckler-Rysth said that would be fine and launched into a detailed description of how to find the place. But there was no need, Backman having already put the address into her GPS.

She let Gunilla finish, even so, sensing that she somehow needed to say it.

According to Backman's list, this woman was over sixty, but she looked younger. No doubt she went to the gym three or four times a week, thought Eva Backman. Slim, elastic and entirely wrinkle-free. Platinum-blonde hair, just the shade for when you couldn't be blonde any more but didn't want to go grey.

Maybe she didn't even need to leave home to stay in shape, in fact; the multi-level detached house, all glass and silvery-grey wood, would be big enough to accommodate both a pool and a workout room, for those who felt so inclined.

But there was no chance of a guided tour. Gunilla Winckler-Rysth emerged to meet her the moment she got out of the car, and it was evident that she was keen to talk. She had a vague aura of unease about her, and Backman couldn't decide if it was acute or chronic. They sat down at a granite-topped table in a kitchen that looked as if it had only been installed last week. Gunilla Winckler-Rysth had already set the table with dark bread, cheese and a salad garnish, plus a carafe of water with slices of lemon. She asked Backman if she wanted tea or coffee; Backman opted for coffee and her hostess started fiddling with a big espresso machine, all gleaming stainless steel. It, too, looked brand new.

'What a lovely place you've got,' said Backman. 'How long have you and your husband lived here?'

'Nearly a year,' came the answer. 'We lived on the outskirts of Gothenburg before. We like the more rural setting down here.'

Her voice, too, had that diffuse edginess to it. A hint of guilty conscience, possibly, or something of the kind. Backman looked out of the window and thought there was bound to be a nice woodland jogging track somewhere on the doorstep. I wish I could have a figure like hers in fifteen years' time, she thought as Mrs Winckler-Rysth frothed the milk. But once the coffee machine stopped hissing, Eva Backman decided it was time to shift her brain from physical exercise to the matter in hand. She switched on her new digital voice recorder and placed it next to a granite candlestick in the middle of the table.

'So you didn't know that Germund Grooth was found dead on Sunday?'

'No, I had no idea. It came as a complete shock when

you told me. In the same place as Maria then . . . is that right?'

'Yes.'

'My God. But why? What's the point of . . .?'

'The point of what?'

'Of – I don't know – of dying in the same place as she did? I mean, it's all so long ago. Thirty-five years.'

'Were you still in touch with Germund Grooth, you and your husband?'

Gunilla Winckler-Rysth set two cappuccinos on the table and Backman noted that her hands were shaking slightly. Not much, just a nervous bird's-wing vibration. She sat down opposite Backman and picked an imaginary hair off her black trousers. 'No,' she said. 'You couldn't say that.'

'Couldn't say that?'

Her hostess thought for a moment. 'Hah, well, how can I put it? He pretty much disappeared from the scene after Maria died, but not entirely. I suppose we've seen each other three or four times since then . . . all told. It can't have been more than that. He lives . . . lived . . . in Lund.'

'I know,' said Backman. 'When did you last see him?'

'Only a couple of months ago, actually,' said Gunilla Winckler-Rysth.

'And in what connection?'

'He came here. My husband bumped into him in Gothenburg, they both happened to be having lunch at the same restaurant. Sometime last spring, it was . . . and, well, Tomas invited him here.'

'When did he come?' asked Backman.

'In June – early June. He was at some conference in Gothenburg and he brought a woman with him.'

'A woman? Was he in a new relationship then?'

'It depends what you mean by relationship. Germund's, er, been with . . . quite a lot of women over the years.'

'But he was never married?'

'No. I don't think he ever even lived with any of them . . . apart from Maria. I wouldn't really like to say. I expect this woman was just the latest in a series of casual acquaintances . . . Sorry, that sounds a bit judgemental, but it was the way he was. I don't mean he just picked her up in Gothenburg; we knew there would be the two of them. He'd told us beforehand.'

Eva Backman nodded. 'I see. What was her name? We might need to talk to her.'

'Kristin something,' said Gunilla Winckler-Rysth. 'She was Danish, at any rate.' Then her face assumed a new expression. 'Why . . . I mean, why would you need . . .? Why did you need to talk to me at all?'

DI Backman waited. She observed that her hostess had some difficulty swallowing as she struggled to put her next question into words.

'How did Germund actually die? You're a detective, aren't you, a . . . a criminal investigator?'

DI Backman nodded. 'That's right. We're investigating the death.'

'But why? Why does it need investigating?'

'Isn't that pretty obvious?'

'You mean . . . because of the Maria thing?'

'Yes.'

Gunilla Winckler-Rysth shook her head and clasped her hands. Could be to stop them shaking, thought Backman. Maybe there was a hidden drink problem in the picture here?

145

Upper-class-housewife-white-wine syndrome? That well-toned veneer started to perforate a little and, when it came to it, self-employed businesswoman could mean absolutely anything. The thought occurred to Eva Backman, her prejudices surfacing.

'But that was such a long time ago,' continued Mrs Winckler-Rysth after a slight hesitation. 'It's been thirty-five years, for God's sake. Do you mean to say . . . you found Germund in the same place?'

'Exactly,' said Eva Backman. 'Gåsaklinten in Rönninge, outside Kymlinge.'

'Gåsaklinten . . .' She unclasped her hands and moistened her lips. 'And Gåsastupan, yes, that was the name. They said it was one of those places where people threw themselves to their deaths in the old days, I remember that. But what happened? Did Germund kill himself?'

'We don't know,' said Eva Backman.

'I mean, he can't have . . .'

'Yes?'

'He can't have slipped and fallen in exactly the same place. It just sounds . . . too unlikely.'

'We think so, too,' said Eva Backman. 'What's your own view?'

'Mine?' said Gunilla Winckler-Rysth, raising her eyebrows. 'Why should I have a view? I haven't the remotest idea about any of this.'

Eva Backman tried to gauge how genuine her surprise was, but reached no conclusion, so she decided to go on the offensive. 'I understand there was some speculation about Maria Winckler's death in 1975,' she said. 'That's right, isn't it?'

'Speculation?' said her hostess.

'Yes,' said Eva Backman. 'Speculation.'

Gunilla Winckler-Rysth said nothing for a while. She looked as if she was trying to decide which way to go. Backman's assessment was that she did not like being made to go thirty-five years back in time.

'You're right to say there was speculation,' she said finally. 'And we've never really stopped thinking about it, of course, Tomas and I.'

'And why is that?' asked Backman.

'What?'

'Why have you never stopped thinking about it?'

'It's hardly that strange, is it? Maria was his sister, and the way she died was so . . . well, I don't know what to say.'

Backman waited again. Gunilla Winckler-Rysth shook her head.

'She was such an unusual person, Maria,' she said. 'It was always so hard to predict how things would turn out for her . . . Incredibly clever, and you always felt she was going to keep on surprising you, but for her to die that way. It just seemed incomprehensible, from the very start.'

'How do you think it happened?' asked Backman.

'I think she took her own life,' said Gunilla Winckler-Rysth after a pause. 'Personally, I'm convinced of it.'

Backman guessed family opinion was divided on the subject, but decided not to go into it for the moment.

'Could you elaborate a little?' she asked instead. 'What makes you think Maria took her own life?'

'Why would she go and slip off a high rock like that? It seems so . . . clumsy. She wasn't clumsy.'

'Do you have clear memories of that day?' asked Backman.

'Well, yes, pretty clear. Some things are hard to forget.'

'And you remember the police investigation afterwards?'

'Parts of it. There was an Inspector Sandin, if I remember rightly. He wasn't very pleasant, actually.'

'Sandlin,' Backman corrected her. 'Yes, he was very keen to get to the bottom of it all, which made things a bit uncomfortable at times, I dare say. Do you remember that some people thought she shouted something as she fell?'

'Yes,' said Gunilla Winckler-Rysth, 'I do.'

'And?'

'To this day, I'm certain that she did.'

'No one cast any doubt on it, as far as I know,' said Backman, 'but there were differing views as to what she shouted, weren't there?'

'Yes, there were,' said Gunilla Winckler-Rysth.

'And what was yours?'

'Haven't you looked through the case file? It must be in there.'

'I haven't had a chance yet,' explained Backman. 'One of my colleagues is working on it.'

Gunilla Winckler-Rysth drank some of her cappuccino, dabbing the froth from the corners of her mouth before she answered.

'I thought the same as Anna Berglund and Elisabeth,' she said. 'We thought we heard her cry "Murderer!"'

'Murderer?'

'Yes. You must know that, even if you haven't read the police reports.'

'Of course,' conceded Backman. 'I do know that a few of you thought that was what she shouted. But I wasn't aware it was all the women. My colleague's busy going through the interviews at the moment, as I said.'

'I see,' said Gunilla Winckler-Rysth. 'A couple of the others thought they heard something like "Die", but Anna and Elisabeth said it was a longer word . . . possibly "Murderer!" I think I felt the same.'

'You say felt, not feel,' said Backman.

'It's just . . . it's just not possible to be that definite about something you heard thirty-five years ago.'

'You've changed your mind?'

Gunilla Winckler-Rysth sighed. 'Not really.'

Eva Backman considered this for a moment. 'I don't quite follow,' she confessed. 'On the one hand you tell me Maria Winckler took her own life, and on the other hand you heard her shout "Murderer!" How does that fit together?'

'It doesn't fit together, I know that,' replied Gunilla Winckler-Rysth, pulling a face. 'But Maria was tricky, you have to remember that.'

'What do you mean by tricky?' asked Backman.

'Unpredictable,' said Gunilla Winckler-Rysth after a few seconds' thought. 'Difficult, sometimes. But terribly clever, like I said.'

'Difficult?'

'Yes.'

'Go on,' Backman encouraged her.

Gunilla Winckler-Rysth raised her hands in a half-hearted gesture of resignation. 'I've been thinking about this for thirty-five years,' she said, and began brushing crumbs off the table. 'Not non-stop, of course. But periodically. I can't . . . I mean I just can't imagine that anyone in that group would have pushed her over. But I can imagine – and maybe this sounds a bit crazy, but there has to be some logic in this . . . if you know what I mean?'

'What is it you *can* imagine?' asked Backman.

Gunilla Winckler-Rysth took a deep breath. 'I'd be grateful if you didn't mention this to my husband,' she said. 'We have very different views on this. But in actual fact I can imagine Maria jumping of her own free will and shouting "Murderer" to . . . well, to put the blame onto one of us.'

Eva Backman was silent for a while. Then she said, 'I understand what you're getting at. Did you say anything about this possibility to Inspector Sandlin when he interviewed you back then?'

'I may have hinted at it,' said Gunilla Winckler-Rysth. 'Towards the end. I don't remember.'

'I can check in the case file,' said Backman, 'but I have to say it sounds rather odd. Your theory, I mean.'

'I know,' said Gunilla Winckler-Rysth. 'But she was an odd person.'

'Odd in what way?'

'I . . . I don't really know.'

'Were you close friends?'

'She was Tomas's sister. We saw a lot of each other at one time, for a few years.'

'Can you describe her in a bit more detail?'

Gunilla Winckler-Rysth glanced at the voice recorder. 'You're recording this, right?'

'Do you want me to turn it off?'

'Yes, please.'

Eva Backman pressed the 'off' button and put the device away.

'She was so young,' said Gunilla Winckler-Rysth. 'We were all so young.'

Eva Backman nodded.

'Sometimes it's hard to think that it really happened. So many years have gone by. Our children are grown up, all three of them; they're older than we were then and . . . oh, I don't know.'

'She was your sister-in-law,' Backman reminded her. 'What sort of relationship did you have with her?'

Gunilla Winckler-Rysth looked uncomfortable. 'I never really understood her,' she said, in a tone that made it sound as if, thought Backman, she didn't really stand by what she had said. 'She was always so absorbed in herself and her own business. Not that she was unpleasant or anything, but she just wasn't interested in other people. Apart from Germund, maybe. I assume they complemented each other in some way . . . I suppose that's the expression.'

'But you and your husband saw a lot of them?'

'Oh yes, they were always part of things. In those Uppsala years, I mean.'

'Go on.'

'Well, what shall I say?' She cleared her throat nervously. 'Tomas loved arranging parties and so on. Trips and group activities; he still does, of course. He's been in the travel business ever since . . . Maria and Germund were always invited, and they hardly ever said no, which was a bit peculiar, when you think about it. I think Tomas felt a sense of responsibility for his sister. He knew what a lone wolf she was at heart and felt . . . it was up to him to encourage her out of her lair – or something like that. He took it hard when she died, terribly hard.'

'And the other couple?' asked Backman. 'Rickard and Anna Berglund, you saw a lot of them, too?'

'Oh yes,' said Gunilla Winckler-Rysth, nodding. 'It was

always the six of us. Sometimes other people as well, but always us six. In Uppsala, I mean. And after . . . what happened to Maria, we'd all finished at university, and then things went the way they did.'

'You didn't carry on seeing Rickard and Anna Berglund?'

'No, we didn't actually. Things didn't turn out that way. We lived in Gothenburg and were so tied up with the children and work, they lived in Kymlinge . . . No, since it happened, we haven't seen much of each other at all. We've chatted on the phone a few times, or Tomas and Rickard have, anyway. Gåsastupan and Maria's death, well, it was a turning point, there's no denying it.'

'When did you last meet up?' asked Backman.

'Must have been ten years ago, maybe even twelve,' said Gunilla Winckler-Rysth. 'Since Anna got ill we haven't seen them at all. Tomas has spoken to Rickard on the phone a few times, but we haven't seen them.'

'And when did she get ill?'

'She was diagnosed with cancer three or four years ago, I think. Maybe longer? She's been having chemotherapy and all sorts of things, but they don't seem to have done any good. I haven't heard how she's doing at the moment.'

Eva Backman decided not to update her on Anna Berglund's condition. 'If we could talk a bit more about what's happened to Germund Grooth,' she suggested. 'Can you think of anything that might explain his death?'

Gunilla Winckler-Rysth took at least five seconds to answer and Backman let her take all the time she needed.

'I've no idea,' she said finally. 'Not the faintest idea. I told you I never really understood Maria and, in fact, the same applies to Germund. They were equally tricky, both of them.

I expect that sounds a bit odd, considering how much we saw of them, but it's true, all the same. Yes, that's exactly it,' she said after a short pause, and nodded a couple of times, as if to emphasize that this was an accurate summary of the case.

As Eva Backman was driving back to Kymlinge half an hour later, she thought about two phrases from Gunilla Winckler-Rysth's final statement.

Not the faintest idea. They were equally tricky, both of them.

Perhaps they were two truths as good as any other. The question was whether there really was anything to investigate. Two suicides. Or an accident and a suicide – what was there to suggest that it wasn't one of those two alternatives? And neither of them was a matter for the CID.

Even if Maria *had* shouted 'Murderer' as she plummeted into Gåsaklyftan thirty-five years before, it didn't prove anything, did it? What had Sandlin's insight been? wondered Backman. Had he bought Gunilla Winckler-Rysth's strange suggestion that Maria was trying to attribute the blame to one of the others? Assuming she had actually mentioned it to him, as she thought she had.

Eva Backman herself found it hard to believe in that version of events. If you wanted to implicate someone else at the moment you took your life, you'd shout a name, wouldn't you?

Or had Maria been trying to implicate the whole lot of them? It didn't make sense, as Mrs Winckler-Rysth had also pointed out.

And was it that word 'murderer' that had led Sandlin to invest so much effort in the investigation?

Or had he just been the sort of terrier who wouldn't give

up until he'd turned over every card in the pack? Surely there seemed to be plenty to suggest as much?

Eva Backman realized the question marks were proliferating and growing rather too disparate. Turn this off for now, she decided. Wait until you're sitting down with Barbarotti and a cup of black coffee.

She put on a Brian Ferry CD and accelerated.

17

Sparrow here. Sunday afternoon.

Everybody's complaining about November. I love November. The rain. The trees undressing and standing naked in the gale. The darkness lingering longer and longer every day, the sinking feeling. It makes demands, and not everyone can live on those terms, but I can.

Germund and I. We're moving in together, and he was the one who suggested it, not me. The petty bourgeoisie in Norrtäljegatan don't want to rent out their spare room any more; I don't know if they just want to be rid of me or if they're planning to bring the loom up from the garage or what. I've got to be out on 1 December, in any case, and when I told Germund, he said I could live with him for now.

For now? I said. What the hell does 'for now' mean, Germund?

Until one of us dies, Germund said. What did you think I meant, my sparrow?

Or both of us? I suggested. Maybe one fine day we should arrange to jump off a bridge or fall over a cliff edge together? That would be splendid, don't you think? Dignified and elegant, landing with broken backs at the exact midway point between pure maths and physical love.

I'd just read Calderas' *A Happy Death*, found it at Viktor's

Books the other day, and thought I knew what I was talking about.

Why not? said Germund. When the time comes. But how about a drop of vodka first, eh?

We had a drop of vodka first.

That was the day before yesterday. Yesterday we were at Sibyllegatan for their autumn dinner. Elk stew with everything the forest has to offer, as Dad used to say. And home-made wine, of course. It tasted of yeast as usual, but after two glasses you get used to it. Something happened between Tomas and Germund, I still don't know what, even though I tried to wheedle it out of him.

I didn't try very hard, and maybe it'll come out later.

We were a party of ten. The four of us, and then Rickard with his new girl, one of those leftie birds who don't bother with make-up, her name's Anna. Come to think of it, I reckon she's not just his new girl, but his first. That's simply speculation, though; I don't really know Rickard. I don't *know* anybody at all; I've never quite got the hang of what it entails.

No airs and graces about her, anyway, Anna the first. She seems strong. Quiet and strong. Maybe I could take to her, but I didn't talk to her much. There were two other couples there as well, some students on Tomas's course and their partners. One of the partners was French and had only been in Sweden just over a year, and it was natural for me to pay her more attention. We smoked a joint on the balcony together, too, though we had to do it surreptitiously because Tomas and Gunilla are conservative where that sort of thing is concerned. They're so bloody bourgeois, as if alcohol's that much better than grass. Her name's Nadal, anyway, she comes from Nantes, and she's in Uppsala to read some niche area of art history. Though I don't think she does that much studying; her parents own a chateau and vineyards in the Loire valley. She invited me to come down for the grape-treading next autumn; I don't know if I really liked her, but it was cool speaking French for a whole evening.

But it wasn't that much fun for Germund. He drank too much and was soon letting one of the economists – not Nadal's guy, the other one – get under his skin. He was called Lars-Inge and he really was insufferable, so I understand Germund up to a point. But he ought to be able to handle this sort of thing much better. There's no need to waste energy putting down people like Lars-Inge.

I'm realizing I don't even know Germund 100 per cent. Not even him. When it's just him and me, I always know where we stand. It's when we're in company he can seem somehow alien to me. It really only happens when Tomas and Gunilla invite us round, in fact. Germund and I are hardly ever with other people in any other context. Perhaps it'll be different now we're moving in together, I don't know. Perhaps it's hard keeping your balance on that tightrope between pure maths and fucking. I'm not sure if this is going to work.

Lars-Inge had a loud voice; I bet he comes from a line of politicians and priests going back fifteen generations. He disapproved of most things: blacks, communists, hippies, pop music, Danes, Finns, religious believers, arts subjects and people who don't get it. After four glasses of wine he did anyway, but before that he just sat there meekly, not saying a word. I assume Tomas hadn't seen him the worse for drink until last night, because if he had, I don't know why the hell he would have invited him.

157

After half an hour at the table, Germund asked Lars-Inge's girlfriend, a woman called Berit with big tits and thick crimson lipstick, where she'd found such a charmless prick. Thinking he was joking, because what else could she think, she said he was the illegitimate child of Hitler and a female chimpanzee, and she felt sorry for him because he'd had such a rotten childhood.

Or maybe she didn't think Germund was joking at all; just because you've got big tits and too much lipstick, it doesn't mean you're stupid. Lars-Inge didn't seem to feel like having a row with his girlfriend; maybe he'd just picked her up for the night and was looking forward to a fuck later, so he decided to go for Germund instead.

Shall I beat you senseless or argue you into the ground, you nosy devil? he asked, and then they sat there trading insults for ages, the way drunken males do. That was when Nadal and I went out onto the balcony for the joint. It was her idea; I never smoke grass by choice. When we came back inside, Germund and Tomas weren't there and everything had gone stale. Lars-Inge was leaning back, puffing on a cigar. Anna and Rickard seemed to be considering going home, even though it was only eleven; they were whispering to each other, at any rate. Gunilla and Busty Berit were busy making coffee in the kitchen, and Nadal's guy Bengt was in front of the bookshelf, studying the titles of the books with his head on one side, looking like a depressed question mark. Led Zeppelin had finished but no one had bothered to put a new record on. Nadal and I were feeling great, though, and we sat on the sofa giggling loudly for a bit, and gradually the mood lightened. We drank some more wine, too, and coffee, and some kind of Ukrainian pepper spirit Bengt had with him, which he'd brought back from a tour of the Soviet Union over the summer, though goodness knows what an economist would be doing in a country like that. And when I eventually asked where the hell Germund and Tomas had got to, Rickard said they'd gone outside for a talk. Rickard seemed entirely sober, he's turned more serious since he got in with that clerical lot, and his Anna wasn't much of a one for stimulants, either. I think she's doing a journalism course, but I'm not sure. She's leftie but seems solid and dependable, as I say.

It was midnight by the time the two absent gentlemen came back in, looking as though they'd spent the intervening time in a ditch. But perhaps it was just the rain. Perhaps they'd simply gone to Rackis, the student pub, for a couple of beers. Neither was prepared to say what had happened or how they'd spent the time. They each had a glass of the pepper spirit and the party broke up shortly afterwards. It's possible I missed part of the evening. I might well have dozed off in my corner of the sofa, but by the time we got back to Germund's it was 1.30 a.m. and I was completely clear in the head.

He wasn't himself. He had a shower and we went to bed. I asked what he and my brother had been up to, out there in the rain, but he didn't answer. He just lay there, staring up at the ceiling with empty eyes, and it seemed to me that if this was how he was going to behave, there was really no point moving in with him. But eventually we fell asleep. We didn't get anywhere near fucking and, by the morning, things were back to normal. More or less.

Apart from the fact that we had breakfast together. And he apologized. Christ, he said, I think I fell down some kind of black hole yesterday.

Was it to do with Tomas? I asked. Or with that Lars-Inge?

Germund said it was mainly to do with himself. A horrible sort of reflux from childhood, it happened to him every so often. Plus a few other things.

Are you going tell me one day? I asked.

Probably not, said Germund. Do you feel like a drop of vodka and some sex?

No, I said. Not today.

Can't say I blame you, he said.

Then I put my clothes on and walked home to Norrtälje-gatan. November, I thought. Naked trees, darkness, sinking down. God's turning his back on us.

Not only me, he's turning his back on everyone. I'm happy with that. There's a kind of cold justice to it. In my next life, I shall be a bare tree in the wind.

18

Interview with Anna Berglund. Kymlinge police station. 29 Sept. 1975. Time: 17.00. Present: Detective Inspector Evert Sandlin, Detective Constable Sigvard Malmberg.

ES: Your name and address, please.

AB: Anna Berglund. My husband and I live at the vicarage in Rödåkra. He's the vicar there, the parish of Rödåkra–Hemleby.

ES: Thank you. Can you tell us about the gathering on Saturday evening?

AB: What do you want to know?

ES: Just give us a general account. Who was there. Why you were meeting up. What the atmosphere was like.

AB: It was me and my husband. Tomas and Gunilla Winckler. And then Germund and Maria.

ES: Germund Grooth and Maria Winckler?

AB: Yes.

ES: And you've all known each other a long time?

AB: Yes.

ES: How long?

AB: About five years. We used to see a lot of each other when we were students in Uppsala.

ES: But you've all graduated now?

AB: Yes. Though I never studied in Uppsala. I was at the college of journalism in Stockholm, so I commuted. I grew up in Uppsala.

ES: I see. And why did you all get together on Saturday?

AB: We hadn't seen each other for a while. And with Germund and Maria having just moved to Kymlinge, it seemed natural. Tomas and Gunilla drove up from Gothenburg.

ES: And you all met at Rödåkra vicarage?

AB: Yes. We live there, as I said.

ES: How did the evening go?

AB: How did it go? Er, it was all fine. We had dinner and talked. Nothing special. We had a nice time.

ES: No incidents?

AB: No.

ES: How long did you go on for?

AB: Until about midnight. Gunilla's pregnant, and she got a bit tired. They were staying the night with us.

ES: And then you decided you'd all go on a mushroom hunt?

AB: No, we'd already decided that, earlier on.

ES: Whose idea was it?

AB: I don't know. It seemed a pretty obvious idea for us all to go out somewhere together on the Sunday. I suppose it was us – my husband and me – who suggested it. And the others agreed.

ES: Can you tell me what happened out at Gåsaklinten?

AB: I don't know what to tell you. I'm at a complete loss to understand it.

ES: I know it must seem hard. But we've got to try to find out what happened, as I'm sure you appreciate.

AB: Yes, of course. I imagine she slipped and fell, but I just don't know how it happened.

ES: Roughly how far were you, at the time, from the place the accident occurred?

AB: I don't know. A couple of hundred metres, I suppose. Maybe a bit closer.

ES: Tell us what happened.

AB: I heard a cry, and realized something must have happened. I ran towards the sound and, when I got there, I saw her lying at the bottom.

ES: Did you see any of the others?

AB: Yes, they were already there.

ES: All of them?

AB: No, not quite. I think Tomas got there just after I did, but the other four were all there. Yes, that's right. Germund and Elisabeth were already on their way down to her.

ES: Could you mark on this map where you were when you heard the cry?

AB: I'm not very good at maps.

ES: Well, just give it a try.

[*AB does so. Time taken: 25 seconds*]

ES: Thank you. When you got up to Gåsaklinten, how did you find out what had happened.

AB: I knew there was something wrong. Though I knew that as soon as I heard the cry, in fact. Gunilla was sobbing and everyone looked shaken. But I didn't know what had actually happened until I got right to the edge and saw her lying down there. I just couldn't take it in.

ES: When did you realize she was dead?

AB: Straight away, I think. I mean, she looked completely lifeless.

ES: Have you seen dead bodies before?

AB: Yes. I worked at a hospital.

ES: Tell me about her cry.

AB: It was just a cry. Loud and sort of sustained.

ES: What did she cry out?

AB: [*After a long hesitation*] I thought it sounded like 'Murderer!'

ES: Murderer?

AB: Yes.

ES: Are you sure?

AB: No.

ES: But you're sure they were words, one or more? Not just some inarticulate sound?

AB: Yes, it sounded like three syllables. It could also have been 'Murder me!'

ES: So am I to understand you as saying it could have been either?

AB: I think so. But it could equally well have been something else.

ES: At what point did you feel sure she had shouted either 'Murderer!' or 'Murder me!'

AB: Sorry, I don't quite follow.

ES: Was it when you heard the cry, or when you saw the body?

AB: [*After some hesitation*] When I heard it, but I couldn't interpret it until I saw the body. It was so unreal.

ES: What was unreal?

AB: For someone to shout 'Murderer!' in the middle of the forest.

ES: Could you hear who it was shouting?

AB: No, I don't think so. Or, well, perhaps I could?

ES: So in principle it could have been somebody else?

AB: I don't understand what you mean.

ES: Are you sure it was Maria?

AB: Who else could it have been?

ES: All right, let's go on. What were you thinking as you went up the hill and over to the edge?

AB: I was thinking that something must be wrong.

ES: Did you think someone had been murdered?

AB: No, of course not.

ES: And what conclusions do you draw now?

AB: Sorry, what?

ES: What are your conclusions now you know that Maria is dead and that she shouted 'Murderer!' or 'Murder me!' before she died?

[*AB shakes her head but does not reply. She takes out a handkerchief and blows her nose*]

ES: Answer my question, please.

AB: I don't want to draw any conclusions at all.

ES: Do you think Maria slipped and fell or that somebody pushed her?

AB: I don't think anybody pushed her.

ES: Do you think she jumped of her own volition?

AB: I can't be the judge of that.

ES: Can you explain why she would have shouted 'Murderer!' unless someone had pushed her?

AB: No.

ES: Did you see anyone else in the forest except your own group?

AB: A man came along with a dog, but that was after we found her.

ES: And you hadn't seen him earlier?

AB: No.

ES: Did you speak to him?

AB: No.

ES: Did any of the others speak to him?

AB: Maybe. Yes, they discussed what had happened, of course.

ES: And what did you talk about amongst yourselves when you found her?

AB: I don't know. We were all in shock.

ES: Who went to get help?

AB: Tomas.

ES: And why him, specifically?

AB: I don't know. It just turned out that way.

ES: Did the rest of you try to resuscitate Maria?

AB: No, it was obvious she was dead.

ES: Did you yourself go over to her, to check?

AB: No, the others had already done that by the time I got down there.

ES: Which others?

AB: I think it was Germund and Elisabeth. They were the first to reach her down there, anyway.

ES: But surely you must have discussed amongst yourselves what it was she shouted?

AB: Yes, everybody had heard it.

ES: Go on.

AB: I don't know what to say. It certainly took a while before . . .

ES: Yes?

AB: Before we got round to talking about what she shouted. Everyone heard it, but Elisabeth and I heard it more clearly. I think perhaps Gunilla, too, actually. Elisabeth thought it sounded like 'Murderer!' or 'Murder me!', or something like that.

ES: What did the others think?

AB: They said they thought it had an 'uuh' sound in it.

ES: Did you, as a group, discuss the possibility of her having been pushed?

AB: No.

ES: Why not?

AB: I don't know.

ES: I don't really understand. There could have been someone else out in the forest. That dog-owner, for instance.

AB: [*No answer*]

ES: Couldn't there?

AB: I'm telling you, I don't know. We didn't discuss it. We were all in a state of shock.

ES: What did you think of Maria Winckler?

AB: I liked her.

ES: How would you describe her?

AB: [*After some hesitation*] She was out of the ordinary. She had integrity. Those are qualities I value.

ES: Did the others feel the same way?

AB: Of course. We're old friends, all six of us. But you'll have to ask the others what they think, of course, not me.

ES: And the seventh person on the excursion, Elisabeth Martinsson, what can you tell me about her?

AB: I've never met her before. She teaches at the same school as Germund and Maria. She seemed nice, but we didn't have much of a chance to talk.

ES: At the moment you heard the shout, could you see any of the others?

AB: Once I got up to the top of the hill.

ES: You didn't see anyone until then?

AB: No.

ES: Are you sure?

AB: Yes, I'm sure.

ES: Do you know if Maria had any enemies?

AB: No.

ES: When did you last see her, before this weekend?

AB: It was in December last year. Before we moved here.

ES: When did you and your husband move here?

AB: January. That was when he took up his post.

ES: And you work at the *Swedish Church Times*?

AB: Yes.

ES: What do you make of the relationship between Maria and her partner Germund?

AB: I really couldn't say. I assume they get on . . . got on
. . . well. They were both rather unusual.

ES: Unusual in what way?

AB: Not very sociable. I suppose that's how I'd put it.
Two individualists. But I never had any problem getting
on with them. They're our friends.

ES: Would you say you knew Maria well?

AB: No, we were never close friends, if that's what you
mean. We never met up, just the two of us. It was always
the group of six. And she was Tomas's sister, too, of
course. Tomas and my husband did their military service
together in Uppsala – that was how they got to know
each other.

ES: Do you know if Maria suffered from depression?

AB: No, I'm not aware of anything like that.

ES: She never said anything about killing herself?

AB: Not as far as I know.

ES: And there was no one in the group who had any sort
of score to settle with her?

AB: No.

ES: And thinking back to Saturday evening, nothing
happened that you feel might have any bearing on her
death?

AB: No, nothing at all.

ES: Is there anything you want to add that you feel we ought to know?

AB: No, I've nothing to add. I'm finding this all extremely unpleasant.

ES: I'm sorry about that. But I'm sure you can cope.

AB: Was there anything else?

ES: No, not for now. But I'm sure we'll want to speak to you again. Interview terminated. The time is 17.22.

19

Rickard Berglund's first accommodation in Uppsala after the Army College for Non-Commissioned Officers was a room in Torsgatan in Luthagen. It only took ten minutes to walk down to the Faculty of Theology and he found it pretty much ideal. His landlady was called Angelica Liffermann; she was eighty years old and had had students lodging with her for a quarter of a century, ever since her husband died. She preferred theology students, after trying their equivalents in humanities and medicine but not liking their tendency to get audibly frolicsome in the room. She preferred gentlemen lodgers, too, because she occasionally needed help with practical tasks and a man was more use for that than a woman.

She spent her days reading, crocheting and solving crosswords, enjoyed a glass of port in front of the evening news programme on TV and had a cat called Miller. The animal was seventeen years old and moved about ten metres a day, at most. Sometimes he made it to the litter tray, sometimes not. There was also a daughter in Kristianstad; her name was Gunvor and Mrs Liffermann rang every other day to scold her. Usually after the glass of port. Rickard could hear her tirades through the thin walls and would think to himself that it must take exceptional patience to put up with such vast amounts of regular abuse.

She never scolded him, though. He never received female visitors in his room and there was never any frolicking. Or not at Torsgatan, at any rate. When he met up with Anna, it was always either in Eriksberg or they met at a pub or some place in town.

About a week into August they went to bed together for the first time. It wasn't a particularly satisfactory coupling, because it turned out they were both virgins. But the embarrassment passed, and a month later they tried again, with rather better results.

Rickard was pleased he was Anna's first, and she was his. Embarrassment shared is embarrassment halved. Thank goodness she hadn't given herself to that anti-Vietnam protester Göran, he thought. This way, they could feel that things were really serious between them. Rickard and Anna; it was rather strange that he could be so sure of it after just a few short months, but such were the convictions of the heart. You knew, without understanding how you knew. Anna had her first proper orgasm the second Friday in November, or that was what she claimed anyway. Practice makes perfect when it comes to sex, too, just as it said in the magazine advice columns that Rickard occasionally consulted in strictest secrecy.

It was after this experience, the November orgasm, that she said she thought she loved him. He hardly slept a wink that night, and the following evening when they were at Sibyllegatan for the elk-stew dinner, he felt they were a real couple. Just as much so as the others: Tomas and Gunilla, Germund and Maria – yes, he felt it deep in his bones.

We'll get married one day, he thought.

We'll have children.

Anna and I.

Rickard and Anna. It had a lovely ring to it.

They decided to make haste slowly. Not to rush into moving in together. To wait a while with the engagement, and so on. There was no need to be in any hurry about meeting each other's parents, either, but when Rickard was back home in Hova for three days over Christmas, he did reveal to his mother that he had met a girl.

She was pleased, he could see, but she found it hard to express the emotion in words.

'Oops!' she said. 'Take care of yourself.'

He promised he would. And he gave her a hug when he left on the twenty-sixth; it evidently took her as much by surprise as it did him. They had never been ones for physical contact. Nor had his late father; there was a boundary between the flesh and the spirit that could not be crossed entirely without punishment.

He didn't know whether Anna had said anything about him to her family in Salabackar, and he didn't want to ask. She clearly didn't get on with them. She'd moved out while she was still at upper secondary, and she hardly ever talked about them. Neither her parents nor her brothers. Hardly ever talked *to* them, either, as far as Rickard could judge. Of course the day would come when he'd have to meet them – just as Anna would have to be introduced to his solitary mother back home in Hova – but there was no need to be in any hurry.

And it was well into January before there were any more declarations of their love for each other. This time, too, it was after a successful coupling at Glimmervägen in Eriksberg, and Rickard began to understand that physical love was just as important and hard to negotiate as they told you in those advice columns.

Perhaps his faith was a stumbling block. There was a split in him that he didn't know how to handle, and initially he took the simplest way out: he didn't handle it at all. He couldn't talk to Anna about God, and he couldn't talk to God about Anna. Or at least he couldn't find any meaningful words in either direction, and this problem, too, he put off for the future. There was no shortage of future for a young student in Uppsala in the early seventies, so there was nothing for him to worry about.

He didn't really see that much of Anna in those first terms, either. She took the train into Stockholm every day, and generally they only saw each other one evening in the week, and at weekends, when he would sleep over at Glimmervägen. Sometimes they had sex, sometimes not. They usually shared a bottle of wine. Red, Vino Tinto or Parador; neither of them was that keen on white. Or on rosé, which had recently shot to popularity.

It was no more than that. And nor did it need to be.

As for God, Rickard met Him on all the other days, at the Faculty of Theology. It wasn't actually all that easy to perceive his presence there, but He was, in principle, a *sine qua non*. Rickard Berglund had this as an axiom deep inside him, and axioms are not open to question. *Axioms never have to make an effort*, Tomas said once, when they were discussing the matter during shooting practice in Hågadalen. *They tend to get a bit self-righteous, it's in their nature.* Rickard remembered them trying to explain what they were laughing at, to an unusually pompous second lieutenant named Norén. They had not succeeded, and had been given a reprimand.

But where, exactly – in his current day-to-day situation – was the living God supposed to find a dwelling in this secularized, left-leaning land, if not in the Faculty of Theology at Uppsala University? Only half a stone's throw from the archbishop's palace, and a quarter of one from the cathedral?

Good question, he would think. Rhetorically elegant. But could you ask it without the treacherous whiff of irony assaulting your nostrils?

The new curriculum stipulated that the theology degree begin with a foundation course in religious knowledge, and the modules you had to pass to amass the required marks were spread over the two terms of the university year. They amounted to an overview of the seven examination subjects: history of religion; the exegetics of the Old Testament; the exegetics of the New Testament; church history and the history of its mission work; dogmatics and symbolics; and ethics with philosophy of religion; plus practical theology. Rickard was diligent; it was in his nature. He worked his way through all the compulsory course material, and tried to do the supplementary reading suggested at his seminars; and he read Kierkegaard in parallel: *Either–Or, Stages on Life's Way, The Concept of Anxiety.* One problem was the difficulty of getting hold of the complete works of Kierkegaard in Swedish. He only had his well-thumbed copy of *Selected Works* and *Concluding Unscientific Postscript Part II* in Danish (which he'd happened across in one of the second-hand bookshops up on

Övre Slottsgatan) – but in spite of that, in spite of all the gaps, every time he immersed himself in these founding texts of existentialism (having understood that was what they were) he experienced something healthy and true and human. So much healthier, truer and more human than Ambretsen and Finck's *History of the Christian Mission*, anyway. But you could probably say that of most things.

At any event, Rickard ploughed doggedly through his set texts, as indeed did most of the other students on his course. With moans and groans and attacks of exam nerves, of course, but they went with the territory. Kierkegaardian choices would have to wait; things were the way they were and to everything there was a time and a season.

Even the return of our Lord Jesus Christ to this earth, presumably. All in all, there was a lot that seemed to lie in a very distant future, and perhaps that was why His presence sometimes seemed rather haphazard.

But one day – and yes, for many days to come, he knew – he would talk to Anna about all this. Of course he would; that, too, was only a matter of time.

20

Barbarotti did not finish going through Sandlin's green files until four o'clock on Tuesday afternoon, but Asunander had postponed their session until Wednesday, so it didn't really matter.

He put the last documents back in place and pushed away the files. He leant back in his chair, put his feet up on the desk and clasped his hands behind his neck.

And thought what a bloody odd story it was.

Well, not odd, that was the wrong word. And it couldn't really be called a story, either. After going through the three last interviews – all conducted on the same afternoon and evening, Monday 29 September 1975, the day after the death at Gåsaklyftan, by DI Evert Sandlin at Kymlinge police station – Gunnar Barbarotti felt he had rarely, if ever, read anything so devoid of real content. Neither Rickard Berglund nor Elisabeth Martinsson nor Gunilla Winckler-Rysth had contributed a single thing to change what he had gleaned from the witness statements he had read the evening before: Germund Grooth's, Tomas Winckler's and Anna Berglund's.

To put it quite simply, they all said exactly the same thing. All six had wandered around the forest on their own, separately, and not one of them had any of the others in their sight when they heard the cry. All of them had headed up to the edge of the crag as soon as they could and been with the dead body of Maria Winckler down below within a few minutes. Tomas Winckler had run for help.

No one could cast any light on anything whatsoever, and if it hadn't been for two of the women claiming the deceased had cried out 'Murderer!' or 'Murder me!' there would have been no grounds for suspecting any kind of crime at all.

Or not until now, thirty-five years later, with the next excursion member lying there.

A death leap, thought Gunnar Barbarotti. If they had never existed, why had anyone invented the phrase?

But it was the consistency of their accounts that seemed strange. The similarity of their evidence. Or was it just that Sandlin was a poor interrogator? Dogged but poor? Had he asked the wrong questions?

It was hard to judge after all this time. Getting them to mark where they were on the map was a smart move, Barbarotti had to admit. Each member of the group had been given an unmarked map to put their cross on, and had evidently had no knowledge of where the others had put theirs, but not even this had thrown up any irregularities. When Sandlin collated all the results on his own map, the crosses were spread over an area of about 400 metres by 300, and it all seemed completely compatible with their statements that they had not been able to see anyone else when the cry rang out.

A smart but ineffective move.

But wasn't that in itself just plain weird? thought Barbarotti. If six close friends – plus one loose horse – have met up after not seeing each other for quite a while, wouldn't it be more natural to talk to each other as they wander round? If not as a group, then at least in pairs? At least some of them? Did they find they'd had enough of each other on the Saturday evening? Did something happen at that dinner? Something they decided to hush up, for whatever reason?

Although it could just as well be pure chance. Elisabeth Martinsson and Gunilla Winckler-Rysth said they were close by each other, two or three minutes before the cry. Anna Berglund thought she'd caught a glimpse of her husband at around the same time. And it was undulating, forested ground, so there wouldn't have been any long lines of sight.

But it meant no one had an alibi. Sandlin had noted the fact in his commentaries on the case, and Barbarotti could only do the same now, thirty-five years later. Any one of the six could have pushed Maria Winckler over the edge.

In principle. The question, of course, was *why*? Why would one of them have done it? Did anyone have reason to?

Was that what had spurred Sandlin to go on with the investigation for three months? Had he scented a motive?

Was it that scent which had made him inspect the crime scene on three separate occasions, the last one as late as December? Inspired him to drag half a dozen DCs and assistants out there to stage a reconstruction? Driven him to interview a further ten people, over and above those directly involved, and caused the police commissioner at the time, one DCI Valfridsson, to demand a written extra memorandum on progress in the investigation, to justify why they did not simply drop the case?

The memorandum was in the second file. It was dated 19 November 1975 and indicated that there were various interviews and investigations still to be done. There was little more to it than that; Barbarotti thought he could sense DI

Sandlin hadn't had much time for his boss, and he also recalled that Valfridsson was reputedly as unpleasant as they come. Even by police-commissioner standards. He retired five years before Barbarotti embarked on his own career with the Kymlinge police – and died not that long afterwards, when his tobacco-related emphysema, not unexpectedly, caught up with him.

Sandlin naturally hadn't spent all his time working on this one case all through the autumn of 1975. Not every single day. Every document was dated and there were breaks of several days and even weeks.

Well, I suppose that's it, Barbarotti summarized to himself and sighed. He decided to hand the whole lot over to Backman, so she could look through it at her leisure. Admittedly they had agreed that he would dig about in the past and she in the present, but surely there was scope for a bit of job swapping?

He unclasped his hands from behind his neck, removed his feet from the desk and was about to stand up when she knocked on the door and stuck her head round it.

'Am I disturbing your brainwork?'

'Good timing,' said Barbarotti. 'No, I'm afraid my brain has run aground. I was about to come in and ask if you'd solved the case.'

'Not exactly,' admitted Backman, taking a seat. 'But I'm getting there.'

'Really?' said Barbarotti.

'Yes, because I don't think there *is* a case. Just as I said all along. She fell and he jumped.'

'Why?' said Barbarotti.

'Which one are you talking about?'

'The jump,' said Barbarotti. 'The fellage doesn't need any justification.'

'Fellage?' said Backman. 'Good word.'

'I know,' said Barbarotti. 'Well?'

'You want me to tell you why Germund Grooth jumped into Gåsaklyftan?'

'I do,' said Barbarotti. 'Enlighten a shipwrecked copper's brain on that point, if you wouldn't mind. Why does he take his life at exactly the spot where his partner died, thirty-five years ago?'

'I think you'll find the answer lies in your question,' said Backman.

'Eh?' said Barbarotti.

'More or less, yes.'

'You mean it's completely normal?'

'Not particularly remarkable, at any rate. If you've decided to die, you probably want to choose the location with a certain amount of care.'

Barbarotti eyed her crossly and considered her words. 'Damned if I know,' he said. 'I've never been close enough to taking that decision to start thinking about the method. Or the location. Have you?'

'In my teens, maybe,' admitted Backman. 'But I wasn't quite right in the head back then. They might both have jumped, actually. Her and him. And perhaps he knew that's what she'd done.'

'All these years?'

'All these years. Perhaps she was his one true love and, after thirty-five years, he simply gave up. Tried to be reunited with her in some way. No, I don't think it's that strange, in fact.'

183

'Who have you spoken to?' asked Barbarotti.

'Two of them,' said Eva Backman. 'Gunilla Winckler-Rysth and Elisabeth Martinsson. Martinsson only by phone. I didn't go in particularly hard, either.'

'How do you mean?' asked Barbarotti.

'I mean I didn't bother with the alibi question, for example. What sort of window of opportunity are we talking about here? Four hours, if I've understood correctly?'

Barbarotti nodded. 'Basically, yes. Saturday between twelve and four, roughly speaking. Ritzén's inclined to think sooner rather than later, but it clearly isn't possible to narrow it down any further.'

'Shame the old bloke and his dog didn't do their rounds a bit more often. That could have been a help.'

'I know,' said Barbarotti. 'But we are where we are. And I think it's a pity you're trying to simplify all this. My body's giving me rather a different message.'

'I didn't know you'd started aromatherapy,' said Backman. 'Or is it Senso Balance?'

'Both,' said Barbarotti. 'Never underestimate science. You haven't spoken to the vicar yet then?'

'He isn't a vicar any more.'

'Have you spoken to the ex-vicar?'

'No. His wife's dying of cancer.'

'Yes, you mentioned it,' said Barbarotti and sighed. 'Hardly the best timing, but I'd still say we ought to do it, oughtn't we? Would you like me to take him on?'

'I'd be grateful if you would,' said Backman. 'But what's in the other scale pan?'

'These,' said Barbarotti, passing her the files. 'But I don't want you to read them with any kind of preconceived ideas.'

'You're talking rubbish again,' said Backman. 'I don't know what preconceived means. When have we got to go through all this with Asunander?'

'Tomorrow afternoon,' said Barbarotti. 'You've got the evening and the morning to get through them.'

'OK,' said Backman. She accepted the files and handed him a thin folder in return.

'What's this?'

'Transcripts of my interviews with Winckler-Rysth and Martinsson. I don't want you at a loose end, if you happen not to be able to get hold of the ex-vicar.'

'Thanks,' said Gunnar Barbarotti. 'You know how to add spice to life.'

'I wrote them in blank verse,' said Backman. 'I hope you'll appreciate the effort.'

'I shall set them to music,' said Barbarotti, 'so we can sing duets for Asunander tomorrow.'

'*Mon dieu*,' said Backman.

Why the hell are we talking like that? he thought, as the door closed behind her.

To brighten up our daily lives, is it? Because we're so tired of our jobs that we can't stand them, otherwise?

And what's this vague itch in the soul that I'm going about with?

A few hours later, he was asking Marianne the very same question.

'I'm going about with this vague itch in my soul. What do you think that's all about?'

It was half past eight in the evening. They had retreated to the study they shared. In actual fact it functioned more as a refuge than a study, he had thought on more than one occasion. Four teenagers at home certainly made their presence felt. Even if they constituted Sweden's future.

'Is it work, or us?' asked Marianne.

'It certainly can't be us, so it must be work,' said Barbarotti.

'Are you sure of that?' said Marianne. 'We've taken on responsibility for four children, so we'd be pretty stupid to want to back out now.'

'Are you mad?' said Barbarotti. 'Who's talking about backing out? I only said I had a bit of an itch in the soul, and that in all probability it's to do with work. I love you more than ever.'

'Good,' said Marianne. 'I love you, too. And the soul needs a bit of discipline, which it's good to remind each other of, when the tiredness sets in. What's eating you at work then?'

'I don't entirely know,' said Barbarotti. 'That gentleman found lying at the bottom of Gåsaklyftan, I suppose. That's what I'm working on, anyway.'

'That incident on Sunday?'

'It actually happened on Saturday. But he was found on Sunday.'

'I see. And why's he giving you an itch?'

'Hard to say,' said Barbarotti. 'Eva Backman maintains there's nothing criminal behind it all, and she's generally right. But I sense something else entirely.'

'Something happened a long time ago in the same place, is that right?'

'Yes, it did,' sighed Barbarotti. 'A woman died there in 1975. And the man found the other day was her partner at the time.'

'What on earth are you telling me?' said Marianne, and

it struck him as unusual that he had not discussed it with her until now. But they had barely seen each other since Sunday, because she had worked an extra shift on Monday night.

'Yes, it's true,' he said. 'A young woman of twenty-five slipped and had a fatal fall out there . . . It's an ancient leap, you know, where old folk threw themselves over the edge when they thought they'd become a burden, although Backman says those leaps never existed. Her name was Maria Winckler anyway. And thirty-five years later her partner, now just over sixty, goes and falls in exactly the same spot. Germund Grooth.'

It took him a moment to register that something was wrong. Marianne had been sitting on the edge of his desk, but now she was on her feet, standing there with one hand raised in a strange, frozen gesture he couldn't interpret. She was staring at him – no, not at him, but at the wall behind him, that Piranesi poster they'd bought in Prague, or maybe just the wallpaper beside the poster – and for a couple of seconds her eyes expressed nothing, nothing at all. Or, possibly, utter confusion.

Then she pulled herself together. She ran her hands through her hair and pulled her shoulders back.

'Go and get a bottle of wine,' she said. 'I think we need to talk about this.'

'What . . . what the heck do you mean?' said Gunnar Barbarotti.

She cleared her throat. 'What I mean is that I know very well who Germund Grooth is . . . or *was*, I suppose I ought to say.'

'How can you . . .?'

187

'One of those Italian ones. And hurry up, for God's sake.'

Gunnar Barbarotti got up, and the thought occurred to him that his itch had turned into something else. But he wasn't sure what.

21

The next morning, Gunilla held him to account. Or tried to, anyway.

Leaving her to cope with the whole gaggle of them? Going out on his own with Germund and abdicating all responsibility? What kind of solidarity was that? What did he mean by it?

'He needed it,' Tomas replied.

'Needed it?'

'Yes. I'm sorry, but you'll just have to take me at my word.'

'So Germund's needs take priority?'

'In that situation yesterday, yes. I had no choice.'

'Why? Why did you have no choice?'

Tomas rested his head in his hands and looked at her across the kitchen table. It was a quarter to ten in the morning and she thought he looked tired, but he didn't sound hungover. Or contrite, as she had sort of been expecting. Instead he was wrestling with his loyalties, that much was clear. Should he tell her or not? She poured more coffee from the Thermos jug and waited. She spread some marmalade on a rusk and tried to stifle her irritation.

'He was going to kill himself.'

'What?'

'Germund was going out to kill himself. That was why I went with him.'

She regretted not having asked him the night before. She had opted to stay silent and feel hurt instead. They got to bed around two, once everyone had gone, and they didn't say a word to each other. They just lay there back-to-back and went to sleep.

And now here he was, claiming to have saved Germund's life. Like hell he did, thought Gunilla Rysth. If he's lying about something like this, things are serious. Really serious.

But why should he lie? He'd had all night to come up with a better lie than that.

'Tell me,' she said, lighting a cigarette.

'All right,' said Tomas. 'Though I promised him I wouldn't say anything.'

She took a drag on her cigarette and waited again. He sighed, and rocked slightly on his chair. Surveyed the piles of unwashed dishes.

'It would be best not to tell Maria.'

'I'm not planning to tell anybody. He was pretty drunk, wasn't he?'

'I know. But it wasn't just the drink talking, you see. That was my judgement, anyway. It was a pity he fell foul of that bloody Lars-Inge.'

'Yes. What were you thinking of, bringing him here? Isn't there anyone better on your course?'

'I'm sorry,' said Tomas. 'I've only ever known him sober. God, he was just unbearable. Makes you wonder how this country's going to look, with people like him in charge of the money.'

'Well, you provide the counterweight. And Bengt wasn't too bad, either.'

Tomas shrugged. She sighed. 'But you don't end your life just because you ran into an obnoxious economist? Do you?'

He shook his head. 'No, hopefully not. I just don't get him. But sometimes it only takes a spark to set things off, doesn't it? And yesterday was one of those times for Germund. It wasn't easy to get anything out of him about the background, except that it wasn't acute, as far as I could tell.'

'What do you mean, wasn't acute?'

'Well, there was no particular trigger, or anything like that. It just seemed to be something he carries inside him, which surfaces from time to time. Maybe it's to do with the death of his parents and sister. As if it's always lurking there somewhere, but I don't know. I didn't like to ask.'

'And what did he actually say?'

Tomas shook his head again. 'He came out of the loo and then he just said: "I've had enough now, Tomas, I'm going out to kill myself. If you wouldn't mind telling Maria I'm sorry."'

'What? He said that?'

'Yes. That's exactly what he said. Word for word. And he sounded completely sober, even if he wasn't. Then he took his coat and scarf and went out of the door. What the fuck was I supposed to do?'

Gunilla stubbed out her cigarette and tried to come up with a spontaneous reaction, but the whole thing felt so bewildering. And murky, somehow. Unwieldy and beyond her comprehension. It came home to her that she didn't actually know Germund Grooth at all. She had never had a proper one-to-one conversation with him, as she had with Rickard and Maria. Not that she understood Maria particularly well, either, heaven knows, but she couldn't relate to Germund in any way at all, that was the fact of it. If they happened to find themselves alone in a room together – not that it happened very often, but once or twice it had – she never really knew what to say.

191

There wasn't the option of any banter with him, either, which she could at least count on with Maria. Moaning about Tomas, for example, half seriously and half in jest.

But Germund Grooth was difficult. Superior, without meaning to come over that way presumably. She didn't dislike him, absolutely not, but he remained a stranger. We're two separate species that don't communicate, she thought. It's as simple as that. A fish and a cow.

She gave a laugh. Tomas's brow creased in surprise.

'What are you laughing at?'

'Sorry. It was nothing. Well, what did the pair of you do after that?'

Tomas put up his hands and gave a sort of shrug. 'We walked. Out to Stabby, a couple of times round the forest and then back. We went over to Rackis, had a beer. There was a blues band on, but they were just taking their break. To start with, he told me to shove off and leave him alone, so he could just get on and do what he was going to do. I told him I wasn't leaving him on his own, and of course I wasn't going to let him kill himself . . . I thought I'd better take him seriously. You have to show respect; I'd be pretty cross if I'd decided to commit suicide and then people wouldn't take me at my word. Don't you think?'

Gunilla nodded. 'Of course. He was drunk, too, and when you're drunk and sad, you want to be taken seriously, even if you start spouting a load of drivel. So you really think he would have gone through with it, if you hadn't been there?'

Tomas lit a cigarette. 'How can anybody know?'

'Are you asking *me*?'

'Yes. You see, it's like this: when we look back, all we can see is what happened, isn't it? Not what *didn't* happen. Maybe I saved Germund's life, but we'll never be able to establish that for certain. The important thing, surely, is that I made a decision. I thought it was crucial not to let him go off on his own, but I'm not expecting a medal for my contribution.'

She made no comment, just sat there looking at him as the seconds passed. He actually looked a bit hurt, and perhaps he had every right to. 'Sorry,' she said. 'You probably acted as you had to. Me getting grumpy about it isn't the end of the world, is it? Being left with that crowd. But what did you talk about? He must have told you why he wanted to end it all?'

'Not in any clear terms,' replied Tomas. 'He said he had an infernal burden to carry.'

'An infernal burden?'

'Yes, those were his exact words. And he told me he thought life was a bloody joke, a theatre, and he didn't feel like standing on the stage any longer . . . well, he went on like that. About everything being a deception, a lie, and when you hit the bottom and see through it all, there's only one thing left to do.'

'End it all?'

'Yes. I told him that was bullshit, of course, and asked him where the sense was in being dead. He laughed and said of course there was no sense in it, and that was the whole point. Anyway he pretty soon stopped talking about actually doing it and we just wandered about in the rain, talking, that's all . . . And then, at Rackis, it got . . . well, it all got a bit pompous, I'm afraid. You know?'

'Young male intellectuals setting the world to rights?'

'More or less. But he isn't easy, Germund. I don't know what that infernal-burden stuff is all about. But it's fucking obvious there's trauma involved. Losing your whole family when you're ten. It's hardly to be wondered at, if you turn out a bit weird.'

'What sort of help did he get, do you know? When it happened, I mean.'

'No idea. I don't think he talks about this to Maria, either, but maybe you could ask her. It wouldn't be a good idea for me to try. But I assume they had child psychologists ten years ago, too.'

'Who took care of him?'

'I don't know. But he came to Uppsala when he was sixteen. He started at Fjellstedska – you know, the private school – and lodged with somebody here.'

Gunilla nodded and mulled this over for a few moments.

'Peculiar phrase, wasn't it? Infernal burden.'

'Yes. He told me something else rather jaw-dropping as well. He's been to bed with twenty-two different women. What do you say to that?'

'What do I say to that? Disgusting, that's what I say. Does Maria know? I thought they were moving in together?'

'They are. She presumably knows about it; he didn't tell me to keep that quiet, at any rate. Only the suicidal thoughts.'

'She's shagged around a bit herself, I dare say?'

'What's that got to do with it?'

'No idea. She's your sister, not mine.'

'And what's that supposed to mean?'

'What?'

'That she's my sister, not yours?'

Gunilla sighed. 'Sorry. Can't we stop this now, Tomas? We're only upsetting ourselves. It was a bloody awful night last night, and sometimes things just go that way.'

He got up. 'OK. Shall we do the washing up instead? I don't think there's a clean teaspoon in the place, is there?'

★

She found herself thinking about it, afterwards. All that winter it kept resurfacing in her mind, not often but from time to time.

Not only what Tomas had told her about Germund – the suicide evening and the many girls he'd had – but also that unpleasant conversation in the kitchen. She had been angry when they started talking, but several times it felt as though they were going to find their way to each other. Yet it didn't happen. They didn't reach out far enough. They washed up and cleaned the flat for two whole hours and barely said a word to each other the whole time. She assumed it was because of what she'd said about Maria. That she was his responsibility, not hers. He'd taken it as an accusation, as if she was somehow holding him responsible for what they got up to, both Germund and Maria. He never put it into words, but his silence – the fact that he didn't even think it was worth discussing, and it was pointless trying to explain it to her – well, that was the part she found hardest to accept.

The way he kept her outside. She didn't know what was inside, what his own thinking on the matter was, but that was because he never opened a door or a window for her to peep through. Into his private space.

Men, she thought. Silence is golden. What a load of crap!

But she had been accusing him, he was quite right about that. She couldn't deny it.

In the middle of January they went down to his parents' house in Spain, as planned. The day before they left, she spoke to Rickard Berglund on the phone, only very briefly, though he'd still had time to remind her that Spain was a fascist dictatorship, but if you had a chance of a free week in the sun, of course you took it. Ibiza in August had given them a taste for more, he supposed.

It wasn't easy to forget that sort of comment – despite the mildly humorous tone in which Rickard had delivered it – and the sun wasn't much to write home about, either. They had bad weather all week, cold and wet; they took the train into Malaga a couple of evenings, and they were the only vaguely tolerable parts of the week. One day they rented a car and went to visit a cave complex in Nerja, but the place frightened her. Tomas liked it, but she thought it was like some enormous grave, an underground cathedral. And an underground cathedral could surely only be built for a certain kind of ruler? A prince of darkness, she suggested to Tomas once they were back in the car, but he gave a snort of derision.

Prince of darkness? What are you wittering about, Gunilla?

On their last day she lay in bed all afternoon, crying in time to the steady rhythm of the rain. She told him she had a headache and needed rest; he presumably didn't believe her, but found it a convenient solution. Truth is a compromise between two people who don't want to argue. He left her alone with her sobs and went out into town on his own. By the time he got back, about nine that evening, it was obvious he'd had numerous glasses of wine.

He wanted to make love to her, of course, and she let him. When it was over and he'd dropped off to sleep, she thought about their relationship, which was clearly at a crossroads. They couldn't go on this way. It was no sort of life.

But when they'd been back in Uppsala for three weeks and the spring term was under way, she realized she was pregnant again. It had happened that last night in Fuengirola. She couldn't explain, even to herself, if she had left her pills at home in the bathroom cabinet on purpose or had simply forgotten them.

But now that it was a fact, it made no difference. She was expecting a baby. It was less than a year since they had lost Lucy.

TWO

22

DI Backman's flat was on the top floor of the block, but she didn't so much as glance in the direction of the lift. She took the stairs as usual and, if she hadn't, she wouldn't have had her sudden idea on the third floor.

She had met Alf Ringgren a few times before; they both moved in around the same time, and they would occasionally stop and exchange a few words when their paths happened to cross. About the weather, or life in general, or their landlord, Kymlinge Fine Homes. Alf Ringgren was probably in his sixties, a quiet man with a slightly battered look; he had moved there for the same reason as she had: divorce on the grounds of fundamental incompatibility. That was how he expressed it, but he'd never gone into detail. There'd been no reason to.

But her motivation for stopping outside his front door was nothing to do with divorces. It was his place of work that was the decisive factor.

He taught at Kymlingevik School, didn't he?

She stood there trying to remember. He told her he'd been there since the Stone Age, didn't he?

If he was over sixty now, as she guessed, that would mean he had taken up his post at the school in the mid-seventies. With any luck, therefore, he would have been on the staff that autumn when Maria Winckler died at Gåsaklyftan. In 1975.

This was her sudden idea. Before hesitation could catch up with her, Backman rang the doorbell.

'That's right,' Alf Ringgren said, with an apologetic smile. 'I started in the autumn term of 1973 in fact. Thirty-seven years at the same school: what do you think of that? I'll gladly take the medal but really, you know, there ought to be a price on the heads of folk like me. Still, I shall cross the finishing line in a year's time, either way.'

'I only have two teachers in my circle of acquaintances,' said Eva Backman. 'I should say *did* have, because they both left the profession before they were forty-five.'

'A lot of people do,' admitted Alf Ringgren. 'But bear in mind that it's rarely because of the pupils. There are other variables that are harder to put up with.'

He turned from the dully gleaming coffee machine – not the same make as the one at the Winckler-Rysths', but she was still sure it had cost him over 10,000 kronor – and put two espressos on the table. A box of After Eights. If I'd come an hour later, he'd doubtless have produced two glasses as well, she thought. There was a shabby sort of sophistication about him.

'It's easier for a man, too, I'm afraid to say,' he added. 'If you're prepared to exploit the fact, that is.'

'My colleagues say the same,' said Eva Backman. 'But perhaps we could have this discussion some other time?'

'Whenever you like,' said Alf Ringgren and smiled. 'Today you'd rather we stick to the autumn term of 1975, right?'

'Exactly right,' said Backman. 'Those two fellow staff members of yours, Maria Winckler and Germund Grooth, do you remember them?'

He nodded. 'But only vaguely. She died, didn't she, an

accident out Rönninge way or something? Fell off some high place and broke her neck. Wasn't that it?'

'More or less,' said Backman. 'What subjects is it you teach?'

'Swedish and history,' said Alf Ringgren. 'Mainly Swedish. I've turned my hand to social studies and geography in my time, too, the way you have to. I think this Maria you're talking about was a language teacher . . . and Grooth, well, I assume it was the sciences. We didn't have any subjects in common, at any rate.'

'Can you recall if they made any sort of impression on you?' asked Backman.

'Why do you ask?'

'Could I possibly ask my questions first?' suggested Backman. 'Then maybe I'll explain afterwards.'

'Maybe?'

'Yes,' said Eva Backman and smiled. There were certain advantages to being a woman, too. And to the fact that, for once, people hadn't already heard the whole story from the papers or the television.

'Fair enough,' said Alf Ringgren. 'I don't really know what to tell you. She died, and he stayed on at the school for the year . . . if I remember rightly. Yes, I'm pretty sure he was still there for the end-of-term festivities in summer 1976. I seem to recall he was in a show that we teachers put on. Just a trifle, some silly little choir thing, but that's why I remember it. I think he came to one or two staff parties, too. After she was gone, I mean.'

Eva Backman took a few sips of coffee. She could sense he knew more than he was saying; there was something in his manner that gave it away. He had some memory of Germund

Grooth that he was finding it hard to reveal, for some reason. Or perhaps it was just wishful thinking. An occupational hazard for a police officer, you might say.

'Can you describe them?'

He adjusted his glasses and thought about it.

'Him maybe, but not her. They'd only been there a month or so when she died, and I don't think I spoke to her once. But she was an attractive girl, I do remember that.'

'Yes, I've heard other people say that,' said Backman.

'They'd just moved to the area. The staff were mainly pretty young back then . . . the average age was about thirty, I'd say. It's different today; there are at least six of us due to retire next summer. Anyway there was a bit more energy around in those days . . . but a lot of waffle, too, I'm afraid. The years of compulsory education in Sweden in the 1970s definitely didn't generate many Nobel Prize-winners.'

'I know,' said Backman. 'I finished mine in 1980 and I certainly haven't had so much as a sniff of a prize. So how would you describe him then? Germund Grooth?'

Alf Ringgren hesitated for some time over this before he answered. 'I don't think I *can* describe him,' he said at last. 'All I really remember is one incident.'

'An incident?' I guessed as much, she thought.

'Well, you could call it that. He clashed with a colleague, sometime in the spring it must have been.'

'What do you mean by clashed?'

'There was this . . . altercation, I suppose you'd call it. His name was Svantesson, the other teacher. I knew him quite well, but he's sadly no longer with us. Stomach cancer – he was only fifty-five. Anyway he punched Germund Grooth. It was after a particularly tough parents' evening, and a few of us were having a beer in the staffroom before we went home. Yes, March or April, I think it was.'

'And this Svantesson punched Germund Grooth?'

'Yes.'

'Why?'

'I didn't see it myself and I'm not sure. It was out in the cloakroom, I think, and Svantesson didn't want to talk about it afterwards. But one of the other teachers told me he'd allegedly been with his wife.'

'So Grooth had been with . . .?'

'Svantesson's wife, yes. I don't know how much truth there was in it. It's not the kind of thing you want to poke your nose into, and it was just that one incident. Nothing else happened. I never talked to Svantesson about it, even though he and I were on quite friendly terms. I felt awkward, of course.'

'And when Germund Grooth moved away, it all fizzled out?'

'You could put it like that, yes.'

'Do you know if Mrs Svantesson is still alive?'

'No, she died last year. Or it could have been the year before that.'

Eva Backman sighed. 'Do you think there are any other staff members from back then who knew Germund Grooth any better?'

Alf Ringgren leant back and pondered again. He ran his hand over his chin and cheeks, as if to check up on his shaving. 'I can't think of anyone,' he said in the end. 'But a look in the files at the school might yield a few more names. Two of the other teachers who are retiring at the same time as me were there in 1975, if I remember rightly. One of them is a science teacher, too. But I find it hard to imagine either of them was friends with Germund Grooth. Or that anyone else was.'

'And why's that?'

'Because . . . because he wasn't the sort to invite friendship.'

'Sounds a bit harsh.'

'Yes, I know,' said Alf Ringgren. 'But that was how it was, even though I can't rely on my memory a hundred per cent after all this time. What's all this about anyway? Has something happened to him?'

'Yes,' said Eva Backman. 'You could say that. Something's happened to him.'

Invite friendship? she thought when she had left Ringgren and gone back up to her own flat. Well, maybe that was one way of describing it.

If you didn't invite friendship, you ended up with no friends.

And the same outcome was to be expected if you went to bed with your colleagues' wives, too. Except for the woman in question herself, that was.

What was it Ringgren had said? In the spring? Which meant that six months after the death of his partner, Grooth found another consort. Albeit a short-lived one. And earnt himself a punch on the nose into the bargain. What was so remarkable about that?

Nothing, thought Eva Backman. Nothing at all. It was just what Ringgren had said it was. *One incident.*

She found the leftovers of yesterday's pasta in the fridge and put them in the microwave, but saw that she didn't have the makings of a salad to go with it. On the other hand, she noted that there was a splash of red wine left in yesterday's bottle, and decided it would be a shame to waste it.

She sat down at her lonesome kitchen table and started on her dismal dinner.

Germund Grooth, she thought. Goodbye. I have no desire to reflect on your supposed character. You jumped off a cliff because you didn't want to live any more. I'm very sorry about that, believe me, but please will you now take a running jump out of my head, too?

And she regretted having paid any attention to that brainwave of hers.

'So tell me then,' said Gunnar Barbarotti. 'What are you trying to say?'

Marianne hesitated.

'I want you to take this the right way,' she said.

'What does that mean?' asked Barbarotti?'

'It means I knew him . . . pretty well.'

'Pretty well?'

Marianne sighed and took a large sip of wine. 'That's right. You remember that physics teacher I told you about?'

'The one you were seeing when we met?'

'*Had been* seeing,' Marianne corrected him. 'It ended about six months before I met you. Longer, even.'

'OK. And?'

'It's him,' said Marianne.

'What?'

'Germund Grooth. I had a relationship with him.'

Gunnar Barbarotti just about swallowed his mouthful of wine without choking. 'What the hell are you saying?' he demanded.

'There's no need to swear at me,' said Marianne.

'I wasn't swearing at you,' said Gunnar Barbarotti. 'I was swearing at things in general.'

Marianne watched him with a slightly anxious look in her eyes. 'Well, that's the long and the short of it,' she said. 'I'm sorry.'

Gunnar Barbarotti stood up and did four circuits of the room.

'What are you sorry for?' he said when he had finished.

'Sit down,' said Marianne. 'I'm sorry he had to crop up again like this. I can see it's thrown you off-kilter.'

Off-kilter? thought Barbarotti, sitting back down. What's she talking about? I don't give a toss about her having been with some moron who's gone over a cliff edge.

'All I remember you saying is that he was depressed,' he said.

'That's right,' said Marianne. 'That was his dominant characteristic. He was as gloomy as a Good Friday. Depressive is probably a better word for it than depressed.'

'All right,' said Barbarotti. He cleared his throat and took another swig of wine. 'So you went to bed with someone else. It was before I came into your life, but I have to admit it feels a bit weird. Now that he's dead and I'm investigating the circumstances surrounding his death.'

Then an image came into his mind and it wasn't easy to get it out again. The image of her lying naked, as she must have done, and waiting for him, parting her legs and taking pleasure in receiving him, just as she did with him, Barbarotti . . . nowadays.

Repeatedly. How many times? Ten? Fifteen? Bloody hell, he thought, what a prat I am. Why has this come into my head?

'How long were you together?' he asked, noticing that his voice wasn't quite itself, either.

'Do you really want us to talk about this?' said Marianne.

'Of course,' said Barbarotti. 'Why shouldn't we?'

'Because it's upsetting you.'

He drained his glass. 'We could be talking about a murder investigation here,' he explained. 'I'll just have to take it on the chin.'

Marianne sat there in silence for a minute, looking at him. He realized he was finding her gaze hard to bear. What an idiot I am, he thought again. I'm as primitive as a male orang-utan.

'We were together for less than a year,' she said finally. 'Or that was the length of time between the first encounter and the last, to be more precise. He was living in Lund; I was in Helsingborg. We first met at the Grand in Lund when I was out with a girlfriend. I suppose it must have been . . . well, no more than ten times, altogether.'

'You went to bed with him ten times?'

'Yes,' said Marianne. 'He was a good lover. There wasn't much else to get excited about, mind. He wasn't any fun. Depressive, like I said. But he had a bit of style to him. If sex was all you wanted, it was perfectly fine, but there's a lot more to life than that. Don't you think, my prince?'

She leant across the table and put her hand over his. Barbarotti closed his eyes.

'Sorry,' she said. 'Though I don't really know what I'm saying sorry for.'

'Nor do I,' said Barbarotti, pouring some more wine into his glass. 'Any more for you?'

She shook her head. 'No thanks. You know what . . .?'

'What?'

'I don't know for sure, but it wouldn't surprise me if he was seeing other women while we were involved with each other. Though I never asked.'

'You just met and had sex?'

'Basically, yes. But if you're going to go on like this, I'm going to bed. You and I were both over forty when we met, and neither of us was inexperienced. We've got five children with other partners.'

Barbarotti didn't answer. He drank some more wine as he tried to collect his thoughts.

'What makes you think he was murdered?' asked Marianne.

'It's because . . .' began Barbarotti, but then found he didn't know how to complete the sentence. 'I don't know,' he said and gave a deep sigh. 'No, there's nothing to indicate he was murdered. Except the link, that is. The fact that his girlfriend died in exactly the same place, thirty-five years ago. But Backman . . .'

'Yes?'

'Backman reckons it adds up, psychologically. Maria Winckler, his girlfriend, possibly took her own life, that other time – or fell, it doesn't matter which – and this depressive physicist now wants to be united with her, somehow. In another world, in some twilight land, how the hell should I know . . .? So this one was suicide.'

'That isn't right at all,' said Marianne.

'Eh?' said Barbarotti. 'What is it that isn't right?'

Her eyes seemed to shift focus for a moment. From presence to absence. From *now* to *then*. 'He wasn't like that,' she said. 'If you believe you can be united with someone after death, you have to have some sort of faith. Germund had no faith. He was completely lacking in anything of the kind.'

'How can you know that? You got to know him well enough for that, you reckon?'

She started to smile, but thought the better of it. 'You can pretty soon tell if people have a spiritual dimension or not. I can, at any rate.'

'Sounds a bit cocky,' said Barbarotti. 'If you'll forgive me. A bit spiritually elitist.'

'You can't help seeing what you see,' said Marianne. 'But there was something else weighing on him, and I seem to remember he even admitted as much. Some sort of guilt, though the same is true of a lot of people of course. And he was the very opposite of cocky, more like mournful and reserved . . . A gentleman in a way, but it all got a bit too boring in the end. And he agreed with me on that. He knew he was a melancholy sort of character and he couldn't see why I would choose to be with him.'

'Nor do I,' said Barbarotti. 'He must have been quite a bit older than you?'

'Fifteen years, I'd say,' said Marianne. 'But it wasn't his age that was the problem. It was his gloominess. I wasn't seeing him constantly over long periods, but it was still very obvious, even so.'

'Only one night at a time?' asked Barbarotti.

Marianne finished her wine and put the glass down on the table.

'You know what, Gunnar,' she said, 'here's a suggestion. If your team needs to know any more about Germund Grooth, I think it would be best for me to talk to Eva Backman.'

'To Eva?' said Barbarotti. 'Not on your life. This . . . this stays between you and me.'

'Sometimes,' said Marianne, 'you can be terribly primitive, do you know that?'

Gunnar Barbarotti didn't answer. So can you, he thought.

Terribly, and especially before you met me. Leave me in peace now. I need a private chat with Our Lord.

And because she could evidently read his thoughts, she got up and went into the bedroom.

23

Sparrow here.

April 1971. I've turned twenty-one. I've come of age, but it doesn't feel remotely different.

This time Mum and Dad insisted on coming here. Tomas booked a table at Taddis and we had something called an 'Indonesian Feast', the usual six of us plus the two of them. Eight of us around a table of at least twenty different dishes; it was the first time they had met Germund, but not the first time they had met Gunilla. I think they're starting to give up on me, or Dad is at least; he's relieved not to have me under the same roof, but he still kept trying to persuade us to go down to their house in Spain. Tomas and Gunilla were there in January and, according to Tomas, it rained pretty much the whole time.

I'm living at Germund's; it's about five months since I moved in. He sticks to his own style, doesn't care about being so damn successful the way everyone else tries to. Or so damn political. He just *is*. And he's bloody clever, of course. We don't talk much, but it feels as though we understand each other. If there's anything there to understand. And the sex is still good, too.

Really good sex, and it's not a bad idea to get used to each other, either; I can turn him on just by taking off a stocking, if I want. I think I'd like to go with another girl sometime, just to see what it's like. I haven't decided whether to mention it to Germund; that might be taking it too far. There's something so simple about boys. They're suggestible and predictable; though with him, that's the way I want it. I like being in control; better the devil you know, that's another platitude from Dad.

It feels like a step in the right direction anyway. Especially for an evil young girl like me, so easily bored by what's normal. I don't know what I'm going to do with my life, I really don't.

It doesn't worry me, but sometimes I think it will do, one day. Worry me, that is. And then I shall be like all the rest of them.

I think Gunilla's pregnant again, but they haven't said anything. Maybe they're afraid it'll be like last time. I don't know what they're playing at. Rickard and Anna definitely aren't expecting a baby, though; they're far too cautious for that kind of recklessness. Rickard and Dad were absorbed in some deep discussion while we were having that Indonesian Feast, or that was how it looked, at any rate. I don't know what it could have been about and it was a bit surprising, of course. Rather than paying attention to his son or daughter and their respective partners, he found the young theologian more to his taste. Maybe it was religion and faith they were talking about; Dad's always been drawn to that sort of thing, even though he's never gone the whole hog. Just the opposite; in fact he's spent his whole life only half doing everything, so he's always had half in reserve, in any situation. I think that must be the way he sees it. It's as detestable as it's unimpeachable. He really hasn't twigged what Ibsen's *Brand* is all about.

Or what anything's all about. Nor has Mum.

I'm through with French. Three assessed courses in three terms, that'll have to do. A distinction in the first two, but not in the third, and I've only myself to blame. I didn't care as much, skimped on the Life and Society module and threw together my Proust essay in just three nights. I'm reading English and history of literature in parallel this term. There's a young American lecturer in the English department – I think he's a Vietnam deserter – who flirts with me a bit sometimes. I've decided to ignore him, even though I actually quite like him. But I also take it as a sign that I'm turning into just some average Swedish girl; I don't like that at all, but it's another thing I can't really take up with Germund.

I do extra shifts at The Prophet occasionally. That was where that madman went on the rampage with a machine gun last year, but it's hardly likely to happen again. I need paid work; Germund and I have expensive tastes, which the student grant doesn't cover, and I don't want to ask Mum and Dad for money. I'm damned if I will, in fact; Mum would like nothing better than to have me eating humble pie.

Germund, meanwhile, has found another way of making some money. He bought a grants handbook at Lundequist's and found a grant that was tailor-made for him. It was set up by some old vicar a hundred years ago, and only orphaned scientists from Gästrikland can apply. The 10,000 kronor was his for the asking, and the best thing about it is he can apply every year, as long as he stays a member of the Gästrike-Hälsinge student club. We're planning a trip this summer, probably to Normandy and Brittany. He's promised to pay part of my share, so why would I refuse? And Paris, of course. I've passed three university modules in French, yet I've never been to Paris, which probably makes me unique. Germund is thinking of buying a summer car on the cheap and selling it again in the autumn. If we set off right after midsummer, we'll have two months. The Spain idea will have to wait.

A few days after Taddis, I met Anna. It was the first time she and I have ever had a proper talk. We happened to run into each other on Kungsgatan, and we went for a coffee because she'd just missed a train to Stockholm and had an hour to wait for the next one. I soon realized I was feeling sorry for her. I don't know why, I don't normally feel sorry for people. The whole of humanity, yes, but not individuals. It was something to do with her wary manner, I think. As if she was cowed by something, and I assume it comes from her childhood – that's the usual story. Some people find it hard to step out of their shoes even when they've outgrown them, that's the thing. When Anna goes into a room she apologizes for her presence. Even if it's just a cafe where she's prepared to pay over the odds for a lousy cup of coffee and an equally lousy pastry. As if she feels she hasn't the right to be there. As if she's taking up someone else's space.

And yet I have this sense of her strength, which is para-doxical, and I remember thinking it when I saw her for the first time. If anyone really were to come along and ask her to move, I can well imagine her telling them to go to hell. Pulling back her shoulders and defending herself.

We didn't talk about any of this, of course. We mainly talked about our studies. She's at the college of journalism in

Stockholm, and communism's the name of the game there. She's left-wing herself, though not one of those bloody champagne socialists like everybody else, but more grounded somehow. It's more about fairness than about politics for her. Global famine and oppression, and all that. I respect her for it, though I'm sure it's based in her own working-class background. I think her dad was some tough union type, before he started overdoing the drink.

Anna and Rickard are thinking of moving in together soon. She never said it straight out but I could still tell, and they suit each other. Or perhaps it's just that people grow more alike when they see too much of each other. They melt into each other like sad jellyfish, whether they mean to or not. I haven't been with any other guys since Germund and I started living together, and I don't think he's had any other girls, either. But I'm sure it wouldn't bother me if he did have himself a fuck on the side. We're not dependent on each other in that way.

We're not dependent on each other in any other way, either, in fact. Though I do wonder why it feels so vital to stress that. Or why I don't give that American a try. Or a girl. Perhaps I'm partway to turning into someone else, I don't know.

Sometimes I feel old. Especially when I look around and see how my peers think and behave. There's a fair dose of pathos in that, although maybe it's just as Germund says: being brainy is no reward in itself. When you see through other people and discover how little there is to them, the shit always splashes back onto you. You end up feeling you're staring into a mirror, and I hate that. I don't want my life to look like other people's.

It still applies as much as ever, that prioritizing of pure maths and physical love.

And beauty, as I said. And pure vodka.

I'm still happy enough in this city, but it's starting to sink in that it won't last forever. And why should it? Nothing lasts forever, especially not life. Anna claimed, when we were sitting in that cafe, that there was a kind of Uppsala snobbery, a sort of academic snootiness that she doesn't come across in Stockholm. Perhaps she's right, and we should go there more often. I think I shall persuade Germund to come along and we'll go to the National Theatre or the Opera House or whatever, fairly regularly if we can; it really doesn't take more than an hour on the train.

Why not now, on the last day of April, for example. All that May Day Eve hysteria gets on my nerves.

Another sign that I'm older than my sullenly accumulated twenty-one years?

Over and out. Sparrow is tired.

24

'OK, let's hear it,' said Asunander, leaning back to the point where his desk chair gave a complaining creak. 'Where are we?'

'We're in two minds,' said Barbarotti.

'Really?' said Asunander. 'And what are we in two minds about?'

'What happened,' said Eva Backman. 'Whether we have a case or not.'

'We definitely have a case,' said Asunander. 'Possibly two. Two falls down the same steep drop, what's more, and you're saying they were both accidents?'

'DI Barbarotti and I have slightly differing views,' said Backman. 'Personally, I tend to think they were accidents. Possibly suicide, or two suicides. Sandlin didn't find reasons to conclude anything else, thirty-five years ago, and the fact that her partner has been found dead in the same place hardly changes Sandlin's judgement.'

'Judgement?' said Asunander. 'Is it judgements we're dealing in here? I was under the impression our job was to focus on facts. Dry, incontrovertible, patiently extracted facts. But please do correct me if I'm wrong.'

He's enjoying this, thought Barbarotti. He would have been better suited to the role of principal at some nineteenth-century girls' grammar school. It was better when he still had the loose teeth that stopped him saying so much.

'We make judgements on the basis of facts,' he said. 'Of course.'

'Of course,' said Asunander. 'So what facts have we got?'

Eva Backman cleared her throat. 'We have two people who take the same fall, but with thirty-five years in between. They were a couple when it happened in 1975, and he's lived alone ever since. Senior lecturer in physics at Lund; we don't know what had brought him to Kymlinge. Other than, potentially, to kill himself in the same place as his partner did.'

'Other than potentially that,' muttered Asunander. 'What do we know about him?'

'We haven't had a chance to take a closer look at him yet,' said Barbarotti. 'We've been concentrating on those individuals who were involved last time, and on the crime scene.'

'Crime scene?' said Asunander, raising an eyebrow.

'I mean the scene of the incident. Gåsastupan.'

'An old clifftop leap, so I heard,' said Asunander.

'That's just popular legend,' said Backman. 'It can scarcely have happened in real life.'

'You think not? Tell me what you've come up with at Gåsastupan then.'

'Not much,' said Barbarotti. 'DI Borgsen's been leading that side of things. No, there's no sign of anything out there. Other than Grooth slipping over the edge, that is. No footprints, no signs of a struggle. It's quite stony just there.'

'Hrrm,' said Asunander. 'But if I understand this correctly, you still see grounds for suspecting a crime? Because you tell me there are differing opinions on the team.'

Gunnar Barbarotti shifted uncomfortably.

'I don't know,' he said. 'Perhaps Backman's right. Perhaps he just wanted to kill himself in the same place. Are you familiar with Sandlin's investigation, sir?'

'Only in general terms,' admitted Asunander. 'She seems to have shouted something about being murdered before she hit the ground, which was presumably what aroused his suspicions?'

'That's right,' said Barbarotti. 'Maybe something beyond that, but it's not obvious from the material in the report.'

'Not obvious from the material?'

'Correct.'

Asunander leant back again. He crossed his arms on his chest and assumed a grim look. 'It's the method I'd choose myself,' he said.

'Pardon?' said Eva Backman. 'What method?'

'If I were going to kill someone,' clarified the chief inspector. 'Push them off a cliff. Or a high balcony. Simple but effective.'

'Leaves no trace,' said Barbarotti.

'Not even a hint,' said Asunander. 'A hand on a back, that's all. As I said. It would be damn annoying if we're actually dealing with two murders. Even if the old one comes under the statute of limitations. Don't you agree?'

'Very annoying,' affirmed Eva Backman.

'My view entirely,' said Barbarotti. 'So, what shall we do? Carry on working on it for a few days and see what we find?'

'What else?' said Asunander. 'Make sure you check out our new victim thoroughly, at the very least. Senior physics lecturer in Lund? That sounds pretty suspicious, for a start.'

Barbarotti nodded. Backman nodded.

'What sort of person is he and what's he been up to recently? Friends and acquaintances, not forgetting his mobile-phone records. Well, I probably needn't spell it out for two such experienced detectives as yourselves?'

'Of course not,' said Eva Backman.

'Leave it to us,' said Barbarotti.

'So you've changed your view?' said Eva Backman, a minute and a half later.

'How do you mean?' said Barbarotti.

'I thought you had this gut feeling that Germund Grooth had been murdered?'

'Mm, sort of,' said Barbarotti. 'I just didn't want to rule out the possibility, that's all.'

'But now you do want to rule it out? Twelve hours later.'

'Not rule it out,' said Barbarotti. 'I simply started to feel you might be right, that's all. One slipped and one jumped, wasn't that what you said?'

Eva Backman sipped her coffee and subjected him to a long stare. Blast, he thought, it's not only Marianne who can see straight through me; she can too.

'And what prompted this rethink?'

'Nothing,' said Barbarotti. 'I haven't had a rethink. It's an open question. You surely think the same, don't you? Strange, but open.'

DI Backman thought about this for a good while. 'OK,' she said finally. 'It looks as though we've got to spend a few more days on this in any case, now Asunander's decided he wants it. The physics lecturer's last days in this life, what do you reckon?'

'Sounds exciting,' said Barbarotti. 'Will you take it or shall I?'

'I'll take it,' said Backman. 'You're more suited to the prehistoric era, hadn't we decided?'

Barbarotti nodded. 'Yes, we had. Though I'd be quite keen to talk to that ex-vicar,' he said. 'I don't know how things stand with his wife, but he could spare an hour surely?'

'Elisabeth Martinsson and Tomas Winckler, too,' Backman reminded him. 'We really ought to have face-to-face interviews with all parties involved. I've only had time to see Mrs Winckler so far. After all, it could still be that one of them is a murderer.'

'So you've changed your opinion?'

'I've never had an opinion,' said Eva Backman. 'Not on this case; you've just been imagining I did. But if I concentrate on the senior lecturer, you can work your way through the rest of them, one at a time. I've already spoken to Martinsson, but only on the phone, as I said. We ought . . .'

'Yes?'

'We ought at least to find out what they were doing on Saturday afternoon. Don't you think? If all five of them have alibis, then we'll know where we stand.'

'Four,' said Barbarotti. 'We won't need to investigate Anna Berglund. The poor woman's in bed, dying of cancer.'

'OK then, four,' said Backman. 'You interview Winckler and Berglund, and I'll take care of the dead lecturer. Are we agreed?'

'Absolutely,' said Barbarotti. 'You're planning a little trip down south then?'

'Oh, you studied in Lund, didn't you?' Backman said as she recalled the fact. 'Might be better if you were to do it?'

'Hardly,' said Barbarotti. 'I've too many preconceived ideas of that particular metropolis of learning. Our loose horse Martinsson, incidentally: what did you arrange with her?'

'Nothing,' said Backman. 'I just said we might get back to her.'

'I'll see if I can fit her in, too,' said Barbarotti. 'While you're having fun down in Skåne, I mean.'

'That's all agreed then,' said Backman. She cast a final appraising eye over him and left the room.

He just sat there at his desk for twenty minutes before he could bring himself to do anything.

I'm an idiot, he thought. Only an idiot can get jealous of a man his wife went with before he even met her. Only an idiot can get jealous of a dead man. Ergo, I'm an idiot.

But on the other hand, he thought after a while, it isn't only love that's blind. Jealousy can be just as blind. That's an extenuating circumstance, so I'm only a semi-idiot.

What was more, it was starting to pass and be replaced by something else. He wasn't quite sure what, and he felt sleepy, more than anything else. He hadn't slept more than two or three hours, and he'd had no further discussion of the subject with Marianne. Neither last night nor this morning. He'd felt pretty rotten about it, but maybe it was just as well.

He hadn't taken the matter up with Our Lord, either, even though he had fully intended to do so. But there was something about Our Lord and Barbarotti that didn't feel the same as usual. Hard to put his finger on it, but when he thought about it, he realized he hadn't sent up any of those existence prayers for quite a few months. Not since before the summer; it had been to do with Sara and Jorge, he remembered that, though not the details, but the prayer had been answered. God had been awarded a plus point and had reached the round number of twenty. Barbarotti had noted it in his book.

Quite a compelling sign of His existence then, even if there were several years of the marathon left to run – but the fact that Barbarotti had stopped talking to Him surely indicated there was something amiss? Marianne read the Bible now and then, and they would sometimes discuss a passage, talk about trust and providence and all sorts of things, but that personal contact he was used to was undeniably not what it had been.

Maybe it was just a question of convenience. They'd talked about that, as well. When all was going well, when it wasn't an hour of need in some way, it was fine to keep God tucked away in the wardrobe. Only taking him out when he was urgently needed. Maintaining the ongoing relationship, perhaps even daily contact, demanded effort, and human beings are naturally lazy. That was the crack the Devil was able to creep in through, thought Barbarotti. The loophole of spiritual idleness.

He sighed and decided it was time to pull his socks up. In his relationship not only with God, but also with his wife.

He determined to forget what she had told him about Germund Grooth – or try to suppress it, at any rate – and revealing to Eva Backman why he had so suddenly and oddly changed his mind would have felt like shooting himself in the foot. The fewer people who knew he was a semi-idiot, the better.

And anyway it wasn't at all clear whether he actually had changed his mind or not. It was just that the frisson of fascination he had experienced out at Gåsaklinten was starting to fade. That tickling sensation, that indefinable something that generally signified things weren't quite right, had gone. I don't give a damn about that Grooth, he thought. Of course he killed himself, just as Backman claims. It's only a question of time until we can shelve this case, but I'm going to work on it with an open mind until then.

I shall be objective and unbiased, just as usual.

He wondered for a moment whether he could call and disturb Marianne at work, but decided against. It seemed excessive to break in on the delivery of a baby just so he could hear her voice. Especially if they were queuing up to give birth, as she claimed. I shall buy a bunch of roses tonight instead, he decided. Gentlemen, when did you last buy your wife flowers?

Content with the outcome of all this finely weighed deliberation, he downed half a mug of coffee and looked up the contact details for Rickard Berglund, former clergyman, now funeral director.

25

Rickard Berglund got to the OK service station in Svartbäcks-gatan half an hour too early. They'd agreed on 6.30, but the sign gave the opening hours as 7–21, so he assumed he'd got it wrong.

It was a cold morning, definitely a few degrees below zero, even though it was only 1 October. There was a mean and persistent northerly wind to keep him company, too; it always seemed to blow from the north in Uppsala; he had often thought that. As if it came from somewhere way up in Norrland, blasted its way southwards with undiminished power and force and anger, and met no opposition until it reached this seat of learning and its cathedral. He wished he'd put on an extra sweater and a pair of gloves; he could really have done with them. He decided to take a walk while he was waiting for the service station to open. Better that than to stand shivering by the pumps.

The first of October 1971, he thought, thrusting his hands into his pockets and setting off along Stiernhelmsgatan. The day I started living with a girl. No, wrong. *The day my future wife and I moved in together* – that was how it should be. Me and Anna. Rickard and Anna Berglund, née Jonsson.

They'd never talked about getting married, of course not, but Rickard still knew that was how it would be. On his private, secret agenda it was an event due to take place in a year or two's time. In 1972 or 1973, there was no need to leave it unnecessarily long. And then they would be able to celebrate their silver wedding before the year 2000. *The big plan*, as Grundenius would put it.

I wonder what I shall be doing by then? he suddenly thought. In the year 2000, when I'm fifty-one! It was a dizzyingly long jump through time. Will I be a vicar then? he asked himself. Will Anna and I be living in a vicarage and have four children? One or two of them could even have flown the nest by then, couldn't they? Grandchildren. It was indeed a prospect that made him dizzy.

And how will the world look by then?

A justifiable question, without a doubt, he thought, lighting a cigarette. Will communism have triumphed? Will the Third World War have laid waste to everything? Will anybody even care about something as trifling and middle-class as wedding anniversaries?

Will there still be churches? And priests? Will anyone believe in God any longer? Will they have come up with a new opium of the people by then?

These were questions that his fellow theology students were fond of discussing, but Rickard had never seriously engaged with them. It was so easy to imagine you lived in the last days, so easy to make things out to be worse than they actually were. As God and the world and every conceivable kind of society had existed for thousands and thousands of years, there was presumably no reason to think everything was about to collapse at any moment. Or within the next few decades. *Dystopias*, that was what they were called, and as the rampant prophets of the left liked nothing better than to compose such dark analyses of the current state of affairs – *late-capitalist Gehenna,* he had seen it referred to in a very prominent position in *Dagens Nyheter* a few days before – it wasn't surprising if people started thinking everything was going to pot. The world was on the verge of destruction, or revolution, or war – but belief in gradual, positive, peaceful progress, no, that simply wasn't a tenable position, with things as they were.

It was almost as untenable to be a Christian. You only had to see how Dag Hammarskjöld's *Waymarks* had been received in influential circles. The most important Swede in the world, consigned to the scrapheap just because he was a believer. It really was astonishing.

Thus thought Rickard Berglund as he stubbed out his cigarette and turned left into Idunagatan. But in any case, there was good reason to keep the *big plan* classified as top secret. Every good reason, he decided, and glanced at his watch. Quarter to seven, time to head back to the service station. To pick up the van and finally get under way with the move. They'd been planning and packing for a week; two days would probably have done, but it wasn't easy to keep your sense of expectation in check.

Not easy at all. Rickard and Anna. Anna and Rickard. Under the same roof, and he felt a shiver of pleasure at the very thought.

There was a slight touch of anxiety, too, but pleasure above all.

The flat was in the Kvarngärdet area. Väktargatan 40, a two-bedroom, ground-floor flat with its own bit of garden space. Seventy-two square metres, which they both found inconceivably huge. It seemed designed for a family with children, not two students, and the whole area was dotted with pushchairs and sandpits. Cats and dogs and all sorts of other things, too, and everyone looked under thirty: especially the children, of course. He and Anna had been there on the quiet a few times to take a look at the surroundings and they both agreed that they liked the place. They would settle in well there and be able to build their life together.

First, he drove the van to Torsgatan, where he and Anna loaded his possessions – just books and clothes, really – in less than half an hour. He took his leave of Mrs Liffermann, who presumably thought it high time for him to move out, now he had a girlfriend, and he also had a chance to welcome her new lodger. They ran into him on the stairs, a first-term theologist from up in Vittangi with a few bits of fluff on his chin; his name was Josef and he was very likely a Laestadianist Lutheran, Rickard guessed. He had that fervent look, as if he was burning inside. As if he had an angry God clawing at his chest. There was something self-consuming about those young Laestadianists; it was impossible to avoid that reflection when there were so many of them in the theology faculty.

At Glimmervägen, on the other hand, there was lots to carry out and try to fit behind the van's blue-and-white tarpaulin sides, and at that point Tomas and Germund turned up, as arranged. Together they all lugged out boxes of glassware, cutlery and household utensils. Chairs and the kitchen table. The worn corduroy sofa and the two plastic armchairs from the charity shop. Bags of books and records; the vacuum cleaner; clothes, coat hangers, lamps and rolled-up posters (but not Mao and Che, who had vanished to God knows where in the course of the year they'd been together – Anna and Rickard, that was to say; Mao and Che had never become an item in that way). It was most definitely Anna who had most to contribute to the joint household; it was amazing how much she had accumulated in the four years she had lived in Eriksberg. There was an imbalance to it, but it didn't signify. Not in the slightest. If you were going to share your lives, then of course you shared everything else as well.

The only new purchase they indulged in was a bed. It was as big as the ocean, bore the name Adam and came from Sencello in the pedestrian precinct. Not chipboard, but a proper bed with a wooden frame, a slatted base and a double-sprung mattress. Once they were done at Glimmervägen they went to collect it in three long, heavy boxes at a pick-up point through a garage on St Olofsgatan, and then it was finally time to go out to Kvarngärdet and set up home.

Tomas felt the urge to sing on the subject as they drove along, 'The gate out front is swinging', and Germund, also an occasional choral singer, joined in with a rousing 'And there's no place like home.'

Then all three of them laughed their heads off as they sat there crammed into the front seat, each with a can of beer. (Anna had already gone off to Väktargatan on her bike) and Rickard decided this was what being happy felt like. This was the way life ought to look, just like this, in motion, perpetual motion – and not in that other sedentary, drearily brooding way.

Tomas left them after an hour of hauling and unpacking at Väktargatan. He took the van back to the service station on his way home. Gunilla was so heavily pregnant that she could give birth any day and ought not to be left on her own for too long at a time.

But Germund stayed on. Rickard realized that it was unusual to be with Germund without Tomas around. It had hardly ever happened before, even though they'd known each other for two years and often met up socially. It was as if . . . as if Tomas was a sort of membrane; a vital airlock or interpreter, through which you made contact with Germund. Rickard had never thought about it that way before, but it struck him now – as they dragged boxes about and unpacked glasses and plates and tried to assemble the marital bed – that it wasn't at all easy to hold a conversation with Germund. He wondered if it was bothering Anna, too, but it didn't look like it.

On the other hand, there wasn't much need to talk, because there was so much practical work to be done. But still; Maria had promised to drop in with some pizzas from Lucullus on Sivia torg after her lecture finished around four, and by two-thirty Rickard found himself hoping she would turn up a bit early.

A few minutes later the phone rang. It was surprising, of course, that it was already installed and ready for use, but it was Rickard's phone, which he'd brought with him from Torsgatan, and he'd managed to persuade the phone company to let him keep his old number.

It was even more surprising that the call came from the Akademiska hospital and was about Helge.

Helge from Gäddede. Rickard hadn't heard a word from him since they were discharged from their military service at the Staff and Liaison College just over a year before.

He didn't hear a word from him now, either, because it was a nurse on the line. She sounded rather brusque, the way they used to in 1940s films, was the thought that randomly popped into Rickard's head.

'Are you Rickard Berglund?'

'Yes. Yes, that's me.'

'It's about a Helge Markström. Do you know him?'

'Helge Mark . . . yes, yes, I do.'

'He's had an accident . . . several fractures. He gave your name as someone we could contact. He doesn't normally live here, apparently.'

'No, he lives in Gäddede. What . . . what happened to him?'

'Run into by a bus. It happened early this morning. They operated and now he's come round. It all went well, so if you'd like to visit, you're welcome to.'

'A bus?'

'As I said. They operated and it all went well.'

The nurse gave him the ward number and told him how to get there. She assured him that Helge was doing pretty well in the circumstances, though he was rather shaken up, and in plaster. The accident had happened on a pedestrian crossing on Kungsgatan, and unless she'd been misinformed, it seemed the bus driver had gone through a red light.

Rickard thanked her and said he would come to the hospital right away. He gave Anna a quick explanation of what had happened and set off.

Helge, he thought. I had no idea you were in town. Why didn't you get in touch?

He had only got there that day, it turned out. He had arrived very early in the morning, on an overnight train from Kiruna. He was actually on his way to Stockholm, where he was due to start a course in cabinet-making, but he had decided to spend part of the day in Uppsala first. Take a stroll around familiar haunts. Perhaps give Rickard a ring in the early afternoon. He had looked up the number in the phone book before he left Gäddede.

'Good job I had the number anyway,' he said with a wan smile. 'Though I'd pictured us having a cup of coffee at Fågelsången. Not like this.'

'Be glad you're alive,' said Rickard. 'Arguing with buses isn't a good idea.'

'I know, I know,' said Helge. 'That's been made very clear to me. I was feeling a bit tired; you never get much sleep on trains.'

'What time was it?'

'Can't have been much after six. I didn't get to see much of the town. I didn't even get across Kungsgatan.'

Rickard looked at him lying there in the bed. He had one arm and one leg in plaster and his face was a greyish-blue colour. He had a little moustache that looked like a new addition.

'That course you were supposed to be starting . . .'

'I'll have to put it off for a while,' said Helge. 'Pity. I'm starting to get a bit fed up with bloody Lapland.'

He tried to smile, but it was more of a wince. 'How are you, anyway?'

Rickard pulled his chair a little closer to the bed. 'Anna and I are moving in together today.'

'What?' said Helge. 'Today?'

Rickard nodded. 'Väktargatan in Kvarngärdet. Out beyond the Migo store, you know. Sorry I didn't write and tell you.'

Helge tried to shrug. 'We're not very good at writing, you and I. Though in my case it's because nothing ever happens. That's the way it is, where I come from.'

'I don't think you can complain nothing ever happens,' said

Rickard, gesturing towards the plastered limbs. 'My God, Helge.'

Helge attempted another wan smile.

'Yes, but this will pass. Thanks for coming anyway. Do you remember I was with you when you met? You and Anna. That protest march.'

'Of course I do,' said Rickard.

'She sprained her foot and now you're a couple,' said Helge. 'Communist girl loses her footing and lands in the arms of a future vicar. It's just too damn good to be true.'

'How are things for you on that front?' asked Rickard. 'Girls, I mean.'

'No girls in Gäddede,' said Helge and heaved a sigh. 'I thought it would be better in Stockholm. But now I shall just have to go back home and wait, I suppose.'

'Wait long enough and something good will turn up,' said Rickard.

'Is that a fact?' said Helge. 'You rogue.'

He stayed at the hospital for over three hours. When he got back to Väktargatan it was 7 p.m. and Anna was on her own. She looked tired, and said Maria and Germund had only been gone about fifteen minutes. There were still three boxes to unpack and Rickard thought now would be a good time to stop for the day and share a bottle of wine.

The bed was all assembled and ready, that was the most important thing. He suggested they put off the rest of the unpacking until the morning and Anna nodded. But she didn't want any wine.

'I think what I need is a walk,' she said. 'If you don't mind, that is.'

'Why would I mind a walk?' said Rickard. 'Where do you think we should go?'

'I think I'd like to walk by myself for a while,' said Anna and looked down at the floor.

Rickard managed to swallow his disappointment. That's the kind of person she is, he told himself. I've got to accept it. No two human beings are alike, and it's childish to imagine they are.

And when she got back, two hours later, they did in fact have a glass of wine each. On the brown corduroy sofa, with two boxes still left to unpack. He felt this wasn't bad going, considering it had been Tuesday ever since that morning.

26

As Gunnar Barbarotti said hello to Rickard Berglund and shook him by the hand, he thought the cancer must be catching. Via some unknown channel it appeared to have transferred itself from wife to husband, and the lanky, grey-faced man who asked him into the flat did not look long for this world.

Barbarotti knew him to be sixty-one, but he looked about ten years older. He moved like a sleepwalker, too, as if against his own will and better judgement – before sinking down into one of two black leather armchairs, one on each side of a low pine table on which a chessboard was set up.

'Sorry,' he said. 'I haven't slept for a few weeks.'

Gunnar Barbarotti sat down in the other armchair.

'I'm sorry to have to barge in at a time like this. I appreciate things must be very difficult for you.'

Rickard Berglund nodded and drank some water from a glass that was standing beside the chessboard.

'It's almost unbearable,' he said, 'seeing your life partner meet death like this.'

Barbarotti wondered momentarily why he had used the phrase 'life partner'. Did it imply something stronger or something weaker than 'wife', which would surely have been the natural expression?

Perhaps Berglund sensed the question even in his exhausted

state, because he added: 'We've lived together for forty years. Two-thirds of our lives; I simply can't reconcile myself to her suffering.'

'I can't claim to understand,' said Barbarotti. 'There are things no one can understand until they have to undergo them.'

Rickard Berglund regarded him with something approaching interest and nodded. 'Quite right,' he said. 'And there's no reason to try to, either. There are things we're not meant to understand – that's the whole point. But why aren't we allowed to die when life is nothing but a torment . . . what's keeping her here – ah, there's a lot to wonder about . . .'

He lost his thread and blinked a couple of times in the direction of the sun, which had suddenly sent a dazzling ray through the balcony window. He pulled himself upright in his seat, seeming to remember that Barbarotti was not there as his spiritual guide.

'Forgive me, I'm not quite myself. You haven't come here to talk about my wife.'

'No,' said Barbarotti. 'There's been an unexplained death and we're looking into it. Germund Grooth. He was found out at Gåsaklinten on Sunday.'

'Yes, I'd heard,' confirmed Rickard Berglund. 'Linderholm told me. A colleague of yours came in to see him.'

'What do you think about it?' asked Barbarotti.

'Sorry?'

'What do you think about Grooth's death?' clarified Barbarotti. 'You see, he was found in exactly the place where his partner, Maria Winckler, died thirty-five years ago.'

'It's unfathomable,' said Rickard Berglund with a slow shake of his head. 'Utterly unfathomable.'

He picked up a black pawn from the chessboard and frowned. Barbarotti waited for him to say something more, but nothing came. He weighed the pawn in his hand and then replaced it on the board.

'There were various aspects of the earlier death that weren't clear,' said Barbarotti.

'Weren't clear?' said Rickard Berglund. 'Yes . . . yes, it was a terrible thing to happen. Terrible for everyone involved – especially for Maria, who lost her life, of course . . . but also for the rest of us . . . and Germund . . .'

He was speaking so quietly now that Barbarotti could hardly make out what he was saying. As if he was literally on the verge of dropping off.

'There were some suspicions on that occasion. Do you remember that?'

'Of course,' said Rickard Berglund. 'I'm not senile, just tired.'

'I apologize,' said Barbarotti.

'The suspicions arose because Maria supposedly shouted something as she was falling,' Berglund went on in a slightly more energetic tone. 'Some people interpreted it as an indication that she'd been pushed . . . or, rather, I think it was your people who interpreted it that way. The police, a colleague of yours whose name was Sandlin, I think . . . he took things a bit far.'

'I've read his investigation report,' said Barbarotti. 'Perhaps you're right, but anyway nothing could be proved. What was your own view of Maria's death then?'

'She slipped and fell,' replied Rickard Berglund, feeling for something on the chessboard again. 'It's possible she jumped of her own free will, but I consider it very unlikely. She definitely wasn't murdered.'

239

'You'd had a party at the vicarage the night before?' asked Barbarotti.

'I thought you'd come about Germund,' said Rickard Berglund. 'Not that old case.'

'I've come to try to establish whether there's any kind of link between the two.'

'It's been thirty-five years,' said Berglund with a sigh. 'Why should they be linked?'

'I don't know,' admitted Barbarotti. 'But the very fact that he died in the same place indicates some kind of link.'

Rickard Berglund nodded. 'Well, maybe. I suppose that was what he wanted.'

'What?'

'To end it in the same place.'

'You mean Germund Grooth killed himself, and wanted to be reunited with Maria in some way?'

Rickard Berglund gave a tired shrug. 'Something like that, yes.'

'Was Germund a believer?'

Berglund looked at him with another slight glimmer of attention.

'A believer?'

'Yes.'

'I don't know what you understand by that concept, but at the time I knew Germund, he had no God.'

'You haven't had any contact with Germund Grooth in more recent years . . . you and your wife?'

'No. We haven't had any contact at all.'

'When did you last see him?'

Another shrug. 'No idea.'

Barbarotti sighed and wondered what to say next. He was starting to feel there wasn't much point to this conversation.

'Ah, wait a minute,' said Berglund. 'I think it was about five or six years ago that we last met. Or maybe even more, but after the millennium, anyway. We bumped into him in Copenhagen, Anna and I. We were there for the weekend and we came across him in Rådhuspladsen, just outside the city hall . . . We chatted for a couple of minutes, but he didn't even have time to come for lunch with us.'

Barbarotti momentarily visualized the scene. Germund Grooth, hurrying across the square in the spring sunshine, bumping into his old Uppsala friends, but he hasn't got time to talk because he's on his way to meet . . . Marianne!

Switch it off! he thought. Dear God, help me master this. Two points, OK?

'Why did you give up the priesthood?' he asked.

He didn't know what made him ask it. It was something thrown up in the wake of Germund and Marianne's fictional meeting in Copenhagen, presumably, and he wasn't quick enough to stop it.

'What?' said Rickard Berglund. 'Why do you ask?'

'Because it interests me,' said Barbarotti. 'It hasn't anything to do with the death of Germund Grooth, of course, but I just wondered.'

Rickard Berglund sat there in silence, looking at him. He seemed to be weighing up whether or not he could bring himself to answer. Whether it could be in any sense worth the effort.

'Sorry,' said Barbarotti. 'Forget I said it.'

Rickard Berglund cleared his throat and sat up straighter in his chair again.

'What about you?' he said. 'Do you have some sort of religious faith yourself?'

'In a way,' said Barbarotti.

'I shan't ask what that means,' said Berglund. Then he gave a sudden laugh, brief and joyless. 'Yes, you're not the first to wonder,' he said. 'What would make you stop preaching, once you'd started? Not many people arrive at that decision.'

'I assume people can lose their faith,' suggested Barbarotti.

'Oh yes, certainly,' said Rickard Berglund. 'But not in my case.'

'Oh?' said Barbarotti, with a fleeting sense of gratitude that he wasn't recording this conversation.

'More the opposite, in fact.'

'The opposite?'

Rickard Berglund nodded and lapsed into silence for a moment.

'You reach a stage,' he said, 'when it simply doesn't work any more.'

Barbarotti again decided it wasn't an appropriate point to say he understood. He picked up a white castle from the chessboard and twirled it between his fingers for a while instead. He waited.

'There is a God,' Rickard Berglund resumed after half a minute or so. 'But He doesn't live in the Church of Sweden. Not in any other kind of church community, either, to my knowledge. It took me thirty years to understand that, but once you've realized, it's impossible ever to stand in a pulpit again. Not in our standard sort of church anyway. God isn't present, and I think . . . well, I think He's ashamed of that state of affairs.'

'Ashamed?' echoed Barbarotti.

'Or deeply troubled, at any rate. But I don't understand why He doesn't take Anna to Him . . .'

Barbarotti nodded and tried to swallow his surprise. 'I never go to church myself,' he explained. 'But I do have conversations with Him sometimes. My wife, too. I mean, she has a faith, but she never goes to church services, either.'

'Religion,' said Rickard Berglund, in a voice poised on a knife edge between resignation and anger. 'It's got nothing to do with the true faith, nothing to do with the God who loves you and is full of grace. Humanity has taken such a wrong turn, got so relentlessly lost . . . the question is whether there's any hope.'

He clasped his hands and looked at the game of chess. 'I play against myself,' he explained, as if this was somehow part of his relationship with God. Barbarotti couldn't really see the connection and decided not to reveal anything more of his own transactions with Our Lord. It wasn't easy to make them intelligible to other people, not even ex-priests – nor was it necessary. But there was something in what Rickard Berglund had said, and the way he had said it, perhaps, that touched him. As if . . . well, as if he actually knew what he was talking about. As if it was based in deep and genuine experience. The fact that he seemed to have come so much further along the thorny road than Barbarotti had done himself.

Abandoning the church, not because you've lost your faith but because you've found it . . . well, it sounded remarkable and, whatever it involved, it would certainly prove a very painful process, even a simple detective inspector could grasp that.

And now the wife – the life partner – of this former priest was suffering the agonies of the cancer that would undoubtedly take her life, but that had evidently decided to torment her to the bitter end.

That more or less summarized the situation, thought

Gunnar Barbarotti to himself. Rickard Berglund's situation. No wonder he looked so old and tired. No wonder he wasn't particularly interested in Germund Grooth.

He decided not to stay any longer; there was no reason to. Berglund had promised him an hour, after which he would go back to the hospital.

Who am I to keep him from Death's waiting room? Barbarotti asked himself and got to his feet. From Cancer's torture chamber?

In different circumstances he wouldn't have minded staying on to talk for another hour, he felt that quite distinctly. There was something about Rickard Berglund that was . . . impressive?

'Thank you for this interesting talk,' he said. 'And I do hope your wife's death will be the kind that leaves you with some sense of meaning, in spite of everything.'

'So do I,' replied Rickard Berglund without getting out of his armchair. 'Just a little chink of light would do, we mustn't ask for too much.'

Emerging into the street again, Barbarotti found that it had started to rain. Heavy, implacable autumn rain that felt well matched, he thought, to the conversation he had just had. He didn't even bother trying to take shelter, but walked all the way back to the police station. Berglund's flat was at the far end of Rosengatan in Rocksta, and it took him twenty-five minutes – just as it had on the way there; opportunities for a bit of exercise were not to be missed – and he was soaked through by the time he got back.

It didn't bother him. Compared to Rickard Berglund, he hadn't much to complain about, but the thought that he would be sitting at Marianne's bedside watching her die, or she at his, would not stop nagging at him.

When? he thought. How many years have we got left together? Thirty? Ten? Three? Why do we let the days just run by without appreciating them properly?

Why am I getting jealous of one of her exes – who is now deceased, what's more – and won't the day come when I curse myself for not having had the sense to live life while it was actually in full swing?

And we've got five children, that's the most important thing.

27

The morning of 11 October. She woke up, and knew within a few seconds what had happened.

She was carrying death inside her. Not life. She cautiously ran her fingertips across the taut skin of her belly and felt the chill inside. The chill, the silence.

And death. She clasped her hands over her navel and stared out into the darkness. Not a single glimmer of day. Not a single glimmer of hope.

She looked at the luminous hands of the alarm clock. Quarter past five.

She looked at Tomas, sleeping heavily at her side. Just a dark outline in the darkness.

And then she screamed.

She gave birth to her dead baby. It was a girl, but this time they had not had a name ready for her. She weighed 2,960 grams and the doctors had no explanation for why she had stopped living, just a week or so before she was due into the world. Some kind of problem with the oxygen supply, they thought. An unlucky accident; apart from the fact that she was dead, everything was in order.

She was buried on 13 October. She got her own little cross

with a metal plate in Berthåga cemetery and a name, finally. Aurora. It meant dawn.

Born 11 October 1971. Died 11 October 1971. A vicar by the name of Holger Eriksson conducted the funeral, and only Tomas and Gunilla were present.

And Aurora.

Afterwards they went straight to a psychiatric ward at Ulleråker hospital.

It had all been arranged.

It was raining.

From her bed, high up in the tall, narrow building, she could see the tops of the trees. Straight, lofty spruces with crowns of green dignity. The sky behind them, perpetually restless, now it was autumn.

She lay there for hours watching those treetops, that sky. Days and weeks. She wished she could have died with her daughter. She had asked to, but they wouldn't let her.

Not Tomas, and not the doctors.

I'm twenty-two years old, she thought. I've already lost two babies; don't they see that death is my calling? Why are they keeping me here in this pointless way?

Tomas visited her every day. Often for hours, though she said she wanted to be alone.

Alone with her sedatives and her treetops. Her restless sky.

He persisted.

October turned into November. Other people came to visit. Anna and Rickard. Germund, but not Maria. They didn't know what to say to her, felt uncomfortable and didn't stay long.

Even her mother and sister came to visit her. They stayed for three hours and cried throughout. Both of them; they said they had made their peace with her now and that they loved her.

In the end, even Dr Werngren came. He still had a polo-necked jumper every time they met, but it wasn't yellow any more. Usually black or a dark, dark navy. He came once a week, and after a while he started coming twice. They went for walks along the ridge, longer and longer walks in the gathering autumn darkness. She liked the darkness. In December, Tomas started coming along, too.

At Christmas she went home to Sibyllegatan and spent two nights there.

In January she was discharged and went home properly.

She had a thick black notebook in which she had been writing down her thoughts for three months. They burnt it in a pan of petrol on the balcony.

She was taking two sorts of medication. Two white tablets morning and night, plus a red one at bedtime.

Tomas said he loved her.

She said she felt a great need of solitude. It was now 1972.

28

Eva Backman decided to drive down to Lund.

It took twice as long as a flight, of course, but she didn't like flying. And it wasn't politically correct to sit alone at the steering wheel for 350 kilometres, just think of the emissions, but this time she really didn't care. There were several things she needed to think over, and there was no better place to do it than in a car with the right music coming through the loud-speakers. The motion and the rhythm. Wavering between Billie Holiday and Edith Piaf, she went for the latter. At least to start with, the first 100 kilometres, say.

Piaf, she thought. The sparrow. Who in some curious way explained what it meant to be a woman here on earth – not by her words or her life, but by her voice. Her sensual French, so beautiful that it brought you out in goose pimples. If I'd been born in France, thought Eva Backman, I wouldn't be a police officer. I'd have become a singer. No doubt about it. But you have to be able to do those rolling r's, or there's no point.

But it wasn't Piaf and her r's she was meant to be pondering; it was other topics, which demanded a bit more concentration and analysis. The current so-called case, to be more precise. The two individuals who had ended their days in Gåsaklyftan out in Rönninge, ten kilometres south of Kymlinge. The deaths of Maria Winckler and Germund Grooth, at an interval

249

of three and a half decades. Elective or not? Accidental or not? There was nothing to point to any criminal action in either of the cases, as she had said to Barbarotti three whole days ago. Practically nothing.

Others had taken a different view. Sandlin had smelt a rat, thirty-five years in the past, but hadn't been able to prove anything. More recently, Barbarotti claimed to have sensed something fishy, but he seemed to have changed his mind. Why? They hadn't had a proper talk about it, and she was now finding herself drawn in the opposite direction. But was she really? There was barely anything concrete to go on, as she'd noted. Not a shred of technical evidence, nothing that anybody had said or done that might indicate someone had pushed Germund Grooth over the edge. Or his partner in 1975. No chain of circumstantial evidence; in fact no circumstantial evidence at all.

Just a feeling and a few peculiarities. That was right, wasn't it? thought Eva Backman rhetorically. *Wasn't it?*

The absence of any vehicle, for example. That was one point to consider. How had Grooth got there? They had checked the local bus routes, and the nearest stop was more than two kilometres from Gåsaklinten. Sorrysen had checked with a few of the bus drivers, but none could remember a passenger getting off at the Alhamra Cross, which would have been the likeliest place. Walking from the centre of Kymlinge, for example, would have taken him over two hours. Two and a half.

It wasn't impossible, of course. If your aim was to kill yourself, perhaps a ten-kilometre walk was neither here nor there.

Could he have had a lift from someone? In that case, who?

Did he thumb a lift? A sixty-one-year-old university lecturer?

She shook her head and listened to Piaf for a while. *Je ne regrette rien.* Fantastic rolled r's.

Why had Barbarotti revised his opinion? There was something odd about it, but she couldn't work out what. He wasn't normally on the lookout for the most convenient solution; she had other colleagues who were known for doing that, and shutting down cases as soon as the opportunity arose – but not Barbarotti.

Nor did she. Passion for the truth was a pretentious phrase, but if there was one thing driving them both, Backman and Barbarotti, it was precisely that. By God, you were going to find out what had happened. That was the lynchpin, and if you didn't have that curiosity, you shouldn't be a detective. Should you?

Annoying, she thought. If nothing else, it's bloody annoying.

She tried to think back to the two conversations she'd had with people who'd been there thirty-five years earlier. Gunilla Winckler-Rysth and Elisabeth Martinsson. Was there anything either of them had said, or even merely implied, that pointed to a crime? Or two crimes? Something she had missed?

She didn't think so, or at any rate she couldn't catch sight of it. She had only spoken to Martinsson on the phone, and she hoped Barbarotti would find the time for a face-to-face interview while she herself was down in Lund. That ex-vicar and Gunilla Winckler-Rysth's husband, too, of course. Tomas Winckler. Though certain tasks would, in all likelihood, have to be delegated to their assistants, Tillgren and Wennergren-Olofsson, and that wouldn't necessarily mean they would be mismanaged, either.

As for what she might get out of her trip to Skåne, that

remained written in the stars, but Germund Grooth was still pretty much a blank page, so it was quite possible things would come to light. A host of irrelevant facts, if nothing else. A life.

Which for some reason – as yet unclear – had ended in the forest outside Kymlinge, 350 kilometres from the place where he lived.

But if he had simply taken his own life, what was there that remained unclear? When it came down to it.

She had booked two nights at Hotel Concordia in Stålbrogatan in the centre of Lund; she had stayed there once before and rather liked it. A hundred and twenty years before, Strindberg had written *Inferno* in the house next door. That alone was quite something. An Inspector Ribbing was due to meet her at four o'clock with an update. He would lay out whatever facts he had managed to gather about Germund Grooth during the day. They had spoken briefly last night and she thought his voice sounded reassuring.

A safe-sounding, southern Swedish voice, and perhaps that was where the reassurance lay.

A tongue touching the soft palate, an 'r' like Piaf's, yet different. Completely different.

She drove out of Jönköping on the Nissastigen road and joined the E6 level with Halmstad. She swapped to Billie Holiday and decided to skip lunch. She had some mineral water, a banana and a Kex chocolate wafer in the car and would make do with them. And some Statoil service-station coffee. If you were on your own you were free to take that sort of shortcut, and she was running a bit late.

*

He was sitting by a grand piano in the foyer, waiting for her. He was two metres tall and probably weighed more than Piaf and Holiday put together; she hadn't been able to hear that on the phone.

But he was full of energy and clearly kept himself in trim. Policemen who look like that don't need guns, thought Eva Backman, and asked for five minutes in her room before they started.

'I've made sure there's a room here at the hotel where we won't be disturbed,' he told her. 'Coffee and a sandwich, would that suit you?'

She said it most definitely would, and at a quarter past four they sat down on opposite sides of a polished oak table in a small conference room. The open sandwiches were the size of Ribbing's shoes, and a girl with a ponytail the colour of ripe wheat served coffee from a china pot and told them it was Zoega, the local brand.

Once she had closed the door behind her, Ribbing took a sheaf of paper out of a folder and cleared his throat.

'This Grooth,' he said. 'He certainly was a solitary devil.'

Backman nodded.

'Doesn't seem to have had any kind of social circle at all. No family, no friends. The information I did manage to get came from a neighbour and some colleagues. His professor in the physics department and two others. The neighbour's a Mrs Zetterlund, who shared a staircase with Grooth for eighteen years.'

'But you haven't been inside his flat?'

'Not yet. I thought we could do it tomorrow. You'd like to be there, I take it?'

'Absolutely,' said Eva Backman. 'Well, what did they have to say, those colleagues?'

Ribbing consulted his papers.

'Not very much. Grooth started in the department as a doctoral student in 1978. Before that he was a student in Uppsala, but that didn't seem to present a problem at the time.'

He winked. Backman knew it was a joke and gave a brief smile. The old Uppsala–Lund rivalry. It went back a long way.

'I know what you mean,' she said. 'Go on.'

'He completed his doctorate in 1983 and got a post in the physics department the same year. First as a research assistant, then as a junior lecturer from 1985, and he finally got a senior lectureship in 1991. Nineteen years ago, in other words. A capable colleague, according to Professor Söderman. Liked by his students, no complaints. He could have gone further, but lacked the right sort of ambition, the academic passion . . . well, that was the way Söderman put it. Grooth's published two books plus around twenty scientific articles since he got his doctorate. That's considered a bit sparse, evidently . . .'

He paused and turned over a page.

'He didn't have much to do with the other staff in his department, certainly not socially, and those I spoke to saw him as the typical loner. One of them told me he played bridge at Lund Bridge Club for a few years in the mid-eighties, but I haven't been able to get hold of anybody from there yet – I've a few names to ring later today. But it only seems to have lasted for a couple of years, probably less.'

'Academic life?' asked Backman. 'Parties and meetings and doctoral ceremonies . . . I thought you were inundated with those in a town like this.'

A slight smile twitched at the corner of Ribbing's mouth. 'There are lots of opportunities for those who feel like it. But

Grooth hardly ever took part in anything like that. He turned up to doctoral disputations when there was a colleague involved, but that was about the limit of it. No academic societies or anything like that. If these work colleagues of his are telling the truth, that is, and why shouldn't they?'

Eva Backman attacked her vast open sandwich, the corner where the prawns were, and took a drink of water.

'And the neighbour?' she asked. 'Mrs Zetterlund, I think you said?'

'Zetterlund, yes,' said Ribbing, scratching the back of his neck. 'She's over eighty, but very alert and keeps her eyes peeled. She generally exchanged a word or two with Grooth when she saw him, she says. He was pleasant and reliable.'

'Pleasant and reliable?'

'Yes. That can mean more or less anything, of course . . . or nothing at all, more likely. He seems to have behaved responsibly, at any rate. Mrs Zetterlund said he always left the laundry room clean and tidy after he used it.'

'Hmm,' said Backman. 'Anything on the computer and phone front?'

'We got into his work computer, the one he had in the department. His emails are virtually one hundred per cent professional contacts, and his mobile . . . well, as far as we understand it, he didn't have any kind of contract. That's quite unusual these days, isn't it?'

'Yes,' agreed Backman, 'pretty rare. But we have information about a woman in Copenhagen. Have you found her?'

'She's on the computer,' Ribbing admitted. 'Two incoming emails, one outgoing. Her name's Kristin Pedersen; we tried ringing her but we didn't get through. We emailed her as well – no answer so far.'

'It's important we get hold of her,' said Backman. 'The sooner, the better.'

She ate a few more mouthfuls of sandwich, from the liver-pâté section, and pondered as she did so. Kristin Pedersen was the woman Grooth took with him when he paid a visit in Lindås – when did Gunilla Winckler-Rysth say that was . . . May–June time? If there was anyone they ought to talk to about the deceased, thought Backman, it was her. Perhaps I ought to take a trip across the Sound, too? she thought. Now I've come all this way.

Well, she'd have to see how tomorrow played out.

'So we're going into his flat tomorrow morning?' she said, and Ribbing nodded in confirmation. 'Yes. We're bound to find something.'

He brushed a few sandwich crumbs from his broad thighs and seemed to hesitate. 'Why are you and your colleagues looking into his death at all?' he asked. 'I don't really get it. What is there to point to . . . well, you know?'

Eva Backman shrugged.

'Not much, really,' she admitted. 'A few details. For instance: it so happens that his partner died in exactly the same spot, thirty-five years ago.'

'What?' said Ribbing. 'Well, I'm damned.'

'Exactly,' said Backman. 'But maybe it's just what it sounds like. Very odd, I grant you, but maybe there's nothing more to it. Nothing criminal.'

Ribbing made no immediate reply.

'He does seem to have been a bit strange,' he suggested after a while. 'We do have quite a few oddballs in this town. Some people say the university functions as a kind of sheltered workshop'.

'Oh, really?' said Backman, thinking how visible that famous divide could sometimes be. The divide between the select academic world and the one inhabited by ordinary people. People like DI Ribbing. Even though his name hinted at some aristocratic roots back in the past, it was plain which side he was on.

Or sympathized with, at any rate. Maybe he's a black sheep, thought Eva Backman. A gigantic black ram. She took a long sip of coffee to hide her smile.

'Yes, well, there we are,' he summarized, slotting his papers back into the folder. 'It wasn't much to offer you, so I suppose we'll just have to see what we find tomorrow. How were you planning to spend the evening?'

Good heavens, thought Backman. He's not thinking of inviting me out to dinner, is he?

'Haven't a clue,' she admitted. 'A walk and a good book in my room, I expect.'

'Let me suggest Martinus,' he said. 'It's the restaurant at the Grand, and the food really isn't bad. A collegial little dinner?'

Eva Backman considered for two seconds. Why not? she thought.

Why on earth not?

29

'What are you talking about?' said Rickard. 'Can you run me through it again?'

'Glad to,' said Tomas. 'It's nothing that special. Just a way of earning a bit of money. Taking out a student loan every term for the foreseeable future makes no financial sense. You must agree, surely?'

'Perhaps,' said Rickard. 'But a bus?'

'Exactly,' said Tomas. 'A bus.'

They were sitting in the student-union cafe on Övre Slottsgatan. One morning in early April. Sleety rain outside the window, coffee and almond tarts on the table in front of them. Rickard had half an hour before his exegetics seminar, but had no idea when Tomas would need to be off to his business-management lecture. He wasn't even sure if it was business management Tomas was currently reading. Maybe it was still economics. Or economic history, or the whole lot at the same time, but who cared?

'So we'll start by getting a bus,' Tomas went on, trying to keep his enthusiasm in check. Rickard was familiar with the tone and knew there was some persuasion on the way. With rationally based arguments, but persuasion nonetheless.

'Then we'll have to see how it goes,' Tomas went on. 'We'll do a recce this summer, an exploratory trip. All six of us.

We'll have to work out a route . . . find campsites, cheap hotels, sightseeing options, you know the kind of thing.'

'Have you tried this out on any of the others?'

'No. I'm starting with you.'

'How's Gunilla feeling?'

'Better. And she could really do with something else to think about. It would do her good to get away for a bit.'

Rickard nodded. Tomas paused and looked thoughtful for a moment.

'I reckon it'll take us a month. Maybe six weeks, if we're going to cover the whole Eastern Bloc . . . well, we'll have to skip the Soviet Union itself, but we'll have time to get round the other countries, no problem. Poland first, of course, the ferry over from Ystad, then Czechoslovakia, Hungary, Yugoslavia, Romania—'

'This bus?' interrupted Rickard. 'How are we going to get hold of a bus?'

'I've already got one lined up,' announced Tomas with a sheepish grin.

'Really?' said Rickard.

'Yep. This guy on my course, his dad had a little coach company out in Bergsbrunna. But he's got heart problems now and has to retire early . . . he's selling his two buses. One's already spoken for, but we can have the other for forty thousand.'

'Forty thousand kronor!' exploded Rickard. 'Are you out of your mind? I mean . . .?'

'Might be able to haggle him down to nearer thirty-six or thirty-seven,' said Tomas. 'If we pay cash. Twelve thousand per couple, in round figures. Though I'm thinking we ought to put in fifteen thousand each as seed capital on top of that, maybe twenty – it's good to have a decent margin . . . We'll register as a company and the trip we make this summer will be tax-deductible, of course. A recce, as I say. What do you think?'

'What do I think?' said Rickard, hardly able to stop himself laughing. 'I think Anna and I would probably be able to scrape together about fifteen hundred if we really put our backs into it. But fifteen thousand, my God!'

Tomas propped himself on his elbows and leant across the table. He fixed his eyes on Rickard and looked like a cat that has backed its prey into a corner.

'Loans,' he said. 'Ever heard of them?'

Rickard shook his head. 'Loans? Which bank do you think is going to lend *us* anything? Poor students who live on macaroni and black pudding.'

'Not a problem,' said Tomas. 'Our parents can stand surety.'

'What?'

'It's just a formality. But as none of us has any security – or so I assume – we need someone to stand surety. It's just a signature on a piece of paper, nothing more. They never actually have to contribute anything, not even their loose change.'

'Possibly it hasn't occurred to you that you have to pay back what you borrow?'

'Ha-ha. I have, as it happens. But you only have to start after twelve or eighteen months. We can get the loan for ten years, so it won't be very much each time. And we're going to make money, trust me, Brother.'

Rickard was silent, thinking. Tomas leant back, had some coffee and waited.

'I don't know,' Rickard said at length. 'You've rather sprung it on me. Of course a trip round Eastern Europe sounds great, but . . .'

'I'll deal with all the practical arrangements,' said Tomas. 'You don't have to worry that it's going to make a ton of extra work. I thought I'd go ahead with Norrland this autumn . . . or Gothenburg.'

'Go ahead . . .?'

'Weekend trips. Students who want to go home for the weekend. The E4 up to Luleå, or something like that. They can get off at stops along the route, wherever they live. We might even manage a couple of return trips before the summer, by the way. Friday afternoon from Uppsala, Sunday evening back from Norrland. Cheap fares. Or maybe Gothenburg, like I said, though I think Norrland looks more promising . . . Half what it costs on the train, of course we'll get people. All we have to do is advertise – *Ergo* and the other student newspapers. And in the student clubs, of course.'

'And then, next summer, Europe?'

'One or two trips, yes. Low-budget . . . for people like us. Students and other poverty-stricken types who want to widen their horizons. The whole bloody left wing, in other words; they're longing to see what socialism really looks like. Prague five years after the invasion, who wouldn't want to check that out? The paradise of Bulgaria! But first I'm really looking forward to a summer in the bus with the whole gang. We could head off at the end of July – a cold beer in Budapest doesn't sound too bad, does it? And another one in Sofia.'

He laughed. Rickard laughed. The travel-agency business? he thought. By bus through Europe? Well, why not? Provided he didn't have to put in too much extra effort, and could make a bit of money into the bargain. See a bit of the world, as discussed.

'I've got a bus driver's licence, you know,' said Tomas. 'If any of you others get yourselves one as well, we won't even need to hire a driver. There have to be two of you on long journeys . . . when you've got passengers, that is. I'm not talking about this summer now. I'm prepared to drive the whole way.'

'I'll have to talk to Anna about it,' said Rickard. 'What does Gunilla think?'

'Oh, she's fine with it,' said Tomas, 'though I haven't really had a serious talk to her about it yet.'

'I understand,' said Rickard.

'Good,' said Tomas.

They lapsed into silence as they polished off their almond tarts.

'I've got to let them know about the bus on Saturday,' said Tomas.

'Saturday?' said Rickard. 'You mean we've only got three days to decide?'

Tomas shrugged. 'I'm worried the old man's got another potential buyer,' he said. 'So it would be a good idea.'

Rickard looked at his watch. 'All right,' he said, 'I'll talk to Anna tonight. I must get off to my seminar now.'

'We'll be in touch,' said Tomas. 'You don't need to worry about this. We've got a great opportunity here, it's as simple as that.'

'I'm not worried,' said Rickard.

Then he put up his hood and went out to brave the April weather.

★

She was more enthusiastic than he'd expected.

If 'enthusiastic' was a word you could ever apply to Anna. He didn't like making space for that reflection – but it came to him unbidden and he banished it without effort. It was a matter of personality, not anything to criticize or try to correct. Anyway, he was much the same sort himself, wasn't he? He seldom, if ever, demanded the powerful intensity of experience – the rush – that many people clearly strove for. Especially young people, chasing after those ecstatic moments. That was no doubt why they took drugs, thought Rickard. He had never felt the slightest temptation to try them; tobacco and alcohol, admittedly, but that was where he drew the line.

Even when they made love Anna was rather quiet, and afterwards he often had to ask if it had happened for her or not. Two times out of three it had, but he could never tell when it did.

So the fact that she now – with almost no time for thought – gave him a positive answer to Tomas's bus proposal, well, it took him unawares, to put it mildly. They had not yet made any plans for the summer, other than that they would both find work for a while – they couldn't get by, otherwise – and he realized that much of his own doubt lay in the expectation of a negative response from Anna. Sensing that she would think it too risky, too expensive and frankly too dull to jaunt about in a bus for half the summer and then be tied to a loan and a company – well, wasn't it precisely that anticipated deprecating response that had muted his own enthusiasm?

But that was the way it had to be in a relationship, he thought. You didn't assess things only from your own perspective, but also from the other person's.

And her immediate 'Yes' made him feel slightly shamefaced.

'I think it sounds fun, too,' he said. 'We can both work for the first half of the summer, and then spend the rest of it in Eastern Europe.'

'But about that loan,' said Anna, biting her lip. 'I shall never get my parents to sign the form. Whoever is in debt is not free – that's what Dad's going to have on his gravestone. He thinks it's bad enough that I take out study loans.'

'It doesn't matter,' promised Rickard. 'I'll talk to my mum, it'll be fine.'

He talked to his mother up in Hova that same evening, and it was fine, just as he had said.

The only thing that bothered him was having to tell her a bit of a lie, but he knew there was no way round it. Standing surety for her son was no problem for her, quite the opposite, but standing surety for a bus was a different matter.

So he told her it was for a flat, and in some vague and mysterious way he managed to hint that they were expecting a baby, and that was why they needed a bigger place. His mother had never been to visit, not to Väktargatan or to Uppsala as a whole, and she had never met Anna – but it went without saying that she wanted to help them on their way if they were now in need of a proper home.

Not with money, because she had none, but a signature on a form didn't cost anything.

And both mother and son intimated to one another, without committing to any firm arrangement, that it would soon be time for the three of them to meet up. There was absolutely no question about it.

The phone call didn't take more than five minutes. As usual,

Rickard felt a pang of guilt after they hung up, and this time even more so than usual, because he hadn't told her the truth. But at the same time he knew she was as protective of the distance between them as he was, and he assumed she experienced a corresponding sense of guilt.

My mother and I, he thought. Two strangers of the same blood.

But as if by magic, Anna produced a bottle of red, the ever-popular Parador, to go with the Bolognese, and they both felt a tangible new sense of anticipation. When they made love later that evening, he was quite certain she had an orgasm, he didn't need to ask.

30

Gunnar Barbarotti met Tomas Winckler at the Gothia Hotel in Gothenburg, just three hours after he had finished talking to Rickard Berglund in Kymlinge. Winckler was in town on business and staying at the Gothia, and they were sitting in the restaurant on the twenty-third floor with their square plates of seafood, looking out onto a twilight that reminded Barbarotti of bluebottle wings. Its colour, that was, which had a strange dull shimmer to it that he assumed was the result of pollution and dirty street lights.

Tomas Winckler looked as if dirt and pollution were strangers to him. He was freshly showered and buffed. He had promised Barbarotti an hour, but then he had to go off to a business dinner. He would be happy to talk to DI Barbarotti again in the coming week, if necessary. Of course. This whole Germund Grooth affair was very peculiar, to say the least. He and his wife had spent quite a few hours discussing it.

'And did you reach any conclusions?' asked Barbarotti, spearing a prawn on his fork.

'Well, what are we to make of it?' said Winckler. He shrugged his shoulders and simulated a moment's reflection. 'Germund has always been an odd customer, but I for one could never have imagined it would end like this for him.'

'Oh?' said Barbarotti. 'Is that the only conclusion you arrived at then? You and your wife.'

He had felt a sudden wave of antipathy rising in him; there was something about Winckler's smartly tailored suit and topped-up suntan that aggravated him. The man's smooth self-confidence and professional amiability. Why was he staying at the Gothia when his own home was only fifteen or twenty kilometres away, for example? A room in a place like this must cost more than the taxi fare, thought Barbarotti as he waited for the other man to chew and swallow a bit of lobster and formulate his reply. Way more.

'Yes, it was, as a matter of fact,' said Winckler. 'We haven't been in touch all that much over the years. As you know, he came to visit us a few months ago and had a woman with him – Danish, I've forgotten her name . . . But that was a one-off. We saw quite a lot of him in Uppsala because he and my sister were together. After she died, our contact dried up. Largely anyway, and we've naturally no idea why he chose to end his days in Gåsaklyftan.'

'You think it was his own choice?'

'Is there any other conceivable explanation?'

Barbarotti couldn't decide if there was a grain of genuine surprise in Winckler's voice. Maybe there was, but his own mild irritation was impeding his judgement.

'There are a number of unusual factors.'

'Factors?' said Winckler. 'What factors?'

'I can't go into it. But the same applied thirty-five years ago. When your sister died . . . it wasn't entirely clear how it happened, was it?'

Tomas Winckler's face assumed a new and sharper expression.

'What are you driving at, exactly?'

Barbarotti speared another prawn. 'I'm driving at the truth,' he said, trying not to sound pretentious. 'I find both these deaths extremely strange. I've read the transcript of Sandlin's interview with you in 1975, for example. You say you are convinced Maria didn't take her own life . . . and you were equally convinced that nobody pushed her. What was it that made you so sure of those two things?'

Winckler sat motionless, studying him for several long seconds. He gave a couple of twists to the large watch on his wrist. Rolex, Barbarotti guessed. Must weigh about half a kilo.

'Because everything else is unthinkable,' Winckler said finally. 'Completely unthinkable.'

'Even her killing herself?'

'Why should she have done that?'

Barbarotti looked out over the city. 'People kill themselves. Every day. It generally comes as a surprise to those closest to them.'

Tomas Winckler had no comment.

'But you don't think anyone pushed her, either?'

'Definitely not. It's a preposterous idea.'

'And now her partner's been found in the same place, thirty-five years later, that doesn't alter your opinion?'

Tomas Winckler took a gulp of his white wine.

'No. He wanted to die where she did. Don't ask me why.'

'When he came to visit you, with the Danish woman, did he show any signs of depression?'

'No. We've talked about that, my wife and I, as I said. He was a bit spiky, but then he always has been. Gloomy and spiky.'

'Gloomy and spiky?'

'Yes, that pretty much covers it.'

Barbarotti sighed inwardly and changed tack.

'This group, I've been thinking about it. So the six of you socialized a lot – knew each other inside out – and then you split up after what happened to Maria. Was that how it went?'

'More or less. But I wouldn't say we knew each other inside out. Some of us, perhaps. Rickard and I . . . at the beginning.'

'At the beginning?'

'Yes.'

'But you were a close-knit group in Uppsala?'

'For some years, yes.'

'You all left Uppsala around the same time, didn't you?'

Winckler leant back and thought about it. 'Broadly speaking,' he said. 'But that's normal, isn't it? Your studies take up a few years and then you move on. My wife and I moved to Gothenburg in August 1974, I think Rickard got his parish in the spring of 1975 . . . and Maria and Germund must have moved to Kymlinge in the autumn of that year. They both got temporary teaching jobs; yes, it was only a month or two before it happened.'

'You're in the travel-agency business, I gather?'

Winckler nodded.

'I have information here that says you first set up a travel company back in 1972. It went bankrupt in 1974. Quality Travel Company Ltd. Is that correct?'

Winckler gave a laugh. 'Yes. It was just a student thing, really. I thought we'd put on a few coach trips to Eastern Europe; it was popular in those days. And some cheap trips within Sweden, too . . . But that's right, we folded after a couple of years.'

'Lose much money?'

'Some. Not a huge amount.'

'But you stayed in the same area of business?'

'I worked at a bank for a few years. Then we started TW Travel. It's grown over the years.'

He smiled a well-earnt smile of success. Modest, but not without pride. Gunnar Barbarotti drank some of his water and looked over to the bar, where two long-legged ladies were just being served some red concoction, complete with drinking straw. I don't like successful people, he thought. That's the bald truth of it.

'You said Germund Grooth was an odd customer. Could you flesh that out for me?'

Winckler looked at his Rolex and appeared to decide there was time for a short exposition.

'He's always been different,' he said. 'Gunilla and I both thought so, even back then. It doesn't surprise me that he became such an eccentric over the years; he found the whole social-interaction thing very difficult. And he didn't feel the need of it, either, as far as I can see. Bloody brainy, of course, could have gone a long way in the research world, but there was something missing there, too . . . Hard to say what. But he was interesting, I can't deny that. And he fitted well with Maria, somehow . . . She was an unusual person as well.'

'Unusual?' said Barbarotti.

'It's hard to describe her. I mean, she was my sister, and we were very close . . . well, there was something different about her, undoubtedly.'

Different? thought Barbarotti irritably. Can't you find a better word to describe your dead sister?

'When you met that evening at the vicarage,' he asked. 'The day before it happened, that is . . . It wasn't just a reunion, was it? There was something else as well?'

It was a shot in the dark, and Winckler didn't oblige him.

'Something else?' he said, raising two innocent eyebrows. 'I don't know what you're getting at.'

'I've read Inspector Sandlin's interviews with you all,' said Barbarotti. 'There are some inconsistencies.'

What the hell am I jabbering on about? he thought. He must know I'm bluffing.

Tomas Winckler thought for a few seconds.

'I don't know what inconsistencies you could be referring to,' he said. 'It was a standard dinner party. Not the best ever maybe, but it was still an attempt at a reunion. We hadn't seen each other for a year or more.'

'And did you meet up again on later occasions? The five of you who were left?'

'No, not all five. I remember we arranged to meet the Berglunds here in town once, it was probably about six months later. And I think we had dinner with them a couple of other times . . . but it was a good while ago. We somehow just didn't stay in touch.'

'But you and Rickard Berglund were good friends in Uppsala?'

Winckler nodded gravely. 'Very,' he said. 'We did our military service together; yes, he and I were really good friends.'

Barbarotti thought he could detect a sense of regret in his voice. Something had been lost and Tomas Winckler was sorry it had turned out that way.

'Why did you stop seeing each other? There must have been a reason.'

Tomas Winckler shook his head. 'I honestly don't know. I don't think my wife Gunilla and Anna Berglund had a great deal in common. It was mainly us, Rickard and me, who held

271

it all together. Germund was always a bit more on the outside somehow, but Maria was my sister, of course, and for those years . . . well, it was natural for us to stick together, that's all. Isn't that the usual way with life: you hang on to some friends and lose others along the way?'

Gunnar Barbarotti contemplated the fly's-wing heavens for a moment before he spoke. 'How long is it since you heard anything from Rickard Berglund?' he asked.

'We email each other now and then,' said Tomas Winckler. 'A couple of times a year maybe. I know Anna's got cancer, and I assume she hasn't got long left now . . . I had an email from him in early August and answered straight away, more or less.'

'Elisabeth Martinsson, are you in touch with her at all?'

'Who's she?'

Again Barbarotti couldn't work out whether the surprise was genuine or feigned.

'Elisabeth Martinsson came along on your mushroom hunt thirty-five years ago – surely you remember that?'

'Oh, was that her name? No, I only ever met her on that one day.'

'I see,' said Barbarotti. 'What were you doing between twelve and four on Saturday?'

'What?'

'I asked you what you were doing on Saturday afternoon.'

Tomas Winckler drank some wine and twisted his Rolex around his wrist again.

'Why on earth do you want to know that?'

'Just routine procedure,' said Barbarotti. 'I don't want to miss anything.'

'I don't understand what you're trying to achieve,' said Tomas Winckler.

'Perhaps you could answer my question, even so,' suggested Barbarotti. 'Last Saturday, that is?'

Winckler thought for five seconds. 'I played golf in the morning,' he said. 'In the afternoon, yes, I was at home.'

'Is there anyone who can verify that?'

'No. Christ almighty, this is going too far,' said Tomas Winckler.

He started to get up from the table, but Barbarotti gestured him back into his seat.

'There's no need to get upset,' he said, allowing himself a friendly smile. 'You realize, I'm sure, that if Germund Grooth has in fact been murdered, we have a legitimate interest in establishing people's whereabouts at the time it happened.'

'Murdered?' exclaimed Winckler, sinking back into his chair. 'What the hell are you saying?'

'It's one possibility,' said Barbarotti. 'You don't think I'd be bothering to investigate a suicide, do you?'

Tomas Winckler had nothing to say.

'Can I interpret that as meaning you were at home alone all afternoon on Saturday?'

Winckler's jaw appeared to grind for a while, yet no comment emerged. Barbarotti waited patiently, but after thirty seconds or so his companion stood up, buttoned his jacket and strode out of the restaurant.

Interesting, thought Gunnar Barbarotti. Though what atrocious behaviour, leaving me here with the bill.

As he now had to pay 660 kronor, he stayed in his seat and finished his seafood salad, right down to the last pea. He rang Marianne while he was doing so and told her he loved her and was a semi-idiot, but it was with the other half of him, the sound and healthy one, that he loved her – and that he would be home by seven thirty and would very much like to cook a delicious dinner for the whole gang, now they had finally made it to Friday evening. If she would help him out by buying the ingredients, and as long as the gang didn't mind waiting that long.

She replied that, for her part, she loved him with approaching 60 per cent of her sound and healthy 100, and she would discuss the dinner question with Sweden's youth, its future.

Cutting across the hotel lobby a short while later, he was just in time to see Tomas Winckler conduct a fur-trimmed female through the front entrance, and he realized the question of why someone wouldn't take a taxi home to Lindås after their business dinner in central Gothenburg most likely had a much simpler answer than he had envisaged.

Well, there we are, thought Inspector Barbarotti. Didn't I get the feeling there was a bastard lurking inside that Armani?

Although perhaps the suit itself was a distinguishing feature of all the bastards in the world? was the next thought that occurred to him – a hallmark, so to speak – but at that point it was time, of course, to take a big step back from the glorious wilderness of prejudice.

In the car on the way home to Kymlinge it struck him that he had forgotten to ask about Rickard Berglund's alibi for the time in question. Tomas Winckler had apparently played golf in the morning, but things were far from clear after that. They had been unable to establish the exact time of Germund Grooth's death; it had occurred sometime between noon and 4 p.m. on Saturday 25 September, it was impossible to narrow it down any further, according to the pathologist, Ritzén. Today was Friday

1 October. Barbarotti noted that roughly a week had gone by; they had been working on the case for five days and, to be honest, they hadn't found much to point to anyone having helped the academic over the edge, out there in the forest.

Several question marks and dubious aspects had come to light, but that almost always happened when you started asking people questions. Coming across a few details that were rather opaque – the occasional overreaction, or someone with an unknown woman in a hotel lobby – did not mean you were hot on the heels of a perpetrator. Far from it.

The term perpetrator presupposed a crime had been committed, for a start, and if you sluiced away all those irrelevant irregularities, there really wasn't anything left to point in that direction.

To be honest, he thought again.

But anyway they had reached Friday evening. He decided weekend peace was now in order – and he wouldn't spare another thought for Germund Grooth or Gåsaklyftan or his own wife's past exploits until Monday morning at the earliest.

But there was something about that blasted group of people, he couldn't help but be aware of it, and it was the first question he would get to work on when he was back at his desk in Kymlinge police HQ.

Plus the others' alibis, naturally. He hoped Eva Backman and her assistants had found out how things stood on that front. And he hoped Backman's trip down to Skåne had yielded something at least, but he could probably take that as read?

Weekend peace came first, though. Lucília do Carmo and fifty minutes' fado to begin with. Liquid sorrow in Portuguese.

31

Maria the sparrow.

July 1972. I've been working at The Prophet for six weeks, tonight's my last night and not before time. I can't take any more of those pubertal males who can somehow afford to sit there night after night, knocking back the beer as their voices get louder and their eyes hazier. Most of them aren't students; the students have gone home to Bollnäs and Piteå and Katrineholm. The town's as empty as after a nuclear war, and the wretches who've escaped the radioactive fallout gather at The Prophet. And there's the sparrow, standing behind the bar and filling their glasses with foaming beer so they can slowly and methodically put their remaining brain cells into a coma as they wait for the final collapse. Christ, how I loathe them. I know I ought to feel sorry for them, but I don't.

Germund has been working at a bicycle-repair shop in Övre Slottsgatan, mending and repainting; the bikes are presumably stolen, or have been fished up out of the River Fyris, but what the hell. You have to take what's on offer, and he's got his grant as well, plus some money he inherited from his parents after they died in that accident, so we can't complain. We can get by. I'm not complaining, I just feel so tired in what was once my soul.

And tomorrow we're off. It's going to be bloody great. When

my golden-boy brother first came up with his idea of a bus company, I thought it was the stupidest thing I'd ever heard, even from him, but I have to say I've changed my mind. The company has three part-owners: Tomas and Gunilla with 51 per cent, and then Germund and me, and Rickard and Anna, with 24½. He wants to be in control of course, Tomas, but it doesn't bother me. They had to put in 26,000 kronor, and we and the Berglunds – they actually got married a fortnight ago and both have the same surname now – 12,500 each.

So Germund and I now find ourselves joint owners of a quarter of a bus. It cost 38,000. Tomas has spent 2,000 on various repairs and we've got 11,000 in capital. The reason I know all these figures is that we had a company meeting at Sibyllegatan yesterday and Tomas went through everything in great detail. Quality Travel Co. Ltd, the bus is yellow and green, and he's taken out loads of the seats and put in curtains as screens and stuff like that, so we each have our own little section as we chug round Europe. But when we start carrying real passengers to and fro, he'll have to fix the seats back in again. They're in a barn out in Lurbo for now; he's got contacts in all sorts of places, my brother.

The plan is to be away for five weeks. We'll be back the weekend before the start of the autumn term and, you know what, it's a long time since I've looked forward to anything the way I'm looking forward to this trip. Though I realize it's mostly to do with The Prophet and the beer morons, and the prospect of getting away from there.

Finally getting away from Uppsala for a while. Germund is actually as enthusiastic as I am, though he wouldn't know how to spell the word. But I can see it in him. He's taken all the undergrad physics courses you can possibly take, and his

277

professor wants him to start on postgrad research, but Germund says he needs to cover a bit more maths first. Maths and theoretical philosophy, that's what he's going to do this autumn. As for me, I'm going to carry on with history of literature, the level-three course, with half the term spent on the dissertation; I'm tending towards Céline, though they really like you to stick to something Swedish. It would have to be Stig Dagerman in that case, but I don't have to decide until the autumn anyway.

It's still working out fine, living with Germund, and I'm starting to think it's to do with what you might call our birth-marks. We're both damaged, him worse than me of course; he lost his family, I just knocked my head and underwent a personality change. There is a degree of difference, but also a basic similarity that we build on. Sometimes, when we look at each other across the breakfast table, it's as if we are seeing each other for the first time.

'Well, hi there, darling,' he might say to me. 'What's your name and how the hell did you get in here?'

I generally answer in French. Say I don't reveal my name to strangers, and if he doesn't get out of my flat right away, I shall ring the police. *Les flics.*

Yes, it's as easy as anything to go back to square one with Germund; I don't know if other people know this, but in fact it's a great advantage. It really turns him on when I speak French, too, so that does no harm, either. Our sex is so good we could almost write a handbook.

They got married in church, Rickard and Anna, but just a side chapel in the cathedral. I've no idea why they decided to go through with it just now; maybe she's pregnant, but I expect that'll become clear during the trip. Afterwards we went for dinner at Skarholmen, the usual group of us plus some close family members. Rickard's mother, and Anna's parents and brothers. A pretty motley crew, in truth, but we were there for two hours and no blood was shed, as Germund put it in his speech of thanks. Nobody had asked him to make a speech, but he was a bit drunk and presumably thought he ought to contribute in some way. Anna's dad certainly didn't seem to enjoy it very much.

Things have been tough for Gunilla since that stillbirth last autumn. She was in Ulleråker for a couple of months for treatment, but she's been at home since January. She hasn't lifted a finger to study, though, just drifts around at home like some kind of sad zombie. I've tried to talk to her, even though helping people sort themselves out isn't really my thing. But she's clearly taken a hard knock, so we'll have to see how she copes on the trip. If there's anyone I'm concerned about, it's Gunilla; she seems more brittle than you might expect and it takes a thicker skin than that to be with five other people for five weeks in a bus. And a string of socialist paradises.

Germund had another of his weird nightmares the other night. I don't really know anything about them, because he doesn't like talking about it. I was woken by him sitting up in bed and jabbering something; at first I thought it might be some kind of physics formula, it sounded incomprehensible, and it took me a few seconds to realize he was talking in his sleep. He suddenly got up, walked straight across the room and started banging his head on the doorpost. Several times, and he kept rattling off the same strange words. Then he just stood there in the middle of the room with his arms dangling stupidly at his sides, but still jabbering, and even though he kept on repeating more or less the same words, I couldn't make any sense of them, not a shred. I'm not even sure he was talking Swedish. He stood there for maybe half a minute and then he fell to the floor and started whimpering. I can't find any better word for it than that – whimpering – and when he'd been going on for a while, I decided it could be time to wake him up. First I said his name and touched him, but that didn't work, so I went out into the kitchen for a glass of water and threw it over him.

He woke up instantly, stared at me and asked me what year it was.

Yes, he asked me what year it was. Twice, the second time in a loud and slightly demanding voice. For a moment I thought he'd gone mad and something had malfunctioned inside his skull, maybe because of the water – what do I know? – like solid rock can be split by heat followed by sudden cold, but then he blinked a couple of times, cleared his throat and went to the loo.

He stayed there for ten minutes, came back, apologized and said he'd had a nightmare. I asked if he remembered sitting in bed jabbering, or banging his head against the door-post, but he said he had no memory of anything like that. He'd been in an interrogation room in wartime, he maintained, and all he'd said was his name and rank, just as you were meant to. Over and over again, even though he was horribly tortured.

I'm not convinced he was telling the truth. I can very well imagine him sitting on the loo and fabricating a plausible dream. There was something about the way he told it. Next time, if it happens to him again, I shall press him a bit harder, but I didn't feel up to it this morning. I'd been working at the bar until after midnight and only had a few hours' sleep in my body.

We went back to sleep and didn't say any more about it.

32

They went into the Prennegatan flat at ten minutes past nine on the Friday morning. It was 1 October and the weather had changed to what Backman supposed one would call an Indian summer. That idea of going over to Copenhagen and trying to find Kristin Pedersen had come back to her at breakfast in the hotel, but she realized this had more to do with the blue sky and warm breeze than with the case itself. A nice piece of meat and a glass of red at one of the restaurants round the old square at Gråbrødretorv in the evening, once her mission was accomplished, was also quite a tempting prospect.

And then she could drive home on Saturday. It wasn't her turn to look after the boys until Sunday, so there was time.

Yesterday's dinner with DI Ribbing, whose first name was Gustaf, had been very pleasant, and perhaps it had given her a taste for more. He had tried it on with her a little, she felt, but he was at least ten years younger than she was and she hadn't encouraged him. She'd just been generally positive and encouraging throughout. She enjoyed two glasses of Sancerre with the sole and a drop of Muscat with her crème brûlée, ending up a touch tipsy but nothing more. She tried to pay her half of the bill, but he wouldn't let her. They parted on Grönegatan outside the Concordia just before eleven.

A quick hug, that was all. Not even that minimally extended eye contact containing the unspoken question.

That's my love life nowadays then, she thought before she went to sleep. Non-existent.

And in Prennegatan the next morning they had an Inspector Larsson for company.

A small flat. A bedroom with a workstation. A living room with Bang & Olufsen stereo equipment and 1,500 books. Not much furniture apart from the bookshelves: a glass table and a couple of tubular-steel armchairs, a touch on the spartan side. A small balcony looking out over the inner courtyard. DI Larsson informed them the block had been built in 1936 and was owned by a housing association. Sixteen flats in all; Grooth's was on the second floor and was one of the smallest. He had purchased it in 1995, when the association was set up. Before that, he had rented it.

Everything was neat and clean. The bed was fairly neatly made, there was nothing left lying around untidily, like clothes or half-read newspapers. Not even anything in the dishwasher. A little drift of post on the hall rug, that was all, and it struck Eva Backman that it looked pretty much as you would want your home to look when you got back after a trip.

Or possibly to create that impression, if you knew the police would be coming in. If you'd killed yourself, for example.

She wondered if Ribbing was reflecting on the same thing, but didn't ask. At any event, they didn't find any kind of farewell letter. Beside the computer in the bedroom lay a desk diary. Backman opened it at the right week. There was a single entry, which made it all the more pregnant.

Or so it seemed to Backman.

Friday 1 October

Paris. Kastrup 10.30

She looked at her watch and nodded to Ribbing, who had just come into the room.

'Look at this. He was due to fly to Paris in an hour's time.'

'What?' said Ribbing. 'What the heck does this mean?'

They discussed what it meant for ten minutes. Although thirty seconds would have been more than adequate, in Eva Backman's view at least. Why the hell would you book a flight to Paris departing a week after you had killed yourself?

Ribbing and Larsson both tried to find a plausible answer to that question, but in the end they gave up.

'He didn't kill himself,' concluded Ribbing. 'It must have happened some other way.'

'Yeah,' said Larsson, on an intake of breath, because he was born way up in Skellefteå and had never really learnt to talk like a Scanian in the thirty years he'd lived there. 'That's the way it looks. Unless he had a very sudden attack of depression.'

'You don't get depressed if you've got a trip to Paris waving at you from just around the corner,' decided Ribbing. 'Is there anything else that points to him having killed himself?'

'There's nothing that points to anything,' said Eva Backman. 'That's the problem.'

'Accident?' queried Larsson.

'His partner died at exactly the same spot, thirty-five years ago,' Backman told him.

'Bloody hell,' said Larsson, inserting a wad of snus under his lip.

★

They stayed there for just over an hour. They made a rather random search of drawers and wardrobes, looking for something – it was hard to know what – that could give them some hint as to why the owner of the flat, sixty-one-year-old Germund Augustin Grooth, senior lecturer in physics, had ended his days in Gåsaklyftan, Rönninge, in the district of Kymlinge. Nearly a week ago now, and more than 300 kilometres from his home.

They didn't find a thing, but they seized the computer – a fairly new laptop, which unfortunately they weren't able to get into, despite Larsson's alleged hacking skills – and the diary. Backman had been through the latter from start to finish, but there were very few entries in it. Two female names, Kristin and Birgitta, featured on various dates, always with a time – as did H-G and Rex; they seemed to be work colleagues of Grooth's. Or that was the conclusion Backman cautiously drew, at any rate.

Hopefully the laptop would contain something of more substance. The three of them reached that optimistic conclusion, and Backman promised to look in at Lund police station after lunch for an update on progress, and to decide whether she would take it back to Kymlinge with her.

Then they parted, Ribbing and Larsson to head back to HQ while Backman went up to the next floor and rang the doorbell of Mrs Zetterlund, eighty-two, who had been told to expect her.

'I don't hear all that well,' was the widow's opening remark. 'But I see like a hawk and I smell like a violet. Coffee?'

'Yes, please,' said Backman.

'It's Zoega. Will that be all right, Miss Backman?'

'Always,' said Backman.

'Eh?' said Mrs Zetterlund.

'Zoega would be lovely,' clarified Backman in a slightly louder voice.

'I'm pleased to hear that,' said Mrs Zetterlund. 'There's no better coffee north of Brazil, and that's what my husband used to say as well. If you take a seat in the living room, Miss Backman, I'll bring it through in a moment.'

It took a while before Backman could get to the point but, after various preliminaries, a cup and a half of Zoega and four or five biscuits, it was her hostess herself who took the initiative.

'It's awful about Mr Grooth. He was the best neighbour you can imagine.'

'Ah, was he?' said Eva Backman. 'Well, I need to ask you a few questions as a result of his death.'

'Was he beaten to death?'

'Beaten to death?' said Backman. 'Why do you ask that?'

'So much of it goes on,' said Mrs Zetterlund. 'People being beaten to death, it happens all the time. And getting shot, and all sorts of things.'

'We don't really know how Germund Grooth died,' admitted Backman. 'That's why we're investigating.'

'Oh yes, I know that,' said Mrs Zetterlund. 'In any case, it's a shame he's dead. He was a fine fellow. He was a university lecturer, you know.'

'Hrrm,' said Backman. 'Now, do you remember when you last saw him?'

'When did he die?'

'We think he died on Saturday. Last Saturday, that is.'

'Yes, I haven't seen him all week,' declared Mrs Zetterlund, 'so that could well be right. But surely he hasn't been . . .?'

'Yes?'

'He hasn't been lying dead in his flat ever since Saturday?'

'No,' said Eva Backman. 'He was found somewhere else.'

'Somewhere else?'

'Yes. Can you remember when you last saw him?'

Mrs Zetterlund leant back and closed her eyes. 'I'm concentrating,' she explained.

'I see,' said Backman and waited.

'Last Friday evening,' said Mrs Zetterlund, opening her eyes. 'I saw him when he got home on Friday. A week ago, that is. Yes, I remember that.'

'Friday evening,' echoed Backman. 'And you're sure of that? I'm sorry for having to ask, but we've got to—'

'Sure as night follows day,' Mrs Zetterlund interrupted her. 'My sister was here. We always meet on Fridays and play cards. We take it in turns, here and at her place. She's rather frail, though she's only seventy-seven. Osteoporosis, she's been short of calcium all her life.'

'And when was it you saw Germund Grooth? Was it while you and your sister were playing cards on Friday evening?'

'Oh yes. We were sitting here by the window, playing Japanese Two-Man Whist as we usually do; I tend to win, I think Sylvia's got too little calcium in her head, too – or maybe too much – yes, that might be it. That must be where it's all accumulated, of course . . . Well, anyway, I saw him cut across the street down there and come in the front entrance. I think I said to Sylvie: here's Mr Grooth coming home . . . Yes, I'm sure I did.'

'What sort of time was that, roughly?' asked Backman.

'Quarter past nine,' said Mrs Zetterlund.

'How can you know that?'

'Because we'd been watching the quiz show, which ends at

287

nine. Then I made the tea and sandwiches, that takes ten minutes – and we'd dealt the cards . . . but we hadn't even started. We go on until eleven, and then I ring for a taxi. Yes, he got home at quarter past nine . . . possibly a couple of minutes before or after. Is it important?'

'Roughly quarter past will do fine,' said Backman. 'Was he alone or was anyone with him?'

'He was alone,' replied Mrs Zetterlund. 'Just him and his briefcase, if I remember rightly. He always has that with him.'

'You seem to have a good memory,' said Eva Backman and drank some Zoega.

'The only thing wrong with me is my hearing,' said Mrs Zetterlund. 'But you speak up, nice and clearly; it's much worse if people mumble. As if they don't really want you to understand what they're saying.'

Eva Backman was thinking. 'And you didn't see Grooth on the Saturday at all?'

'No.'

'He lives alone, we understand. Do you know if he often has visitors?'

'Do you mean women, Miss Backman?'

'Yes, although not just them.'

Mrs Zetterlund closed her eyes again. Five seconds passed. 'I've seen him with a couple. But no more, over all these years.'

'A couple of women?'

'Yes. Wasn't that what we were talking about?'

Backman nodded.

'I've run into one of them a few times. I think she's Danish. She even said hello once. The other . . . well, it was only the once, but she was coming out of the flat as I went past. Dark-haired. Certainly not Danish, a skinny little thing.'

'And when was this?'

'The skinny one?'

'Yes.'

Mrs Zetterlund shrugged her shoulders. 'A couple of years ago . . . or it could have been three. The Danish woman has been around for longer. She's better-looking all round. She must be ten years younger than him, but he's well preserved, really well preserved.'

'Thank you,' said Eva Backman. 'And what about male friends? Do you know about any of those?'

'I don't think I've ever seen a man visit Mr Grooth,' declared Mrs Zetterlund after another brief contemplation behind closed eyes. 'No, not as far as I can remember. He was a pretty solitary type, really. But a gentleman, I want to stress that. Fine and decent. Shame he's dead.'

Interesting summary of Germund Grooth, thought Eva Backman as she left Prennegatan. Fine and decent gentleman, unfortunately dead.

But if Mrs Zetterlund's information was accurate, he had returned home at a quarter past nine on the evening of 24 September. The following day, Saturday the twenty-fifth, he was lying dead at the bottom of Gåsaklyftan outside Kymlinge, 300 kilometres away.

What were his movements in between?

Why and when had he travelled up to Kymlinge?

And how?

But, above all, why? Why, in heaven's name?

She sat down on a bench in a pedestrian precinct, took out her mobile and rang Sorrysen.

'Have you been able to get hold of Grooth's phone records?'

DI Borgsen confirmed that he had. They were on the desk in front of him in fact.

'Anything startling?' asked Backman.

'I don't know what you mean by startling,' said Sorrysen. 'If we take just the last week of his life, we've got eleven calls in all. Not much to go on, in other words. I'm not talking about his work phone here, but his home landline. He didn't have a mobile. All the numbers have been identified except one.'

'Except one,' said Backman.

'Except one,' said Sorrysen. 'To his home phone from a mobile. Pay-as-you-go, so we can't trace it.'

'When?' said Backman.

'Saturday morning at seven twenty-two,' said Sorrysen. 'The call lasted just over forty seconds. Forty-three, to be precise. It hasn't been kept; too much time has elapsed.'

'Interesting,' said Backman.

'Perhaps,' said Sorrysen. 'But I don't think you could call it startling.'

'And the other ten?'

'Not a single one to a private individual,' said Sorrysen. 'Or from one.'

'I see,' said Backman. 'I guess I'll take a look at it for myself when I get back. Thanks very much.'

'Don't mention it,' said Sorrysen and hung up.

She checked out of the hotel, grabbed a bite of lunch at a hot-dog stand near the central station, and at a quarter past one she met Larsson and Ribbing in the latter's room at Lund police HQ.

'There's good news and bad news,' said Ribbing.

'Bad first, please,' said Backman.

'We haven't got into this laptop yet,' said Larsson. 'But it's only a matter of time, of course. Our computer whizz is out working on something else at the moment.'

'OK,' said Backman. 'And the good?'

Inspector Ribbing cleared his throat. 'The good news is that we've found Kristin Pedersen,' he explained. 'She's in the Seychelles, but she'll be back in Copenhagen on Monday. We can interview her then, if you think it's important.'

'It's extremely important,' said Eva Backman, with a brief stab of annoyance that her trip to Denmark was off the agenda. 'I want you to record it and I'd like to send you some questions beforehand.'

'That'll be fine,' said Ribbing. 'You've got the whole weekend to formulate them. Do you want to take the laptop up with you or shall we get it sorted here?'

Backman considered this. 'Would it be possible to copy the whole lot and send it up to us?'

Larsson shrugged. 'Of course. Would you like us to do that then?'

'Yes, please,' decided Backman. 'I assume it's only the emails that are of interest, but send the whole lot once you get into it.'

'Kotkas will have it fixed in an hour,' promised Ribbing. 'He's phenomenal, you'll have Grooth's secrets on a silver platter by the time you're back in Kymlinge. Is there anything you need help with at the moment? We'll keep in touch anyway, as we discussed.'

'Yep, we certainly will,' Larsson chimed in.

Eva Backman thought about it, but couldn't recall anything else on her current wish list. She thanked her Scanian colleagues and promised she'd contact them again after the weekend.

She made her way to the police-station car park, climbed into her car and ten minutes later she was out on the north-bound E6.

She decided to give Piaf and Holiday a rest and reflected that at least she wouldn't be returning empty-handed from her sojourn in the southerly provinces. Far from it.

Matters were coming to a head, essentially.

Germund Grooth had a trip to Paris booked for a week after his death.

He had been at home in his flat in Lund as late as a quarter past nine on the evening before his death. Probably until eleven, if it really was the case that the Zetterlund sisters had been playing cards in the bay window above, with at least one pair of eagle eyes fixed on the street.

The next morning, the last of his life, someone had rung him from an untraceable number. At twenty past seven.

Suicide? DI Backman asked herself. Forget it.

Accident? Forget that, too.

So that was two question marks straightened out, she noted.

But the new ones that had arisen in their place were more crooked still and she beat her head against them until it bled, all the way back to Kymlinge.

Metaphorically, of course.

33

They drove off the ferry at the terminal in Świnoujście in the early morning of 24 July. None of them had slept very much during the crossing, but that didn't stop Rickard Berglund feeling intensely wide awake as he looked out through the bus window at the unfamiliar, dirty grey buildings of the port area. Apart from a couple of short visits to Denmark and Norway, it was the first time in his life he was beyond the borders of Sweden, and something that might be described as a quiet sense of exultation was growing in his breast.

He could recall a similar feeling from a time long ago. When he was twelve, to be precise, in the summer between primary and lower secondary. He had gone with his classmate Sune to the boy's summer cottage in Malung up in Dalarna, and that car journey – well, his recollection of it was as clear as anything; he and Sune had sat in the comic-strewn back seat of the Stridsbergs' black Volvo PV on their way through unknown forests with their mouths full of Trixi and Tuttifrutti sweets – and it was then, then he had felt that sense of embarking on an adventure ticking inside him. The same feeling as now.

Even though he was now a grown man – basically twice the age he had been then – newly married and halfway to his theology degree and ordination. A much later stage along life's path, to speak in Kierkegaard's terms. Yet it was still just as overwhelming, that seductive lure of whatever you wanted to call it: adventure, the unknown, freedom and all the unpredictable experiences waiting round the corner.

Childish or not, he did nothing to try to quash that vague sense of excitement. *Carpe diem*, he thought, and when he cast surreptitious glances at his fellow passengers, he could see it was the same for them.

Tomas at the steering wheel. Gunilla in the passenger seat beside him, with a big map open on her lap and a half-eaten banana in her hand. Anna: she was sitting back-to-back with him in their *autobus-pied-à-terre*. It was Maria who had invented the word; everything sounded better in French, she claimed, and perhaps she was right. It consisted of a big wooden crate with a mattress and pillows on top and storage space beneath. Maria and Germund had one, too, at the back of the bus. Tomas and Gunilla lived on another one in the front; they were rustic but practical. They had also installed curtains running across the bus to make private night-time territory, but now the curtains were all hitched up to the roof because it was morning.

Yes, it was their first morning on foreign soil, on a journey that would last at least thirty-five days and thirty-five nights and take them to countries and places that until now – until this July morning in this year of Our Lord 1972 – had not been much more than empty names and abstractions. You can't be sure Rome exists until you've been there and seen it for yourself, Germund observed, and there was a lot of truth in that.

But first of all, Świnoujście and Szczecin! They had sat in a cafe on the ferry at some late hour, eating sauerkraut and something called *bigos*, drinking beer and trying to pronounce those tangles of consonants. A rather drunk long-distance lorry driver called Marek had helped to guide their unpractised tongues and told them a few things in broken English about Poland, the first country awaiting them on the other side of the Baltic Sea.

And then: Prague. Balaton. Budapest. Vienna. Zagreb. Et cetera, et cetera. Rickard had started keeping a travel diary when they left Uppsala, as had Anna, and she was taking it rather more seriously than he was, planning to write it up as a reportage for publication. She'd had half promises from *Vi* magazine and *Dagens Nyheter*, but no firm undertaking to pay her a fee, because naturally they wanted to see the result first. Anna was only a second-year student at the college of journalism, not a recognized name in reporting circles. Still, she had invested in a new system camera, a Nikon; a travelogue without pictures naturally wouldn't do. And if Rickard's notes and reflections could be of use in any way, that was all to the good, of course.

They were a twosome, they were newly married. The world lay open and the possibilities were boundless.

The first day they got as far as the town of Jelenia Góra. It was dusk and they had been travelling more or less all day, with Tomas and Germund taking it in turns at the wheel. Germund had managed to get himself a bus driver's licence in just a few weeks, and it was undeniably useful that they could share the driving. They could basically be on the road all day and all night if they wanted.

Not that they did want to, of course. It was important to stop and give themselves time to look around and soak things up. Register and experience them. This first day they had stopped for a couple of hours in Poznań and bought in supplies, mainly fruit, drink and dry goods; they had no way of keeping things cool on the bus, but of course the Eastern Bloc was a civilization that provided everything its citizens needed in the way of fresh food. It would be the same as other civilizations in that respect, and thinking otherwise was just imperialist prejudice. They could buy milk and butter every morning and, with six of them, they would have no problem consuming it all the same day, before it went off. Or they could do it the other way round, buy provisions for dinner and breakfast at the same time, in the evening, and take advantage of the cooler temperatures overnight.

They had also bought beer and vodka in Poznań, at almost laughably low prices, and as they sat around a fire at the campsite with food and drink in the warm darkness, and with the silky female voice of an unfamiliar Polish singer streaming out of the transistor radio, the word 'magical' sprang very readily to mind.

'Thank you, Tomas,' said Anna. 'Thank you for coming up with this trip. We're going to have our horizons well and truly widened. It feels amazing to be part of this, don't you all think?'

She laughed because she was a little drunk. Rickard found himself wishing she would be drunk a bit more often, it had such a liberating effect on her. He took a pull on his beer, had a mouthful of bread and sausage and wished he could stop the clock. Right there, right then.

'Eat and drink, my friends,' said Tomas, lighting a cigarette. 'Especially eat, because this sausage will be a goner by tomorrow.'

'Are you sure it isn't already?' said Rickard.

'The beer's cheaper than water,' remarked Germund. 'It would be a shame not to drink that up, as well.'

'Can't you choirboys give us a serenade?' suggested Maria. 'We can turn off this Polish nightingale.'

'The summer hymn,' requested Gunilla. 'Then we can all join in.'

And so it was. They sang in four parts and the much-loved hymn rang out in the darkness. Rickard felt Anna's hand creeping cautiously up his thigh and he knew that this moment – this evening at an obscure campsite on the edge of the Polish town of Jelenia Góra – was something he would never forget.

They made the quietest love they had ever made, and once Anna had fallen asleep, he pulled on his tracksuit and sneaked out of the bus.

He took a pee behind some bushes and then stood stock still, listening out into the darkness. The croak of the frogs and the burble of the water were all that he could hear. The half-empty campsite spread down a long, gradual slope to a murmuring stream; he hesitated for a moment and then made his way down to sit on a rock beside the water.

He put his hands together and had a strong sense that God could see him now. That He could see them all – himself and Anna, Tomas and Gunilla, Maria and Germund – and was holding His protective hand over them. He didn't often have thoughts of that kind; studying theology and sensing God's presence were rather different things, and it wasn't the first time he had reflected on the fact. Like baking bread without eating it, you could say, or practising swimming strokes without water. But now he was suddenly filled with an intense and naive experience of God which – like that joyous sense of expectation at the ferry port that morning – had clear echoes of childhood. It was simple and pure.

And he prayed. Prayed for them all and for the rest of their European trip to be meaningful, and there was something about the flowing water, and perhaps the croaking frogs as well, which all at once presented him with the sensation of God's voice coming to him through that unexpected medium.

It was an experience that was totally and utterly his own, what was more. Nothing from which he could wring images or metaphors for use in his future role as a vicar, and he wondered why this boundary seemed so evident and so crucial. But as he knew only too well, there were some things you understood without knowing *how* you understood them.

He thought about Anna, too, of course, and the way they had become a married couple so precipitately. He still wondered what had impelled him to propose, that evening at the start of May. Anna had revealed how it had felt for her: she had been as taken aback by his proposal as she had by her own acceptance. They had both laughed about that and agreed this was how things should go in life; it was spontaneous and unreflecting actions that won out in the long run.

Things had been going pretty well for Anna all through the spring and early summer. It wasn't only marriage that deepened their relationship; perhaps in fact mere passage of time was doing the work for them. You grow together, Rickard would often think. You learn each other's habits and idiosyncrasies, that's the way enduring love is built. What was more, Anna had a few articles published, in *Our Home* and *The Metalworker*; it was unquestionably important to her to win approval on the professional front as well. She was even offered a summer job upcountry on the *Östersund Post*, but the question of accommodation and the fact that she would be expected to stay on until the end of August made her turn it down. She went back to her hospital assistant's job at Akademiska for six weeks instead. Rickard took temporary work at a post office in Svartbäcken for the same period; barring unforeseen circum- stances, they ought to have enough in the kitty for the trip, at any rate. And with any luck, some left over to make their study loans go a bit further in September.

The first payment on the bus loan wasn't due until January, but that felt pleasantly distant. If everything worked as Tomas had calculated, they would also be making some money from the cheap trips they would run to Norrland in the autumn. Tomas and Germund could take it in turns to drive at the weekends, and maybe Rickard could get himself a bus driver's licence, too, eventually.

He thought about the others as he sat there by the flowing Polish stream, and asked himself what sort of effect a trip like this was likely to have on relations within the group. It wasn't easy to predict. Gunilla and Tomas's relationship was as much a given as his own and Anna's, of course, but Gunilla had been through a tough year. After the stillbirth in October she had spent a few months as a patient at Ulleråker; she'd come home to Sibyllegatan in January, admittedly, but as far as Rickard knew, she'd had a doctor's certificate for the whole spring term. She certainly hadn't been studying, and although Tomas didn't like talking about her condition or complaining to other people, Rickard could see it was hard going for them. There was a kind of fearfulness and fragility about Gunilla, characteristics there had been no hint of in the attractive, independent girl he had met three years ago. He remembered envying Tomas and thinking he could never find a woman to match Gunilla, but now he felt rather differently. It was hard not to feel sorry for them; they had lost two babies in two years, neither of them even making it across life's threshold, and of course that must be painful. Incredibly painful. Rickard and Anna still hadn't talked about bringing babies into the world, but he could sense that the sadness of Gunilla's two unsuccessful pregnancies had made Anna even more hesitant than she might have been on her own account.

But even if things happened and situations changed, he knew it would still be Tomas and Gunilla. It was different where Maria and Germund were concerned. Radically different. Tomas's way of putting it was that they were two exceptional individuals, and whatever he meant by that, it was quite an apt description. Rickard had known them for three years, too, or to be more precise, three years had gone by since he first met them, because nobody could really claim to *know* people like Germund and Maria. They were erratic, and maybe saw it as a badge of honour to be that way; it was impossible to predict what they would say, or how they would react, in any given situation. Rickard knew they had virtually no social circle beyond the quartet making this trip with them – but other people, and relationships with other people, did not seem to bother them, or to occupy any space in their mental universe at all. This could just be an act, of course; striving to be special and out of the ordinary wasn't such a rarity among young people. Rickard had encountered a lot of them in the theology faculty – the weirder, the better, it sometimes seemed – but in Maria and Germund's case there was no sign of that kind of trivial posing. None at all.

Exceptional individuals to a tee.

Leaving the water, the frogs and the voice of God behind him, he walked across the dewy grass back to the bus. He opened the door nearer the back, and on the other side of the curtain to his left he could hear them having sex, Germund and Maria. He and Anna had stayed as quiet as they could, and it had undeniably added a bit of spice, but the exceptional duo showed no such consideration. Rickard could hear Maria groaning quite loudly, whimpering and enjoyment rolled into one, and he felt himself getting another erection and was aware that he would have liked to watch them.

Yes, he would have liked to peep behind that curtain, see Germund penetrate Maria, watch their shameless and highly audible fucking. He felt so ashamed of the thought that he blushed, but the erection was still there. He slipped into bed beside Anna and lay there for a long time, trying not to listen to this uninhibited erotic music. But it was fruitless. By the time it finally sounded as if Maria had climaxed, Anna was awake, too. She turned to him and he could hear from her voice that she was smiling in the darkness.

'Again?' she whispered. 'It's actually a bit of a turn-on, hearing them.'

And for the second time on that first night in a foreign land they made love. Not quite as silently as the first time, and Rickard thought it was the best sex they had ever had.

He also thought that his wife was a wonderful mystery. From the front of the bus, not a sound was heard all night.

34

Assistant Detective Claes-Henrik Wennergren-Olofsson had the longest signature in Kymlinge police station, and as he also liked to add his title – before or after his actual name – it often took him half a minute and two lines to complete the job.

Alexander Tillgren, who had the same rank but a service record that was six months shorter, had good grounds for considering Wennergren-Olofsson an idiot. He thought they were good, anyway, but his colleague was bigger and stronger and, moreover, armed with a preening, if totally unjustified self-confidence, so Tillgren often chose to keep his views to himself.

Not that it was always easy. Wennergren-Olofsson liked to teach him things whenever the opportunity arose, and a two-hour car journey from Kymlinge to Strömstad indubitably provided the opportunity.

I'm going to puke, thought Tillgren, long before they were even halfway there. If he doesn't shut up in a minute, I'm going to sock him on the jaw.

'So I told him to watch himself bloody carefully,' said Wennergren-Olofsson. 'And do you know what the blighter did?'

'No,' said Tillgren. 'What did the blighter do?'

'He tried to hit me,' said Wennergren-Olofsson.

Good, thought Tillgren. 'He never did?' he said.

'Oh yes. But then he found he'd tousled with the wrong man.'

'Tussled,' said Tillgren. 'Not tousled.'

'Eh?' said Wennergren-Olofsson.

'Wrong word,' said Tillgren. 'But forget it. What do you think about this case then?'

Why am I even asking that? he wondered. I'm just as much of an idiot.

Wennergren-Olofsson seemed to ruminate on the vocabulary question for a moment, before giving up on it. 'Complicated,' he said, 'but not impossible to solve. I have my theories.'

'That sounds exciting,' said Tillgren, prompting a suspicious glance from his colleague. It was sometimes hard to judge quite how much irony he could slip into his replies without getting caught out, and he liked to sail as close to the wind as he possibly could.

'Yes, well,' said Wennergren-Olofsson. 'And what do you think? Have you combed through the whole case?'

'Not exactly,' said Tillgren. 'But, I mean, it is pretty odd for two people to lose their lives at exactly the same spot with such a time interval.'

'Pretty odd?' snorted Wennergren-Olofsson. 'Let me tell you that if I'd been in charge of those interviews, I would've had this sorted. From the very beginning, I mean. It's important to be in on the ground floor, so to speak. It's obviously one of them.'

'Who did what?' said Tillgren.

'Who murdered them both, of course,' said Wennergren-Olofsson. 'This Sandlin who handled the case in '75 knew that something didn't add up, and that the Winckler babe was murdered. He just couldn't prove it.'

'Is that a fact?' said Tillgren.

'Yes,' said Wennergren-Olofsson. 'It is.'

'Have you read Sandlin's case notes?'

'Skimmed them,' said Wennergren-Olofsson.

'So you think it was one of the group members who killed Maria Winckler and Germund Grooth?'

'Yep,' said Wennergren-Olofsson. 'Make a note that it was me who said it.'

'I will,' said Tillgren. 'But who, then? And why?'

Wennergren-Olofsson inserted some snus under his top lip and thought for a moment. 'Damned if I know,' he said. 'I haven't met them, like I said. You kind of have to have them there in front of you – we've talked about that. Then you can always spot where the cracks are, and when they're lying. A focused detective with a bit of psychology in his skull can see a thing like that.'

Mein Gott, thought Tillgren, who had once had a girlfriend from Wuppertal. What a bloody clown. If I ever commit a crime, I shall demand to be interviewed by W-O.

'Exactly,' he said. 'But now we've got a chance to talk to Elisabeth Martinsson. That's something, at least. She was on the spot in '75.'

Wennergren-Olofsson nodded enthusiastically and turned his wad of snus. 'This is how we'll do it,' he declared. 'You ask the questions, and I can concentrate on observing her. Detecting that little hesitation, you know. That little crack.'

'Smart thinking,' said Tillgren. 'We've got Barbarotti and Backman's list of questions to follow, so that won't be a problem. A tape recorder, as well.'

'The tape recorder's a bloody helpful tool,' said Wennergren-Olofsson. 'So you can listen back and analyse. We'll double up, to be on the safe side.'

'Double up?' asked Tillgren.

'Use yours and mine. Backman and Barbarotti want a tape and a transcript, don't they? But I can keep my recording and make my own assessment. Probably the safest way.'

'Brilliant,' said Tillgren. 'Mind if I take a nap for half an hour? Bit of a late one last night.'

'Slacker,' said Wennergren-Olofsson. 'But OK, we've got to be razor-sharp when we go in for the attack.'

Two hours in the car on the way back, too, groaned Tillgren inwardly, shutting his eyes.

Elisabeth Martinsson lived in a poky little flat near the harbour in Strömstad. The pokiness was the result not only of its limited floor area, but also of the fact that it was over-furnished. As if she'd moved from a big detached house and forgotten to dispose of anything, thought Tillgren as he said hello to one of the two dachshunds, which went by the name of Malte. Malte's mother was called Brynhild and she couldn't have cared less about the police intruders. She was sixteen going on seventeen, according to her mistress, and was very happy to stay in her place, reclining on a tasselled cushion on top of a yellow piano, enjoying a leisurely retirement.

But how the blazes would a dachshund get onto the top of a piano in the first place? Perhaps she was lifted up there every morning? Tillgren decided not to ask. He didn't think he'd ever seen a yellow piano before. And definitely not one with a dachshund on top.

'Have a seat,' said Elisabeth Martinsson. 'Sorry about the mess. But I've no excuse for it, it always looks like this.'

Tillgren looked around him. In the middle of the room stood an easel with a large oil painting on it, three-quarters finished, by the looks of it. He scrutinized it for a few seconds and got the impression of a ruined watermill and a collection of goats, but decided not to ask about that, either. The walls were covered in a large number of paintings, hung so close together that they were touching, from one corner of the room to the other and from floor to ceiling. Quite a lot of naked men in contorted positions, but also a few landscapes of a more traditional kind. Strong colours. Tillgren could imagine himself hanging one or two of these paintings in his own little flat back in Kymlinge, but it was hard to get a proper impression because they were all so crowded together.

'I had a studio once,' explained Ms Martinsson, as if reading his mind, 'but it got too expensive in the long run. This useless council doesn't see fit to spend even a few kronor on its suffering artists, don't you forget that.'

'We won't,' said Wennergren-Olofsson. 'Forget it, I mean.'

'Good,' said Ms Martinsson.

They sat down in two small armchairs, plastic and tubular steel, by a table cluttered with tubes of paint, brushes, news-papers, jam jars and paperback books. Elisabeth Martinsson pulled out the piano stool and sat down opposite them.

I hope she doesn't offer us anything, thought Tillgren. I hope we get this over with quickly.

'I would have offered you something,' said Elisabeth Martinsson, 'but I've nothing in.'

'We stopped on the way,' lied Wennergren-Olofsson. 'We haven't come here to drink coffee.'

'I do realize that, thank you,' said Elisabeth Martinsson, donning a pair of glasses with thick black frames. Tillgren thought she looked pretty well preserved for a suffering artist of past sixty. Kind of French, with that short black hair, and lithe even though she was obviously no keep-fit freak. There was a blue packet of Gauloises among the jumble of items on the table, but the flat did not smell of tobacco smoke, so perhaps it was just another artistic prop.

'We're investigating two unexplained deaths,' announced Wennergren-Olofsson in an authoritative voice. 'I and my colleague Tillgren are going to ask you a number of questions, which we want you to answer as fully and honestly as you can.'

'I spoke to another officer a couple of days ago, said Elisabeth Martinsson. 'A woman . . . Backlund or something like that.'

'My colleague Backman,' Wennergren-Olofsson corrected her. 'That's right, but we want some more detail now and we have to do it a bit more formally.'

I thought he was going to be the silent observer, thought Tillgren. Though maybe the actual interview hasn't started yet.

'We've got a list of questions, which we'll go through in order,' Wennergren-Olofsson went on, with a nod to Tillgren. 'It's going to simplify things if you just answer, and don't start wondering why we're asking that particular question. So, you work as an artist?'

'Is that question part of the interview?' queried Elisabeth Martinsson, regarding him sceptically over the top of her glasses.

'Not really,' said Wennergren-Olofsson.

'Oh?' said Elisabeth Martinsson. 'Well, in that case, my answer is this. Look around this bolthole of mine. What the hell do you *think* I do?'

'Um, right . . . got you,' said Wennergren-Olofsson.

'Let me put it this way: I work as an illustrator to live, but I live to paint. Do you follow?'

'Ah hah?' replied Wennergren-Olofsson, frowning. Tillgren took out the list of questions Backman had given them. Better start before this gets out of hand, he thought. He put the little tape recorder next to the packet of Gauloises and pressed the 'play' button. Wennergren-Olofsson did the same with a smaller and sleeker device.

'Two recorders?' asked Elisabeth Martinsson.

'Just covering all eventualities,' Wennergren-Olofsson politely explained.

'Yours is buzzing.'

'It's meant to do that,' said Wennergren-Olofsson. 'It means it's on.'

Tillgren cleared his throat. 'Right then,' he said. 'Interview with Elisabeth Martinsson in her flat in Strömstad. The time is thirteen twenty-two. It's Friday 1 October 2010. Present are Assistant Detective Tillgren, Assistant Detective Wennergren-Olofsson.'

'Get started,' said Elisabeth Martinsson, lifting Malte onto her knee. 'I haven't got all day.'

Just over an hour later they were in the car and heading back home.

'We made a good job of that,' observed Wennergren-Olofsson. 'I expect you saw the point of my interventions?'

'No,' admitted Tillgren. 'Not really.'

'Sometimes you need to confuse them,' explained Wennergren-Olofsson. 'Make them lower their guard. Disrupt their focus so you can coax out that little slip of the tongue.'

'But leeches? I haven't come across any leeches in this case.'

'That's the whole point. It puts them off their stroke.'

'I hear what you're saying,' said Tillgren. 'And what did you get out of it then?'

'It's too early for analysis,' said Wennergren-Olofsson. 'I want to listen to the tape in peace and quiet first. But we might as well check how it sounds right away.'

He took out his recorder, pressed the button and told Tillgren to hush.

For the first ten seconds there was nothing to hear. Wennergren-Olofsson switched off the device and tried again. He turned up the volume and again urged Tillgren to keep a) his mouth shut and b) his eyes on the road. They had switched places before they left Strömstad; Tillgren was driving, with Wennergren-Olofsson beside him in the passenger seat.

After thirty seconds there still wasn't a sound from the recorder.

'Oh God,' said Wennergren-Olofsson. 'There's been some kind of glitch.'

'I'm afraid so,' said Tillgren.

Wennergren-Olofsson wound some way forward and tried for a third time. Not a sound. He switched it off.

'This is precisely why it's always a good idea to double up,' he declared. 'We'll have to listen to yours instead.'

Tillgren fished his recorder out of his breast pocket and pressed 'play'. There was an instant humming sound. Then, very faintly, a voice that Tillgren vaguely recognized as his own. Then another, which he assumed to be Elisabeth Martinsson's.

It was impossible to understand a single word. Presumably it would have been intelligible if the persistent hum in the foreground had not blanketed all other sound.

'I think,' said Tillgren, accelerating slightly, 'in fact I'm sure, that it's your buzz my machine has recorded there.'

'Oh, come off it,' said Wennergren-Olofsson. 'What useless make of recorder is it anyway?'

'What I'd like to say,' said Tillgren, raising his voice a little, 'is that if your damn equipment hadn't been buzzing like that, my recording would have been first-rate.'

'What the heck are you raving about?' objected Wennergren-Olofsson. 'I mean, it's bloody obvious . . .'

Tillgren was suddenly aware of something happening inside him. Hard to say exactly what, but it was like a dam bursting. Surrendering to something powerful and wild, something that came welling up irresistibly like a . . . yes, like a stream of lava, and at a stroke, within a second or two, his relationship with his colleague Wennergren-Olofsson underwent a radical change. Totally and utterly radical. It felt distinctly odd and distinctly wonderful.

'Can't you shut your mouth for one moment, you complete idiot,' he said.

'Eh?' said Wennergren-Olofsson.

Tillgren cleared his throat. 'You forgot to check the batteries in your recorder,' he told him. 'Fat lot of use it's been to us, ruining my recording of the interview as well. It would have been better if I'd been left to get on with this by myself. Don't try to defend yourself, I'm fed up to the back teeth of you throwing your weight around.'

'I'm damned if—' started Wennergren-Olofsson, but Tillgren slammed a hand down on the dashboard and shut him up.

'That's enough,' he announced. 'I don't want to hear another word. You can start writing out the interview from memory right away. You were just sat there listening the whole time, so something must have stuck. But I want to check it before you hand it in – I'm not leaving anything to chance. Fucking dimwit!'

Assistant Detective Wennergren-Olofsson's Adam's apple bobbed up and down like some overheated, old-fashioned tachograph, and the colour of his face deepened to scarlet, but not a word emerged from his mouth. Not a single little squeak.

So there we are, thought Tillgren, switching on the radio. Every cloud has a silver lining.

'Look lively,' he said. 'You've got an hour and three-quarters to get it done. I can lend you a pen and paper, if you want.'

35

It was like the winter ice slowly thawing out of the ground.

A slow and slightly erratic thaw, rather like the ones they had at home on the little roads of Värmland. Coming and going, and sometimes the cold would return overnight and the ground would be more frozen when you woke up in the morning than it was when you went to bed. But it crept forward, in a process as inexorable as the changing of the seasons: after winter comes spring.

That was how she described it to Tomas and she also said she felt sorry for him. He had lost two babies as well, but she had taken all the pain upon herself. The right to grieve and yearn and sink into her own misery. He told her she needn't worry about that, as long as the thaw was moving in the right direction in the longer term, there was no need to hurry it. She was a woman, he was a man, it was crazy to expect everything could be weighed on gender-free scales; that just wasn't how relationships worked.

She had her own views on the subject of male and female, but she didn't voice them. It was enough to feel the frozen chill inside her gradually melting and life feeling its way back in, finding she could suddenly laugh and take an interest in new things. Discovering the unfamiliar, teeming world that was constantly around them on a trip like this one. People who actually lived their lives in places she had never heard of, soldiering on although their daily lives clearly consisted of constant toil from morning till night. That was how it looked, at any rate, in some of the places they were seeing. She had never believed in socialism, or communism – whatever the difference was – and now that she could see it with her own eyes at close quarters, she found no reason to revise her opinion. There was a greyness and drabness to the countries of Eastern Europe they travelled through, especially in the dismal housing blocks of the suburbs, which they did not visit as such, but found themselves sweeping past, and it struck her that those trips they were planning to run would be sure to give more than one radical tour-party member pause for thought. Perhaps that was Tomas's intention in fact, if he had any motive in setting up his bus company beyond making a bit of money. It wasn't easy to tell, and perhaps he didn't really know himself. She didn't ask; they had enough to worry about with themselves, and with repairing what had fallen apart in October. One night in Prague they made love for the first time in six months; well, it was longer than that in fact, because those fumbling attempts in January and February barely counted.

It was outdoors, in a park: a slightly daring and impulsive coupling behind the cover of some bushes. They had left the others in the bus at the campsite, and they took a long walk through the city afterwards. Over the Charles Bridge and up round the castle and cathedral. The air was warm, and they bought hot dogs and Czech beer in a bar that was still open, even at half past twelve at night. Even the most deep-frozen ground in Värmland, Gunilla thought, can't resist anything and everything. If you just take the decision to carry on with life, then life returns to you.

They got a taxi back to the campsite; it took the driver a while to find it but the fare was almost nothing, and once they had slipped into their bed at the front of the bus, Tomas came to her again.

They spent three days in Prague, and the same number in Hungary, at various places around Lake Balaton. Then they made their way back through Czechoslovakia and into Austria. The bus ran like clockwork. At a little Co-op store in Wiener Neustadt, Germund made a real find: three one-litre bottles of Stroh rum, 80 per cent proof – the co-operative movement at home was renowned for its temperance-supporting views, and they all agreed it was a sensation – and from that evening onwards they fell into the habit of drinking *Jägertee*. It only took one cup of the strong, sweet, spicy rum and tea to get you a bit drunk. Certainly if you were Gunilla or Anna anyway, and this was undoubtedly another factor in the gradual thaw.

On the morning of 4 August they drove over the border with Yugoslavia at Graz, came to a town called Osijek and decided to stop for two nights. It was Tomas's birthday the next day; he thought he would like to mark the occasion with something special for dinner, a whole beast of some kind if possible, spit-roasted over the open fire, and a considerable amount of beer, and no one had any objections to his plan.

Fruit salad and cream for dessert, with Stroh rum. No birthday cake, it was too bourgeois.

They all went into the centre of Osijek together in the morning, to lay in provisions. They were able to park the bus on a street just off the old square, and divided into two parties for their trip round the shops. Maria, Germund and Tomas in one, Gunilla, Anna and Rickard in the other. When Gunilla's group got back to the bus with their purchases, the others had not yet returned, and she decided to take a little walk on her own. Leaving Rickard and Anna at a cafe table, she wound her way through decaying back alleys in the heart of the old town. After a few minutes she emerged onto a little square with a church, its doors standing open.

She hesitated for a few moments before she decided to go in. She didn't normally visit churches, but there was something that appealed to her about the way the sun was catching an old tiled roof and sending its rays in through the dark entrance. It was also quite something, she thought, to go into a church in a country where the official doctrine was that all religions were a bad thing and would be abolished in the long run.

But they hadn't been abolished yet, not the places of worship themselves and clearly not the underlying beliefs, for that matter. Maybe it was just a question of time, but she found it hard to imagine it. A world without faith, without churches? Or half a world, at least, if the divide between East and West were to prove an enduring one.

There were about ten people dotted around the pews, as some simple organ music played from the gallery above, and at the altar a black-cassocked priest was busy with some devotional task. The church interior was not large, and it was almost devoid of decoration; perhaps a socialist compromise, thought Gunilla. You could carry on, but you weren't allowed to draw attention to yourself. Away with all the finery and ornament.

She stood at the back, hesitating. She let her eyes rest on the squares of light and dark created by the slanting sun, streaming through the windows. The dust, dancing in the rays of sunlight. There was something about this simple scene that held her captive. What are these people doing here? she thought. Why have they come here this morning? Roughly half men, half women. They were scattered in their individual places and at least some of them seemed deep in prayer. All at once she found herself envying them, but it was a strange sort of envy she could not even explain to herself. As if they – even though they were so much worse off than she was – knew something about life that she had not yet arrived at. She assumed they were worse off, anyway; the two women in front of her looked poor and shabby, and she suddenly wished she could talk to them. Sit on the pew between them and ask questions. If only they'd had a common language. What were conditions like for them? How had their lives been, what were their cares and sorrows, and why were they here, praying? Had they lost parents or siblings? Who were they praying for, and did they really believe anyone was listening?

She realized these were naive thoughts – and intrusive ones. She suddenly felt like an interloper. Who was she to come in here, questioning and interfering? An inquisitive foreigner with no God and no faith; two stillborn babies and yet no faith, was that not strange? Or perhaps the very opposite? If you lose two babies, don't you also lose your God?

If she had ever had one. She decided to go out into the sunshine, sensing that melancholy was threatening to get the better of her, but just as she was about to turn and go, her eyes fell on one of the backs in a seat over to the right, quite near the front. It belonged to a tall man, sitting there with his head bowed, and there was something in his posture that revealed him as considerably younger than the rest of

316

the churchgoers. As he momentarily turned his head to glance towards the priest at the altar, she saw that it was Germund.

She didn't mention it. Not to Germund, or to any of the others. She had vaguely intended saying something to Tomas, but there was something about the whole scene inside the little church that held her back. The atmosphere and the stillness, the light and the dark and the backs of bowed heads. And her own thoughts while she was there.

And there was nothing that remarkable about it, either, of course. Germund had gone into a church and sat there for a while – maybe in search of a bit of peace and quiet or to cool down. It was already really hot, even at eleven in the morning; no, it would have been hard to explain what she found so unusual about it. Or why that brief interlude had made such a strong impression on her. Talking about it – and above all with Germund – could so easily spoil it all. Perhaps that's the way with experiences, she thought, with all experiences: when we start putting them into words, they fall apart. Or they seem different and sullied somehow.

They become something else.

If you want to preserve them, you have to keep them to yourself.

Do other people have thoughts like these? she wondered that evening as they sat round the obligatory campfire, waiting for the little suckling pig they had bought to be ready to eat. Am I the only one who's so brittle and emotional and so careful about life? Fearful about life? Even if the thaw continued and achieved the desired effect, there would still be that disparity. Between herself and the others. Between herself and Tomas.

Something that couldn't be bridged, and shouldn't be bridged, either, because that was the point.

Every human being is alone, she thought. Even at a birthday party with a suckling-pig centrepiece, a mug of *Jägertee* in your hand and your best friends around you, you were alone.

36

'So if we could just try to summarize,' said Eva Backman. 'And buck up, while we're at it. I have to say I'm not making head or tail of this business.'

It was Monday morning. They were sitting in Barbarotti's office, each with a cup of horrible coffee. The rain was beating down onto the metal windowsill, and the brief flirtation with an Indian summer had fizzled out over the weekend, to be replaced by low pressure in a series of depressions, evidently queuing across the North Sea ready to sweep in across the west of Sweden.

Barbarotti blew his nose and nodded.

'Bucking up sounds a great idea,' he said, 'but I'm afraid I have to admit I'm feeling pretty clueless myself.'

'No more than I expected of you,' said Eva Backman. 'But be that as it may, there's something about Germund Grooth's death that doesn't add up. The notion that he died a natural one, that is.'

They had spent half an hour on the phone to each other on Sunday afternoon. Barbarotti had filled her in on his meetings with Rickard Berglund and Tomas Winckler, and she had told him what she'd been up to in Lund.

'You're thinking of that Paris trip?' said Barbarotti.

'I'm thinking of all sorts of things,' said Backman. 'Him

being at home late on the Friday. Him getting an untraceable phone call on the morning he died.

'Us not having a clue how he got up to Kymlinge, still less how he got out to Gåsaklyftan . . . And yes, that Paris trip, as you say. If I were going to commit suicide, I'd allow myself a Paris trip first. Or do it there.'

'Jump off the Eiffel Tower?' suggested Barbarotti. 'Instead of Gåsastupan?'

'Maybe,' said Backman. 'I know we haven't so much as a sniff of forensic evidence, but if you or I or anybody else were to push someone off a cliff – or an Eiffel Tower – and then leave the scene, well, there wouldn't be any forensic evidence, would there?'

'The prosecutor isn't going to like this,' said Barbarotti.

'What's wrong with you?' demanded Eva Backman. 'I couldn't care less what the prosecutor says. I want to know what happened. Why have you changed your mind?'

'I haven't changed my mind,' said Barbarotti, staring grimly into his coffee. 'You've changed yours. Your assessment was that Maria Winckler slipped and Germund Grooth fell, don't you remember?'

'I was wrong,' said Eva Backman. 'It doesn't happen every day, but when it does, I'm the first to admit it.'

'OK,' said Barbarotti. 'Let's assume you're right and there's something fishy about both these deaths. How do we take it forward?'

'We indulge in a bit of conjecture,' said Eva Backman. 'We're good at that, after all. If we assume the opposite of what we've been assuming up to now, and say both of them were murdered, where does that take us?'

'It depends whether we make other assumptions as well,' said Barbarotti.

'How do you mean?

'Well, whether we assume the perpetrator to be one of that group, for instance. It could actually be someone else.'

'Who happened to be out in the forest thirty-five years ago *and* last weekend,' asked Backman.

'Who had planned to be there,' said Barbarotti.

'Our friend Elis Bengtsson, for example?'

Barbarotti shook his head. 'I find it hard to see what he could have to do with it. Though the fact that he was on the scene both times is a factor to consider, of course.'

'Let's forget him,' said Backman after a gulp of coffee, a grimace and a short pause for thought. 'In the role of murderer anyway. We might need to talk to him again. Ask if he saw anyone else out in the forest, for example.'

'He didn't,' observed Barbarotti. 'Not last time, at any rate. Sandlin pressed him pretty hard on that. So shall we, for the sake of this discussion, assume it's someone in the group?'

'We're only conjecturing,' said Backman.

'I know that,' said Barbarotti. 'Maybe we could try the elimination method?'

'Not a bad idea,' said Backman. 'Who do you want to eliminate first?'

'Hang on a minute,' said Barbarotti. 'Are we presuming it was the same murderer both times then?'

Eva Backman sighed and leant back in her chair. 'I haven't a bloody clue,' she said. 'Maybe our conjecture would go better if we took one murder at a time. I get the feeling . . .'

'Yes?'

'. . . that in that case we ought to take the latest incident first. If Maria Winckler does turn out to have been murdered, that case comes under the statute of limitations.'

'There ought not to be any limitation on murder cases,' said Barbarotti.

'I agree with you,' said Eva Backman. 'We've talked about that before. But let's try to concentrate on Germund Grooth, and if we assume for now he was murdered by one of the other group members, who would you propose excluding first?'

'Does Elisabeth Martinsson count as a group member?'

'That's up to you to decide.'

'All right. We'll say she does. The first person I propose excluding is Maria Winckler. My justification is that she's been dead thirty-five years.'

'Smart thinking,' said Eva Backman. 'I accept your argument unconditionally.'

'Your turn,' said Barbarotti.

'Well, I'm going to exclude Anna Berglund. I admit I haven't met her and none of us has spoken to her, but if you're bedbound in the final stages of terminal cancer, you don't go around pushing people off clifftop leaps.'

'I rather thought you said there was never any such thing as clifftop leaps,' said Barbarotti.

'I'm not sure about it,' said Backman. 'And, as usual, I admit the fact. In any case, we can count Anna Berglund out. Do you agree?'

'Without any shadow of a doubt,' said Gunnar Barbarotti. 'So that leaves us with a trio. A quartet, if we include Elisabeth Martinsson . . . How did the interview with her go, by the way?'

'I think W-O and Tillgren are busy writing it up,' said Backman.

'I hope we'll be getting the tape as well.'

'There was some glitch with the tape recorder, I gather.'

Barbarotti yawned. 'Why am I not surprised?'

'There's nothing wrong with Tillgren,' said Backman.

'I'll give you that,' said Barbarotti. 'But if I've got to eliminate one of the four, I suppose it had better be Ms Martinsson. She just happened to tag along on the mushroom hunt, and didn't have anything to do with the others in the gang. If we're also assuming there was some kind of motive behind the murder . . . or murders.'

'As things stand, before I've had a chance to read our assistants' interview with her, I agree,' said Backman. 'Let's cross her off the list. Three left. Purely for the sake of argument in this discussion.'

'Three left,' echoed Barbarotti. 'This is going swimmingly. If we can keep up this pace, we should have narrowed it down to the murderer in about two minutes' time.'

'But this is where it gets problematic,' said Backman. 'We have the trio of them to choose between – Tomas Winckler, his wife and Rickard Berglund – and if I'm not misinformed, any one of them could have done it.'

'Theoretically,' said Barbarotti. 'How far have we got with checking their alibis?'

'Not very, I'm afraid,' sighed Backman. 'We've been a bit slipshod there. I forgot to ask Gunilla Winckler-Rysth when I went to see her . . . or, rather, I didn't think there was any point in asking her. But I rang her yesterday, and she claims she was shopping in the centre of Gothenburg for most of that Saturday. She was pretty vague about timings – she didn't meet friends or anything like that . . . didn't have lunch with anybody – and she was surprised that I was asking, to put it mildly.'

323

'Not much of an alibi then?'

'Probably not. How about your two gents?'

Gunnar Barbarotti scratched his head. 'I've been a bit remiss, too,' he admitted. 'I didn't raise the question with Rickard Berglund because his wife's at death's door, and one thing and another. He spends most of his waking hours there with her. But we had a very interesting talk . . . He's an interesting person. He stepped down from his vicar's job so he could keep his faith, pretty much. I suppose I'd better have another word with him.'

'You do that,' said Backman. 'And Tomas Winckler?'

'Says he played golf in the morning and was at home on his own in the afternoon.'

'While his wife was in town shopping?'

'I assume so. But I haven't checked it out. There's another aspect, too. How long should we allow?'

'Elaborate,' said Backman.

'Well,' said Barbarotti. 'If we factor in the time it takes for a perpetrator to convey Grooth from here to Rönninge, in a car, say, and then get him up to Gåsaklinten, push him off and come back – well, it would take a good hour, presumably. It depends on circumstances we know nothing about, of course. But if they also had to go to Lund to get him first . . . well, that puts an entirely different complexion on it.'

'You're right,' said Eva Backman. 'So the shortest window of time would be if they simply had a date out in the forest. If Grooth arrived there in his own vehicle, and the murderer then . . . you know, got rid of it somehow. When he'd finished.'

'Or she,' said Barbarotti.

'Or she.'

'Doesn't sound particularly plausible,' said Barbarotti.

'No, it doesn't. Do you know what's just occurred to me?'

'No,' said Barbarotti. 'What's just occurred to you, Detective Inspector?'

Eva Backman coughed to clear her throat. 'What's occurred to me is that all three of our suspects – or four, for that matter – will be able to come up with watertight alibis for that Saturday, or large chunks of it anyway, and we're just conjecturing away our young lives here.'

'Which leaves us looking pretty stupid,' said Barbarotti. 'But it wasn't me who started it.'

Eva Backman gave a laugh. 'Oh well, it makes no odds. We might as well finish this game, so which of these three do you want to eliminate?'

Barbarotti gave it ten seconds' thought. 'I don't think it's Rickard Berglund,' he said.

'I don't think it's Gunilla Winckler-Rysth,' said Eva Backman.

'So that just leaves Tomas Winckler,' said Barbarotti. 'Do you think we should drive over and arrest him?'

'What impression did you get of him?'

'Rather unpleasant,' said Barbarotti. 'But then I can't stand successful people, so I'm not objective. I think he's being unfaithful to his wife, by the way.'

'How can you know that?'

'I made an observation.'

'You saw him with another woman?'

'How can you know that?, to quote a super-sleuth.'

'Intuition,' said Backman with a smile. 'Anyway, it isn't illegal to be unfaithful to your wife. For some reason. So, can you visualize Tomas Winckler in the role of murderer?'

Gunnar Barbarotti pondered.

'Not really,' he acknowledged with a sigh.

Eva Backman got to her feet and watched the rain through the window for a moment. It was easing off a little; perhaps there was some hope of drier weather by Christmas. She turned round to offer a summary.

'So there we are. Back to square one, I'd say. We've no plausible murderer, we've made no progress and we've eliminated everything. Shall we just decide Germund Grooth died a . . . a relatively natural death?'

'Good way of phrasing it,' said Barbarotti. 'Relatively natural death. But I don't believe that, either. What's that name for someone who doesn't believe in anything?'

'Nihilist,' said Eva Backman. 'You're a bloody nihilist, and you've got to pull yourself together. We need to get this sorted out.'

'Where shall we start?' asked Barbarotti.

'We'll start by stopping all this conjecture,' ruled Backman.

37

Sparrow on her travels. August 1972.

Day fourteen today, if I haven't lost count. We crossed the border into Romania this morning. It took an hour, but we're starting to learn the ropes. The customs officers like detaining us, poring over our visas with magnifying glasses and searching the bus for goodness knows what, but all they really want is cigarettes and a bit of Western currency. It's the same at every border post. This time they seized a copy of *Expressen* that had been lying around the bus ever since we left Sweden. They claimed it was pornographic material, and Tomas didn't help when he explained it was the biggest-selling daily paper in our country. But we were happy to surrender that rag of course, and if they can extract any enjoyment from a few topless models, they're more than welcome.

It's a bit of a strain hanging out with these other people in this constricted space, and Germund and I aren't the only ones who think so. You have to try to mark out your own territory as best you can. What I like best is just sitting by a window, watching the scenery go by. Or reading; our communal library amounts to about thirty books and I've already read about half of them. In the next big town we shall have to make sure we find a decent bookshop to refresh the selection. I assume they'll stock books in English and French at least, even in Romania, but the only question is whether there are towns of any size. Since we crossed the border we've been travelling through countryside, just farming villages and the occasional small town. We're heading straight up towards Transylvania. Tomas is reading about Dracula, or Prince Vlad Tepes, to give him his proper name. Tomas claims he was a folk hero and was misunderstood by the whole of the Western world. I don't know, it sounds like exactly the sort of thing my golden-boy brother likes to say.

I'm getting a bit tired of drinking. We're knocking back beer, wine and rum every single day. Germund bought Stroh rum in Austria; it's so fucking strong you're drunk after just a couple of mouthfuls. You can't drink it neat; we dilute it with tea, but it doesn't help. The other ladies get woozy almost every night; it doesn't take much with them, but I think they like being a little bit drunk. Rickard and Tomas like them in that state, too; they're a lot more unbuttoned under the influence of alcohol, no doubt about that.

We've vaguely discussed treating ourselves to a couple of nights in a hotel soon. A decent shower, a proper bed and a bit of privacy. But whether this country can provide something like that is another question, of course. By Captain Tomas's calculations, we're on our way to a town called Timişoara. We ought to make it by this evening, he reckons, but the roads are bad, and narrow. We keep getting stuck behind tractors and all sorts of other agricultural machinery; it's hard to over-take and I shouldn't think we're averaging much more than forty to fifty kilometres an hour.

If we really do find a hotel somewhere, I'd have nothing against a single room. I'm not sure how I would justify it to

Germund, but perhaps he's feeling the same. These past few days he's spent most of his time with his head in a book called *Husserl, Lobachevsky and the Hundred and One Rabbits*, which he assures me is some kind of mathematical-philosophical master-piece, whatever he means by that. Anyway, it makes him even more inaccessible than usual, but I'm not suffering as a result. Just the opposite.

As for the others on the trip, Gunilla seems to be gradually thawing out. They've started having sex in their section of the bus at nights at least, and that's definitely a good sign. If you're interested in the welfare of your fellow human beings, that is, which I'm not always. But it's easier travelling with people who aren't depressed, it's as simple as that.

Anna and Rickard aren't remotely depressed. They're both keeping diaries and seem to take everything that happens in deep, optimistic earnest. Everything is interesting, everything is worth noting down, even if it's just some filthy old peasant beating his even filthier sow with a broomstick beside the roadside.

Tomas is as he is, I shan't bother wasting any words on him.

I'm longing to see the sea, but right now it's such a long way off, damn it. Tomas maintains it'll take us three or four days to get through Romania and out to the Black Sea. But at our current speed I reckon it'll take us more like a week. Though perhaps we'll decide to try driving through the night; I suggested it, but nobody took it up. Germund and Tomas could take it in turns to drive, after all, but for some reason Tomas insists we're not in a hurry. He's planning for next year's trip with actual passengers, but he can't fucking well make people pay actual money to crawl along behind clapped-out agricultural equipment in the socialist paradise of Romania. I think he'll have to make do with the paradises we've already ticked off the list: Poland, Czechoslovakia, Hungary and Yugoslavia. That really ought to be more than sufficient for anyone with an urge to study the Eastern Bloc.

I shall be getting my period tomorrow, so I feel like telling the whole human race to get lost.

Just one episode with Germund, before I finish.

It was last night. We'd retired to bed behind our curtain and he asked me if I felt like fucking. I said I'd be on my period any time now and suggested we skip it.

'OK,' said Germund. 'I'll read instead then.'

'Go ahead,' I said. 'I think I'll get some sleep.'

But before I fell asleep I had an idea. 'About the death of your parents,' I said. 'I think there's something you're not telling me. Am I right?'

I don't know where that suddenly came from, it just did.

'What the hell do you mean by that?' asked Germund.

'I mean what I say,' I said. 'I'm sensing there's something you haven't told me.'

He shut the book he'd just opened. Rolled over onto his back, clasped his hands behind his head and lay there staring at the roof for about a minute. No words came, but I could tell from his breathing he was thinking hard. I lay there in silence, too, and thought: either he'll come out with it or he won't. Finally he gave a deep sigh and said: 'That's right. But I can't tell you what it is.'

'Not even me?' I asked.

'Not even you,' said Germund. 'Not yet, anyway.'

'I'll take that as a promise for the future,' I said.

'Take it how you like,' said Germund. 'Is there anything else you want to ask?'

'No,' I said. 'There's nothing else.'

'Right then,' said Germund and opened his book again.

38

Interview with 471111-4666 Elisabeth Katarina Martinsson (EM) at her home in Strömstad. Date: Friday 1 October. Present: Assistant Detective Alexander Tillgren (AT), Assistant Detective Claes-Henrik Wennergren-Olofsson (WO). Interview commences at 13.22.

AT: State your name and address, please.

EM: Elisabeth Martinsson. My address is Badhusgatan 14, Strömstad.

AT: Thank you. So, I'm Alexander Tillgren, from the Kymlinge police. With my colleague Wennergren-Olofsson here, I'm going to ask you a few questions, which we want to you to answer honestly. This is in connection with two deaths we're currently looking into. Maria Winckler, who died thirty-five years ago at Gåsaklinten in Rönninge, outside Kymlinge, and Germund Grooth, who was found dead in exactly the same place last week. Are you aware of these two deaths?

EM: Of course I am. I was there when it happened in 1975, and I've already been questioned by another police officer. It was on Tuesday, if I remember rightly.

AT: Can you tell me a bit about what happened in 1975?

EM: Certainly. It's not the sort of thing you forget, and I had a chance to refresh my memory just the other day, as I say.

AT: I'm sorry we have to go through this again.

EM: No problem. I'd just started a job at that school, Kymlingevik School, I think its name was. Teaching art. I was only there a couple of years, then I moved on to something else. We went on a trip one Sunday; a couple of other new teachers invited me to join them. Well, Maria Winckler and Germund Grooth, as you know. We went to look for mushrooms out at a place called Gåsaklinten and, when we'd been looking for a while, Maria fell off a high rock and died. That's basically it.

AT: Why was there a police investigation?

EM: She shouted something as she fell, that was the thing. Nobody saw her fall, we were spread out all over the place, but everyone heard her shout something. There was a long 'uuuuhh' sound in it. Like in Murderer! A detective asked me about it at some length back then. His name was Sandelin, or something like that.

AT: Detective Inspector Sandlin, yes. We've read his account.

EM: Oh. Well, why are we sitting here then? I haven't changed what I think in the meantime.

AT: We're sitting here because Maria Winckler's partner, Germund Grooth, has now been found dead in the same place, you know that. What did you do when you heard Maria cry out?

EM: Have I really got to go through all this again?

AT: Yes, please.

EM: All right. I ran in that direction, of course. At first I didn't realize what had happened, but then I looked over the edge and saw her lying down there. I was the first one on the scene, but the others turned up just after me. We climbed down to her as quickly as we could – we found there was a little path. I suppose we were down there beside her in about thirty seconds; no, maybe a bit longer. I think I realized right away that she was dead, but I started giving her mouth-to-mouth resuscitation anyway. I gave up almost at once, though; I could see it was useless. And then all the others arrived.

AT: Who got there last?

EM: What?

AT: Did you notice who was the last to reach the spot?

EM: No. Why should I have? I was in shock, and so were the rest of them. They were all there within a minute, I'd say.

AT: What did you think? You knew she'd shouted 'Murderer!' What did you think had happened?

[*Ten seconds' pause from the interviewee*]

EM: I don't know what I thought. I don't recall even thinking about what she'd shouted.

AT: But surely you must have thought something? Surely you tried to visualize what might have happened?

EM: [*After more hesitation*] It took a while, I know that, but of course then the thought did go through my mind. That somebody pushed her, I mean.

AT: You thought that?

EM: Yes. What the hell was I supposed to think? But it definitely wasn't until a bit later, when we were all stood there, waiting and wondering what to do. She was lying there and we were standing around her, and of course your brain starts racing.

AT: Do you mean you started thinking about whether any of the others could have pushed her?

EM: Yes, or even someone else. Some lunatic out walking in the woods, say. And I wondered whether she could simply have slipped. But mostly I thought about the others, I suppose.

AT: Go on.

EM: I mean, I didn't know any of them. They were a group who'd known each other for ages. They'd had a party out at some vicarage; one of them was a vicar. Germund and Maria taught at the school, of course, but we were only about a month into the new term. It was Maria who asked me if I wanted to come along.

AT: When did she ask you?

EM: We were in the smokers' room, chatting. I think it

was only a couple of days beforehand. Well, as I said, there I was in the forest, bilberry twigs underfoot and what-have-you, with four people I didn't know and one dead body. Maria's brother went for help, but the rest of us stayed there to stand guard, or whatever you might call it.

AT: What did you talk about?

EM: Not much. As I remember it, we were pretty quiet. That was what came most naturally, somehow. But eventually someone raised the question of the shout. The fact that she cried out as she was falling. There were various different views, but no, we didn't really talk very much about that, either.

AT: And when you were all down there with Maria, did Germund help with the mouth-to-mouth resuscitation?

EM: No, he just stood there, or knelt really. He fell to his knees after a while. I assumed he was in shock. He seemed sort of dumbstruck.

AT: If we can just go back a bit, how did you all get out to Gåsaklinten?

EM: By car, of course. I went with the vicar and his wife, and Maria's brother and *his* wife.

AT: So that must mean Germund Grooth and Maria Winckler drove out there on their own.

EM: Yes. It felt a bit awkward, being picked up by four people I'd never met. But it was because my place was along their route. Maria and Germund would have had to make a detour if they were going to give me a lift . . . Yes, I'm pretty sure that was why.

AT: I see. And what was the mood of the group?

EM: In the car or in the forest?

AT: Both, if you wouldn't mind.

EM: A bit muted, is how I'd describe it. They didn't talk much. In the car it was only Tomas who said anything after we'd introduced ourselves. And there was no interaction in the forest to speak of, either. We were supposed to be meeting back for coffee after two hours, but we never got that far.

AT: Maria was dead by then?

EM: Yes.

AT: And the mood was muted, you say? Even before that?

EM: It certainly felt that way to me. Everyone kept themselves to themselves in the forest, too. They didn't exactly behave like old friends.

AT: But there were no arguments?

EM: None that I noticed, anyway.

AT: Would you say you got to know Germund Grooth? At school, I mean.

EM: No, I didn't know him.

AT: But both of you carried on working there for the rest of that school year?

EM: Yes, but that doesn't necessarily mean you see much of each other. There must have been at least fifty teachers on the staff. I disliked most of them, if I'm honest.

AT: Did you dislike Germund Grooth?

EM: I didn't like or dislike him. We barely exchanged a word, beyond hello.

AT: In spite of that experience in the forest?

EM: Yes. I got the impression he didn't want to talk about it.

AT: Did you go to Maria's funeral?

EM: No. I was invited, but it was up in Sundsvall. Her parents lived up there, it's where she grew up.

AT: How did your invitation to join them on the outing come about? Maria Winckler invited you, I think you said?

EM: Yes, but I didn't know her, either. It was sheer chance, I think, because she happened to mention it. I probably said it would be nice to get out into the country, and then she asked me along. I don't really remember. I think I would have liked her; she didn't seem to fit in with the other staff, either. She was a bit of an oddity, and so was Germund, come to that.

AT: Which of the others could you see when you heard Maria cry out?

EM: Not one of them. I was on my own. The same seems

to have applied to the others, too. But I assume I was the closest, because I got there first.

AT: Can you tell me about the incident in which Germund Grooth was punched on the nose?

EM: What?

AT: Grooth clashed with a colleague. You knew about that, surely?

EM: Clashed with a colleague? I don't know what you're talking about.

AT: In the spring term. You can scarcely not have noticed?

EM: No, wait. This is the first I've heard of it.

WO: If I say 'leeches', what do you say?

EM: Leeches?

WO: I'm going to have to ask you for a quick answer. When I say 'leeches', what do you say?

EM: What I say is that you're nuts.

WO: Noted.

AT: Excuse me, if we could go back to Germund Grooth, this incident with a fellow staff member, you weren't aware of that?

EM: No, and I don't see where leeches come into it, either. Has your colleague got a screw loose?

AT: Let's move on. Did you ever meet Germund Grooth after he left Kymlingevik School in June 1976?

EM: I saw him, but didn't speak to him.

AT: On several occasions?

EM: Only once. But I remember it, because it was quite striking.

AT: Could you tell us about that?

EM: Of course. It was on one of the ferries over to Finland, the Silja Line, I think. I did a trip with my husband; we've been divorced for years now. One of those weekend mini-cruises. It was winter time, early eighties, before our daughter was born. And, well, Germund Grooth was on the same boat.

AT: And what was so striking about it?

EM: It wasn't *that* out of the ordinary, I suppose, but he was sitting at a table in the restaurant and he had two very stylish ladies with him.

WO: Two of them?

EM: Yes.

WO: Stylish?

EM: Exactly. If you catch my drift. And he was keeping them both entertained, you might say. When they left the table, he had an arm round each of them. I mean what the hell do I know, but they were a bit pissed and my husband said his bet was they were heading down to the cabin for a nice little threesome.

WO: Blimey.

AT: And that was it?

EM: He was sitting with his back to us, so he didn't ever catch sight of me. And I'm not sure he would have recognized me, anyway. It was some years since we'd last seen each other in Kymlinge, five or six, I'd say. But I could see it was him straight away. We passed their table as we were going in to sit down.

AT: I see. What about the rest of the group, did you bump into any of them again, after 1975?

EM: I saw the vicar and his wife a few times while I was still in Kymlinge, but after that, no, I don't think so.

WO: Don't think so?

EM: I'm pretty sure I didn't meet any of them.

WO: Interesting.

AT: All right. Just a couple more questions. Did Maria Winckler ever strike you as suicidal?

EM: No.

AT: Did Germund Grooth ever strike you as suicidal?

EM: No, but I know very few people you might call suicide risks, so I don't really know what I'd be looking for.

AT: What were you doing last Saturday? Saturday 25 September, that is?

EM: Why do you ask?

AT: It's just a routine question. I have to ask it.

EM: Do you think I went out into the forest and pushed that damned Grooth over the edge?

AT: No, of course not. But I'm sure you understand that I have to ask the question. And encourage you to answer it.

[*Ten seconds' pause from the interviewee*]

EM: Well, wouldn't you just know it, I was here painting all day. That one. [*Points to a large painting on an easel in the middle of the room*] Yes, I started that masterpiece on Saturday, that's right.

AT: Were you alone?

EM: You bet your bloody life I was alone. You don't think we paint in groups, do you?

AT: Did you meet anyone else at any point during the day?

EM: [*After a brief hesitation*] I had coffee with a friend of mine in the morning. Down at Strands. We meet for breakfast there sometimes.

AT: And then you came home and painted?

EM: Yes, then I came home and painted. Is there anything wrong with that?

AT: Of course not. Can you give me the rough times between which you were at home?

EM: Christ, I haven't a clue. From ten in the morning, maybe. And then for the rest of the day.

AT: Did you speak to anyone on the phone?

EM: Not that I can recall. I usually switch off the phones when I'm working.

AT: I see. Right, I've no more questions. Is there anything you want to add that you think might be of use to us?

EM: No, I can't think of anything. So you mean you think somebody pushed Grooth off that rock in the forest on Saturday?

AT: It's one possibility. Ruling nothing out in our investigation.

EM: And what makes you think he didn't jump of his own accord?

AT: We can't go into that.

EM: Well, there's a surprise. Still, I wish you all the best with your investigation. Was there anything else?

WO: Excuse me, Miss Martinsson. I get the feeling you're keeping something from us. Correct me if I'm wrong.

EM: Keeping something from you? What rubbish. I happened to be out in a forest when someone died there, thirty-five years ago. Apart from that, I've nothing what-soever to do with Maria Winckler or Germund Grooth.

WO: You're not lying to us, are you, Miss Martinsson?

EM: [*Turns to* AT] Listen, could you just take your colleague and go now? And try to teach him some manners in the car on the way home. I assume you understand what I'm referring to.

AT: Thank you, Miss Martinsson. Interview ended. The time is 13.47.

Written record made on 4.10.2010 by Alexander Tillgren, Assistant Detective.

39

It was 8.30 p.m. by the time they finally got to Timişoara, and it was starting to get dark. It was 8 August, and Rickard wrote in his diary that it was the anniversary of the day the peace treaty was signed between the victorious powers and Japan after the Second World War – a date he had gained marks for remembering in a school history test and would presumably never forget – and the first day there was any discernible bad feeling in the group. He also noted it was a Tuesday.

Generally speaking, his antipathy to Tuesdays had waned in the course of his Uppsala years; if he thought of it at all, it was mostly as a superstitious reflex, more or less as you avoid walking under a ladder, or spit three times if a black cat crosses your path. A sort of lingering atavism, but as they drove along the dark, unfamiliar streets of a strange town that looked anything but inviting, it returned to him. We've got to get through this evening, he thought. We've got to find somewhere to make camp for the night. It will sort itself out, and tomorrow the sun will shine again and we'll continue on our way to the Black Sea.

Childish incantations, he realized that, but as he gazed out through the window of the bus, he had a palpable sense of something hostile. Something brooding. As if they had encroached on forbidden territory, and as he looked at his fellow travellers he could see that they seemed to feel the same. Nobody had any comments to make on their cheerless surroundings; they all sat there staring out over the empty pavements and darkened fronts of buildings without saying a word. Barely any of the street lighting was on, and the few dirty yellow lights hanging on their overhead wires were tossing in the gusty wind and seemed to absorb more darkness than they dispelled. As the rain fell, Rickard had the strange impression of a threat hanging over the whole town. Germund was at the wheel and gave no sign of wanting to stop; he concentrated on manoeuvring the bus slowly and steadily over slippery, bumpy cobblestones, over cracked, uneven tarmac, over protruding tram tracks; he seemed to be turning left and right without hesitation, as if directed by some inner guidance system, but for some reason no one queried where he was going.

There had been a charged atmosphere in the bus all afternoon. There were differences of opinion as to whether they should stop before they got to Timişoara or try to get there by that evening – yet the opinion did not divide itself into two camps, but seemed to exist as a split running down each one of them. A tired and cantankerous sort of indecision that was further fuelled by the terrible roads and constant sudden encounters with tractors and other agricultural vehicles that were virtually impossible to overtake. There was nothing for it but to crawl along behind and wait for them to turn off into the next field or at a road junction in the next village. Rickard had studied the map and calculated that their average speed had been less than forty kilometres an hour. They had been on the road for eleven hours and had covered 380 kilometres.

And their goal at the end of it all was this Timişoara, which looked like a town cowering in the expectation of an imminent bombing raid. Rickard drew the same parallel in his diary and, when he showed it to Anna, she nodded and copied it onto her notepad.

Germund finally pulled up beside something that looked like a large storage facility. If they had ever actually found the central districts of the town, they had certainly now left them behind. The street where they found themselves was narrow and deserted, with big, unlit buildings looming in the darkness on either side, and about ten metres ahead of them they could make out a pair of barred metal gates standing open, and some dimly illuminated warning signs. Rickard realized that was what had made Germund stop. It was a dead end; there was no way out, other than by turning the bus.

'Go on,' said Tomas. 'Turn round. We can't very well park here.'

'Don't feel like driving any further,' said Germund. 'What's wrong with spending the night here?'

'Here?' said Gunilla. 'Are you out of your mind? We can't stop here.'

'The bus is the same wherever we park it,' said Germund. 'Or were you planning to sleep in the open air?'

'I thought we were getting something to eat,' said Anna.

'How many restaurants did you spot on the way through this ghost town?' asked Germund.

'There must be a campsite,' said Tomas. 'Timişoara's a big town, you know.'

'I've never seen a more miserable and forbidding dump,' said Maria. 'Is there a state of emergency in force here, or what?'

'Right, let's focus,' said Tomas. 'We'll just have to ask the way. Do you want me to take over, Germund?'

'OK,' said Germund, extracting himself laboriously from the driving seat. 'But I don't see what's wrong with staying here. We've got beer and fruit for supper. I don't think I saw any food shops. Answer the call of nature on the pavement – when in Rome, and all that.'

'I can't see any pavements,' said Gunilla.

'You'll just have to hold on until morning then,' said Germund and went to sit right at the back of the bus.

Crisis, wrote Rickard Berglund in his diary and closed it again.

Before Tomas started the bus, he and Rickard opened out the map in front of them and studied it. It was meant to be a Timişoara town map, and they had bought it at the border crossing, but they gave up after five minutes. There were no campsites marked on it, and not much else either, and they had no idea which district they were in.

'I'll drive through those gates up ahead and turn round,' said Tomas. 'We'll just have to see as we go along.'

'I'm not sure it's such a bright idea to drive into that area,' cautioned Gunilla. 'Those signs certainly tell us we won't be welcome.'

'I can't see any guards,' said Tomas. 'I'm only going in there to turn.'

He started the engine and eased the bus through the open gates. Immediately inside there was a sort of compound between some corrugated-iron huts; he was backing round so that he could drive out again, but before he had time to straighten up the bus, they were surrounded by four men in some kind of military get-up. Two of them planted themselves right in front of the bus, their machine guns trained on Tomas.

'Kalashnikovs,' said Tomas. 'Fuck, they've got Kalashnikovs!'

One of them shouted something and gestured with his rifle.

'He wants you to get out,' whispered Gunilla, and she suddenly sounded to Rickard like a terrified animal in a comic strip. 'I said we shouldn't have come in here.'

'It'll be all right,' said Tomas. 'I'll tell them we lost our way slightly and just came in here to turn round.'

He stepped down from the bus and went over to the two of them standing there in the glare of the headlights. The man who had gestured with his Kalashnikov went on waving it.

'I think,' said Rickard, noticing he was finding it hard to keep his voice steady, 'I think he means we've all got to get out.'

'Take your passports,' urged Anna. 'They're bound to want to check them. A few cigarettes wouldn't harm, either.'

'Well, fuck me, this is ideal,' said Maria. 'These nice boys will know where there's a good campsite. See how helpful they look?'

They lined them up against a wall. From the very first moment it felt to Rickard as if what was happening wasn't for real. It was a game or a play or some ridiculous prank, that was all. This sort of thing simply didn't happen, or not with this cast. Six unsuspecting Swedes suddenly finding themselves a long way from home, without a clue how they ought to behave.

Or what lay in store for them. Once the passports had been scrutinized at length – by three of the men, while the fourth stood there with his weapon slightly raised to make sure none of the group tried anything unwise – one of them, perhaps it was the leader, he looked a bit older, thrust them into the breast pocket of his uniform jacket and said something to the others. Two of them nodded; the third, who looked significantly younger than the others, could even still be in his teens, gave a loud laugh and earnt himself a reprimand. Tomas started to say something in English about wanting the passports back, but was silenced by the leader letting out a roar, raising his Kalashnikov and making a sweeping movement along their line.

That was clear enough. Rickard felt Anna trying to slip her hand into his, but he was worried it might be inappropriate and pushed it away. The men were engaged in a discussion. Three of them had lit cigarettes; no, it wasn't a discussion, it was more like the leader giving orders. He was the one doing most of the talking, the others just nodded and put in the occasional short response. The youngest laughed again – an abrupt and joyless laugh that sounded more like the bark of a dog – but received no reprimand this time.

Several minutes passed. An eternity of time, it seemed to Rickard. The six Swedes with their backs to the wall, the four Romanian soldiers, or whatever they were, about five metres from them, smoking and plotting. A dirty light high on a wall cast a sinister gleam on the whole scene. Gunilla was crying now, unobtrusively but persistently. The bus engine was still growling. Rickard closed his eyes and started reciting the Lord's Prayer silently to himself. And the steady drizzle continued.

40

'I had a thought,' said Eva Backman. 'If we really are dealing with two murders here – or one, at least – what would the motive be?'

'I haven't the faintest idea,' said Gunnar Barbarotti. 'And I bet you haven't, either.'

'You're dead right there,' said Eva Backman. 'Not the foggiest. But the worst thing is, I find it very difficult to imagine one at all. Especially if we're talking about two murders. Why wait thirty-five years? What kind of crackpot would kill two of their friends at that sort of time interval?'

'Assuming it's one of them.'

'Assuming that, yes. Though it doesn't make a lot more sense if it's someone from outside. Does it?'

'It gives us a few more candidates to choose from, at least,' said Barbarotti. 'But maybe he didn't plan to kill them both. From the outset, I mean.'

'He?' said Eva Backman.

'He or she. If Germund Grooth really was pushed down Gåsaklyftan, something must have happened later on to . . . well, to trigger it.'

'Trigger it?'

Barbarotti sighed. 'Christ knows. But can you envisage a plan that revolves around you killing two people? One today and one in thirty-five years' time.'

'It sounds far-fetched,' said Backman.

'Yes, that's what I'm saying,' said Barbarotti.

'And I hear you,' said Backman. 'But why would Grooth be so stupid as to go out into the forest and get himself murdered at all? Seeing as his partner died there, a hundred years ago, you'd have thought he might have smelt a rat? He wasn't thick, after all.'

'I thought we were going to give up speculating,' said Barbarotti.

'All right. But there's something about that group of people.'

'I know,' said Barbarotti. 'There *is* something. Sandlin suspected as much in 1975 and now we do, too. Shall we go through them all again, one more time? Those who are left, that is.'

'Why not?' said Backman. 'Paying more attention to the subtleties this time maybe, that wouldn't hurt. And on that note, what did you get out of the Martinsson interview?'

'Wennergren-Olofsson's a total prat.'

'Well, we knew that. Anything else?'

Barbarotti shrugged. 'Not a great deal, to be honest. I imagine it was like she said. She just happened to come along on that outing all those years ago. She had nothing to do with the rest of the group. But what do you think?'

Backman sighed. 'Her alibi's pretty poor. But I agree. She seems very peripheral. So what have we got? What have we actually got that points to Grooth being murdered?'

Barbarotti thought about it. 'A pre-booked trip to Paris, and a phone call,' he said. 'It's not much.'

'The absence of any means of transport, too,' said Backman. 'But it still isn't much. Do you think it's time to go to the prosecutor?

'No, it's a bit too soon,' said Barbarotti.

'Do you think we should shut down the whole thing?'

'No, it's a bit too soon,' said Barbarotti. 'That phone call, by the way. I talked to Sorrysen, and it turns out the phone number in question has only ever been used once. What do you think that tells us?'

Backman was silent for a moment. 'It tells us you're right,' she said. 'It's too soon to shut this down.'

'OK then, let's do what we said. Run through the candidates one more time.'

Eva Backman leant back in her chair and pondered. 'We ought to take a closer look at the alibis, anyway. See if we can get them verified. I'm keeping in touch with Lund, too. A bit more flesh on the bones where Grooth is concerned wouldn't hurt, would it? They'll be talking to that woman, Kristin Pedersen, today. Maybe one of us will need to do the same, but let's see.'

'And what about Grooth's laptop?' asked Barbarotti. 'Any joy with that?'

'Apart from the emails, it's pretty uninteresting,' said Backman. 'And they haven't yielded much, either, in fact. Sorrysen's going through it all, and there are a few people we'll want to question. Two women he emailed over the past six months, or who emailed him. Kristin and Birgitta, he clearly had some kind of relationship with each of them. We've located Kristin, and Sorrysen's working on the other one.'

Barbarotti nodded and yawned.

'He hadn't downloaded any files of note,' said Backman, 'and nine out of ten of the emails were about work, Sorrysen says. He wasn't in touch with any of the old Uppsala gang by that route, anyway. Except for one short email to thank Tomas

Winckler after they met in May, that is. He received an equally brief one in reply.'

'He wasn't due to go to Paris with this Birgitta?'

'Nothing to indicate it in the emails, as far as I know. But we'll have to check with Sorrysen.'

'Excellent,' said Barbarotti. 'Even if you're a lone wolf, you're still not totally isolated.'

'You talking about Sorrysen?'

'No, Grooth.'

'Ah,' said Backman. 'No, it's hard to be a hermit in this day and age. If you've got a computer, that is. So we can get on with checking the alibis while other mills are grinding away?'

'We might as well,' said Barbarotti. 'I'll get hold of Berglund and Winckler again. Think I'll start with Berglund, as he's local.'

Backman seemed to be hesitating. 'One other thing,' she said.

'Yes?'

'You don't seem quite yourself. Is anything the matter?'

'I don't know what you mean,' said Barbarotti.

Rickard Berglund picked up after only one ring.

'I hope I'm not disturbing,' said Barbarotti after giving his name. 'How are things?'

'Thanks for asking,' said Rickard Berglund. 'Anna died this morning.'

Barbarotti swallowed. 'I'm sorry,' he said. 'I didn't know . . .'

'It was only a question of time,' said Berglund. 'She's gone now, anyway.'

'I don't want to intrude at a time like this, of course,' said Barbarotti. 'Please accept my condolences, and I'll ring back next week, if I may.'

'You're not intruding,' said Berglund. 'The funeral's on Saturday. There isn't actually as much to do in these days leading up to the burial as people think. And I've been waiting for this for quite a long time, of course.'

'I understand,' said Gunnar Barbarotti. 'But I still don't want to . . .'

'It's a feeling of both relief and sadness, now it's all over,' Rickard Berglund went on. 'And it's better to talk about it than bottle it all up inside. Sorry, what was it you wanted?'

I wonder when he last got an hour's sleep, thought Barbarotti.

'I . . . I just wanted another quick word with you about the death of Germund Grooth,' he explained. 'The same thing as last time, in other words. A few little details, but they can wait.'

'I can do tomorrow,' said Berglund, 'if that would suit you.'

'It would,' said Barbarotti. 'What time?'

'In the afternoon?' suggested Rickard Berglund, and they agreed to meet in the police-station foyer at 2 p.m.

Remarkable, thought Barbarotti after he hung up. Nothing to do while you're waiting to bury your wife? Although Berglund was in that line of work now, so he was presumably well versed in the practicalities.

And he had certainly had time to prepare himself. All too much time, presumably.

Eva Backman rang down to Skåne and learnt that Ribbing and Larsson were sitting waiting for Kristin Pedersen, who was due back from Copenhagen. They would be in touch as soon as they'd finished the interview. Later in the day they would be talking to two of Germund Grooth's colleagues.

Eva Backman thanked them and hung up. She couldn't make

up her mind what to do next, but it didn't take her long to concede that she didn't feel like staying in her room. The sky outside the window had lightened a touch, the rain looked as if it was about to stop, and sometimes you simply have to follow your intuition.

It sounded just about acceptable when she tried to justify it to herself in operational terms. *Following your intuition*. Much better than acknowledging that you were playing truant because you needed to get away and be in motion, for instance.

She checked out a car from the pool down in the police-station garage and drove up the ramp. She wound her way across town and five minutes later she was out on the 256, heading towards Rönninge. The rain had moved on and there were patches of blue showing through the cloud cover.

I can't abide sitting still, she thought. That's the plain fact of the matter and it's getting worse from year to year. It just makes me dull in the head. If my body can't move, how on earth am I supposed to keep my brain going?

It took a while to find her way out to Gåsaklinten, even though it was only just over a week since her last visit. Luckily she had remembered to bring a map. An orienteering map, no less, with a scale of 1:25,000; she remembered the look of them from school.

Although the sun was now poking through, the forest was still sodden. What was more, some of the paths were a lot better on the map than they were in real life, and she was wet to the knees by the time she was finally up on the edge of the crag.

She stood looking down to the bottom of the drop, where Germund Grooth's body had been found, eight days before.

And Maria Winckler's thirty-five years before that.

Germund would have been twenty-six at the time, she calculated. She tried to imagine what it must have felt like. How it
must feel to suddenly lose your life partner when you were no
older than that. They weren't married, but they had been
together for four or five years, even so. They lived under the
same roof, in Uppsala and then for a few months here in
Kymlinge. It must leave its mark, thought Eva Backman. Its
indelible mark. There were signs indicating Germund Grooth
wasn't the easiest of people to deal with even back then, and
losing Maria in such a brutal way would hardly have improved
things.

Had it been haunting him for thirty-five years? Ought they
to give the possibility serious consideration after all? Life
wasn't a straight path from one point to another – nor unto
the third and fourth generation, and all that. It went in waves,
in fits and starts; perhaps it had some sort of direction – she
liked to think so anyway – but there were always troughs, and
old stuff could resurface in those troughs. Trauma and grief
and all sorts of things we haven't entirely managed to sweep
under the carpet. It's when we are at our weakest that our
birthmarks can start to bleed, I know that, she thought. That's
when dark memories from the past catch up with us and project
their shadows onto us.

So we find it hard to go on.

So we maybe decide we don't want to carry on living? Not
even if we've a trip to Paris beckoning us into next week.

Because it just isn't worth the effort.

Could that have been the way it happened, after all? She
looked out over the treetops and down to the base of the
sheer drop and mused. Did Germund Grooth simply decide
he'd had enough, that Saturday morning? For some wholly

self-contained reason? Or as a result of that phone call? Making him take the train or a taxi or something and do the deed?

To be united with Maria. The one he had loved and lost when he was just twenty-six. The only woman in his life?

Eva Backman started down the steep little path. The one they had used thirty-five years ago, the one they had used last week. It was a bit slippery after the rain, but not particularly difficult to climb down.

What if he actually did take a taxi? she thought. Imagine if he had. From Kymlinge, or even all the way up from Lund . . . and was dropped off somewhere near here. The Alhamra Cross, or whatever it was called – didn't that seem the likeliest solution?

Had they checked the taxi firms?

In Kymlinge, yes, but had they spread the net any wider? He could have got a taxi from some other place, even if he didn't come all the way from Skåne in one. Gothenburg or Trollhättan, or anywhere, really.

She jotted it down in her mental notebook. *Check taxis!*

That phone call could have been anything at all, couldn't it? A wrong number, say.

Though you probably didn't spend – what was it? forty-three seconds? – on the line to someone who happened to dial the wrong number?

She came down to the spot where Germund Grooth had been lying. There was no trace of the fact, eight days later. She knew the CSI team had done a methodical search, both down here and up on the cliff. They would have been meticulous. But they found nothing, with the exception of Grooth's wallet, which had evidently slipped out of his pocket and wedged itself in a gap between two rocks when he fell. It had taken more than twenty-four hours to identify him, but there was nothing remarkable in that.

There was nothing remarkable in any of it, frankly, she told herself. There was nothing left out here to provide even a hint of what might have happened. No matches or cigarette butts, like in old detective novels and films; no, if Germund Grooth really had been murdered, the murderer hadn't lit up as he stood out here by the clifftop leap, waiting for him.

Always assuming such clifftop leaps had ever existed, and that remained a moot point.

No footprints, either. Not a week ago, and especially not now. The ground up on the cliff edge was quite hard, and it was stony where he had hit the ground; if it hadn't been, they might both have survived, she thought. Maria Winckler and Germund Grooth. She scanned the vertical wall of rock and tried to estimate the height of the drop.

Twenty, maybe twenty-five metres, she thought; the exact figure was doubtless recorded somewhere. Perhaps you could survive a fall like that if you had a relatively soft landing. You wouldn't escape without a few broken bones, of course, but surely a reasonable-sized lingonberry bush would cushion your fall enough for you to escape with your life? Or a spruce sapling.

She shrugged her shoulders and set off up the path again. It was actually easier going back up than it had been coming down, and she was soon back at the spot from which – as far as anyone could judge – the two victims had taken their step into death. Their *plummet*.

The abyss. The leap?

Or they had lost their footing. Or been pushed. She turned round and surveyed the surrounding forest. She tried to visualize the mushroom hunters as they came running that time. Out of breath and from all directions – they'd all heard the shout, of course, and must have sensed something had happened and . . . and all of a sudden, Eva Backman knew what the next move in the investigation had to be.

The map. Inspector Sandlin's map of where they'd all been when Maria Winckler fell.

Because it really was bloody peculiar that not a single one of them had visual contact with anybody else, wasn't it? Surely at least someone ought to have had a glimpse of someone else? Why had they been spaced out in such a studied fashion? It seemed almost like . . . an agreement.

No, Eva Backman chided herself. Now I'm speculating again.

But Sandlin's map still wasn't a bad idea. Happy that the trip had led her to one decision, at least, she retraced her steps to the car.

41

It kept on raining and the wind came in unrelenting gusts.

Gunilla stood between Tomas and Anna, trying to keep count of her heartbeats. She kept her hand tucked under her left breast and could feel them as clearly as anything. She didn't know why she was doing it, but she knew that if she didn't have something neutral to focus on, she was going to faint.

And it wouldn't help the situation at all if one of them fainted.

The men were still in their huddle, conferring. They nodded to one another, smoked and kept an eye on the group. When Tomas cautiously tried to whisper something to her – or perhaps to them all, she never managed to make out what he'd said – one of them bellowed. He was clearly the leader; he threw out a string of threatening words, entirely incomprehensible to them. But their essence was clear. They were to shut up.

If they knew what was good for them, they would stay where they were, backed against the wall, and shut up. Remain still and obedient. The leader gestured with his weapon. Yes, the essence was crystal-clear.

She started her counting again. She never got beyond fifteen or twenty before losing her thread and having to go back to the beginning. She could almost feel the others' heartbeats as well, or at least those of Anna, standing close beside her. The pulse felt somehow intensified by the rain. *The pulse of fear.* The water was streaming down her face, running off her hair and shoulders; it was the same for all of them, of course, and Gunilla realized she had sensed this coming. There'd been something ill-fated about the day from the start. Something about the atmosphere, about that unbearably long drive on those dreadful roads, about the whole thing.

Dear God, she thought, let them decide we're free to go. Let us get away from here.

But she wasn't praying, they were just thoughts without force or any real will, she was aware of that. She had no God, after all. Perhaps she had been on the verge of saying a prayer the other day, when she was in that church in . . . she'd forgotten the name of the town. Looking back, it felt like a moment she had somehow let slip. She'd been feeling that ever since. An opportunity she had failed to make the most of.

Another of those strange thoughts. Or perhaps it was exactly the kind of thought appropriate for here and now. In the darkness, in the rain, pressed against a wall in a strange, disquieting town.

Anything to keep the fear in check, she thought. Anything at all.

She started counting again.

After a period of time that could have been ten minutes – or five, or twenty – the men in uniform had reached agreement.

The leader – who was not very tall, probably no more than

170 centimetres, but stockily built – came striding over to them and stopped about two metres away. He started to address them, still in Romanian – Gunilla assumed it was Romanian anyway – but laced with a few comprehensible words in English. She heard *forbidden, police, document, passport, arrest, problem, prison, territory.*

When he finished, Tomas again tried to say something, but was silenced with a cuff round the ear. One of the other men came over to deliver it. Gunilla felt as if she was going to be sick, and Anna gave a terrified cry.

The man who had cuffed Tomas moved on to Anna. He planted himself right in front of her and raised his hand. A few seconds later he lowered it again and resumed his position behind his leader.

'Come!' said the leader, indicating the direction with his Kalashnikov.

They were made to file across the compound. As they passed the bus, the leader held out his hand and said, 'Key!' Tomas replied, 'In bus', and one of the soldiers climbed in to switch off the engine. When he came back, he handed the key to the leader, who said, 'Forbidden territory', and they walked on to a squat concrete box, a windowless building with a tall chimney.

One of the men unlocked a heavy metal door and they were herded inside. Three of the soldiers came with them, including the leader; the youngest of them stayed outside. The leader switched on the light, a single, grubby light bulb suspended from the roof in the middle of the room.

It was a big, bare space. Concrete floor, concrete walls. A few benches right at the back, under another light bulb that wasn't working. A wall-mounted handbasin in the corner. A few metal containers, possibly petrol cans; the place smelt like a garage or a petrol station, thought Gunilla. Another smell, too, that she couldn't identify. Perhaps it was just a sort of general smell of dirt. Or mould.

They were ordered to sit down on the benches. Once they had done so, the leader stood right in front of them again, feet wide apart, and regarded them impassively. The others were two metres behind him with their weapons ready to raise, and for a moment she thought they were going to be shot.

They were going to be killed, it was that simple.

Here and now, in this filthy concrete bunker on the edge of the town of Timişoara in the country of Romania, they were going to die. She felt the gag reflex again, but just as she thought she would vomit, the leader cleared his throat and said:

'Stay here.'

Then he did an about-turn and marched out of the building with his comrades. As if on some blurry filmstrip – for it didn't feel remotely real – Gunilla saw the heavy door shut and heard it being very thoroughly locked, and then they were alone.

No one said a word for about a minute. Anna was crying. Gunilla started crying because Anna was.

'They're just trying to scare us,' said Tomas. 'Presumably they've gone off to find someone who can take authority. We stumbled into a restricted military area, that's all.'

'Well, they're making a very good job of it, is all I can say,' said Maria. 'Scaring us, I mean. Can't you two stop howling? This is nothing worth wasting tears on.'

'For God's sake,' said Anna. 'You've no tears to call on, of course.'

'More than you can imagine,' said Maria. 'But I'm saving them up.'

'Wouldn't it be an idea to try and pull through this together?' suggested Rickard. 'I mean it would be pretty stupid of us to fall out just now. I'm not so sure they're soldiers.'

'What do you mean?' said Tomas.

'Those uniforms. They look more like some kind of police. Or security guards. They haven't got any indication of rank, as far as I could see.'

'What is this place?' said Anna. 'Jesus Christ, Tomas, he actually hit you.'

'Kalashnikovs,' said Germund. 'Nasty little things. We ought probably to be thankful as long as they limit themselves to their fists.'

'It was the palm of his hand,' said Tomas. 'A clip round the ear, it was no big deal.'

'Do you have to be so fucking optimistic all the time?' asked Maria. 'Someone punches you in the face and you think it's OK. We get locked in this damn bunker, and you still think it's OK. Things are looking grim here – try to get that into your skull.'

Tomas got to his feet and went over to Maria, who was still sitting on a bench. 'Will you please just shut up,' he said sharply. 'It doesn't help anybody, meeting trouble halfway. Why don't you try being a bit constructive for once?'

'Constructive?' said Maria with a dry laugh. 'How the fuck do you see anyone being constructive in this place, exactly?'

She thrust out a dismissive hand and shook her head. Tomas stood there for a moment in a state of obvious indecision, and

Gunilla wondered if he actually felt tempted to follow the soldier's example and administer a cuff round the ear. In the end he went over and sat down beside Rickard.

'What the hell shall we do?' he said.

'I don't know,' said Rickard. 'Wait, I suppose.'

It couldn't have been more than fifteen minutes until the men came back, but no one was timing them.

There hadn't been much talking in their absence. Gunilla wondered why, but didn't find it that surprising. What was there to say? Tomas and Rickard had been all round, examining their detention space, and that was all that had really happened. It wasn't particularly big, about seven metres square; three metres high and windowless. The walls were rough concrete, the door was steel and there wasn't the slightest chance of getting out.

The cans were empty, which Tomas ascertained by kicking them.

And what would they have done if they *did* get out? There was a spare ignition key in the bus, under Rickard and Anna's bed, but what was to say their captors weren't keeping the bus under surveillance? Perhaps they were combing through it right now. Hunting for pornographic daily newspapers or cigarettes or whatever. Money, of course.

And they had their passports. It'll be fun when we arrive at the Romania–Bulgaria border without passports, Tomas had declared, and even Maria had agreed with him on that.

But otherwise they'd just stayed quiet. Unusually quiet; when Gunilla asked Anna if she was thirsty, no answer was forthcoming, only a shake of the head. It felt as if each of them was personally engrossed in coming to terms with the situation; it was some kind of necessary process before they could actually start discussing their position.

Germund kept his head bowed and looked very much as he had done in the church in that town, thought Gunilla. She still couldn't remember its name. Maria was lying stretched out on a bench, eyes closed, but she wasn't asleep, of course. She had been irritable all day, perhaps it was premenstrual tension, but you never knew with Maria. Gunilla thought again how difficult she and Germund were to understand. Tomas was absolutely right.

They were the exception to every rule, those two.

But of course her mind was not really on Maria and Germund, or on any of the others. Fear was ticking away inside her, and she felt the same way she sometimes had in her months at Ulleråker. Through the lonely, wakeful nights. She was out walking across the thinnest of ice that had formed overnight, and at any moment it could give way. At any moment her foot could go through and she would plunge into the darkness again.

She wished she could transfer some of her terror to Tomas. Or, rather, make him aware of it, but it wouldn't do. Tomas was the one responsible for the group; the collective is more important than the individual, he couldn't be expected to deal with everyone's individual distress at a time like this. Not even hers, unfortunately. He's so used to looking after me, she thought. Used to it, and sick and tired of it. She watched him pacing around the room like a caged animal, throwing out pointless comments. Trying to analyse the situation, kicking the petrol cans again, exchanging the odd word with Rickard, who went with him on some of his circuits round the four bare walls. But in between he would sit down beside Anna. It was Tomas who was the leader, Tomas who had arranged the whole trip, and if anyone ought to try to get them out of this fix, it was him. Gunilla knew that was how he would be thinking, and even as she struggled to fight down her own fear, she couldn't help feeling it was a bit childish. A bit Scout leaderish.

She leant a little closer to Anna. Tucked her hand under her breast and started counting heartbeats again.

She didn't get far. All at once, the men were back.

There were only two of them this time. The leader and one of the others, not the young lad. The other man locked the door and stayed on guard beside it, Kalashnikov at the ready. The leader gestured to Tomas and Rickard to sit down on the benches. Maria sat up. The leader lit a cigarette before he spoke.

'Woman,' he said.

His face betrayed nothing. He took a drag on his cigarette.

'One woman, one hour. You choose.'

With his gun, he pointed at Anna, Gunilla and Maria in turn.

'One woman, one hour. Then free. Then free,' he repeated.

It took a few seconds for Gunilla to understand what he meant. Presumably it was the same for the others, too. There was a sharp intake of breath from Anna. Tomas swore. Rickard and Maria seemed dumbstruck, and it was only Germund who was able to react in words.

'No,' he said simply. 'No way.'

The leader took no notice. He repeated his order.

'One woman, one hour. Then free. If not . . .'

He raised his weapon and made a sweeping motion across the whole group. So as not to wear out his vocabulary.

'One woman. You choose.'
He looked at his watch.
'Back in fifteen minutes. One woman with me.'
And after that, they were left on their own again.

THREE

42

The call came in at exactly 13.30. He realized he had written it down while he was listening, and afterwards he wondered why. What on earth made him do it?

It took a while for him to work out what was going on, too.

'Am I speaking to Gunnar Barbarotti?' asked a bright female voice.

'Yes, that's me.'

'I'm ringing from the hospital.'

'Oh yes?'

'Marianne Grimberg, I understand she's your wife?'

'Yes . . . yes, she is.'

'She works in the maternity and gynaecology department here at the hospital?'

'Yes. What's this about?'

'There's been an accident.'

'An accident?'

'Yes, but the situation is stable. She's on her way to Sahlgrenska in Gothenburg.'

'What?'

'Yes, she had a little mishap. They'll operate at Sahlgrenska.'

'At Sahlgrenska?'

'Yes.'

'Operate . . . What the devil are you telling me? What's happened?'

'She passed out. But there's no need to worry, her condition is stable. To be on the safe side, the neurosurgeon at Sahlgrenska is taking care of her. We haven't got that kind of specialism here in Kymlinge. It's probably a minor bleed on the brain.'

'A bleed on . . . You mean, like a stroke?'

He was suddenly finding it hard to breathe. The T-shirt he had on under his shirt felt far too tight. He grabbed at the neckline with his free hand and yanked wildly.

'Yes. They did a CT scan here and Dr Berngren decided she needed an operation. But don't worry, it could easily be something very insignificant. She's on her way there now.'

'Hang on . . . I mean, when did this happen?'

'About two hours ago. In the maternity unit where she works. She lost consciousness and—'

'Two hours? Why didn't you call me sooner?'

The breezy female voice took on a slightly more authoritative tone.

'We dealt with the patient first. That's the procedure. We tried calling you a while ago, but there was no answer.'

Gunnar Barbarotti remembered that he'd left his phone in his room when he went in to talk to Backman. He sat in stunned silence. His head felt like a pinball machine inside. *Marianne . . . bleed on the brain . . . neurosurgeon . . . stable condition . . . Sahlgrenska.* He tried to assemble it all into a comprehensible message, but it simply didn't work. It was a jigsaw puzzle with bits that didn't fit together.

'What . . . what shall I do?' he spluttered finally. 'What shall . . . We've got four children, too – no, five . . .'

'Dr Berngren suggests that you come here first, so we can fill you in on the background. And that you let your children know, too, of course.'

'Oh?'

'Your wife will be having her operation in Gothenburg and isn't likely to be conscious for some hours. We can arrange transport for you and the children, but you won't need to leave for a couple of hours.'

'I . . . I see. I'll ring the children and we'll come in. Where do we go when we get there?'

'Ward thirty-five. In building number thirty. I'm Jeanette Möller, and I shall be here until six this evening. Ask for me at the reception desk. Is that OK?'

'Yes . . . that's . . . OK,' stammered Gunnar Barbarotti and hung up.

He managed to get hold of Sara first, and that was probably just as well. She was the eldest, all of twenty-two years old, and the most sensible. Once she had got past the shock and taken in the message – and realized her father wasn't really in a fit state to deal with the situation – she took the reins.

'I don't think we all need to go down there,' she decided. 'Not right away. I'll collect up the others at home and we'll talk it over. Jenny and Johan might want to go straight there, but we can't be sure. It's best if we let them decide. But you feel free to get going, and I'll take over on the home front in the meantime.'

'But . . .' objected Gunnar Barbarotti.

'No "buts",' said Sara. 'Trust me, and don't worry about it. Go and be with Marianne.'

'Thank you,' said Barbarotti. 'I don't know what I'd . . . thank you, Sara.'

'One more thing,' said Sara. 'Don't drive yourself. The hospital was going to arrange transport, weren't they?'

'Yes, they said they would.'

'There you are then. We'll keep in touch on our mobiles.'

'I love you, Sara,' he said.

'I love you too, Dad,' said Sara, and they rang off.

Jeanette Möller was dark-skinned and about twenty-five. It's funny that you can't tell the colour of a person's skin from their voice, he thought. But why was a thought like that cropping up in a situation like this?

'Hello. I'm Jeanette. We spoke on the phone.'

'Yes, of course,' said Gunnar Barbarotti.

She put her hand on his arm. 'I know it must have come as a shock,' she said. 'That's only natural. But if you come with me, you can talk to Dr Berngren.'

She walked ahead of him to the lifts in the vestibule. They went up to the fifth floor. There was something familiar about it, he thought. It wasn't the ward he'd been on when he broke his foot two years ago, that was a different block, number twenty. But it felt identical. The surroundings, that is. Nothing else was even remotely identical.

'What happened?' he asked again as they stood in the lift. 'You must realize how worried I am.'

'It's quite normal for you to be worried,' she repeated. 'But I don't know very much, I'm afraid. Only that she lost consciousness. And that would be associated with a bleed on the brain.'

Normal? he thought. What did she mean by that? There wasn't the tiniest fraction of this that was normal.

'She fainted?'

'Yes. And she didn't come round.'

'Bleeding?'

'Yes.'

'Where?'

'In her brain. But I don't know exactly where. Right, here we are.'

The lift doors opened to let them out and he followed her into ward thirty-five. She asked him to take a seat; the chair was green. She went to get Dr Berngren. The thoughts were screaming round in his head.

Dr Berngren was a man of ruddy complexion, probably in his forties. He shook Barbarotti by the hand and asked him to come into a consulting room where they could sit undisturbed. He asked Barbarotti if he wanted anything to drink. Barbarotti declined, even as he realized his mouth was so dry that a glass of water wouldn't have gone amiss.

'My wife?' he said. 'How is she?'

The doctor crossed one leg over the other and gave a little cough.

'Quite well, in the circumstances, I should say. But it's too early to be sure. I shall try to tell you what we know in as much detail as I can.'

'Thank you,' said Barbarotti. 'Please do that.'

'It's probably a minor bleed in the brain. Minor, but serious. We did what we call a cranial CT scan here and decided an operation was needed. They'll probably need to remove any excess blood from the brain. That procedure has to be done by a neurosurgeon and only large hospitals have those. So that's why we've sent her to Sahlgrenska.'

'Minor but serious?' repeated Barbarotti mechanically,

noting that he could feel his own pulse in his temples. I'm going to get one, too, he thought.

'Yes. We think it was simply a small blood vessel bursting. An aneurysm. They're more usual among older people, of course, but they can occur in any age group.'

'She's forty-five,' said Barbarotti.

'I know,' said Dr Berngren.

'I want to go there,' said Barbarotti. 'I've got to be with her.'

'We can get you transport right away,' Dr Berngren assured him. 'But there isn't really any point being in too much of a hurry. She's going to be under anaesthetic and in a respirator until the operation. It's important to minimize all brain activity so as not to worsen her condition. Were you thinking of taking your children with you? You have several, I under-stand . . .'

'They're staying at home for now,' said Barbarotti. 'My eldest is looking after them. She's twenty-two; we've got it all arranged. Or . . . if you think . . .?'

'Sensible move,' said Dr Berngren. 'It's usually better if they visit once the patient has woken up. There's also the possibility Gothenburg will send her back to us as early as tomorrow – it depends on how things stand. But it's a decision for you and your family whether you all go, of course.'

'Of course,' said Barbarotti.

'Here's a contact name for you,' said Berngren, holding out a folded piece of paper. 'See them when you get to Sahlgrenska. They're in the neurosurgery department. And there's a phone number, too.'

Barbarotti took the paper and stuffed it into his breast pocket. 'Thanks,' he said. 'And there's . . . there's nothing more you need to tell me?'

'In most cases the patient suffers only very minor after-effects, if any,' said Dr Berngren, 'especially if they are young and the bleed is small. But it has to be taken seriously, of course, and I can't offer you any prognosis. We passed her on to the specialists, which is what we always do in these cases. Sister Möller will help you with the transport.'

'Thank you . . .' said Gunnar Barbarotti. 'Thank you very much.'

What am I thanking them for? he thought. They might not even pull her through.

The taxi ride from Kymlinge to Sahlgrenska hospital in Gothenburg took barely an hour and a half, but it was the longest journey of his life.

He sat in the back seat, behind the driver, to avoid any chance of eye contact. Before they even got as far as the Rocksta roundabout, some lines from the Bible floated to the top of his mind. They spread themselves like balsam over the mosquito swarm of panicky thoughts, and he tried to let them do their work.

In the midst of life we are in death. In the days of your vigour, you walk hand-in-hand with the angel of death. But be not afraid.

He couldn't remember where it was from and he wasn't sure that he had the words exactly right. It wasn't particularly consoling, either; perhaps it was Ecclesiastes. Marianne was quite partial to its sombre preaching, for some reason, and as he sat there trying to regain some kind of control over existence, he felt sure that was just what she was in the habit of saying.

Life is going on, here and now. We must make the most of it. Death is our nearest neighbour; one second we are alive, the next it could all be over. We don't get any warning.

But she wasn't dead, of course.

Marianne was alive. She was in the neurosurgery department of Sahlgrenska hospital in Gothenburg, being looked after by people who knew how to treat this kind of thing. Minor bleeding to the brain. People who opened up the skull, sucked the blood out of the way and made sure the patient got well and suffered no after-effects . . .

He wondered what sort of after-effects could arise. His experience of – what were they called? – aneurysms . . . was virtually non-existent. Could you be paralysed? Bed-bound for the rest of your life? Have speech problems?

Would Marianne be so changed that they barely recognized her? Or she them? Him and the children? Sweden's youth, its future. A tragic figure sitting in a wheelchair all day, with no power of speech? For twenty or thirty years?

The images bombarded him and he wondered how many people there were in Sweden who ended up in positions like this. Couples going through life, and suddenly something happens to one of them and, in a split second, everything changes. Life alters course so swiftly that you don't have time to prepare yourself.

Or say those things while there is still time. Those things that have been left unsaid.

And the fact that a little blood vessel could suddenly burst like that? At any moment in life. The thin vessel wall that suddenly gave way, having an impact not only on the life it was part of, but also on many others around it. Six, in this case.

Not to mention friends and colleagues.

It isn't fair, thought Gunnar Barbarotti.

But fairness had very little say in matters of life and death.

He ought to have learnt that in his line of work, if nothing else.

Because there is death in the midst of life. *In the days of your vigour, you walk hand-in-hand with the angel of death.*

And he prayed.

Another sort of prayer this time. Definitely very different. Our Lord came and sat beside Barbarotti in the back seat of the taxi from Kymlinge to Gothenburg and they talked to each other in a new way.

That old agreement we had, said Our Lord, the one that meant I had to keep proving my existence to you over and over again, perhaps it's time to ditch it?

Without a second's hesitation, Gunnar Barbarotti said yes, that was certainly the case. Time to ditch it.

Because there's something else in play now, said Our Lord. Isn't there?

Yes, that's exactly it, replied Gunnar Barbarotti. Something else entirely. From this point onwards. If you can just make sure—

No, interrupted Our Lord. There you go, bargaining again. Believing in me isn't a question of trade-offs. You're not allowed to lay down conditions. If I do this and that, then you'll concede that I exist. That's all over now; I'm sick of it.

You're sick of it? said Barbarotti.

Yes, heartily sick. I give you all my love, that's my message, and if you accept that love and stand on my side, I shall stand on your side. But I'm not all-powerful. I don't control everything – that's an old misconception. I have no power over people's free will, or over whatever the Devil comes up with. I am the power of good, but there's also a power of evil. And it wasn't me who invented religion and churches and the Pope; that was you mortals. Do you understand?

Gunnar Barbarotti assured Him that he did. To some extent, anyway.

When it comes to Marianne, all we can do is have trust, Our Lord went on. Both you and I. Death and life really are neighbours, just as you were noting in your terror-stricken state just now. But humans are actually the only beings capable of contemplating the beauty of life and finding joy in it. Imagine it being so hard to comprehend that.

I comprehend it, protested Barbarotti. It's just that—

You're starting to quibble again, Our Lord broke in. Stop that now. Have trust and keep Marianne in your thoughts, that's all you need to do.

Then He was gone. The taxi driver switched on the radio, and Barbarotti decided to do just as he'd been advised. Have trust and think of her.

Trust, though? What was that?

Probably the only really effective medicine for the white-hot terror pounding inside him – that wasn't hard to grasp. But holding on to it was another thing. Not worrying, and instead putting your faith in . . . well, what? That was a good question. A very good question. Trust is like a bar of bath soap, thought Inspector Barbarotti in his bewilderment. Almost impossible to get a firm grip on.

And that six-year-old agreement with Our Lord suddenly didn't apply any more. It was punctured once and for all. The odd thing was, it didn't feel the least bit odd.

From this moment on, everything's changed, thought Gunnar Barbarotti. Dear God, let her live.

43

The silence that fell once the door had clanged shut felt like a living creature. For a good ten seconds no one moved so much as a finger, or uttered a single word. It seemed to Rickard that no one else was even breathing. He certainly wasn't. The significance of what the leader had just said was slowly seeping into him, but it was a message that was almost impossible to take in.

One woman with me.

One of them – Gunilla, Maria or Anna – was to be designated to go with the four men. Spend an hour with them. You didn't need much of an imagination to understand what they intended to do. You didn't need any imagination at all.

Four of them. Rickard realized that was why nobody was saying anything. Each and every one of them understood precisely what that meant. There was no scope for interpretation.

If they didn't get a girl, they would use their Kalashnikovs.

It couldn't be more explicit.

The first one to say anything was Maria.

'Why aren't you saying anything, dear brother?' she said. 'Have you lost control now?'

Tomas didn't reply. He got up and prowled around the room.

'What shall we do?' whispered Gunilla. 'Surely you're not . . .?'

'No,' said Anna. 'Of course we'll have to . . .'

Neither of them could find any way to end their sentence. Rickard watched the others. Germund sat staring at his feet. Maria sat motionless, with her eyes shut, and presumably hadn't even opened them to ask Tomas the question, but he wasn't sure. He looked at his watch. One minute had passed.

Fourteen to go. And if Tomas doesn't say anything, I shall have to take responsibility here, thought Rickard. It was a thought that took him by surprise; panic was ready and waiting inside him, fear was dancing, yet he knew he couldn't just sit there, paralysed and unable to act as the minutes ran out.

Like cattle. That was another surprising thought.

Why don't I say a prayer? he wondered. But something held him back.

'We've got to do something,' he said.

'Do something?' responded Maria. Without opening her eyes; this time he saw it. 'And what do you suggest we do?'

Tomas came back and sat down on one of the benches. As if he had reached a decision, thought Rickard.

'If we don't choose, it'll be worse,' said Tomas.

'What do you mean?' said Gunilla.

'I mean we might have nothing to gain by opposing their demand, say.'

'You're excelling yourself this time,' said Maria.

'So you're saying we should let them have one of us?' burst out Anna. 'You mean we should sacrifice Gunilla or Maria or me?'

Her voice broke. She got up and went over to the wall, where she stood with her back to the rest of them. Rickard hesitated. Then he followed her. He put a cautious hand on her shoulder. She turned her head and stared at him.

'Go to hell,' she hissed. 'Go to hell, Rickard.'

He could barely understand what she was saying. Had he misheard? He looked at the others to check. No, none of them seemed to have heard.

Gunilla was weeping. She was leaning forward with her hands clasped round her head, shaking with sobs. Rickard took his hand from Anna's shoulder and checked the time.

They had twelve minutes left.

'We must try to stick together through this,' said Tomas. 'It'll only make things worse if we argue.'

'Good,' said Maria. 'Let's stick together. And resist.'

'I don't know,' said Tomas. 'I'm not sure that's the best approach. What do the rest of you think?'

'I think,' began Rickard, but then realized he didn't know what he thought. Or maybe he did, but it just wasn't possible to say it.

'What do you think yourself?' asked Anna. Her question was directed at Tomas, not Rickard. 'It would be interesting to hear. You think we should agree to their demands then?'

'I didn't say that,' said Tomas. 'I just said it could be a mistake to refuse out of hand.'

'Refuse out of hand?' said Maria. 'What in Christ's name does that mean?'

'It just means we ought to talk it over,' said Tomas. 'Let everyone express an opinion before they're back again. It's an atrocious situation, but none of us can do anything about it. We're victims of something we can't control. It's nobody's fault and we've got to try to keep our composure.'

'OK,' said Maria. 'I'm composed. All us girls are composed. Gunilla, Anna and me. One of us is going to be raped by four

385

soldiers for an hour. Of course we're fucking composed, what do you expect?'

Gunilla let out a scream and threw herself on the floor. Tomas made a clumsy attempt to lift her, but then left her lying there.

'Look how nice and composed Gunilla is,' observed Maria. 'I'm sure she'll be cool and calm after the event, as well.'

'Shut up, Maria!' bellowed Tomas. Rickard saw him clench his fists and watched a blood vessel throbbing visibly on his temple. He knew he ought to do something or try to step in and help somehow, but those hissed words of Anna's had left him dumbfounded. She had told him to go to hell. He didn't know why, or he didn't want to know. Perhaps he suspected deep inside him that she was right and he ought to have protected her in some way, but how would that have been possible? Later, he thought, when this is over – in some miraculous way this is over – I must talk to her about it. She had thrown out an accusation, heaving an unjust lead-weight of guilt onto him, but of course . . . of course it wasn't him she was telling to go to hell; it was a sort of projection, that was all . . . Yes, once the nightmare was over, they would talk it all through and resolve everything.

But right now, while they were in this hateful place, with the seconds ticking by and no solution in view, he had no words in him. No words with any meaning.

He was sitting on the bench now, his head in his hands. Tomas and Anna were on their feet. Gunilla was lying on the dirty floor, rocking to and fro, while Maria and Germund sat motionless, as they had throughout.

'I assume we haven't got a volunteer,' said Tomas, and that was when Maria went over and spat on him.

*

Afterwards, Rickard couldn't say for sure how the idea had come up, but it must have been the result of some kind of collective agreement. In spite of all that had been said and done. Maybe there was no other way. Maybe each of them recognized that this way left them with some kind of dignity. They took a decision, but left it to chance. Their tormentors and chance.

Solidarity? thought Rickard.

By his watch, they had less than three minutes left as they drew the lots.

Three matches, one of them broken. Tomas held them, ends hidden, between the thumb and forefinger of his left hand, and the girls took it in turn to pick.

First Anna.

The match was whole. Rickard could see she was finding it hard to conceal her relief. And so was he. If it had been her, he thought . . . if it had been her, then . . .

He excised the thought. It just couldn't be thought to its conclusion. It was too much.

Maria drew her match. She hid it in her hand without looking to see if it was whole or broken, and as she stood there in utter stillness, looking at the others with eyes almost cat-like, Tomas suddenly burst into tears.

Two short, loud sobs and then he regained control.

His sister or his wife, thought Rickard. One of the two. A few seconds elapsed. The monster of silence reappeared, teeth bared.

Maria showed her match. It was unbroken.

Gunilla let out a shriek.

It sounded barely human, thought Rickard.

*

This time there were three of them. The youngest was left outside on guard. They didn't bother locking the door, simply pulled it to. The leader took a few steps forward and stopped under the dingy light bulb.

His eyes scanned his cluster of prisoners. They were now seated in a neat row along the bench. He lit a cigarette and took a drag on it.

'One woman now.'

Several silent seconds passed. Then Gunilla got to her feet, wrenching herself free from Tomas and taking two steps towards the leader.

Then her legs gave way. She collapsed onto the floor in front of him. Not a sound came from her lips. The leader signalled to the men over by the door. One of them left his place and went over to Gunilla. He grabbed her by the arm and started dragging her across the floor. All that could be heard was the faint rasp of her clothes on the concrete.

'Stop it!'

Germund was on his feet. The soldier let go of Gunilla's arm. The leader raised his rifle. Germund walked slowly towards him with his hands stretched well out from his body. What the hell is he doing? was the thought that flashed through Rickard's mind.

'Stay or I shoot!'

Germund did not stop. He leapt at the leader and, in the same instant, there was a volley of shots.

Rat-tat-tat.

Three shots, no more. One of the men by the door had fired them, not the leader. Germund crumpled at the knees and clapped his hand to his shoulder. His white T-shirt was rapidly turning red.

It all seemed to Rickard to happen in a surreal kind of slow motion. The sense of unreality felt almost physically suffocating. The whole sequence of events couldn't have lasted longer than ten or fifteen seconds, but he still felt – sitting there as a stunned observer, but afterwards, too – that it must have gone on for minutes on end.

The leader's order. Gunilla's few steps. Her fall. The dragging and Germund's shout, his confrontational advance across the room.

The leader's warning. Germund's attack and the shots. *Rat-tat-tat.*

And with Germund still on his knees, clutching his bleeding shoulder – and Gunilla still huddled in a ball on the floor, a metre away from him, and the sound of the shots still reverberating in the room – Maria stands up.

'OK,' she says. 'I'm the one.'

She exits the stage with the three men.

They lock the door with care and silence descends again. A different kind of silence. Rickard finds its name at once.

It's called *Shame*.

44

'I was under the impression I'd be talking to Inspector Barbarotti,' said Tomas Winckler, taking a seat on the other side of the desk.

'Something came up,' explained Eva Backman. 'But I'm as familiar with all the details of the case as he is, so it makes no difference.'

'Really?' said Tomas Winckler. He straightened the crease in his smart, pale trousers and put on a pair of minimal rectangular glasses. 'Well, I've no idea why you're all so keen to root around in this.'

'Let me enlighten you,' said Backman. 'It isn't that odd really. We have good reason to believe that Germund Grooth was murdered. And that the same applied to your sister, thirty-five years ago.'

She watched his reaction. She'd hoped for some clear sign, but there was nothing like that. Just a pair of raised eyebrows and a mildly quizzical shake of the head. He tweaked his trouser crease again, it was true, but she didn't want to fall prey to over-interpretation.

'I find that hard to believe,' he said. 'But I realized something like that must be in the pipeline, after I spoke to your colleague. What makes you think they were murdered?'

'I can't go into that,' said Eva Backman, and wondered how

many times she had said that particular phrase. *I can't go into that.* 'But suspicions were raised even after your sister's death, weren't they?' she added.

'Yes, apparently,' said Tomas Winckler with a shrug. 'He investigated it for months, that Sandlin. I talked to him several times, and so did Gunilla.'

'Do you find it strange?' asked Backman. 'That he should investigate it, I mean?'

'I don't know,' said Tomas Winckler, with a faint and fleeting smile. 'It was so long ago. But it was because of what she shouted, I assume. I'm not at all au fait with how the police think and work.'

Perhaps there was a touch of irony in that last sentence, but it wasn't easy to tell. Eva Backman turned the page of her notepad and left a pause. Winckler didn't fill it with any words, but just sat there calmly, waiting.

'You know I spoke to your wife last week?'

'Of course. She told me about it.'

'I'd actually like to start by going back to the events of thirty-five years ago,' said Eva Backman. 'That get-together at Rickard and Anna Berglund's the evening before it happened, to be precise.'

'I understand,' said Tomas Winckler.

Really? thought Backman. And what is it you understand? That we've every reason to look into what happened that evening at Rödåkra vicarage? That something happened there that points forward to the fatality the next day, and that you couldn't be more conscious of it?

Or was it just an innocent remark? She didn't know; once again, it was balanced on a knife-edge. *Either–or.*

'Were you really all such good friends as you made out?' she asked.

'I don't really follow you,' said Winckler. 'Neither Gunilla nor I tried to claim we were particularly good friends in 1975. We saw quite a lot of each other in Uppsala. Rickard and I met when we were called up for military service, and Maria was my sister. But when we met up at Rickard's vicarage, it was a long time since we'd last seen each other.'

'How long?' asked Backman.

'It must have been over a year since all six of us had been together,' replied Winckler after a few moments' thought. 'Gunilla and I left Uppsala in August 1974. I think we had them round to our place sometime that spring . . . 1974, that is. Along with a few other people, not just those four. That must have been the last time in Uppsala.'

Backman made a note, but said nothing. Tomas Winckler cleared his throat and went on.

'We met at Anna and Rickard's that time because four of us happened to be in the Kymlinge area by then. And we were in Gothenburg – it only takes an hour to get there in the car . . . an hour and a half, maybe.'

'So there was no special reason for you all to meet up?'

'No, no reason beyond having dinner together. And having a little outing on the Sunday, before Gunilla and I went back to Gothenburg. Rickard and Anna invited us and we said yes, it was as simple as that.'

Eva Backman nodded. 'So your regular socializing with the other two couples was restricted to a few years in the early seventies? If we're being strictly accurate.'

'Quite right,' agreed Tomas Winckler. 'Between 1969 and 1973, I can confidently say.'

'And it came to an end while you were all still in Uppsala.'

'Yes, I would say it came to an end. We drifted apart, basically.'

'Was there any particular reason for that?'

'For us drifting apart?'

'Yes.'

All at once he seemed unsure of himself. He sat there in silence and stroked his thumb and forefinger over his chin. Adjusted his glasses.

He's wondering what the others might have said, thought Backman. There is something, and he doesn't know whether I'm aware of it or not. Excellent!

Although if it's important, he would have checked that, surely?

Talked to some of the others?

Unless there was something to prevent him having those conversations, that was.

But just counting those who were still alive, her train of thought went on, there were only two of them. His own wife and Rickard Berglund.

Plus Elisabeth Martinsson, if she needed to be included.

'You're hesitating,' said Eva Backman.

Tomas Winckler nodded and then seemed to come to a decision.

'We went on a trip together,' he said. 'In the summer of 1972. After that we didn't see very much of each other.'

'A trip?' said Backman.

'We travelled round the old Eastern Bloc,' Winckler explained. He straightened up in his chair and put a hand to his glasses again.

He must have bought them yesterday, thought Backman. He's not used to them.

'For over a month, in fact,' he said. 'You get very close to each other in circumstances like that. A bit too close sometimes. Yes, maybe that was what happened.'

★

393

He spent about ten minutes telling her about the trip. They bought a bus together and toured around the countries of Eastern Europe. Poland, Czechoslovakia, Hungary, Yugoslavia, Romania and Bulgaria. He and Germund shared the driving, because they were the only ones who'd managed to take the test for the licence. And how poor and wretched they found many of the places they visited in the socialist paradise.

They stayed a week on the Black Sea, went swimming. The roads were terrible, it was quite a gruelling tour, and on the way back they happened to get to Munich on the day of the Olympic Games opening ceremony – the games that had gone down in history for the murderous terrorist attack on seven Israeli athletes; and, well, it had put a lot of strain on the whole group. Six young Swedes, thrown so close together in a world that largely felt quite alien to them all.

Eva Backman located a sheet of paper.

'That bus, was it connected with the travel agency you registered as a business?'

'Yes,' said Tomas Winckler. 'We did trips to Norrland for a few years, but it never really worked financially. We went broke at the start of 1974.'

'But you carried on in the travel business yourself, later?'

'Yes.' He gave a practised smile, vaguely apologetic. 'But on slightly more orderly terms.'

'Oh yes?' said Eva Backman and decided to change tack. 'Can you tell me a bit about Germund and Maria?' she requested.

He coughed and took another few seconds' thinking time. 'They were different,' he said. 'Both of them – unusual, different. She was my sister and I loved her, but I can't say I ever understood her. And Germund wasn't easy, he was an odd customer in some ways. But they suited each other, they really did. There's been a lot of time to think about it since.'

Telling his story had softened him, noted Backman. She hadn't said much while he was relating the bus adventure, just put in a question here and there, but it suddenly felt like an ordinary conversation, not a formal interview. She decided to try to sustain that tone.

'So, how was the reunion at the vicarage?' she asked. 'It must have been quite nice to meet up again, in spite of those earlier tensions?'

'I wouldn't say Gunilla and I went there with particularly high expectations,' replied Tomas Winckler after some thought. 'And I remember we said to each other afterwards, when we went to bed that night, I mean, that it all felt a bit stiff.'

'Stiff?'

'Yes. Or at any rate, it didn't feel like an old gang of friends relaxing into being together again. It felt . . . awkward, somehow. I can't describe it any better than that. Gunilla was pregnant, too, only four months gone admittedly, but she got tired easily. She had a couple of unsuccessful pregnancies behind her, but that time it all went well. Our first daughter was born in February 1976.'

'The two of you have three children, is that right?'

'Yes.'

'But nothing out of the ordinary happened that evening at the vicarage?'

'No. We had dinner and made conversation. I don't know that anyone particularly enjoyed it. Sometimes it just turns out like that, doesn't it, even when people show up with the best will in the world? Things just don't feel right. We'd grown apart, evolved in our different directions, it's the sort of thing that happens.'

Eva Backman pondered. If he did happen to be hiding something, he was making a very good job of it. On the other hand, it wasn't particularly difficult to cast a slightly deceptive veil over something so long ago. If a murder really had been committed the day after that vicarage dinner party, it now fell well and truly under the statute of limitations. And had done for ten years.

'What were you doing on Saturday 25 September?' she asked. Time to abandon the friendly, conversational tone. 'Ten days ago, that is.'

Tomas Winckler put up his hands. 'And if I ask you why you want to know, you'll tell me it's just a routine question, right?'

'Of course,' said Eva Backman. 'So, where were you?'

'I played golf in the morning. Then I went into Gothenburg. I suppose I was back home in Lindås by around ten p.m.'

'I assume you were with people who can confirm this?'

'Yes and no.'

'What does that mean?'

'I played golf with an old friend of mine. Vassunda golf club; I'm a member there. We were done around eleven, I suppose. As regards Gothenburg, I could arrange for someone to vouch for me, but I'd rather not. Not for the time being, anyway.'

'And why's that?' asked Eva Backman, just as she put two and two together.

'It's a woman,' said Tomas Winckler. 'It's difficult. I don't want her put in a tight corner.'

'Or is it in fact that you're worried about being put in a tight corner yourself?'

Tomas Winckler gave a dismissive shake of the head. 'My

wife knows about her. She accepts it. We're modern people. But this woman is, unfortunately, married to a . . . less-than-modern individual.'

That's quite a phrase, thought Eva Backman angrily. Right down to the little pause for effect. He must have practised it in the car on the way here.

A less-than-modern individual.

'Noted,' she said. 'And I assume she'd back you up, if it came to it? Even if the two of you weren't actually together?'

Tomas Winckler took a deep breath and gave DI Backman an anxious look.

'I didn't kill Germund Grooth,' he said. 'I don't think anybody did. Though I could be wrong, I admit.'

Eva Backman nodded.

'Why did he come to visit you in June? That must have come as a surprise. Bringing a woman with him, as well.'

'It certainly did come as a surprise,' agreed Winckler. 'I just said it without thinking, when we ran into each other in Gothenburg. The way you do. Come and see us sometime, you know . . . I naturally didn't expect him to take me up on it.'

'But he did?'

'Yes, he did. But I've already told Inspector Barbarotti about the visit. My wife has told you. I'm sure neither of us has anything to add.'

Eva Backman nodded. 'I'll accept that for now. I only really have two questions left. Firstly, why on earth did you all spread out like that in the forest and each keep to yourselves, that day? None of you could even see any of the others. Doesn't that strike you as strange?'

'No,' replied Tomas Winckler.

'You didn't all happen to have agreed it in advance?'

'Agreed it?'

He didn't seem to understand the question.

'No, definitely not,' he continued, after taking his mobile out of his breast pocket and staring at it for a moment. 'But I remember Sandlin thought it was odd as well. I initially thought he might have a point. But the more I thought about it, the less odd I decided it was. When you go out looking for mushrooms it's stupid if you all go hunting in the same place. You usually start in small groups of two or three, but as you wander round in the forest you kind of automatically pick out your own bit of territory. You all spread out and, after about ten or fifteen minutes, you're on your own, basically. If you think about it, I think you'll see I'm right.'

Eva Backman gave it brief consideration. She couldn't make her mind up one way or the other; he might be right. She shot out her final question.

'Anna Berglund died early this morning. Did you know?'

Once he had left, she sat on in her room for a while, trying to decide whether he had given a sigh of relief or not. He hadn't said anything on receiving the news of Anna Berglund's death, at any rate. He had simply shaken his head a little, and she would have needed a film camera to know for sure.

But the conversation was only in her head and on an audio recording, and sighs were pretty soundless. Especially if you were trying to suppress them. Shoulders rising and falling. A ribcage expanding slightly for no apparent reason.

Not much to lay before a prosecutor, but perhaps it would have been visible on film.

She gave a sigh of her own and rang Barbarotti.

No answer.

She sat there a while longer, then lifted the receiver and called her colleague in Skåne.

45

Sparrow, afterwards.

I shall never talk about it.

They should have killed me while they were at it, but they didn't care. I meant so little that they didn't even bother to kill me. If I ever get the chance to kill one of them, I shall do it. I wouldn't hesitate, I'd delight in doing it.

But I shall never get the chance, of course.

They returned me as agreed and we left Timişoara. I didn't say a word to any of the others and eventually they accepted my silence. When we stopped some hours later – it was still the middle of the night, with no sign of dawn, and Tomas was driving – I wrote them a note: *Take me to the Black Sea. Don't stop anywhere.*

They tried talking to me again, but I curled up under a blanket at the back of the bus. I was in such terrible pain. Germund tried to touch me, but I hit out at him.

He's got a big flesh wound on his shoulder, but I still hit out at him.

When a child is born, it triggers a hormone that makes it forget. I've read about it. It's among the first things that happen and it has a purpose. The experience of being born, of being pushed out of the womb and into the world, is so intense that it can never be compared to anything else. So it has to be forgotten, or it would get in the way of all future experiences.

I wish I could have a dose of that hormone. I lay under my blanket thinking about it, that first night.

Give me oblivion. Wipe those hours from my life.

Wipe the memory of them thrusting into me, one by one. Fumbling and forcing me open with their dirty fingers. Taking me two at a time and putting a gag on me because I bit them. A rag they found in a corner, stinking of petrol.

Pumping me full of their hateful sperm from their dirty pricks and laughing.

Two of them laughed. The other one was ashamed. The leader's face was expressionless throughout, but he nearly throttled me when he finally came. I didn't try to stop him, but he let go of me too soon.

I shall never be the same. Give me that hormone. I don't want to go anywhere near another human being.

I didn't eat anything for two days and nights. We never pitched camp. Without a word, I forced them to drive day and night.

My period started on the way there. I had to get to the Black Sea to wash myself clean.

We get to Mamaia. I walk along the beach alone. I don't speak. I don't meet anyone's eye.

Along and back again, along and back again. A line of tourist hotels, a sandy beach, a sea. Pasty, flabby package-holiday tourists sunbathing. The whole area marked off by barbed-wire fences. No shops; the flabby tourists have all their meals in their hotels.

We don't fit in. We're sleeping in a bus at a campsite, just within the barbed-wire perimeter.

But I don't care. I eat barely anything. Just a few nuts and a bit of fruit. I walk endlessly along the beach, backwards and forwards, from morning to night.

I drink water. I wash myself in the sea. It isn't enough. Sparrow is too badly damaged.

We leave a few days later. We drive for a whole day and cross into Bulgaria. We come to another package-holiday resort.

I walk along another beach. I don't speak. They are worried about me, but they leave me in peace. Germund puts his hand on me sometimes at night and I let him hold it there.

Occasionally he whispers something to me. I let him whisper.

But I don't speak.

I know what they're thinking. She was peculiar before. This hasn't helped.

They're dead right. This hasn't helped.

I walk and walk. Wash and wash myself in the sea.

46

She was on a respirator.

He sat on a chair alongside, watching her. There wasn't much else to do but watch. Nothing that he did or said would have any effect on the course of events. Nothing that was running through his head. Nothing.

It was half past seven, and they wouldn't be bringing her round for hours yet. Not until the next morning, presumably. The operation was complete. It had gone according to plan, said the surgeon, Dr Hemmingsson. Barbarotti had talked to him for twenty minutes, but he still didn't know what *according to plan* meant.

Well, he knew what it meant, but not what it implied. Nobody would know that until the patient emerged from the anaesthetic. Said Hemmingsson.

It had been a relatively small bleed. They had removed the blood and cauterized the blood vessel to seal it off. There was nothing to indicate any major damage.

But it was difficult to make any prognosis, where the brain was concerned. Nor was there much point in trying to do so. It was simplest to let the patient wake up and then see the actual evidence.

Said Hemmingsson.

In some hours' time then. Nurses came in at regular intervals to check her consciousness levels, jabbing their pens into the area round her nails and pressing her hands. They looked at the readouts on the screens. He had spoken to the anaesthetist as well. Her name was Mousavi and she came from Iran. Everything was proceeding normally, Mousavi explained. The next important step was to take the patient off the respirator at the right time.

But in all likelihood not until early the next morning.

Said Mousavi.

He held her hand some of the time. Talked to her. Wondered if she was aware of it at all.

Presumably not; there was no perceptible reaction, and nor could there be, according to medical science. If you couldn't breathe without the help of a respirator, you couldn't communicate with those around you, either.

That was what Gunnar Barbarotti assumed, but it didn't stop him holding her hand or talking to her.

He had talked to the children, too. On the phone. To Sara a couple of times, and to Jenny and Johan. Jenny and Johan above all; it was their mother lying in the bed beside him. Marianne was Lars and Martin's substitute mother too, of course – and Sara's – but it would be foolish to assume there wasn't a difference. They had been living together at Villa Pickford for a year now, but blood is thicker than either water or time.

It went well, he told them. They did the operation, but she might not wake up until tomorrow morning. What would the two of you like to do?

Jenny didn't know, and Johan found it very hard to say anything coherent at all. Barbarotti could hear that he was fighting back the tears.

He suggested they took the first train in the morning. He'd ring again right away if anything happened during the night, of course, but if they got to Sahlgrenska the next morning, that would be soon enough.

Wouldn't it?

But if you want to come right away, that's fine, too.

They decided on the early-morning train.

Lars and Martin would stay with Sara in Kymlinge for now. Try to carry on as normally as possible.

But it might also turn out that Marianne was being brought back to Kymlinge the next day, he added. In that case, Johan and Jenny wouldn't need to come down to Gothenburg at all. If all went well, that was.

He didn't know what *all went well* meant, either.

He felt he didn't really know anything at all.

He surveyed the room where he was sitting. And where Marianne was lying. It was clinically white. The respirator itself was a tangle of tubes, cables and screens monitoring the patient's condition. She had a tube down her throat to help her breathe, another up her nose and another one that seemed to vanish into her stomach somewhere. A fourth was taking her pulse. At short intervals, nurses came in to check all her functions. One of them had explained it all to him in broad outline, but he realized he hadn't been particularly receptive to the information.

Blinds drawn down over the windows. Every so often they asked him if he wanted anything to eat or drink.

No, he didn't want anything.

*

Those words from the Bible came back to him, and his conversation in the taxi with Our Lord.

In the days of your vigour, you walk hand-in-hand with the angel of death.

Trust.

He still didn't know quite where in the Bible that came from, and trust was still as slippery as a bar of soap. Maybe it was only possible to have trust for short periods – a few minutes now and then – to feel a sort of safe but fleeting assurance that everything would turn out all right.

Or, at any rate, that you couldn't influence the course of events and therefore had to leave them in the hands of others.

Of medical science? Of higher powers?

But only for a limited time. The darkness was always waiting around the corner, wasn't that so? Brooding and patient.

But what the hell does it matter how I feel? he thought with sudden fury. Why aren't I concentrating on her? I sit here, wallowing in my own misery. What kind of moronic self-pity is that? Of course I should be putting all my energy into thinking only of Marianne.

He took hold of her hand again. Squeezed it cautiously and tried to persuade himself she could feel it. It would be good if she could, because he realized there was something he very much wanted to say to her. To convey, in some unfathomable but functioning way.

A whole load of things, naturally, but one that was more important than all the rest. It was to do with Germund Grooth, and it felt like a thorn sticking into his flesh.

The fact that he'd had the whole weekend to iron out the results of his tactlessness, but had failed. The fact that he'd felt jealous of someone who was dead, who'd had a relationship with her years earlier, long before he himself came into her life. The fact that he'd virtually held her to account for it. It was absurd. Moronic had been the right choice of word.

When he talked to her on the phone on his way home from Gothenburg on Friday evening, he was under the impression the problem had been dealt with, or would be dealt with as soon as he got home – but it hadn't happened that way. Somehow it had hung there between them the whole weekend. Simply because they hadn't talked about it. He hadn't brought up the subject of Germund Grooth and nor had Marianne.

But then it hadn't been Marianne's business to bring it up, had it? Of course not. The ball had been in his court.

Nor had he mentioned it to Eva Backman. He hadn't told her his wife might be able to provide a few useful pieces of information about the university lecturer they were putting all their efforts into nailing down.

Because Marianne had been in a relationship with him for a year.

That was preposterous of him, too. You could hardly think of a better character witness, and wasn't that what lay at the heart of this matter? Germund Grooth's character. It could well be. Its importance certainly shouldn't be downplayed.

And now this witness, his own wife, was lying here in a sterile hospital room, robbed of the power of speech as the result of a stroke. Would she ever be able to speak again?

A sudden wave of despair came washing over him, and he rested his head on the edge of the bed and wept.

A nurse came in. She scanned her machines, and Marianne and him, for a while. She pinched the patient's fingers a few times and then left them in peace.

47

They left the Black Sea on 16 August and started the drive back.

Right across Bulgaria. All the signs were in Cyrillic script, making it hard to navigate.

And the roads were no better than in Romania. They generally covered no more than 300–350 kilometres a day, and their transit visas expired while they were still in Sofia.

Rickard had stopped keeping a diary after Timişoara, but Anna continued with a kind of dogged earnestness. She took pictures and made notes. She had that series of articles to think about, of course, it wasn't just an end in itself. They didn't talk to each other very much and they didn't make love.

The idea of making love while Maria was with them seemed impossible. While she was lying there at the back of the bus, mute and paralysed. For the first time since reaching puberty, Rickard had no sexual desire. It was as if all that now felt forbidden, taboo, and he imagined it was the same for the whole lot of them.

Germund had got his wound looked at by a tourist doctor in Mamaia. The doctor asked how it had happened, but they gave no details. Maybe he understood, even so, and maybe he didn't want to know. It was going to be all right, anyway, it was only a flesh wound. Germund had been lucky, amazingly lucky. Two of the bullets had missed entirely, the third only grazed him.

The damage done to Maria was different. Its healing process was one that lay beyond all prognoses. She hadn't spoken since what happened in Timişoara and she seemed to want nothing to do with them. Not even Germund.

Gunilla wrote her letters. She sat at the front of the bus, filling page after page of her notepad. She put them in envelopes and gave them to Maria.

Maria accepted them, but Rickard wasn't aware of them ever being read. Gunilla certainly didn't receive any answers in return.

Gunilla was the one Maria had sacrificed herself for. Rickard tried to imagine how that must feel for her. She would have been raped by four men, but escaped scot-free because Maria took her place.

For some reason. It was impossible to comprehend, but then the whole course of events in Timişoara was impossible to comprehend. It was two hours out of their lives, for each one of them, and it seemed to have changed everything. Not just for Maria, but for all of them. They had passed through some kind of portal, some membrane of evil, and on the other side the world looked different. It would never be the same.

But it was worst for Maria, of course. Different, in a way they simply couldn't imagine.

They had discussed going to the police. No, not discussed. Someone had mentioned it – maybe Tomas – but Maria had shaken her head. Rickard remembered it; once the ignition key had been turned and they were driving out through the gates, she had shaken her head and some of the others had joined in. Not the police. Wasn't that exactly what those men were: police?

Maria had passed them a piece of paper. Later that first night. *Don't stop anywhere.*

They didn't stop anywhere. Or only for as long as it took to buy provisions. It was a miracle the bus held together.

But they got to Mamaia in two days and two nights and there, finally, was the sea.

After a day and a half in Sofia they continued westwards, making for Skopje in Yugoslavia. On the winding and unbelievably bad mountain roads they started getting punctures. They changed a wheel every day, watched by a flock of laughing children from the surrounding mountain villages. The children were begging for chewing gum, but they had long since given it all away. As soon as they reached the next little town, the first thing they had to do was find a little repair place that could mend their spare tyre overnight. Every day it was the same. *Vulk* was the only word they needed. People were used to punctures in those parts.

From then on, they often decided to spend the night at a hotel rather than in the bus. It cost virtually nothing and they got dinner and breakfast for a pittance, too. Rickard knew he would always remember those little towns that all looked interchangeable; of course there couldn't have been more than three or conceivably four of them before they reached Skopje, but time and place felt unreal and elusive there. It was the same with the low-key palaver at the border post after their visa had run out. They paid a few Deutschmarks and a couple of packets of cigarettes and were allowed to drive through.

411

As if the situation, the sense of what had happened in Timişoara still hanging in the air, *demanded* it. As if Maria's silence infected the others with silence. Or forced them into it. Solidarity, a hitherto unknown form of the concept.

They barely spoke to each other in that time, no more than was strictly necessary; sometimes it almost felt to him as if language itself had become something shameful, something to avoid using.

Yes, that was how things stood. Rickard tried to strike up some kind of conversation with God a few times, but soon discovered there was nothing but silence from that quarter, either. As if He had observed Maria's sacrifice and preferred to stay aloof for now.

We've got to get back home, thought Rickard. Nothing can be even remotely normal until we're back home.

They reached Skopje, still bearing the scars of its earth-quake. They drove through Sarajevo and Dubrovnik, and on 24 August they left the Eastern Bloc behind them at beautiful Poreč on the Istrian peninsula. Sheer cliffs plunging straight down into the Adriatic; crystal-clear water, but they only stopped for an hour to swim. They drove into Trieste in Italy, and Rickard felt a kind of relief come over him. Life suddenly seemed comprehensible again. All at once he *understood* what was around him.

Or he imagined he did, at any rate. Perhaps the dynamic between the travellers aboard the bus improved too, but it wasn't by much. Maria still wasn't talking. On arrival in Tolmezzo in the Italian Alps, the others decided to go out for dinner to a rather upmarket restaurant they saw. It was one last attempt to restore normality, but it wasn't particularly successful. Germund and Maria didn't go with them, and when Tomas tried to talk through what had happened, nobody else wanted to. Words still felt too uncomfortable. They came to an agreement of sorts – that was about all. Never to tell anybody what happened in Timișoara. Not a soul. It felt an obvious decision to make, and they all thought so.

They left the restaurant after less than two hours.

Early in the morning of 26 August they drove through Munich, where the opening ceremony of the Olympic Games was to be held that day. It was still two weeks until seven Israeli sportsmen would be murdered and the air was bright and clear.

They spent the night at a campsite outside the university town of Göttingen in Lower Saxony, and late in the evening of 27 August they just caught the last ferry from Puttgarden to Rødby in Denmark. They drove more or less non-stop through Denmark, crossed the strait of Øresund on the Helsingør–Helsingborg ferry and half a day later they were home in Uppsala.

It was midnight on 28 August. They had been away for thirty-seven days. For the past week they had spent virtually all their time in the bus. That had hardly been the plan, and Rickard felt that what he wished more than anything was to sleep for a week in his own bed and wake up to something else.

As for Anna, what she felt and wished were a closed book to him. But he hoped they would start talking to each other again.

48

Eva Backman didn't get hold of Barbarotti until nine-thirty in the evening.

He'd switched off his mobile, he explained, because he was at Sahlgrenska hospital in Gothenburg.

'Sahlgrenska?' queried Backman. 'Why are you at Sahlgrenska?'

'It's Marianne,' said Barbarotti. And then there was a long pause before he was able to get the words out and tell her about the stroke.

Backman's pause was, if anything, even longer. They listened to one another's breathing for what seemed like an eternity.

Marianne. Stroke. This was information that simply refused to find a hold in her brain. You didn't get strokes when you were only . . . What age was she? Forty-five? It was the sort of thing that happened in the autumn of your years, not in the middle of your life. Not Marianne, it simply wasn't possible. Was it?

'Oh my God,' she said at last. 'I didn't know . . .'

'They operated,' said Barbarotti, 'but she hasn't woken up yet. They're probably not going to bring her round until first thing tomorrow.'

'How did it happen?' asked Backman. 'I just can't believe it.'

'An aneurysm,' said Barbarotti. 'A little blood vessel bursting in her brain.' He had to take another pause before he could go on and, when he did, she could tell from his voice that he was finding it hard to keep things together. 'It can happen any time apparently. To absolutely anybody. She was at work and she lost consciousness . . . Yes, that was how it went. That was how it went,' he repeated for some reason.

'It sounds mad,' said Backman. 'Has there been . . .? How will it affect her, I mean – what do they think?'

He cleared his throat. 'They can't say anything until she wakes up. So I'm here waiting.'

'You must be in shock,' said Eva Backman.

'You're right there,' said Barbarotti. 'I've been in a state of shock for over seven hours now. But this isn't about me, it's about Marianne.'

'Yes, it's about Marianne,' agreed Eva Backman and suddenly felt existence tilt and sway. A moment's mental earthquake; slightly delayed, she assumed, as a minute had passed since the epicentre. She sat down, thinking that she ought not to be particularly surprised. Neither by the earthquake nor by the delay. Barbarotti wasn't saying anything, but she could hear his breathing.

'How are the children?' she asked.

'Johan and Jenny are coming down first thing tomorrow,' he said. 'Well, it's not quite definite. Sara's with them for now.'

Eva Backman nodded, then wondered why she'd done it, given that they were on the phone. But words suddenly felt too insipid. What was there to say? What on earth was there to add?

'Aren't the doctors giving you any information?' she asked. 'They must have told you something, surely?'

'Not much,' said Barbarotti. 'But it wasn't a major bleed, anyway, and they say the operation went well. They tell me there's every reason for optimism, but I don't know . . . Hang on, a nurse has just come in and she wants a word with me. I shall have to go.'

'Take care of yourself,' said Eva Backman. 'I shall be thinking of you all, tonight.'

'Thanks,' said Gunnar Barbarotti.

She sat there in the corner of the sofa for a good while before she could bring herself to move. She felt as if the phone call had driven some sharp object right into her. A big, rusty nail. To think . . . To think that life could be so horribly fragile. That anything could happen, at any time.

And to anybody. Manifestly. She clenched her fists and closed her eyes. Images of Marianne danced on her retina. Especially that dinner they'd had at Villa Pickford a fortnight before, with the seven teenagers in attendance. There'd been no signs then, had there?

No, none at all, she told herself, and that was probably the scariest thing of all. The fact that it happened without warning. It just happened. Wonderful, warm, generous Marianne.

Her next thought was that there was no point meeting trouble halfway. Marianne was alive, after all. She might wake up and be her normal self again? Or suffer only minor after-effects.

But what might those be, if so? She had no idea. I know nothing about this subject, Eva Backman had to admit to herself. What can happen after a stroke.

Parts of the brain must have been affected, however small the bleed had been – anyone could work that out. But could other parts take over the function of those that had suffered damage? She felt she'd read something along those lines, and fairly recently. The brain's ability to self-repair, especially if it was a relatively young person who—

The front door opened and Jörgen and Kalle made their entrance. Dumping their sports bags in the hall, they shouted hello. The evening's unihockey training session was over.

Backman extracted herself from the sofa corner and took a swift decision not to tell them anything. Better to wait until the morning, when she would know more. Better to pull herself together a bit first. But idle chat round the kitchen table was more than she could face.

'There's bread and a pasta salad in the kitchen,' she told them. 'I need to put in an hour's work, so you can get it for yourselves, can't you? Viktor's sleeping over at the Zetterbergs'.'

'We'll manage just fine, Mother dear,' said Kalle and gave her a bear hug.

'Ow!' protested Eva Backman. She left her sons to it and shut herself in the bedroom.

It doubled up as a study, an arrangement they'd put in place when she was still married, and the desk was still where it had been, two years later.

Everything looked just like before the divorce, in fact; she found it a lot harder to function in the house than she did at the flat in Pampas, and that was hardly surprising. Not surprising at all; her marriage to Ville was preserved in every coffee cup, every flower on the wallpaper, every goddamned stain on the wooden floor in front of the sink. But in a couple

HÅKAN NESSER

of years it would be over, she thought, and there was really nothing to complain about. At least she . . . at least she hadn't had a stroke.

She knew it wasn't going to be easy to sleep. Not after this. Not with Marianne and Barbarotti at Sahlgrenska; the tremors of the earthquake were still vibrating inside her.

Better to devote herself to something meaningful and wait for sleep to call, she decided. Or for him to ring with further news.

Although he wouldn't do that, of course. If there was any news from the hospital, the children would be first on his list. Johan and Jenny above all, but the others, too.

No, there would be no more phone calls with Barbarotti this evening or tonight, Eva Backman was clear about that. She found her briefcase and switched on the desk lamp. She fished out Sandlin's files, but then had a better idea.

She went out to the kitchen and her indoor-hockey stars. She made herself a pot of tea, told them she didn't want to be disturbed and returned to her desk.

Right, let's concentrate, she thought. Let's put Gunnar and Marianne in a dark corner of our head and focus on Gåsastupan.

No, not dark, it would have to be dimly lit, that corner, and have plenty of padding.

She started with the map. That was where her thoughts had led her when she was out in the forest that morning, anyway.

To be more precise, she would try to get a proper fix on the positions of the mushroom hunters, that September Sunday thirty-five years ago. She wasn't exactly sure what purpose it

418

would serve, but now she had put that question mark into her skull, it would be just as well to straighten it out.

She had no more than sipped her tea when it struck her there was not just one question mark involved, but several.

Could she rely on Sandlin's map, for example?

Not 100 per cent, she supposed, but maybe enough to draw some real conclusions from it, even so. Presuming . . . presuming, on the one hand, that Maria Winckler really had been murdered but, on the other, that it wasn't by common consent – a thought that had flitted through her mind a few days before, she remembered, or was it just that morning? – well then, perhaps she could make the assumption that everyone except the murderer had put their cross in roughly the right place. *Where were you when you heard her cry out?*

Couldn't she?

She studied the map and considered. Cross number one indicated Maria, out at the cliff edge; the rest were scattered in an uneven semicircle to the south and south-west of the crag. One of them – Anna Berglund's – a little to the east; as Eva Backman looked at the map and compared it with her mental image of the terrain in real life, she thought it looked pretty natural. They had come through the forest from the south, fanning out, without any of them necessarily being aware of the overall pattern, but it did look a touch regular. They had slowly made their way north, up onto the high ground; the cliff edge itself was no more than fifteen or twenty metres wide. Further to the east it was also fairly steep, but to the west it flattened out more. She held the image in her mind and calculated lines of equidistance on the map. If the group had wanted to continue its forward movement, it should have been bearing left, towards the west, so that it bypassed the highest ground.

But they never got that far. The sheer drop had put a stop to all further movement.

In the commentary accompanying the map, Sandlin had worked out the distances between the various positions. It was hard to know whether it was of any real significance, but the person who seemed to be closest to Maria Winckler was Elisabeth Martinsson, about 100 metres away, directly to the south of her. Then Germund Grooth, about 150 metres away and a bit further east. The furthest away, about 300 metres and furthest to the west, was Rickard Berglund.

She pondered this, noting that at least it seemed to fit with when they each got to the edge of the drop. Elisabeth Martinsson first, closely followed by Germund Grooth. The fact that Rickard Berglund seemed to have got there a little ahead of Tomas Winckler naturally didn't necessarily mean anything.

Which was also the conclusion Inspector Sandlin had come to in his commentary.

But the big question – if there really was one big question amid this hotchpotch, thought Eva Backman despondently – was of course whether any of them had marked their position wrongly. Put their cross 100 or 200 metres from Maria, when they were in fact right up there with her on the edge.

Where they pushed her over, before seeking cover behind a clump of spruces or something, and then joined the shocked band of other mushroom hunters when the time was right.

Mushroom hunters. Really? Eva Backman hadn't found reference to anybody finding so much as a single chanterelle. But in light of what subsequently happened, maybe that wasn't a particularly vital question.

She sighed, drank some tea and read through Sandlin's comments. It didn't take her long to see that he'd come to the same conclusions as she had. Or, rather, to the same further set of question marks. As each group member had been asked to mark their position on an empty map, not knowing where the others had put theirs, the murderer's tactic would have involved a certain risk. Even though the sightlines in the forest weren't very good, it wasn't just one massive thicket, and putting a random cross that wouldn't be too close to the other five – position unknown – well, it was undeniably chancy.

But it wasn't impossible to pull off. Especially if the person was able to observe which directions the others came running from when they heard Maria scream. Crouching there behind a barrier of spruce branches, say.

Not impossible at all.

In Inspector Sandlin's view.

In Inspector Backman's view, thirty-five years later.

She sighed, had some more tea and let her thoughts return for a moment to Sahlgrenska hospital.

She spent the next half hour on other things that had arisen during the day.

Tomas Winckler's account, for example. She turned on the recorder and listened to a few minutes of it, but realized it was so fresh in her mind that she didn't need to carry on. So she switched off the tape and leant back in her chair with her feet up on the desk instead.

What had he actually told her?

That he was having a relationship with a married woman and it didn't bother his wife. So he had claimed, anyway. Not very nice, thought Eva Backman, but scarcely criminal.

His alibi for Saturday hinged on that woman. Maybe she would support him unconditionally, regardless of whether they'd been together or not. Maybe she was prepared to lie for his sake.

But what motive could Tomas Winckler have had for killing Germund Grooth?

What motive could he have had for killing his own sister, thirty-five years earlier?

I haven't the faintest idea, thought Backman, drinking more tea. And that story of his about the group of them, how did that fit in, and was it important? There could be something lurking there, she thought. The group had broken up after that tour of Eastern Europe in . . . what had he said – the summer of 1972? That was three years before the incident at Gåsaklyftan, if so.

That dinner party at the vicarage hadn't been a great success, according to him. The old gang had grown apart, their Uppsala days were long gone. But was it something more? Backman asked herself. Was he downplaying the whole thing? Admitting the mood hadn't been great, to conceal something considerably worse?

Could that be the case?

Speculation, she thought. Pure speculation.

But when you have nothing concrete to go on, what else is left?

Maybe I had it right from the very beginning, she told herself. One slipped and the other jumped. Why am I racking my poor old brains over it?

Oh yes, so I don't have to think about Sahlgrenska.

She turned her thoughts to Lund instead. They'd drawn a blank there, too. She had rung DI Ribbing, only to hear that Kristin Pedersen had simply failed to show up at the appointed time. They had called her repeatedly on her Copenhagen number, but there was no reply.

Perhaps it wasn't just a blank, in fact, Eva Backman corrected herself. Perhaps it was something more? Something significant. Anyway her colleagues down in Skåne were going to try again in the morning, presumably with the help of the police on the other side of the Sound.

But they had spoken to a couple of Grooth's university colleagues. A Professor Lindskog and a lecturer by the name of Törnell. They had both known and worked with Grooth for many years, and both basically confirmed the picture of him that various others had already painted.

A loner. Competent and unexceptionable in his work alongside them in the physics department, but not the sort of person you got to know more closely or socialized with. Grooth had preferred keeping himself to himself, and that sort of thing raised no eyebrows in the academic world.

Ribbing had sent over the recordings of the interviews, but she hadn't found time to listen to them. She would make do with his summary on the phone for now.

Well, that was about it, thought Eva Backman with a glance at the time. Quarter to eleven, and her eyelids were starting to droop, after all. She put away Sandlin's files, skimped on her evening toilette and was soon in bed.

The hazy, barely comprehensible images of Barbarotti and Marianne in a room at Sahlgrenska came back as soon as she turned off the bedroom light. With a mighty effort she restored them to their dimly lit corner and devoted her last waking thoughts to the case.

There's some hidden business here. There has to be. Business we've come nowhere near to yet. That's it.

49

Gunilla bumped into Anna at the checkout in Lundequist's. They were both buying books, Anna some kind of course material and she a Georges Simenon paperback; she was getting it as a birthday present for a new friend, a girl on her Spanish course.

It was Saturday 21 October, and it struck them both that they hadn't actually seen each other for a couple of months. There was a slight sense of shame in their surprise. On Gunilla's part, anyway.

And it was presumably the slight sense of shame that made her ask Anna if she wanted to go for a coffee. At Güntherska just round the corner, maybe?

To compound her shame, she realized she was hoping Anna would say no. But she didn't. She looked at her watch and said yes. She had an hour to spare before she was meeting Rickard, so why not?

'How are you both?' she asked once they both had their coffee and cinnamon bun in front of them.

'Fine,' answered Anna.

That was the problem with Anna, thought Gunilla. She never took the initiative in a conversation. You had to keep it going yourself. Put new logs on the fire. If you didn't start on some subject or another, ask questions or make assertions, the conversation soon lapsed.

It could feel like a mild reproach, she sometimes thought. Because it was hard to cope with those who wouldn't speak; Tomas had told her that during her own difficult period last year. Those months at Ulleråker, that time of strain and silence.

It feels as if you're holding me responsible for everything, he said to her at one point. It isn't fair.

It wasn't as bad as all that, neither in her own specific case when she was ill, nor with Anna Berglund in general, but uncommunicative people did hold some kind of advantage, it was undeniable.

'And how's your course going?'

She gestured to the book Anna had taken out of its plastic bag and placed beside her coffee cup on the table.

'All right.'

'You must be in your last year now?'

Anna nodded and bit into her bun.

'I've started a course in Spanish,' Gunilla said, to keep the information flowing. 'I enjoy getting to grips with a new language – you learn so much at the start. And Rickard's studies are going well, too?'

'Oh yes. Have you heard anything of Maria?'

A question, at least. Gunilla shrugged. 'Not much. Tomas tries to keep in touch, but he doesn't get very far. They are as they are, she and Germund. And what happened didn't help, of course . . . Tomas and I have talked a bit about whether all six of us should get together sometime. But maybe it would be best to leave it a bit?'

Anna nodded.

'I read your articles about the trip in *Dagens Nyheter*,' Gunilla went on. 'It was very well written. And well done you, for being able to face writing them up, what with . . . well, what with everything.'

'If you're going to be a journalist, you have to be able to write.'

'Yes, there is that, of course.'

There was a moment's silence.

'Tomas has got the bus sorted out, anyway. He's doing the first trip up to Norrland next weekend.'

'So I heard,' said Anna. 'Rickard told me.'

'We'll just have to see how it goes. He reckons he'll go up every other weekend. If Germund joined in, they could go every week. Until Christmas, that is. It would be great to bring in a bit of money for the company.'

'The company, yes,' said Anna.

Gunilla waited, but there was nothing more.

'He's not doing the Eastern Europe tour, of course. Next summer, I mean. But nobody was expecting he would, presumably?'

Anna shook her head. Gunilla sipped her coffee and decided she would keep quiet for a bit, too. She leant back in her chair and gazed out of the window. It had started to rain. People were hurrying past on the pavement, looking glum. Saturday stress, she thought. Irritable people who had only come into town to spend money on things they imagined they needed. A mother with a pushchair swathed in a plastic rain cover stopped right outside the window, picking up her screaming child to try to find out what was wrong with it. That was how the scene looked from inside anyway, as she turned the child this way and that before restoring it to its plastic bubble.

Could have been me, thought Gunilla suddenly, and noted to her surprise that she experienced no pang of pain. If nothing else that had happened lately had made much sense, at least she could now look at a baby without that tightness in her stomach. Especially when the baby was bawling and needy.

'I've got to go now,' said Anna. 'I remembered there's something I've got to do before I meet Rickard.'

'OK,' said Gunilla. 'Think I'll sit here for a bit longer and wait for the rain to ease off. Let's stay in touch, shall we, and see if we can arrange a reunion? It would be nice to see your photos.'

'You can give me a ring,' said Anna and left the coffee shop.

Gunilla looked at her watch. They had barely been there fifteen minutes.

But there was no reunion. The autumn months passed. Gunilla and Tomas discussed the subject once or twice, but each time something else got in the way. And they knew that the onus was on them. If Tomas and Gunilla didn't take the initiative, nobody else would, either.

But they did manage four trips to Norrland in the course of the term. Tomas drove three times, Germund once. Gunilla went too, on the last of Tomas's trips. They spent the night at a fairly basic hotel in Luleå. Their combined total of passengers over the four trips was seventy-eight. The price was about 60 per cent of what it cost on the train with a student discount; everyone who went was happy with it, but the bus could carry fifty and the profit was very modest. Tomas had calculated that they would need at least thirty passengers on each trip for it to be cost-effective. Ideally they would make a run every weekend, so people knew they could just hop on the bus when it got to Friday afternoon. And that they'd be back in Uppsala by late Sunday evening.

But it was only a trial term, of course. In the spring they would do more advertising and really put their backs into it. Maybe try to find a third driver, too; Germund hadn't seemed particularly enthralled at the prospect of driving up and down the E4 every other week, and Tomas said he had a couple of likely names in mind.

It was very difficult to know how to approach Germund and Maria, really. To start with, when they got back to Uppsala at the end of August, it seemed only natural to leave them to themselves, in view of what had happened – but gradually, as they got into November and December, Gunilla, at least, began to feel it was odd that they were no longer meeting up. Maria was Tomas's sister, after all, and they'd assumed – or she had, anyway – that the upset of events in Timișoara would start to subside.

Because that was the point of their tacit agreement, wasn't it? They wouldn't mention it, and it would fade away.

And perhaps it was doing so, but the problem was that she didn't know. She'd tried ringing Maria for a chat, in September and again in October, but had never got an answer. She wasn't even sure whether Maria had started speaking again or was still electing to stay mute. And if you weren't speaking, you naturally didn't answer the phone.

But she hadn't seen her even once, all autumn, and when she happened to run into Germund and asked him, he just told her Maria was OK.

She had written a letter, too, like she'd done on the bus, but had received no reply that way, either.

'Are we even sure she's still in town?' she asked Tomas one

day in early December, and he nodded. So he was keeping tabs on her.

That was a phrase of his. Keeping tabs. Gunilla didn't really know what it meant, but Tomas clearly didn't want to talk about it. Maybe he was meeting up with Maria and not telling her. She couldn't tell – nor could she decide if it was because he felt guilty that he didn't want to talk to her about his sister. But it was all the same to her; she had her own guilt problems, and they were quite enough to cope with.

Because the fact was that Maria had offered herself up in her place on that disgusting evening in Timişoara, and Gunilla knew that if she hadn't, she herself would have fallen apart. If she'd had to go with those soldiers for an hour, she would have been an in-patient at Ulleråker for good. She had Maria to thank for the fact that she was still functioning at all.

It was as simple as that.

But she couldn't help feeling resentful about it. Why should she feel guilty, when the guilt lay with those men, and them alone?

There was no question that Maria's action had been self-sacrificing, but did it have to mean Gunilla was obliged to feel grateful? For all eternity?

Of course not, she would think, when she tried to look at it through clear eyes – and to be fair, Maria had never painted it in those colours. She had never uttered a sound on the subject. Or written a word. Nobody had, it was all inside her own head. And it wasn't easy to get rid of.

Especially as Maria had been inaccessible since it happened. Totally and utterly inaccessible. All the way back in the bus, and ever since.

It's the things that stay unexpressed that are the most intractable, thought Gunilla. If we can't put them into words, they can never be resolved.

Every now and then through those autumn months she would wake in the middle of the night and not be able to get back to sleep. She would lie there in their swish double bed from Asko Finncenter, staring out into the darkness and trying to think about it. No longer with those really black feelings from her time in Ulleråker, it was true, but still with a deep sense of unease.

No more than three and a half years had passed since she left home in Karlstad, but it felt so very far away.

Why does it keep happening? she would ask herself. What does it mean, this succession of misfortunes?

The suicide of a former fiancé? The loss of two babies? Ulleråker? The Timişoara incident?

It's all happening too fast, she thought. I can't live like this.

Germund and Maria? Where had they got to?

And Rickard and Anna, had they vanished, too? Tomas and Rickard met up occasionally, she knew that. But never here at the flat in Sibyllegatan, like it used to be. Always in town, at a cafe or student club. That was how things were now, and it felt as if . . . well, what?

On the other hand, they had a new circle to socialize with. From the very start she'd got on well with Britt-Marie and Karin, two other girls on her Spanish course. Britt-Marie was the one who'd be getting Simenon's *The Snow Was Dirty* for her birthday. The two of them became regulars at Sibyllegatan. They both had boyfriends; Karin's was an American named

Dave, who'd left the States so he wouldn't be sent to Vietnam, and Britt-Marie was with a standard Swedish boy called Jörgen, who came from Hammerdal in Jämtland.

Tomas also did his bit, bringing home various new people. Ulrika and Dennis, for instance, who lived just a few streets away from them in Luthagen and had a kid and a dog, even though they were only twenty-one and twenty-two. The dog was an enormous and very placid Leonberger that answered to the name of Johansson, the kid a one-year-old boy called Torsten.

The first time Gunilla babysat Torsten was in mid-January 1973, and that was the evening she realized she'd got over the sadness of her two pregnancies. She'd lost Lucy and Aurora, but these were not traumas that had marked her for life, after all. Thank goodness.

She remembered those thoughts she'd had six months earlier about the ice in the ground starting to thaw. There were signs that the process might now be complete.

It was January 1973, too, but right at the end of the month, when the six travellers to the East finally came together again. It was at Sibyllegatan – where else? – and it had become more or less unavoidable by then. Not least because of the state of the finances at Quality Travel Co. Ltd.

50

He awoke with a start.

Three women in white were standing there looking at him, and for a moment he didn't know where he was.

But then it came back to him. He must have lain down on the empty bed next to Marianne's at some point during the night, because that was where he was now. In a foetal position, with his hands tucked between his knees. Someone had put a blue hospital blanket over him. He swung his legs over the side of the bed and sat up. Everything went black for a moment but he recovered himself. He wiped his hand over his chin and cheeks; he could feel he'd been dribbling in his sleep. It was a long time since he had felt so unsavoury. Like some old drunk after a night in a ditch.

'I'm glad you had a bit of sleep,' said one of the figures in white. He recognized her then; it was Dr Mousavi, the anaesthetist.

'Er . . . yes?' said Barbarotti.

'We're going to wake your wife now,' Mousavi explained. 'She's almost regained consciousness of her own accord, and that's a good sign. But we'll have to ask you to leave the room while we do it.'

The two nurses at her side nodded. Barbarotti rubbed his eyes with his fists.

'You can have a wash and brush up outside and grab a bite of breakfast. We'll need half an hour or so. We'll call you when you can come in again.'

He got to his feet and studied Marianne. He couldn't see any obvious change, but was sure they knew what they were talking about. He stroked her arm and went out into the corridor before his feelings got the better of him.

A glance at his watch showed him it was a quarter to six in the morning.

It took them three-quarters of an hour. He had time for a shower and two cups of black coffee. He couldn't face anything to eat.

He wondered about ringing home to Kymlinge, but decided to wait. Silly to wake them if he didn't have any news, he thought. The first train down to Gothenburg was at eight, so calling just after seven would give them time enough.

Dr Mousavi came out just after half past six, and Gunnar Barbarotti realized he was able to read the situation in her features in the half second before she said anything.

Marianne was alive.

That was something.

And presumably more than that.

'You can go in to her now,' Dr Mousavi told him. 'She's breathing for herself, and she's conscious. But she's terribly tired, so don't expect her to start talking to you. She needs to sleep, but we've taken her off the respirator.'

'And that means . . .?' asked Barbarotti.

'That means everything appears to have gone well. All vital functions are working, and we haven't detected any serious

434

after-effects. But complications can arise and she'll need a long period of rehabilitation.'

'I understand,' said Barbarotti.

'One more thing,' said Mousavi. 'These patients tend to be quite irritable. All she needs at the moment is sleep. She doesn't remember anything of what happened, and you won't be getting any immediate displays of affection.'

She looked at him over the top of her brown-tinted glasses and gave him a pat on the arm.

'It doesn't matter,' said Barbarotti. 'Thanks. Thank you so very, very much.'

Then he went in to see her, with the tears streaming down his face. The two nurses smiled at him, but he didn't notice.

He spoke to Sara.

Then he spoke to Johan and Jenny, telling them they wouldn't need to come down to Gothenburg as their mother was very likely to be moved back to Kymlinge hospital that afternoon.

'Is she going to get better?'

'I think so,' said Barbarotti. 'There are no signs to indicate she won't. But it's going to take time.'

They were both so glad that they didn't know whether to laugh or cry, and before he gave way to the same thing himself, he suggested maybe they should go to school as usual, knowing that was exactly what their mother would have said.

They promised to think about it.

After that he spoke to Lars and Martin, each of them separately, and then to Marianne's sister, and to her brother, whom he'd also rung late the previous evening, and finally – because Marianne was still asleep – he called Eva Backman.

'Please say it went well,' begged Eva Backman.

'It went well,' said Gunnar Barbarotti.

'Thank God,' said Eva Backman. 'How well?'

'It's too soon to know,' Barbarotti told her. 'Time will tell. But she's conscious and she knows who I am. When she's not asleep, that is, but she sleeps all the time.'

'Well, you can thank your creator you've still got her,' said Eva Backman.

'I do, every single second,' Barbarotti assured her. 'We may be able to come back to Kymlinge this afternoon. They're short of beds down here. But she'll have to stay in the rehabilitation unit for a few weeks.'

'Of course,' said Eva Backman. 'Do you know . . .?'

'Yes?'

'Do you know, I've never been so scared in my whole life as I was last night. I woke up at three o'clock and couldn't get back to sleep. It was as if it had happened to my own children. If there'd . . . no, I don't know.'

They were both reduced to silence and Barbarotti had a distinct feeling Our Lord was looking down on them from his puffy cloud. Or on him, at any rate.

'Yes, I know,' he said. 'I remember.'

'Pardon?' said Eva Backman.

'Sorry, I wasn't talking to you,' said Barbarotti.

He stroked her cheek with the backs of his fingers. She opened her eyes and looked at him.

She parted her lips slightly as well. As if she was trying to say something. But no sound emerged, of course.

'We're going back to Kymlinge soon,' he said. 'In about an hour, the doctors say.'

She closed her eyes and gave a deep sigh. He took hold of

her hand, squeezing it gently, and thought he could feel a slight pressure in return.

'I know you're not up to talking,' he said. 'But you can hear what I'm saying, can't you?'

He thought he detected a little nod.

'Anyway I want to tell you that I love you and that I shall do everything to protect you from now on.'

She opened one eye and closed it again.

'We shall live together until we're a hundred, and I won't waste a minute of it.'

She sighed.

'You won't have to lift a finger in the house until Christmas. I've talked to the kids and we're going to work out a rota. All you've got to do is rest and get better. We'll look after you day and night. Can you hear what I'm saying?'

She smiled.

51

There is a special providence in the fall of a sparrow.

I think it was Shakespeare who wrote that, and he's wrong. There is no providence whatsoever in my fall. Twice my life has imploded – yes, that's exactly the right word, *imploded* – the first time when I hit my head as a child and my personality changed, the second when I was gang-raped by four soldiers in Timişoara.

I'm glad I elected not to speak. It was an instinctive reaction, a defence mechanism. If you don't speak, you don't get spoken to, either. Maybe to start with, but after a while they give up.

I just wanted to be left alone, and I still do. I especially don't want to see any of the others. If there's one thing I can't bear, it's the urge to go over it all again and analyse what happened. I'd be obliged to paddle around in their clumsy concern and supposed attempts to set things to rights. To help them get in touch with their own convulsions. It simply doesn't work; they just sat there like stupid mice in a trap, trembling and petrified and feeling sorry for themselves. Germund and I were the only ones who took action. Who offered any kind of resistance and tried to achieve anything.

I feel ashamed for them, have done ever since. They would never understand it and I'm not going to bother trying to explain it to them. I don't want to see them again. I know it's not going to be feasible to avoid them entirely, but let it subside first. Let them get a bit of distance, too.

Germund understands this without the need for words; our relationship has grown stronger, yet more fragile, both at the same time. What's making it fragile is mainly my not being able to have sex any more, and I honestly don't know if that's going to pass or not. We've tried a few times, but I feel such revulsion rising in me that I want to throw up. I need to switch off that whole aspect of my life for now.

How long? asks Germund.

How the hell am I supposed to know? I answer.

I'm speaking again, obviously. Not much, but when I have to. I took the supplementary-level course in literary studies this autumn, and I didn't need to say much there. Only when I had the viva for my extended essay on John Cowper Powys really. I gave up the Céline and Dagerman. I don't think my supervisor, a lecturer called Linnell, really got Powys, but he gave me the top grade anyway. A brilliant piece of work, he said. More brilliant than you can ever know, I thought.

This spring I'm doing the pre-Masters course. Two modules, the nineteenth-century novel and the twentieth-century novel, an excellent way of passing the time for a sparrow that's fallen to earth. You read a novel and meet once a week to analyse it to shreds, it's as simple as that. The other day, when I was walking home across the Old Cemetery, I could sense Hjalmar Söderberg turning in his grave; when he wrote *The Serious Game* he never intended it to be treated like this. I told him I agreed with him, but it wasn't worth getting worked up about.

439

And yes, I do know Söderberg's buried in Stockholm. It was just a train of thought.

I'm working on my next essay, too. It's on the French surrealist poet Grimaux, who won the PSCP Prize in 1930 and killed himself in New York three years later. It was nothing to do with the prize, it was because he lost his wife and daughter in a boat accident off Collioure. What I'd really like is to focus on what he wrote in New York – about twenty poems, dark but full of elucidation of the real structure of life – but my supervisor says the material is too limited.

I've pointed out to him that people have written whole doctorates on ten lines of Racine or Shakespeare, but he turns a deaf ear to that. He claims not all poets are suitable for that. Not all scholars, either, I assume he means.

Germund's still reading philosophy. Theoretical philosophy, mostly stuff to do with mathematics and logical, watertight systems. We were talking about our old obsession the other day: pure mathematics and physical love.

Are you fucking anyone else? I asked him.

Germund said he preferred not to discuss it.

I would completely understand, I said. If you were.

OK, said Germund. It has been known to happen.

When we get going again, I want you to stop all that.

Of course, I get it, said Germund. I can stop right away, if you like.

As long as you keep me well out of it, you can carry on, I said. But I don't want to be able to tell that you've been with anyone else. Don't ever come home reeking of cunt. I shall leave you, if you do.

I could see it disturbed him. He wandered round the room for a long time, tugging his hands through his hair. I thought how attractive he looked. It reminded me of some old film noir. Moody young man attempts to reach a decision.

I love him, I thought.

I've started thinking that from time to time.

When he'd finished pacing, he stopped and looked at me with burning eyes. I think that's how John Cowper Powys would have put it, anyway. *Burning.*

I never want to be without you, Maria, he said. All other women are like lukewarm water compared to you.

I wondered if that was what his pacing had been about. Fashioning those words. But in any case, I liked them and told him that if I ever decided to start fucking again, it would be with him.

It felt as though we sealed a pact that night.

Without words, obviously.

We've only met up with the others once since last summer.

It was a few months ago, at the end of January, or it might have been early February. At Tomas and Gunilla's, of course, in Sibyllegatan. I was sorely tempted to feign flu or something and let Germund go on his own, but that would have been too selfish. Germund's no more interested in that lot than I am. That's just the way it is.

The reason we had to get together was that bloody bus company. Germund and I own a quarter of it, after all, and the idea when we started was that there'd be some profit in it, of course. But it hadn't turned out quite like that, my golden brother informed us as we sat down at the table for our chilli con carne and the ubiquitous Parador. It was in our glasses and in the chilli recipe, too. We'd made a bit of a loss, he said, strewing the table with his sheets of paper, but that was a good thing, really, because it meant we wouldn't have to declare any profit for tax. And we could offset this year's loss against next year's gains.

He went on like that for a while and gave us various forms to sign. On reflection, I think it was just as well we had something neutral to keep our minds on. We didn't go anywhere near the subject of Timişoara, it was as if it had never happened, and we had never even gone on a trip together, but I noticed the others found it hard to look me in the eye. Gunilla more than anyone, of course; she wrote me a stream of letters over the autumn, and I've read about half of them but not answered a single one.

At any event, said Tomas, it would be good if we could each put a couple of thousand into the company. Another couple of thousand, that was to say. We were going to focus entirely on the runs to Norrland this year; he had a guy who was willing to drive at least every other weekend, so, if all went well, we'd have recouped our losses by the summer. He asked Germund if he felt like carrying on as a driver, and Germund said he didn't want to set foot in that goddamned bus ever again.

Rickard said he and Anna would find it hard to scrape together 2,000 kronor, especially if they were to start making repayments on the loan they'd had to take out to buy their share in the bus in the first place, but he and Tomas decided to discuss that later, just the two of them.

We only stayed a couple of hours. Germund was nervy and on edge as we trudged home, and I tried to get him to tell me what the matter was, but he didn't want to talk about it. I stopped bothering him then; we both respect each other's need to be left in peace. Solitude is the most fundamental of human needs, that isn't news to anybody.

Dreams are a plague. Everything I manage to build inside me in the course of the day comes crashing down. Grimaux writes about that experience, too. It makes not a shred of difference what wise thoughts we may have when we're awake; we can cover vast stretches on our journey to mental healing, but the minute the dreams break loose, all we've achieved is thrown to the wind.

I feel them over me again. Their hard breathing. Their sweaty bodies and filthy cocks. Grubbing around in me. I can't even make myself wake up; I know it's a dream, every time, but it's something else as well. An old piece of waking reality that belongs to me in the same way as a hand or a foot, and that I can't just chop off. Because it actually happened, it isn't really a dream, but part of my mental landscape, and it seems I shall be expected to spend time there quite regularly. To walk there some nights, so I don't forget.

The last poem Grimaux wrote before he committed suicide – it was dated two days before – is about being visited by his wife and daughter in the night, every night for weeks on end, and they are utterly dead and in an advanced state of decay; and about this finally driving him to try to kill them again, to escape their visitations.

The thought occasionally recurs that I ought to go back and kill my rapists, but how would I find them? How would I go about it? The gods know I wouldn't hesitate for a second if I got the chance. Some choices in life are simple.

There's really only one medicine that works for me at

443

night: if I smoke a bit of hash before I go to sleep, they stay away. That seems to be the case, anyway; I've tested it three nights in a row now, and it's always worked.

Germund doesn't like the smell, but he puts up with it. And he never smokes any himself, he says it just makes him stupid.

In a week's time it's the Mayday Eve holiday, and we've decided to take a trip to Stockholm and spend the weekend at a hotel.

52

In the early morning of 6 October a band of squally rain blew in over Kymlinge from the south-west and stayed there all morning. At about nine o'clock Gunnar Barbarotti was nursing a cup of coffee on the top floor of building thirty in Kymlinge hospital, contemplating the angry, leaden sky through a big picture window and thinking that nothing could have worried him less.

Marianne was in the room, asleep in a bed just a few metres away from him. She wasn't worrying him, either. Not by comparison with how things might have been, anyway. He had stayed there overnight again and had talked to half a dozen different doctors and nurses. They all told him basically the same, and everything pointed in the right direction. Marianne wasn't going to be left with any lasting impairments as a result of the stroke she had suffered two days before, at her place of work just 150 metres from the room where they now were. Not serious ones. It was too soon to make any definite pronouncements, of course, but with a mind to how things could have turned out, there was no scope for anything but cautious optimism.

Their five children had just left the hospital to get on with the regular tasks of the day, meaning school and college obligations of various kinds, but he didn't intend to go into work until after lunch. Before the children left, they'd all stood around Marianne's bed holding hands, the whole family. She herself had only summoned a tired smile, but that was enough.

Oh yes, more than enough.

He assumed she still wasn't aware of what had happened to her, but that wasn't anything to worry about, either. It would gradually come back, so Dr Berngren and several of the other medical staff had assured him, and there was absolutely no rush.

No, the only thing that was vaguely worrying Inspector Barbarotti this rainy autumn morning was the conversation he was due to have with Eva Backman when they met in her room at police HQ at 1.30 p.m.

They had agreed the time and place, and he had alerted her to the fact that he had something important to impart.

Something important to impart? she asked. You've just told me Marianne's doing fine. What else could possibly be important, in comparison to that?

It's to do with the case, he'd admitted. The death at Gåsaklyftan. And . . . well, with Marianne, too.

In a way.

But I'll come to that when I see you.

Good grief, Eva Backman had groaned. Have *you* been at the oxygen, too?

'It's probably just as well if I come straight to the point.'

'Good idea,' said Eva Backman.

He swallowed, and coughed to clear his throat. He stood up from his chair and sat down again.

'What is wrong with you?' said Eva Backman. 'You seem to have ants in your pants.'

'It feels so bloody ridiculous,' said Barbarotti.

'I can see that you think so,' said Backman.

'It's just that . . . that Marianne . . . my wife, in other words . . .'

'I do know she's your wife.'

'That she had a . . . how can I put this? A relationship with Germund Grooth.'

Eva Backman's coffee cup fell to the floor.

'I told you it was bloody ridiculous,' said Barbarotti.

'Are you pulling my leg?' That was the first thing she wanted to know, once they'd cleared up the floor.

'No,' said Barbarotti. 'Don't be daft. Why would I pull your leg about something like that?'

'You're right,' conceded Backman. 'Go on then, for goodness' sake! Give me the details! When?'

'Ages before she and I met, of course,' said Barbarotti. 'That is, quite a long time before,' he corrected himself. 'They were together a few times over the course of a year, more or less.'

'Oh yes?'

'I should have told you, of course, but I felt so damned . . . Well, I know I've been a stupid idiot, but I felt too embarrassed, basically.'

'You *are* a stupid idiot,' said Eva Backman.

'That's what I'm telling you,' said Barbarotti. 'Nice to have you on my side for once.'

'You're welcome,' said Backman. 'But this means we know a bit more about Germund Grooth then? Or that you do, at any rate?'

'Hmm,' said Barbarotti. 'We didn't talk about him very much.'

'What?' said Backman. 'You didn't talk about him? What do you mean?'

'I mean what I just told you. We didn't really talk about him.'

Eva Backman raised her eyebrows and her voice. 'So here we are, moving heaven and earth in our search for informants to put us in the picture about this blasted Grooth, and all the while there's Marianne—'

'Things got a bit tense,' Barbarotti broke in.

'Tense?'

'Yes. Between Marianne and me, that is.'

'Why did they?'

'Because . . . because I got a bit jealous.'

Eva Backman's jaw dropped. Then she shook her head.

'I told you I was a stupid idiot,' said Barbarotti. 'But I love her, and that gives a person the right to be an idiot.'

'So you were jealous of a man she was with before she met you?'

'Yes.'

'Who's now dead, what's more.'

'Yes.'

'Men!' said Eva Backman.

'I know,' said Gunnar Barbarotti. 'We are as we are – you and I have talked about this before.'

'We have,' agreed Eva Backman. 'But this means Marianne's sitting on various bits of information about Germund Grooth. How long were they together, did you say?'

'Barely a year, she says,' said Barbarotti. 'But they were never a couple, as such. They just met up once a month or so. Marianne lived in Helsingborg before we got together, you know.'

'Oh yes, I remember,' said Eva Backman with a sigh. 'Well,

anyway, this is all very irregular. But it might not get us much further, when it comes to it. So the two of you really didn't discuss him at all?'

'No, basically.'

'Unbelievable. And now it's going to be impossible for quite a while, of course. I have to say there are times . . . times when I can't help feeling there's someone coordinating all this. A director.'

'I *know* there's a director,' said Barbarotti. 'Actually no, not a director. More of a . . . supervisor.'

'A supervisor?' said Backman.

'Something like that.'

She shook her head again. 'Sometimes you're a complete riddle. But solving it is beyond me. I'll leave it to Marianne. What about this current mess? I think you'll just have to get a grip on yourself and talk to her, when she's up to it . . . What have they said about that? The doctors, I mean.'

'She needs rest,' said Barbarotti. 'She'll be in the rehab unit for a couple of weeks at least. But of course I can still talk to her . . . in a day or two. Maybe tomorrow?'

'You be sure to do that,' said Eva Backman. 'But go easy, we don't need to hurry into this. After all, it's only going to be a . . . a character judgement, isn't it?'

'I assume so,' said Barbarotti. 'Though my feeling is . . .'

'Yes?'

'My feeling is that it'd be best coming from you.'

Eva Backman subjected him to a long, hard stare.

'I get it,' she said. 'And yes, I think you're right.'

She checked the time.

'I'm seeing Asunander in half an hour. He wants to know how we're getting on.'

'Aha,' said Barbarotti. 'And how *are* we getting on?'

'Not very well,' said Eva Backman. 'Do you want me to fill you in on what you've missed?'

'Yes, please,' said Barbarotti.

'We've spoken to them again. Mainly to double-check on the alibis, as discussed. Nobody can be completely ruled out, if we're sticking to those hours on Saturday afternoon. But I haven't been able to see Rickard Berglund yet. I was meant to do it yesterday, but then . . . well, things got in the way. And it's his wife's funeral on Saturday, so I don't really know.'

Barbarotti nodded. 'We're no further forward then?'

'Not strictly speaking, no. Though there is one thing: they finally got hold of Kristin Pedersen in Copenhagen. They said they'd send up her interview statement by this evening. So that might give us a bit more on Grooth's character, anyway. Quite apart from the Marianne angle.'

Barbarotti got to his feet. 'I'll ring Berglund and ask when we can have a chat. I'd better do it, as I was the one who spoke to him last time. He might want to wait until after the funeral, when he's got his thoughts a bit more in order.'

'Could be,' said Backman. 'You're planning to be at work then?'

'It's more sensible for me to take time off once she comes home,' said Barbarotti.

Backman nodded.

'Sara's decided to stay with us for a while, too. I don't think things are that great between her and Jorge, so it suits her in a way.'

'How long have they been living together?' asked Backman.

'Two years, give or take,' said Barbarotti. 'It's a shame really. I like him.'

'You're not the one living with him.'

'Well spotted. Is there anything else? I was thinking of popping back to the hospital for a while.'

'Yes,' said Backman, getting up. 'There is something else. Give my love to Marianne, and tell her she's going to be fine. But she needs to take her time. I'll come and visit in a day or two . . . and not only for that thing we talked about.'

'I shall pass on the message,' promised Gunnar Barbarotti. 'My regards to the boss.'

'I shall pass on the message,' said Backman.

53

'There's a fundamental difference between chasing happiness and chasing meaning,' declared Rufus Svensson, scratching his beard. 'We need to be clear about that. It's simpler to look for happiness, but we belong to the crazy crowd who've chosen to look for meaning. Correct me if I'm wrong. No, actually, I'm not wrong, I know that, but please say something anyway.'

They were sitting in Ofvandahls cafe. In the smoky, tobacco-stained inner room, which had become something of a regular haunt in recent months. The oval table and the sofa beneath the portrait of the illustrious founder, also known for his third-rate verses. It was half past six in the evening and they'd been ensconced there ever since the end of Professor Hallencreutz's lecture at around four. Rickard Berglund went to get his fourth cup of coffee, or it might even have been his fifth, and thought to himself that he really ought to go home soon.

But on the other hand, he liked sitting here. They were a quartet; apart from himself and Rufus Svensson, the party also comprised Matti Kolmikoski and Sivert Grahn. They'd been reading theology together for almost six terms now, but it was only this term that they'd started socializing in any sort of regular way. Rickard had wondered from time to time why that was. Why hadn't he played a more active part in student life in his years in Uppsala? Why hadn't he met more people? And in fact this particular gang of four didn't have much to do with student life in the generally accepted sense, he thought. Four future clergymen, all of them members of the Skåne student club, which meant they saved 500 kronor a year and didn't have access to any of the actual student clubs.

Which of course meant they saved even more money. Going out to a student club meant getting drunk, and even if the beer, wine and spirits cost a fraction of what you'd pay at a normal restaurant, they weren't free of charge.

It had been a simple enough choice on Rickard's part, and Anna had supported him in it. She was born and bred over on the east side of the river, in the part of town that had nothing to do with academic Uppsala. For her, the university world meant snobbery and exclusive friendship groups and private parties. She had experienced it from a very young age as a world of closed doors, and her studies at the college of journalism had very little to do with the traditional world of academia. Meanwhile, the left was winning everywhere, even in Uppsala. Maybe times were changing, Rickard and Anna would say to each other. Maybe the punch parties and student serenades and all the other hollow rituals were on their last legs; two weeks before, there'd been considerably more students on the workers'-rights demos on 1 May than there had been at the formal dinners held on the same date, traditionally marking the arrival of spring.

'Our friend Rufus is quite right in what he claims,' said Matti Kolmikoski once Rickard had returned to the table. 'But he hasn't gone to the root of the matter. As usual, I'm tempted to say.'

His Swedish came with very definite Finnish intonation, a

fact that somehow had the effect of making his words seem more considered and charged with meaning than they really were. It wasn't the first time this had occurred to Rickard. If you were intending to spend your life standing in a pulpit, you had it made if you spoke Finland-Swedish. Or had a Norrland accent; there was some kind of solidity to those versions of Swedish that the idioms of the south and middle of the country lacked.

'It's not an absolute given that we're talking about a state of opposition, you see,' Kolmikoski went on. 'Between happiness and meaning. I, for example, could never be happy unless I were free to devote my life to seeking meaning. I find the overall concept of happiness in general to be woolly and overrated. Utilitarianism is too simplistic, if you ask me.'

'That may well be,' nodded Rufus Svensson, combing his fingers through his luxuriant beard again. 'But there's hardly going to be anyone round this table professing themselves an adherent of utilitarianism, is there now? I thought I was among Christian folk.'

'And so you are,' put in Sivert Grahn. 'But I completely agree with Matti. I'd go further and say that, for me, the two are well-nigh synonymous. If I can't devote myself to the search for meaning, I can't be happy for a single second.'

He was the most interesting member of the group, Rickard thought. Understated and serious, but not weighed down by the Laestadianist melancholy that afflicted so many of the theology students. He was modest and intelligent, rarely put himself forward, but didn't follow the crowd, either. He always took his own stance on important issues. Rickard hoped they wouldn't drift out of touch after the end of the course; he could almost see them in his mind's eye, running into each other over the years. All four of them, meeting up and comparing their experiences of different parishes and appointments. Discussing questions of faith and life and ethics, twenty or thirty years from now. Remembering their Uppsala days.

'You're right, Sivert,' he said. 'To live is to seek meaning. That isn't necessarily the case for all people – we all have a free choice. But for us, it has to be that way. Believing there's a God means trying to understand him, which is exactly what Mulholland and Erasmus tell us.'

The others nodded. Rickard had noticed that he was pretty good at this sort of thing. Keeping slightly in the background – perhaps he'd learnt that from Sivert, in fact – and listening to the others' points of view before stepping in to summarize the discussion, when the time came.

'Whoops,' said Rufus Svensson, looking at the old silver fob watch he'd just fished out of his pocket. 'This wretched time-piece has run away with itself again. I'm sorry, Gentlemen, but I must be getting along home for the evening milking.'

The others laughed. Rickard thought to himself that Rufus would undoubtedly make a splendid vicar. Old-school; if you'd developed that sort of joviality by the age of twenty-four, things could only continue in the right direction.

They parted outside the cafe and he set off along St Olofsgatan, heading home to Kvarngärdet. It was the middle of May, the bird-cherry was coming into bloom, it was a beautiful early-summer's evening and there were just two more weeks of term to go.

A single exam, to be precise, right at the start of June, and then he only had another year left. If was a strange thought, really. Four years had gone by since he first arrived in Uppsala, and he vividly remembered his own emotions that day. Getting off the train at the station and walking through the town with a feeling almost like reverence ticking away inside him. Locating the now-familiar landmarks – the River Fyris, the cathedral, the theology faculty, the university library, the castle and the road sloping down from it – and first meeting Tomas at Cafe Fågelsången.

And the year of military service at the Staff and Liaison College, with all that it involved. Helge from Gäddede; meeting Anna as they were watching the demo along Drottninggatan, standing outside Viktor's Books.

Her tumbling straight into his arms, just like that, him helping her get back home and them gradually becoming a couple. They'd been living together for . . . well, it would be two years, come the autumn. And married for nearly a year. It felt both longer and shorter, somehow.

The greater the distance he put between himself and the centre of town, the nearer he got to Väktargatan, the more his thoughts dwelt on her. Or on their relationship; there was no distinction between the two, when it came to it.

She would be graduating from the college of journalism in a few weeks' time. She'd landed a summer stand-in job at the local newspaper, *Upsala Nya Tidning*, potentially with the prospect of a more permanent arrangement, come the autumn. For his part, Rickard was going to take a temporary job at the post office, just like last summer. Sivert Grahn, Matti Kolmikoski and Rufus Svensson all had the final year of their theology degrees ahead of them, as he did, and Rickard looked forward to socializing with them at Ofvandahls even more often in the two terms they had left. After that there would be at least one more term to prepare for ordination. He couldn't deny it felt reassuring. He wasn't entirely ready to turn his back on Uppsala yet, but perhaps in another eighteen months he would be. He and Anna had talked about it many a time and agreed they were both willing to move somewhere else, preferably far away from this seat of learning – but they hadn't quite reached that juncture. There would be plenty of time to start looking round the country for posts they could fill.

And, after all, there were churches and newspapers in most places, so things were sure to work out when that day came.

We're doing fine, Rickard unexpectedly found himself thinking as he crossed the dual carriageway at the Mobil filling station. This is what marriage looks like. A bit up and down; and it was right what they'd been saying at Ofvandahls just now, in their discussion of happiness and meaning. When you applied it to a relationship, that was to say. It was idiotic to expect everything to be sweetness and light the whole time. Or that *happiness* would be ever-present. Day in and day out, morning, noon and night, no, things simply didn't work like that. You had to seek out meaning in your life, and it was just the same in a marriage, he thought. Together you negotiated a winding road through both troubles and joys, and there was no need to imagine the grass was much greener for anybody else. Or that you should always be striving to reach it.

They'd talked about having children, but had decided to wait a while. Wait until they'd left Uppsala, at least, and were earning a regular income. Things were a bit shaky in that department at the moment. Quality Travel had turned out to be a costly gamble – even before they factored in the cost of last summer's trip round Eastern Europe, which had barely been mentioned between them once Anna's article had been published – but they had just about coped without recourse to Rickard's mother, so far. The Norrland trips in the spring term had gone fairly well, Tomas had reported, but the bus needed some repairs over the summer and unfortunately the payout they'd been expecting was out of the question for now.

They rarely saw Tomas and Gunilla these days. Apart from the meeting about the bus at the end of January, they'd only met up once. The four of them had gone out for dinner at Guldtuppen on Kungsgatan one evening in April, but it hadn't really felt like before. Perhaps it was the shadow of Timişoara still hanging over things; that, at any rate, was what Anna and Rickard concluded on their walk home afterwards.

He and Tomas spoke on the phone now and then, and they'd had a very occasional coffee together, but that was all. He didn't know what courses Tomas was taking at the moment, but assumed they still centred on economics.

And Maria and Germund? He had seen neither hide nor hair of them since January, and he was pretty sure Anna hadn't, either.

But things were as they were, he thought as he cut across the grass to the other end of Väktargatan, and there was a time for everything.

Meeting. Parting. And dying.

She was writing when he came in. She nearly always was; he could hear her tapping away on the keys as soon as he came into the hall. He took off his jacket and hung it on the hook as he shouted hello.

'Hi there!' Anna called back. 'Where have you been?'

He could hear she was in a good mood. She was probably just finishing off an article she felt happy with.

'Ofvandahls,' he said, going into the kitchen, where she was typing.

'Christ almighty, haven't you just?' said Anna. 'You stink like a smoked herring.'

'I walked all the way home,' said Rickard apologetically. 'And we did have a window open.'

'If four theologians each smoke four cigarettes an hour,' said Anna, 'for four hours, how much will they reek of old smoke? I assume it was the usual gang?'

'Correct,' said Rickard. 'Four bishops in the making. Why don't you write a piece about us?'

Anna laughed and he thought about the happiness-and-meaning thing again. The fact that there were times when you didn't need to look for the meaning.

'Would you like a cup of tea?' he asked. 'I'll make it.'

'You know what: I could fancy a glass of wine,' responded his wife. 'I think there's a bottle in the larder, isn't there?'

And for some reason, this almost brought tears to his eyes.

54

They'd arranged to meet at ten and he went straight from the hospital. He'd spent two hours that morning in the rehabilitation unit, spoken to an array of doctors and nurses and experts – and, above all, talked to Marianne.

Today it had been possible. She was still incredibly tired but there was a definite improvement, compared to the day before. He felt as if she was being born back into life, in a slow but unstoppable process; he'd no idea where that image had come from. She had no memory of what had happened, no memory of the journey to Sahlgrenska and back, or of anything to do with the operation, and it wasn't clear if she would ever remember anything about it.

But it didn't matter. She understood what had happened to her; the hospital was her natural working habitat, after all, and even if there was a difference between childbirth and a stroke, this was, in a sense, all commonplace to her. She wasn't at all concerned about her own situation – nor was there any reason to be, according to Dr Berngren and assorted other people. Though she *was* a bit worried about how they would manage at home. Particularly how Jenny and Johan would cope with the fact that their mum had had a stroke.

But having spoken to them – and they had popped in for a while before school again that morning – and having had assurances from the two of them and from Barbarotti that things were going fine at Villa Pickford and that they also had Sara there to help them, she felt reassured. They all held hands again before she fell asleep; it had been a moment for them all to carry with them through the day, thought Barbarotti.

And not only through the day.

But now he was standing outside the front door of a man who had lost his wife just three days before. He resolved to keep comparisons out of his mind and rang the doorbell.

Rickard Berglund looked a bit less haggard than the last time they met. He was wearing jeans, a thin black polo-necked sweater and a pair of felt slippers. He shook Barbarotti's hand and invited him into the living room. He apologized for being a bit behind with the cleaning and asked if his visitor would prefer tea or coffee.

'What are you having?' asked Barbarotti.

'Coffee.'

'Then I'll join you.'

He took a seat in the same armchair as on his previous visit. The chess set was still on the table and Barbarotti didn't think any of the pieces had been moved. But he couldn't swear to it, of course. Rickard Berglund disappeared out into the kitchen and was soon back with a pot of coffee and a plate of dry almond biscuits.

'You've read a fair amount,' said Barbarotti, indicating the bookshelves that took up two whole walls. There must be getting on for 2,000 volumes, he estimated.

'There are twice as many again down in the cellar,' said Berglund, sitting down in the other armchair. 'Yes, I've read a word or two over the years.'

'I apologize for having to bother you at a time like this,' said Barbarotti. 'I was very sorry to hear about the death of your wife.'

'Her last days were nothing but suffering,' said Berglund. 'We shouldn't be sorry that they're over now.'

'But it's still a very tough time for you,' said Barbarotti.

'I heard your wife had some kind of collapse,' said Berglund deflecting the question. 'Your colleague mentioned it. How is she?'

Gunnar Barbarotti realized he had no inclination to talk about it, but he could hardly avoid it, considering Rickard Berglund's own circumstances and their conversation the previous time.

'They think she's going to make a full recovery,' he said. 'We were lucky.'

Berglund nodded. 'There is such a thing as providence,' he said.

The idea wasn't for them to get caught up in matters of philosophy of life, either, but Berglund had used that particular word now and Barbarotti couldn't let the opportunity pass.

'Is there?' he asked. 'I mean to say, I believe there's something like that, too, but I . . . I don't exactly know the nature of it.'

'Maybe we're not meant to know,' replied Rickard Berglund, taking off his glasses. 'A providence that we can understand immediately turns into something else, doesn't it? Something to calculate and have expectations of. The point is to put your suffering into other hands, isn't it?'

Barbarotti registered that this was a question and wondered what he ought to say. He had come here to establish what Rickard Berglund had been doing one Saturday nearly two weeks ago – and possibly to fish around a little in what had happened at a vicarage dinner party in 1975 – but suddenly, and right from the start, there seemed to be other things that were much more fundamental. Or at any rate you couldn't just shut the door on them once you'd opened it.

'I'm only an amateur in matters like this,' he said. 'But I admit it interests me. I mean, it seems stupid to go through life imagining it isn't important.'

'Yes, that would be one way of putting it,' said Rickard Berglund, running one hand contemplatively over his cheeks and chin. 'Have you read Kierkegaard?'

'No,' admitted Barbarotti. 'I haven't read Kierkegaard.'

'He was my household god for many years. It's about the stages of life, among other things. From passion via ethics to faith and fulfilment, but I shan't take up your time with that now. Anyway, it leaves one question unanswered.'

'One question unanswered?' asked Barbarotti.

'We all have it inside us, but most choose not to confront it. How to actually relate it to our lives. To our actions and our responsibilities. Christianity has gone so wrong, so hopelessly wrong. We need to turn the clock back two thousand years to find our way again. It's sad, unspeakably sad.'

Barbarotti recalled a similar phrase from their previous conversation and was again unsure how to reply. Rickard Berglund put his glasses back on and drank some coffee.

'I can't help noticing you're not recording this conversation or making any notes,' he said. 'Why did you want to talk to me, in actual fact?'

'It's the Germund Grooth incident,' said Barbarotti and gave a series of coughs, trying to cover his own confusion. 'We really want to get to the bottom of it. Why he died . . . and in addition, possibly, what happened to Maria Winckler all those years ago.'

Rickard Berglund said nothing and appeared to be thinking. Barbarotti took a biscuit and waited. He wasn't feeling on top form for this kind of conversation, he thought. Something in his brain wasn't really working the way it normally did. Berglund's question was justified, without a doubt. Why *was* he sitting here talking to this dropout vicar who had just become a widower? Really?

But *really* was a treacherous kind of word, and he had thought so on many occasions. It implied that what was going on was in fact concealing something else and there was a sort of focus, an insistence on drilling down to some essential core.

But there wasn't always anything to drill down to, however much you liked to imagine it.

'There are so many questions without answers,' said Rickard Berglund eventually. 'So many connections we never discover. I remember you telling me last time you were here that you had some form of faith, or have I got that wrong?'

For a split second Barbarotti could see Our Lord watching him with a furrowed brow and a demanding look.

'That's right,' he said. 'I have a faith. That is, in my opinion there is a God. And I have a relationship with Him. But I wouldn't call myself religious in any conventional sense.'

'I'm glad to hear it,' said Rickard Berglund, with a twitch of the mouth that was almost a smile. 'Yes, I know I abandoned my calling some years ago. But I didn't abandon my faith; we talked about this, didn't we? You'll have to forgive me, but I've been so tired lately. My memory's letting me down. I haven't slept properly for months, in fact . . . And I couldn't until she finally found peace. Yes, there's been a difference over just these few days. I found a kind of peace, as well.'

Barbarotti thought for a moment. 'On Monday I didn't know if my wife was going to live or die,' he said.

Berglund nodded. 'It's only in the mirror of death that we can really see life clearly,' he said. 'It's only there that we can really value things and separate the wheat from the chaff. I hope that doesn't sound too sanctimonious. I don't want to sound sanctimonious; I did more than enough of that when I was giving sermons in church.'

He gave a brief, dry laugh, and Barbarotti found it hard not to smile himself.

'Well, there are a lot of things that *are* sanctimonious,' he said. 'And there are a lot of things one can never discover the truth about. Take us, and our current investigation into these strange deaths; I'm fully aware that we may never know the answers. How and why they died, that is. What do you think?'

Rickard Berglund leant back in his seat and ran his hands along his thighs.

'Should we look for happiness or meaning?' he said. 'That's one question that has followed me over the years. Should we really be striving to understand everything? What good does it do? Perhaps the knowledge we've striven for will hurt us when we finally find it? What's your image of God like? What qualities does your God possess?'

Barbarotti suddenly started to wonder if the man opposite him was in his right mind. He was certainly much more on the ball than the last time they had met, but there was something odd about him, to put it mildly. Or was it just because Barbarotti himself was on the defensive?

'My image of God,' he said when he'd chewed through half

his biscuit and washed it down with some coffee. 'Well, there are only three things I'm sure of. He's a gentleman, he's got a sense of humour and he isn't omnipotent.'

Rickard Berglund gave another hoarse little laugh. 'Is this something you've worked out for yourself?' he asked. 'From personal experience, I mean?'

'How else?' said Barbarotti.

'Good,' said Rickard Berglund. 'Very good. There's basically no other way. But you've missed the most important thing. His boundless love.'

Barbarotti nodded, but before he could steer the conversation onto the right track, Berglund spoke again.

'It happened the same day then?'

'What did?' asked Barbarotti.

'I lost my wife the same day yours had a stroke. That's a rather strange coincidence. Well, we ought to be in a position to understand each other at any rate, don't you agree?'

Barbarotti took another gulp of coffee and tried to concentrate. 'This wasn't really what I came here to talk about,' he said. 'It's Germund Grooth we're interested in. And the death of Maria Winckler in 1975, too, to some extent.'

'Sorry if I'm straying,' said Rickard Berglund. 'I'm not exactly myself at the moment.'

'It's hardly surprising,' said Barbarotti. 'But if I could just go back to that fateful day, thirty-five years ago, what actually was it that made you and your wife organize the dinner party at the vicarage? As I understand it, your group had more or less fallen apart by then?'

'How do you know that?' asked Berglund.

'We've talked to Mr and Mrs Winckler. They told us the six of you barely socialized at all in that final year in Uppsala.

Tomas Winckler says it all ground to a halt in the autumn of 1972, after a trip round Eastern Europe – my colleague talked to him about it the other day. I assume you can confirm this information?'

Rickard Berglund put his hands to his cheeks and massaged them, just once up and down. 'Yes, something happened,' he said slowly and thoughtfully. 'But I think actually we would have drifted apart in any case. Yes, I'm sure we would. A month in a hot bus just accelerated the process, that's all.'

'But you and your wife invited them to the vicarage that Saturday in September?' observed Barbarotti. 'Even though you weren't really seeing each other any more. Why did you do that?'

Berglund shrugged. 'It was my idea, I'm afraid,' he said. 'I ran into Germund in town and he explained they'd moved here. I told my wife, and as Tomas and Gunilla had moved to Gothenburg a few years before, we thought . . . well, what's the point of living in a vicarage, if you can't throw a party there?'

He gave a quick smile, but was instantly serious again. 'It was a terrible thing to happen, of course. But I've never, not once in all these years, entertained the idea that anyone could have pushed her. It was what that Sandlin was angling for, though. That was his name, right?'

'Inspector Sandlin, yes,' confirmed Barbarotti. 'But Germund Grooth's death two weeks ago, hasn't that made you revise your view at all?'

Rickard Berglund thought for half a minute. If not longer. Barbarotti let him think, remembering the old rule that you shouldn't be afraid of silence and wondering whether Berglund had really taken on board that they suspected Grooth had been murdered. But he had clearly been living with the puzzle of Maria's death, so he ought to, oughtn't he? At any event, Barbarotti knew he had to find a way to approach the alibi question; perhaps he'd just have to ask it straight out. Even if it felt brutal.

I'm too soft, he thought. I feel sorry for him. I'm not entirely sure why, but I assume it's because his wife's funeral is coming up on Saturday.

'I haven't had time to reflect on it,' Rickard Berglund said finally. 'It does seem very odd, I grant you that. But I didn't know Germund. I never have, not even in the Uppsala years, not really. He and Maria were such a strange couple, very strange.'

'And how strange was that evening at the vicarage?'

Berglund gave a sort of shrug. 'It was pretty much as usual, I'd say . . . well that is, it wasn't really a success. But we wound up quite early. Gunilla was tired, what with the baby on the way and everything else. If we hadn't arranged the picnic in advance – planned the food, and so on – we probably wouldn't have gone ahead with it.'

'Oh?' said Barbarotti.

'No, I don't think so. But it was all agreed, so to speak.'

'I see. And was there any sort of incident at the dinner party the night before?'

'Incident? No, definitely not.'

'And what about on your Eastern Europe trip . . . When was that now? 1972?'

'1972, that's right,' said Berglund. 'No, I don't think anything particular happened on that, either. We'd had enough of each other, that was basically it. Drifted apart. And to this day I try to avoid long trips by bus.'

Barbarotti decided there was no way round it.

'What were you doing, the Saturday Germund Grooth died?' he asked.

Rickard Berglund again took time to think. But only a few seconds.

'I haven't the faintest idea,' he said. 'I suppose I was with Anna at the hospice. That's where I've spent nearly all my time this past month.'

'Have you any way of checking that?'

Rickard Berglund put on his glasses and leant a little closer to Barbarotti.

'I suppose one could ask the staff,' he said. 'But why on earth do you want to know?'

Barbarotti could have answered 'routine procedure', but for some reason it felt so inadequate that he chose to say nothing at all.

We shall close this case now, he thought. There's no point pursuing it any further.

55

Gunilla woke up, turned on the bedside light and looked at the clock.

It said 03.35. It also told her it was Thursday 22 November 1973. What had woken her? A noise? She turned her head and saw that Tomas wasn't there. Hadn't he come home yet? she wondered. Where had he got to? Why wasn't he lying there on his side of the bed?

At half past three in the morning! She couldn't remember precisely where he'd said he was going yesterday evening – something at his student club most likely – but he hadn't said anything about being out half the night . . .

She heard the noise again. A sort of scratching. A faint sound from the hall, metal on metal if she wasn't mistaken, and fear was just seizing her by the throat when she realized what it was. Mainly because he had finally managed to get the key in the keyhole.

She heard him turn the key and stumble into the hall. He closed the door, with much huffing and puffing. It *was* Tomas, wasn't it?

Yes, she recognized his cough, and heard him mutter something as he kicked off his shoes and hung up his coat. A coat hanger hit the floor. Then the miasma of alcohol reached the bedroom, and she didn't have to wonder any longer.

It was Tomas. He had come home at half past three in the morning and must be totally smashed. She briefly considered putting out the light and pretending to be asleep; she was sure he hadn't noticed it was on. But then she decided it was her duty to go out there and receive him, so she kicked off the duvet and called out to say hello.

He stood there in the middle of the floor, swaying. He tried to focus his eyes on something, possibly on her. Then he opened his mouth and closed it again.

Jesus Christ, thought Gunilla. I've never seen him as drunk as this before.

'Hello, Gunilla . . .' he managed to say, almost toppling over with the effort of it.

'Hello, Tomas,' she said.

He used one hand to prop himself against the wall and took a deep breath.

'Sorry, but I'm a bit drunk.'

Or that was roughly what it sounded like. And it fitted the evidence before her eyes.

'So I see,' she said. 'Come and lie down. Or do you need a minute in the bathroom first?'

'Bath . . . room,' replied Tomas, as if he wasn't really familiar with the concept. But his brain finally caught up. 'The bathroom . . . is . . . a great . . . great . . . idea! I'll go to the . . . bathroom . . . first!'

He started taking off his jacket, but got stuck halfway and she had to help him. As she struggled to do so, he tried to put his arms around her, but it was easy enough to slip out of the embrace.

'Right, you pop into the bathroom and then come along to bed.'

471

He just stood there again, swaying gently and presumably trying to remember where the bathroom was. Then he headed in the right direction, went in and switched on the light.

'There you go,' she said.

'Bathroom!' said Tomas, his face lighting up for a fraction of a second.

He staggered in and she closed the door. She heard him slump onto the toilet and start muttering to himself again. She gave a sigh and went to hang up his jacket in the hall, and she had just inserted the coat hanger when she saw some banknotes sticking out of one of the pockets. She took them out and saw that there weren't just a few. His whole pocket was stuffed with cash.

Hundred-kronor notes.

It was the same in the pocket on the other side. She felt something knotting inside her as she took them all out. Note by note. A hundred kronor at a time.

There were enough to fill both her hands. She went into the kitchen and sat down. Switched on the light over the table and started to count them, her mind racing.

It came to almost 20,000 kronor.

She went back to the bathroom, put her ear to the cool wood of the door and listened. There was the sound of a tap running, but nothing else. She waited a few moments, then opened the door a little.

Water was gushing into the handbasin.

Tomas was lying on his back in the bathtub, fast asleep with his mouth open. He had managed to take his trousers off, but that was all.

It'll have to wait until the morning, she thought. She turned off the tap and put the light out.

She forced him out of the bath and into bed at around seven. She almost had to carry him.

At a quarter past eleven she marched him unsteadily back to the bathroom and made him take a shower, and by twelve on the dot they were both sitting in the kitchen over cups of black coffee.

The banknotes were on the table between them.

'Well?' she demanded.

'Some bloody idiot was offering round a bottle of 1946 Calvados,' said Tomas.

'I don't care what you drank or why you did it,' said Gunilla. 'Where has this money come from?'

'I need another Magnecyl,' said Tomas.

'It's not a good idea to have more than two,' said Gunilla. 'And they take a while to start working. Drink your coffee. The money?'

'Hrrm,' said Tomas and scratched his temple. 'I sold the bus.'

'You *what*?'

'I sold the bus.'

'But you can't just . . . I mean, why?'

'Who gives a damn,' said Tomas. 'I'm sick of it.'

Gunilla looked at the piles of 100-kronor notes. One pile of a round 100, one of 97: 19,700 kronor.

'Twenty thousand in cash,' said Tomas. 'Who gives a damn?'

'But oughtn't we . . .' said Gunilla, 'oughtn't we to have asked the others first?'

'The others?' said Tomas. 'Why should I have asked them?'

'Because we all own the bus together . . . owned.'

Tomas swallowed a mouthful of coffee and pulled a face.

'We paid thirty-eight for it,' she added.

'I know how much we paid for it. I was the one who did it. But we've done seventy thousand kilometres in it. I'm the one who had to sort out every bloody detail in this company. Why the hell should I have to consult any of them? You and I own fifty-one per cent of it, don't we?'

He stopped talking and went across to the sink to gulp some water straight from the tap. She wondered why he was being so aggressive; it wasn't like him. Was it because of the hangover, or did he know at heart that he'd sold the bus too cheaply? She decided not to probe him on that.

'OK,' she said. 'I suppose you're right, in a way.'

'I'm going to do two more trips and get paid to drive,' said Tomas. 'We agreed that.'

'Who did you sell it to?'

'A guy called Pontus. Law student. Sharp as a knife.'

'But why did he pay you like this, for God's sake? I mean . . . you were carrying it loose in your jacket pockets.'

'That was the way we decided to do it,' said Tomas. 'And on the receipt it says ten thousand; it's best, for all parties.'

Is it? thought Gunilla, realizing this was some subtlety she didn't fully understand.

'But surely we've got to share the money with the others?' she said.

'Sure,' said Tomas. 'They'll get two and a half per couple . . . plus a quarter each of what we've earnt this autumn. They'll be happy with that.'

'Two and a half?' queried Gunilla.

'The receipt says ten thousand,' repeated Tomas.

'Oh, but,' said Gunilla, 'this can't be—'

'Can we get one thing straight?' he interrupted.

'What thing?'

'That I'll be the one in charge of the finances in this family from now on. It's simpler that way.'

Gunilla rested her chin on the knuckles of one hand and looked at him. He looked back with bloodshot eyes. He didn't seem remotely bothered by either matter.

Neither that he'd come home as drunk as a lord at half past three in the morning, nor that he'd sold the bus and was intending to cheat the others out of 10,000 kronor.

'We'll share out the money in good time for Christmas,' he said. 'In a fortnight or so. They'll like that. Then we can declare the company bankrupt in the new year.'

'I don't like this,' said Gunilla.

'Has anyone, apart from me, lifted a finger to make this work?' said Tomas.

'Maybe you're right, but . . .'

'Next time we'll have to be a bit more careful who we choose as project partners,' said Tomas.

'Next time?' queried Gunilla.

'Next time,' said Tomas. 'I mean it. But right now I need to grab another hour's kip. It was that bloody Calvados . . . 1946 vintage, did I say? Just after the war.'

'We promised to go to Ulrika and Dennis's this afternoon for some cake,' said Gunilla 'It's Torsten's second birthday.'

'You'll have to go on your own,' said Tomas. 'Sorry, but I just can't face it. You can say I've got a cold and don't want to pass it on.'

He got up and stumbled back to the bedroom. Gunilla just sat there, staring at the piles of notes for a while. Then she stuffed them into the nearest kitchen drawer and phoned Ulrika.

56

When Eva Backman got back from seeing Asunander, the printout of the Kristin Pedersen interview was lying on her desk.

In a manila envelope, with a note from Sorrysen to say he hadn't had time to read it through.

She took the sheets of paper out of the envelope, saw that there were thirteen of them and decided to take them home with her for evening reading. It was a quarter past four and she'd promised to make a lasagne for her sons' dinner.

They'd need it on the table by about six, ideally, as two of them had a match at eight.

She thrust Miss Pedersen into her briefcase, spent the briefest of moments tidying her desk and left the police station.

It was half past eight by the time she was able to turn her attention to the transcript. Truth to tell, she was a bit reluctant to get down to it; a creeping suspicion that it wasn't particularly important any more had started gnawing away at her. Asunander had asked prosecutor Månsson to attend the afternoon's meeting, and both of them had been singularly unimpressed with the results of the operation so far.

Had they in fact come up with even the merest hint that pointed to Germund Grooth's death being murder? the prosecutor wanted to know. In my personal opinion, Asunander had declared, that's about the measure of it. *The merest hint.* They had had that much for a week now and, as he understood it, they'd accumulated nothing more. Or was he mistaken?

Backman said that was roughly how things stood, unfortunately, but they were still actively working on it.

And that merest hint, Månsson wanted to know, what did it comprise, exactly?

Backman thought for a moment and then said it had two ingredients. *Two* hints, you might say. First, Grooth had received an anonymous and untraceable phone call on the morning of the day he died. And second, it was virtually impossible to comprehend how he had got from his home in Lund to the isolated rural location of Gåsaklinten, 300 kilometres away. If they assumed he had done it under his own steam, that was.

Was that all? the prosecutor asked, scowling at her.

Yes, that's it, she replied, thinking that what she most felt like doing was tugging at his hair – it looked rather like a wig, but opinion in police HQ was divided on the subject. Those are all the particulars, which was what you asked for, wasn't it?

But before Månsson could answer, it struck her that no, actually, there was one other thing she'd forgotten. She told them about the trip to Paris he had booked for a date six days after he died. So taking all those things together, it seemed a little hasty to conclude that he'd killed himself.

She didn't like Månsson and she didn't know anybody else who did, either. But even if he couldn't dispute that last finding she'd presented, he had still made her feel dubious about the whole undertaking.

And that was presumably why she didn't feel much like sitting down with Ribbing's transcript of his interview with the elusive Danish informant Kristin Pedersen.

Driving back from Lund five days previously, Eva Backman had been convinced of Grooth's murder, she remembered that very clearly. But now she felt anything but sure.

Not because there had been any developments of note in the case over the past five days, but because there had been none at all.

Still, the show must go on, thought Eva Backman. She turned her attention to the first page and bit into an apple.

It tasted sharp, almost sour.

Ribbing had been thorough. His account of proceedings was closely typed and every last detail, however insignificant, was included in full. Her age and profession and place of residence, and how much she was claiming for her train fare across the Sound to Lund.

The reason Ms Pedersen had failed to show up to the previous meeting was that it clashed with her dental appointment; she had realized too late, but a Danish dentist always took priority over a Swedish police officer. Over a Danish police officer, too, come to that.

Kristin Pedersen eventually explained that she had known Germund Grooth for about four years. They had met on a ferry between Frederikshavn and Oslo. Backman recalled that someone else had reported seeing Grooth in a similar setting, but couldn't immediately summon to mind who it had been, but perhaps it was a favoured strategy of his. This was the sort of place where he picked up his women; she made a mental note to ask Marianne where the two of them had met –

although she found it hard to imagine Marianne on any kind of cruise, for some reason. Certainly not as a pretext for picking up men.

There had been no talk of the two of them moving in together or anything like that, Kristin Pedersen elaborated; she'd had enough of that sort of relationship in her life. She wanted to live alone, but felt the need of a man now and then. Was that so strange?

Ribbing said it wasn't strange at all, and Ms Pedersen went on at some length about the advantages of having a partner you knew you could call on, as it were. Or a couple of partners, even. So you didn't have to start from scratch every time you got the urge. Ribbing said he understood perfectly what she was talking about.

But he'd seemed such a tormented soul, Germund, was the next thing Kristin Pedersen said, and that made Backman read more slowly, her frown of concentration intensifying.

GR: Tormented?

KP: Yes, I can't find a better word for it. Germund had some burden to carry that was a torment to him.

GR: What sort of burden?

KP: He never told me. But he admitted there was something.

GR: And how did this torment manifest itself?

KP: He'd seem sad and very down. Only periodically, though. There would be no point seeing someone who's gloomy the whole time.

GR: But you say there was a specific reason? Something he didn't want to talk about?

KP: I think so. I almost got the feeling it went back to some event in the past.

GR: What event would that be?

KP: Like I told you, I don't know.

GR: Were you aware that he lost his partner in an accident, a long time ago?

KP: Maria, yes. He told me. She slipped off a cliff and died.

GR: Did you talk much about that?

KP: No. He only really told me about it once, and touched on it again onc other time. So just twice, as far as I can remember.

GR: Could that have been the event that triggered these depressive tendencies of his?

KP: I've no idea. It's possible, I suppose, but it could equally well have been something else. Something . . .

GR: Yes?

KP: [*After a long hesitation*] I might be wrong here, but it could have been something that went even further back. Something that happened when he was a child.

GR: Did he ever tell you anything about his parents?

KP: Yes, he said they'd both died when he was quite

young. Only twelve or thirteen, I think. A car accident, I believe he said.

GR: Could that be the event underlying this?

KP: I don't know.

GR: But you had a sense of some kind of trauma in his background, anyway?

KP: I'm pretty sure there was, yes. It seemed to be at the root of all his torment. Could have been something to do with his parents' death, could have been losing his girlfriend like that – I've no way of telling. Could have been a combination of the two or something else entirely. He never wanted to talk about it when he was in one of his low moods.

GR: I see. How did you hear about his death?

KP: I found out the other day, when the police rang.

GR: When did you last see him?

KP: We were together one weekend at the start of August.

GR: Where?

KP: At my place in Copenhagen. It was the last time I saw him.

GR: How did he seem?

KP: His usual self.

GR: How did you spend the time?

KP: How do you think?

GR: I see. Did you notice any of his torment, as you call it? That last time you met, I mean.

KP: He would often lie awake for a long time after we went to bed at night. For an hour or more. I'm pretty sure he did it that time, too. But I didn't think of it as anything out of the ordinary. Tormented men can be quite attractive as well, you know, but maybe that's beyond your range of experience?

GR: I wouldn't say that, Ms Pedersen. What do you make of his death?

KP: Excuse me?

GR: You do know how he died?

KP: No. Your people said it was a car accident.

GR: I apologize, there must have been a misunderstanding. We said it was an accident. But no cars were involved.

KP: Oh? What kind of accident was it then?

GR: He fell off a cliff.

KP: A cliff?

GR: Yes.

KP: Him as well?

GR: Yes. You really didn't know this?

KP: No. How could I? I've been in the Seychelles for three weeks.

GR: We're aware of that. Well, Germund Grooth was found dead in exactly the same place as his partner, who died thirty-five years ago.

KP: What?

GR: Yes. That's why we're taking an interest in the circumstances of his death. So tell me: in your opinion, would Germund Grooth have been capable of taking his own life?

KP: He died in exactly the same place?

GR: Yes. Do you think he had suicidal tendencies?

KP: [*After a brief hesitation*] Not really.

GR: What do you mean by that?

KP: He had that tormented side, certainly, but if he'd been going to take his own life, he would have done it long ago. He was past sixty. And what's more . . .

GR: Yes?

KP: What's more, he was off to Paris, I remember. We spoke on the phone just before I went to the Seychelles – that's right – and he told me he was going to Paris for a week at the start of October. This week, I think it was meant to be. You don't top yourself a week before you're due to go to Paris.

GR: We've also noted that particular. Tell me, do you know if he was going to Paris alone or in company?

KP: I find it very hard to believe he wouldn't be meeting up with someone else.

GR: And why is that?

KP: My dear inspector, I was far from the only woman in Germund Grooth's life. I've never imagined I was. But to think that he went and died in the same place as she did.

Tormented and attractive? thought Eva Backman, looking up from the transcript for a moment. Well, yes, maybe there was some truth in that. Particularly if you were talking about a passing attraction, and that was presumably the case here. A whole series of passing attractions.

Trauma? They couldn't be sure that was right, but if it was, it certainly provided food for thought. His parents' death and then the death of Maria Winckler. Could there be a third? But why would it take a third?

She shook her head and read on. Ribbing went on a bit about how often they'd seen each other, and whether Kristin Pedersen knew any of the other women in Grooth's circle of acquaintances (which she didn't, and had no interest in doing), and came back to the question of Grooth's burden of torment and depressive tendencies, but it didn't seem to Eva Backman that he gleaned anything of substance.

Ribbing went on to ask – just as she had instructed him – about the time she and Grooth paid a visit to the Wincklers in Lindås in June, but the only thing Kristin Pedersen had to say about it was that they'd stayed the night with a couple of well-heeled petty-bourgeois Swedish schmucks. They were as boring as hell but they served some very nice wines. She didn't remember what they'd talked about. If there'd been any kind of animosity between Grooth and the hosts, then Kristin Pedersen hadn't noticed it.

But she had enjoyed a glass or two, she had to admit. She'd fallen asleep on the sofa, if she wasn't getting it confused with some other occasion.

Eva Backman reached the end of the report and gave a sigh. She put the papers back in the envelope and reminded herself what she'd been thinking the other day.

There's some kind of story hidden behind all this. A story we have yet to get anywhere near.

Is that really the case? she thought now. Or is it just that we like to imagine it? That *I* like to.

On the other hand, Ms Pedersen had found it hard to believe Germund Grooth would kill himself. What with his Paris trip coming up and everything.

She had said it in as many words.

I just can't get my head round this, thought Eva Backman. But I'm tired of it. I shall go in and see Barbarotti tomorrow and tell him he's got to get a bloody move on and solve this case now.

Or we'll simply close it, which is what the powers that be would clearly prefer.

57

Sparrow.

It wasn't easy to find out any information about the boat accident in which Bernard Grimaux lost his wife and little daughter, but I did it in the end. My supervisor praised me for my literary detective work, as he called it, and said he'd seldom read such a brilliant essay as mine.

I know, I thought, but when he suggested I move on to a doctorate in the spring term, I said a polite but firm no.

Neither Germund nor I had any intention of stranding ourselves in the academic backwater – or that was what we used to tell each other, anyway. But when I think about Germund, I do wonder which world he's ever likely to find his niche in. We're both odd customers, but Germund is even more afflicted than I am, in a way.

But back to Grimaux first, and I have it from two French papers – or magazines, to be precise. They both interviewed the poet a few months after the accident, before he decided to cross the Atlantic.

They revealed that Bernard was with his wife and daughter when it happened. They were literally all in the same boat, and all three of them were thrown overboard. Grimaux survived, but his wife and daughter drowned, and that's the crux of it. Neither of the magazine interviews says it outright, but if you read them alongside various other things he wrote in his final year in New York, a clear picture emerges. He tried to save them, both of them. He battled with the waves for a long time, but the point came when he gave up. He decided to save himself rather than carry on trying to rescue them.

If he hadn't taken that decision, all three of them would have perished. Three dead instead of two. But it kind of doesn't help. Life doesn't allow such pure mathematical simplifications – I'm going to discuss this with Germund one day, of course. In his dreams and his poetry Grimaux comes back time and again to when he actually abandons them – the moment in which he decides, and it's a moment, and a decision, that refuses to leave him in peace. They come back and implore him to help them; they haunt his dreams – but even, it seems, when he is wide awake. He finds it excruciating: a drowning wife and a drowning daughter crying out for his help, and in the end he realizes there is only one way to be rid of them. He will have to kill them again to be free of his guilt and his torment. In his very last poem, the one dated two days before his own death, he carried out this act, and it is the darkest, most beautiful and most inexorable poem I have ever read.

But now I'm leaving Grimaux behind me. It's January and there's a perishing wind blowing in Uppsala. Germund and I have discussed whether we really want to stay here much longer; he claims he needs another year; he wants to get back to his physics, he says, and I assume that's the way things are going to be. I don't know where we'd go, or what we'd do, if we moved away. My life has no direction. I'm going to be in paid employment this spring, at any rate, and initially that's going to be in the cemeteries department, at the Old Cemetery and possibly out at Berthåga. I saw an advert in the paper saying they needed people, so I called them and got the job right away. It's for six months; they might decide to extend it in due course, but there's no guarantee. I'm looking forward to it; pottering among the graves with my rake instead of just studying all the time, yes, it's going to be a nice change. I start on 1 February.

I don't really know what to expect from Germund at the moment. But maybe I never really have. It frustrates him that we haven't started fucking again. He sees other girls now and then – it's no secret – but we don't talk about it. I don't want to know, and tell him I'm not bothered by it.

But it's a torture to him that I can't let him in; I've asked him if he'd prefer me to move out, so he can start bringing home other women, but whenever I do that, he flies off the handle.

It's you and me, Maria, he said the other day. It's you and me forever, isn't that what we decided? Can't we go and talk to someone?

Go and talk to someone? I said. Who were you thinking of? Who would we go and talk to? And about what?

About this, said Germund, throwing out his hands in some kind of appeal, though really he was gritting his teeth in anger. About you and me. About the fact that we love each other, but never fuck. About what happened in goddamned Timişoara. I don't suppose you're the first person in the history of the world to be raped?

I thought for five seconds about what the hell to say in reply. Then I hit him. I happened to catch his eyebrow with my ring, it started to bleed and we had a few very pleasant hours of making up afterwards.

We drank vodka and lay naked in each other's arms, and I helped him climax later on, but that was as far as we got. It's too early, still too early.

My parents are forever badgering us to visit them down in fascist Spain, but I keep stalling. Badgering *me*, I suppose I mean. Maybe I could face going down there if I could be left in peace, so I shan't discount the idea entirely. If I worked through the summer I could go down for a couple of months in the autumn, but it would have to be on condition they weren't there themselves. Or not the whole time at least. I shall have to negotiate that with Mum; they have still got the house in Sundsvall, after all, and spend at least half the year in Sweden. So no, I won't rule out the possibility. You don't have to just lie on the beach the whole time, there are places like Granada and Ronda to visit, and various other things.

My pig of a brother has sold the bus and that's probably for the best, but I think he swindled us out of our fair share. I don't care, we'll get by anyway. Germund is still getting his quaint old grant and, once I start work, I expect they'll pay me some kind of wage, too. But things are a bit tight for January, which is a bloody awful month at the best of times, God knows.

I saw Gunilla in town yesterday, going round the fruit stalls at St Erik's torg, and I'm more or less convinced she was pretending not to see me. She averted her eyes in that transparently obvious way people only do when they see someone they don't want to speak to.

I wonder what that's a sign of, and I wonder if I ought to

take it up with her. A bit of harmless confrontation; I don't like being treated that way. Not by anyone and, above all, not by her.

The dreams aren't recurring as often now and I'm always unprepared. But at least once a month I'm back in that room. It's as vivid and painful every time. I understand how Bernard Grimaux felt in New York, I really do.

58

'Have we forgotten anything?' asked Eva Backman.

It was Friday. It was raining. They were having lunch at the King's Grill, where she'd opted for Baltic herring fillets with lingonberry sauce, while Barbarotti went for slow-cooked veal with dill sauce and potatoes.

'Forgotten? I don't know. I can't remember.'

She let that one pass. 'We can't keep working on this for much longer,' she said. 'Except in the standard, going-through-the motions way. There's nothing to justify putting any resources into it, Asunander and Månsson were quite clear about that, weren't they?'

'Sorry,' said Barbarotti, 'but what could it possibly be that we'd forgotten? We seem to have left no stone unturned.'

'I feel the same,' said Backman.

Barbarotti drank some of his fizzy water and leant back. 'OK, listen to this,' he said. 'If it does so happen that Grooth was murdered, we're never going to find any forensic evidence. We'll presumably never find out who did it, and even if we do get that far – if we stumble across a solution, say – we won't be able to get him convicted. Or her.'

'Glad you're so optimistic. That was what Månsson meant, the lack of forensic evidence. But it would be nice to know how it actually happened, don't you think? Whatever else we can or can't find out? It's so frustrating.'

Barbarotti concentrated on his veal for a while and said nothing.

'What's up with you?' continued Backman. 'Have you lost all sense of curiosity? I'd actually been planning to say that you'd got to get on and solve this bloody case, because I was tired of it. Are you with me on that?'

Barbarotti swallowed and thought.

'I'm with you,' he declared. 'Of course I wonder what happened. To both of them.'

'Right then,' said Backman.

'I just don't see where we take it from here. We've spoken to all the parties twice. We can hardly do another round.'

'A thought keeps coming back to me,' said Eva Backman. 'There's a hidden story here that we still haven't got anywhere near.'

'A hidden story?'

'Yes. In that group of people. There's something only they know about, something they don't talk about. And that lies at the heart of it all.'

'Go on,' said Barbarotti.

Backman put down her knife and fork and dabbed her mouth with her serviette. 'Well, as I see it, there were six of them – perhaps seven – at the outset. Now only three of them are left. Or four, but I don't really think so. These three, that is the Wincklers and your ex-vicar, have simply decided not to tell us. It's some kind of pact, written or unwritten . . . What do you think of that idea?'

'Sounds like the script of a bad film,' said Gunnar Barbarotti.

'Maybe life is a bad film,' said Eva Backman. 'Weren't we talking just the other day about there being a director running the whole show?'

'Yes, we were. But why should they be a *bad* director?'

Eva Backman gave a sniff. 'There's plenty to point in exactly that direction, wouldn't you agree? But we're losing the thread again. That's what always happens when I talk to you these days. How's Marianne today?'

'Slowly improving,' said Barbarotti.

'Mmm?'

'They say everything's fine, but I just don't get how she can be so tired. However, she sends her regards and says she'll be happy to see you. Sometime over the weekend, if you can fit it in. I mentioned the Grooth thing, too . . . And she's fine with talking to you about that.'

'Great,' said Backman. 'I'll go on Sunday, once I've handed the boys back to Ville. How did it go with the vicar yesterday, by the way? All you said was that nothing emerged.'

Gunnar Barbarotti gave her a brief account of his conversation with Rickard Berglund. Or tried to, at least, but he could hear how unstructured it sounded.

'We ended up talking about all sorts of stuff,' he explained. 'I suppose it was partly because of the circumstances. Marianne's stroke, and him just losing his wife. It didn't . . . it didn't seem an appropriate time for a proper interview. Maybe I was sloppy and just let it go.'

'What do you think you let go?'

Barbarotti shrugged. 'I don't know. No, maybe there wasn't anything to let go of. But I didn't even manage to pin him down on his alibi. You might at least have expected that . . . But I'm going to check it with the hospice at the hospital.'

'Was he with his wife that Saturday?'

'It seems so. But he can't remember precisely. He's been there with her pretty much night and day for over a month.'

'All right,' said Eva Backman. 'You'd better follow that up. Both the Wincklers have got flimsy alibis, and so has Elisabeth Martinsson. It's pretty damn odd that none of them have ruled themselves out, isn't it?'

'And that none of them did thirty-five years ago, either,' said Barbarotti. 'Yes, it is odd, and you have to wonder if it's co-incidence or not. What are you up to this afternoon?'

'Going through the rest of the reports from our colleagues in Skåne,' said Eva Backman with a sigh. 'I shall know more about Germund Grooth than Marianne does, by the time I see her on Sunday.'

Barbarotti nodded but had nothing to say.

I'm losing my mojo, he thought once he was back in his room. I don't recognize myself.

Perhaps it was because of Marianne? Dr Berngren had spoken to him about that. Keep an eye on yourself, he'd urged. Delayed shock isn't unusual in situations like these.

Though what he felt was more of a general dulling. Perhaps that was how it manifested itself? Lars had noticed it at the breakfast table this morning, at any rate, or was it Martin? Morning, Dad, is there anyone at home in your head today?

He couldn't remember what he'd answered, or even if he'd answered at all. But it said something, didn't it? He didn't feel entirely with it, and people could tell. When he was at Marianne's bedside he was fully present, certainly, at least while she was awake. Perhaps that was where he should be spending all his time at the moment? Just like Rickard Berglund had.

But he wasn't doing anything useful there. Not most of the time. If he was needed anywhere, it was at home. He and Marianne were responsible for five children, and it was lamentable that his mind wasn't more engaged, with things as they were.

I shall be more on the ball from tonight, Inspector Barbarotti decided. I've had enough of this shock-related woolliness. My most important task . . . my most important task is to keep myself together and look after them. Make sure they can see I care about them, as well. Make sure it *comes across*. They're going to remember this time for the rest of their lives.

He glanced at the clock. Half past one. He yawned. There were documents from four different cases to go through. Not counting the Gåsaklinten business, but then no new reports had come in on that one anyway. He shuffled through a couple of the piles, but found it hard to raise any real enthusiasm.

He yawned again. Looked out of the window.

The weather didn't look entirely miserable, he noted. The band of rain had gone over and the cloud was beginning to break.

He clasped his hands in front of him on the desk. A little trip in the car? he thought. A little trip out Rödåkra–Rönninge way? All of a sudden it seemed more than justified. It was never wrong to take another look at the scene of the crime. Quite the opposite, in fact: it was the most classic of methods.

He crept past Eva Backman's door and opted out of putting his head round it to tell her how he intended spending his afternoon. What was it she'd said?

A hidden story?

59

When Rickard Berglund looked back over the year 1974 – in those days between Christmas and New Year, when it was definite that they would be leaving Uppsala – he had a sense of it being a year somehow bulging with events.

He took it as a sign that they had made the right decision. The profusion of events in itself pointed to it being time to leave the university environment and make their way out into real life. Neither he nor Anna had any second thoughts about taking the next step, as they had assured each other the minute they finished reading the letter – the letter to say he'd secured the position he had applied for and could take up his post on 1 February.

He had collected his theology degree in June, but by then the major event had already occurred: his mother's death. It had come completely out of the blue at the start of April. She had the first stroke on the evening of the eighth, and another when she was taken into hospital in Mariestad in the early morning of the ninth.

Ethel Berglund's funeral was held at Hova church on 18 April; if she'd waited another eight months, he could have officiated himself. The first stroke had happened on a Monday; the second, which ended her life, on a Tuesday. He couldn't help registering the fact.

Even though he had never been close to his mother, her death put a sort of retroactive damper on his ordination in Uppsala Cathedral during Advent. He was aware of wishing she was there. And that his father, the free-church pastor, could have been there, too, but he drew a degree of comfort from knowing they were now reunited and could be together to watch their son's elevation to his sacred calling from their shared puff of cloud up above. He was sure neither of them would have any objection to that perspective.

He sold the house in Hova at the end of May, and he and Anna treated themselves to a month's holiday in the Greek islands. They took little ferries between the islands of the Cycladic archipelago, each lovelier than the last in the blue, blue sea, and they told each other, half in jest and half in earnest, that God had created boats while buses were the Devil's work.

Like Rickard's mother, Quality Travel Co. Ltd was a mere memory. Tomas had sold the bus and they had shared out the meagre assets before declaring themselves bankrupt in February. When Rickard came to think of it, that was the only time the six of them were all together that year. With Tomas and Gunilla's move to Gothenburg in August, Sibyllegatan was now ancient history as well. Yes, 1974 had undeniably been a year of leave-taking.

The period of practical training that led up to ordination had given him the opportunity to try things out in earnest in a few parishes outside Uppsala: Vittinge, Almunge and Knutby. And even though he had given no more than four sermons in total, it had been a chance to experience what the gravity of liturgy involved. And what it felt like to stand in a pulpit with the congregation listening below him. The first time, in the beautiful church at Vittinge, he had suffered such nerves that he had hardly been able to ascend the stairs.

But it had been a good autumn that had taught him a lot; he had met wise and kindly clergymen with many years' experience in the field, and now that he was about to take charge of Rödåkra–Hemleby parish over in the far-away west of Sweden, he felt ready for the task in spite of everything. Ignorant and inexperienced, that went without saying, but ready nonetheless.

Anna had also had a year that fitted well with approaching departure. Her contract at *Upsala Nya Tidning* had been extended, it was true, but after her fill-in job last summer they transferred her to the local office out in Östhammar. It meant long days and long travel times. They bought their first car, an old three-gear Volvo PV that cost them 2,400 kronor, so at least she didn't have to go on the bus, but it still meant two hours on the road every day. Her new job at the *Swedish Church Times* was something she'd found without his involvement or influence; it was a part-time post, working half the week and focusing on western Sweden, and her bosses told her it would be fine for her to be based in Kymlinge, although she'd be expected to make trips to Gothenburg and other places when required, of course.

And she was more than ready to leave the town where she'd grown up – Rickard had no reason to doubt her word on that point.

Perhaps there were a few other things that ought to be causing him a little concern, but he tried to put them out of his mind as best he could. It was as if there was a room inside Anna to which she wouldn't grant him admittance. He had described it to himself in just those terms on quite a few occasions. *A private room*. There were times when he almost felt he didn't know her at all, and that he couldn't really be surprised at her.

But perhaps it was like that with all women, with all human beings? You couldn't just put things in *italics*, and perhaps you weren't intended to, either. Perhaps that was the challenge? He was never quite sure what Anna thought deep down about a whole range of things; she claimed she had some sort of faith, for example, but they seldom talked about it. He could rarely persuade her to come along to any church event. They never prayed together and, in all the years they'd been a couple, they probably hadn't been to a church service together more than three or four times. One of those was a service he'd taken himself, the one at Dalby church. He'd basically stopped asking her if she wanted to come with him.

Because of course he would have liked to discuss questions of faith with his wife – not at quite such length as in his quartet at Ofvandahls, but still. On the other hand, perhaps it was just him being over-sensitive; they did talk, and not only about the practicalities of the here and now – but she would often break off a conversation like that, just when he thought it might get a bit more profound, and say she didn't really want to discuss that at the moment. He rarely understood why, and had no sense in advance of when they were approaching those stop signals; the silence that descended between them after one of those rebuffs made him feel uncomfortable. It was as if she was winning small victories simply by not saying anything. By closing the door to her inner room. To language, even.

Perhaps he should be worried, he didn't know. But in any

case, it was nothing that needed sorting out while they were still here in their flat at Kvarngärdet in Uppsala. In January a new future would start, they both knew it, and new conditions would apply.

Up to now they had been young, he would think to himself. In Kymlinge, with their own parish and their own vicarage, they would be grown-up.

Stages on life's way.

They had more or less stopped meeting up with Tomas and Gunilla in the course of the year. Particularly since the Wincklers moved to Gothenburg, of course, but he did sometimes ask himself why it was. He never found any answers and he never seriously discussed it with Anna. Maybe that Timişoara incident was still lurking in the background somehow, and possibly the defunct travel company, too. Quality Travel Co. Ltd had been Tomas's idea from the start and, with hindsight, you could see it hadn't been a particularly successful venture. Exactly how much money Rickard and Anna had lost altogether was hard to say, but now he had the inheritance from his mother it didn't bother him any longer. He and Anna had both taken out study loans and would have to start paying them back sooner or later, but it was the same for everyone. From January they would both have permanent jobs; they had a vicarage and were already considering whether to get a better car. Admittedly the Volvo had run like clockwork ever since they bought it from a retired elementary-school teacher out in Morgongåva, but maybe Rickard's new professional role called for something a bit more up-to-date. Though now he remembered there'd been an old vicar with a PV back home in Hova–Gullspång, and the image rather appealed to him, somehow.

He had barely seen Maria and Germund. He assumed Maria was still down in Spain; before they moved in August, Tomas had told him on the phone that she was going to spend a few months that autumn at their parents' house down there. He'd also said he didn't think she was in a very good state. That was the way things were, and it had its explanation, of course. As for what Germund was up to, neither Tomas nor Rickard could say – some kind of advanced theoretical physics, presumably. Rickard had only seen him twice over the autumn; one of those times he'd been in the company of a woman and they were in the Fyris cinema, sitting two rows in front of him and a bit to one side; they seemed to be quite closely acquainted.

Oh well, Rickard had thought, it's none of my business. The only odd thing was that when he mentioned it to Anna, she flared up and said of course it was their business, and they ought to try and get in touch with Maria down in Spain. Rickard had asked if they could even be sure the two of them were still together, but Anna had dismissed the idea with a sniff.

But they hadn't bothered to contact either Maria or Germund, and Rickard realized once again that there were sides to his wife he still couldn't read. On the other hand, he thought, what is there to say she understands all that much more of me?

They'd been together for four years. And a thought suddenly came to him and made him break into a broad smile inside: four more years down the line, we shall have four children and we'll have forgotten all about this time.

Well, maybe four kids in four years was pushing it a bit, but surely they could reckon on two?

Two children, who would grow up in a vicarage in the country. It was a pretty picture of the future and he all too readily summoned it up when he found himself not getting to sleep at night.

The parish of Rödåkra–Hemleby. He liked the name, too. And maybe my calling will be to work there for the rest of my life, he thought.

And we'll be there soon. Just one more month.

He remembered the vague sense of excitement he had felt on those first days of their Eastern Europe tour, but the sense of expectation he felt now, in those quiet days between Christmas and New Year, was something else entirely.

The *big plan*. The time had come.

60

It was Saturday evening and he was sitting beside her bed.

The five children had been there, too, but they said they knew the grown-ups needed a moment to themselves as well. Or perhaps Marianne had suggested it when he popped out of the room to get a drink; that was just as likely, of course.

'Weren't you scared?' he asked.

'I was unconscious,' said Marianne. 'I don't think you can be scared and unconscious at the same time.'

'But weren't you scared when you woke up? Didn't you wonder what had happened or where you were?'

She shook her head. 'I was just terribly tired. It was as if I belonged to sleep and nowhere else. I still am tired; I sleep sixteen hours a day, don't I?'

'Are you feeling tired now?'

She smiled. 'Stay a bit longer.'

'I was scared,' said Barbarotti. 'I've never been so scared in all my life. I thought you were going to leave me.'

'I understand that,' said Marianne, 'but I've no intention of leaving you.'

He took her hand and held it between his own, as gently and protectively as if it were an abandoned baby bird. He sat there, looking for the words. 'Life is so fragile,' he said. 'It's so fragile that . . . it's almost impossible to handle.'

She nodded but said nothing.

'I mean, how can we actually live when everything could end at any moment? I've thought about this before; I've seen plenty of dead people in my time, but on Monday it suddenly came home to me with absolute clarity. Do you understand what I'm saying?'

'Are you still scared?'

He thought about it. 'I don't know. I feel sort of dulled. Berngren says I could be suffering from delayed shock; it can go this way sometimes, apparently. But this isn't about me, for goodness' sake. It's about you, and our children. If you can just promise me we'll be able to live together for some – no, I mean many – many more years, then I'll be able to relax.'

Marianne looked at him in silence for a few seconds. She looked as if she was remembering something.

'There's a poem by Philip Larkin,' she said. 'Our English teacher in upper secondary gave it to us on a handout. That teacher, he had some kind of incurable illness.'

'Oh?' said Barbarotti.

'He died six months later, and we had a stand-in for our final year. Well, there are a few lines of it that I've never forgotten.'

She took a drink of water. Barbarotti waited; he could see she was running through it in her mind first, to make sure she hadn't mislaid any of the words.

'It goes like this. It's about death, you know, when it comes:

'And so it stays just on the edge of vision
A small unfocused blur, a standing chill
That slows each impulse down to indecision
Most things may never happen: this one will.'

'You remember it word-for-word?' asked Barbarotti.

'It's called "Aubade",' said Marianne. 'We all learnt it off by heart. The girls did, anyway. Do you get it?'

'I think so,' said Barbarotti.

'There are no guarantees,' said Marianne. 'But I shall get through this crisis, I can feel it.'

'Good,' said Barbarotti.

'But it's not the number of years that matters. It's the hours and days we make sure to use well. Isn't it? You can live a meaningless life that lasts a hundred years, but what would be the point of that?'

'I give you that,' said Barbarotti. 'But I want the children to get a bit older.'

'Have trust,' said Marianne.

He leant over the bed and kissed her. Then subsided into the chair again.

'I've talked to an ex-vicar a couple of times,' he said. 'His wife died the same day you had the stroke.'

'Is this for the case? The Germund Grooth one?'

'Yes.'

'I think Eva's coming to see me tomorrow?'

'That's right,' said Barbarotti. 'She's coming tomorrow afternoon. But this vicar, you see, he's been sitting at his wife's bedside for . . . well, several months anyway. Maybe years, I don't really know. And now she's gone. They haven't got any children, or anyone else close to them, it seems. It must feel . . . well, I really can't imagine how it feels.'

'And that frightens you?'

'Yes,' said Barbarotti. 'It frightens me. *Most things may never happen: this one will* . . . wasn't that what you said?'

Marianne nodded and had another drink of water. 'Life and

death are like brother and sister,' she said. 'Or like – what do you call them? – Siamese twins, in fact. If we're afraid of one, we'll be afraid of the other. Do you understand what I mean?'

Gunnar Barbarotti thought about it and said that he did. But he didn't know if reason and words had any weight; perhaps they were nothing but air. It was Marianne's turn to take *his* hands. 'It's going to be all right,' she said. 'Go home and have a game of cards with the kids. I think I'll take a little nap now.'

He sat there for ten minutes. His thoughts felt like straying butterflies, filling his head. Just on the edge of vision. A small unfocused blur? When he was sure she was fast asleep, he went out to the ward sister and asked his way to the hospice.

They'd taken trouble to make it nice in the hospice section, Barbarotti noticed. This was where people came to die. And their families came to say a dignified farewell. There were armchairs, and pictures on the walls. Pot plants and book-shelves. Even a glass cabinet with some alcoholic drinks: port, Madeira and brandy. He was pleased to see it; there seemed to be a kind of warmth and common sense here that went way beyond laws and council regulations.

Dignity in the closing stage of life.

And it was staffed around the clock. He said hello to the large, elderly lady doing a crossword behind the reception desk. He introduced himself and explained why he was there.

'Anna Berglund?' replied the woman. 'Yes, that's right. She was with us for quite a long time. But she died on Monday.'

'I know,' said Barbarotti. 'It was her funeral today. I'm here on a matter that feels slightly . . . indecent is perhaps the word. In the circumstances. You keep it very nice here.'

'Yes,' said the woman. 'Most people appreciate that. I could imagine dying in a place like this myself. I've worked here for fourteen years. What is it you wanted to know?'

'It's to do with Rickard Berglund, Anna's husband. He spent a lot of his time here, if I'm not mistaken? At his wife's deathbed.'

She nodded. 'That's right. I think they loved each other deeply, and I do hope he's going to be all right on his own now.'

'What we're investigating isn't directly to do with either of them,' said Barbarotti, 'but it would make our job easier if we knew where he was on the Saturday before last . . . 25 September, that is.'

'The Saturday before last?'

'Yes.'

'Why don't you ask him yourself?'

'I did, but he's been here so often it's all blurred into one, he says. Which is understandable, in view of—'

'It's perfectly understandable,' the woman interrupted, but she looked slightly worried. 'We don't actually keep any kind of record of visitors in this department. There's no reason to . . . but wait a minute and I'll have a look.'

She leafed quickly through a desk diary.

'Saturday 25 September . . . yes, I was working that day. The morning-to-afternoon shift. That means I would have come on duty at seven and finished at four.'

She shut the diary, put her hands on her hips and seemed to be thinking.

'I don't really remember,' she said. 'Although, hang on – I do, as it happens. Fancy that. When I changed over with Magdalena in the morning she'd been on night duty, she said Berglund had stayed till two. We were getting to know him quite well, since his wife was here for so long . . . It's normally only a few weeks, but Anna Berglund was with us for almost three months, it was as if she didn't want to die . . . as if she wouldn't let go. Anyway, I thought to myself: I suppose I won't be seeing Berglund today at any rate, but he turned up just before I was due to go home.'

'What time would that have been?' asked Barbarotti.

'Just before four. Yes, that's right. How funny that I should remember it.'

'And you're sure this was Saturday the twenty-fifth?'

'Oh yes,' she assured him. 'I work every other weekend. We're talking about a fortnight ago, aren't we?'

'We are,' said Barbarotti, preparing to leave. He thanked her for the information and apologized for disturbing her.

'Don't worry about that. A bit of a diversion is always welcome. Not very much happens here actually.'

He pondered as he drove out to Kymmens udde, heading home.

Not him, either, was the first thing he found himself chewing over. Not even Rickard Berglund seemed to have a watertight alibi for the critical time period.

Not Tomas and Gunilla Winckler down in Gothenburg. Or Elisabeth Martinsson in Strömstad. Or Rickard Berglund in Kymlinge.

Not now, or thirty-five years ago, just as Eva Backman had pointed out. It really was extremely curious.

But on the other hand, if Berglund had been at his wife's bedside until two in the morning, it was entirely reasonable for him not to show up again until around 4 p.m. the next day, wasn't it? And maybe he'd met someone on the Saturday who could confirm where he'd been. Out shopping, at the barber's or anything, really.

But unfortunately there was only one way of getting that confirmation. Another conversation with Berglund himself, applying slightly more pressure than he had been able to on his last visit.

A job for DI Backman, thought Barbarotti. She, after all, was the lead investigator in all this. She was even going to interview Marianne tomorrow.

Well, maybe *interview* was too strong a word.

Before he got sidetracked into wondering what that conversation might contain, and before he was back with the horde of youngsters waiting for him at home, he turned his thoughts to his trip to Gåsaklinten the day before. Whatever the point of that had been.

None at all, seemed the most obvious answer. He had wandered about in the forest for an hour. He had stood up there at the cliff edge and tried to conjure up in his mind's eye what had happened there thirty-five years back in time. And two weeks ago. Two people – lovers once – had each stood up here and looked down, with that long, long gap in between. Then something had happened . . . either they had reached a decision or they had felt an unexpected hand on their back, pushing them forward . . . Barbarotti could almost feel that little push himself. It was all too easy to kill someone that way. The question, the eternal question, was of course w*hy*? Why on earth had Maria Winckler and Germund Grooth died?

He had climbed down the little path and walked around for a while down there amongst the rocks, too, but was driven back by the rain. The light showers he had divined from the look of the sky before he got in his car in the centre of Kymlinge had proved a chimera. He had forged his way back up the steep track and returned to the car, but it had taken him the best part of fifteen minutes and he was soaked through by the time he was behind the wheel.

This evening it was dry, though. Clear and cold, with the temperature probably somewhere around zero. There was a light on in almost every window of the house as he pulled up in front of Villa Pickford. I shall leave the dead in peace now, he thought as he got out of the car.

Now I'm focusing on Sweden's youth, its future. And canasta.

And I'm going to thrash them.

61

Sparrow.

El gorrión. That's the word in Spanish. So, not *moineau* like in French, they come from different roots. But it's masculine in both languages, which is a bit misleading, I think. Piaf and I are both decidedly female. I had some problems with Spanish when I first got here, four months ago, but it's coming along. I'm getting better and better; my French is pretty perfect now, so I can derive basically everything from that. It just takes time, that's all.

At the bar where I work you can get by with a pretty limited vocabulary anyway. And English, of course. Half the customers are non-Spaniards.

Torremolinos. It's an expanding tourist trap in Franco's dictatorship, but I've sort of settled in here. I couldn't care less about politics and when the generalissimus dies, democracy will take over. Everybody says so. I wouldn't exactly say I'm happy here, but then I wouldn't be happy anywhere else, either. When Mum and Dad came down at the end of November and said they were planning to stay in the house until March, I realized I had to look round for somewhere of my own. I decided to leave Fuengirola as well – best to put a bit of distance between us, even if it's not that far away. I found a little flat very close to the bar, no more than a room really, but it's all I need. If I agreed to go to bed with the landlord I probably wouldn't have to pay any rent, either, but I won't do that.

I don't go to bed with anybody. I've more than enough to contend with when I'm on my own. On my days off, I walk along the beach for hours. Back and forth, back and forth, and though it's not at all like the Black Sea beaches, I can find myself thinking I'm back there. I don't know what's going on inside my head, but it's certainly something. Mum's afraid I'm losing it, going crazy, and will end up locked away in a Spanish mental hospital. I can see it in her. We don't see each other that often, maybe once every couple of weeks. She comes to see me; I never go to Fuengirola, however much she pesters me to.

She comes on the train and she brings food with her. Fresh vegetables, fresh bread that she buys on the square just down below, fruit, tinned food. She's afraid I shall starve to death, and I suppose that's a reasonable assumption. I've lost seven or eight kilos since I came down here, but I'm not feeling any the worse for it. I eat very little. Just fruit, really, but I drink masses of water. Litres and litres a day, but never a drop of alcohol, even though I'm behind a bar five evenings a week.

I sometimes smoke a joint when I get home from the bar, which is usually about three in the morning. It's like before – whenever I do that, I can sleep dreamlessly right through to late morning.

There are plenty of guys trying it on with me, of course; I'm still good-looking, even though I'm so skinny. But there's something in my eyes that makes them give up pretty quickly. I think I scare them; they discover there's something dark inside me, something they don't want to know because they wouldn't be able to handle it. A couple of weeks ago there was this girl who came on to me as well, there are plenty of gay people down here. I actually went back to her place with her and we lay naked on her roof terrace and fondled each other for a while, but she was too drunk and I felt this wave of disgust. I left, and she swore at me, but the next night she came to the bar and apologized, pale and contrite. I think she wanted to subject me to another try, but I told her to go to hell. I didn't actually say it, just gave her my black gimlet stare.

Perhaps Mum is right, when it comes down to it. Perhaps I am losing control. I consume a lot of books, but sometimes I find I've read fifty pages and put a book aside, and five minutes later I can't remember a single word I've read. I don't even have any memory of it when I leaf back through the pages, and I wonder where I was in the course of those fifty pages.

Germund has sent me three letters. Short, and I sense a slightly bitter tone. Or perhaps he hasn't quite mastered the art. Of writing, I mean; I've answered all three of them, anyway, and we've spoken on the phone four or five times. He wants me to come back, but I told him it was too soon. Something needs to change in me first; it would just be counterproductive for me to go back to Sweden in this state.

Well, I'll come down there then, says Germund. He started saying it back in November and in the end I gave in. Maybe it would be just as well for us to meet again; after all, he's the only man I could sleep beside and feel safe. No, safe is the wrong word; what I mean is that he's the only man who wouldn't fill me with disgust. That's just the way it is.

He's coming at the end of February and I suspect he'll stay until we can travel back together, even if he hasn't said it outright. He did some teaching during the autumn term, in one of the physics departments, I think, and he says he's got a reasonable amount of money. I suppose we'll just have to squash in together in my one room and see how it goes. And, actually, perhaps Mum and Dad will go back to Sweden in April, in which case we'll be able to stay in their house.

There's a little abandoned girl who hangs around the square here, and I've started talking to her. She claims to live with her grandmother, but I've never seen any sign of a grandmother. If she hasn't actually been abandoned, she's certainly pretty much alone.

She can't be more than ten. We always meet in the evenings, when I'm on my way to the bar. She comes up the steps from the seafront and every day she's wearing the same tatty old dress and cardigan. She goes barefoot, even though the weather isn't very warm. When I say talking to her, that's not strictly true, because we really don't exchange that many words. Sometimes we say nothing at all. But we've got into the habit of sitting on one of the benches outside the church, watching the pigeons; she's terribly shy, but we sit there and sort of keep each other company.

She told me her name was Miranda. I don't ask her any questions because I can see she doesn't want me to, and she doesn't seem interested in learning anything about me, either. We both like this quiet way of going on, and the thought has occurred to me that if my life looked different – and if my head did – I could actually adopt her.

It was only yesterday I had that thought, but it's been with me ever since. I suspect it's dangerous and I could get obsessed by it, and this evening when I went out and sat on the bench, Miranda didn't turn up.

I'm standing here behind the bar, feeling something grow inside me. It could be a scream, it could be something else. I haven't eaten anything since yesterday.

I don't think it would be a good idea to lock myself away in a Spanish hospital. I wish Germund were here. But it's still two weeks until he arrives.

62

'This feels a bit weird,' said Eva Backman, 'and that's putting it mildly.'

'I feel the same,' said Marianne.

'Two weird things, actually. What happened to you, and what I want to talk to you about.'

Marianne nodded. She moistened her lips with her tongue and hesitated. 'Gunnar's finding that very difficult. It was why I suggested you do it instead.'

'Yes, I know,' said Eva Backman. 'I expected to find you in bed, by the way.'

'It's easy to get bedsores,' said Marianne. 'And blood clots and all that sort of thing. I'm supposed to stay as mobile as I can. But I still sleep like a koala . . . they're the ones that snore away three-quarters of their lives, aren't they?'

'I think so,' said Eva Backman. 'Perhaps we'd better get started then, before you doze off?'

'Definitely. So, Germund Grooth?'

'Germund Grooth,' echoed Eva Backman and switched on her recording device. 'What would you like to tell me about that particular acquaintance of yours then?'

Marianne drank some water and sighed. 'I've thought about it, you know. Both before and after . . . all this.' She indicated her head. 'It is a remarkable coincidence – I mean, there are

517

nine million people in this country, after all, and I really haven't had that many men in my life . . .'

'I've had four,' Eva Backman chipped in.

'Me too,' said Marianne with a fleeting smile. 'Another coincidence. But for Germund to be involved in something you and Gunnar are investigating, well, it feels most peculiar, that's all. It even occurred to me that . . .'

'Yes?'

'. . . that maybe it isn't a coincidence.'

'Interesting,' said Eva Backman. 'I wondered something along the same lines. And when you start seeing it like that, where does it lead you?'

'Before I had . . . this . . . I think I decided it had to be. Sheer coincidence, that is.'

'I concluded the same,' said Eva Backman. 'Otherwise the whole thing just gets even less comprehensible. But what was he like? What would you say about Germund Grooth?'

'It would depend,' said Marianne and took a deep breath. 'It would depend what you were looking for. He was a good lover. Tender, you might say, and attentive at all the right times. And I suppose that was what I was looking for, nothing else at that juncture. I found it hard to imagine him stepping in as the father of my children. I don't think we met more than ten times – it only went on for a year or so. The problem was . . .'

She stopped herself and bit her knuckle.

'What was the problem?'

'The problem was that it was purely a matter of sex. We'd see each other for a day and a night and have sex, and that was basically it. I wouldn't be able to talk to Gunnar about this, but that really was all. Does that seem bizarre to you?'

'I don't think it's bizarre. Not in the slightest,' said Eva Backman. 'Why did you call a halt?'

'For that reason,' said Marianne. 'Because there was never any more to it. We never went to see a play or a film, or talked about going on holiday anywhere, he never wanted to know anything about my life. He didn't ask about my children . . . well, you know?'

'I know,' said Eva Backman. 'No, it simply doesn't work. But you asked him about his life?'

'I tried,' said Marianne, pulling a bit of a face. 'But he wasn't particularly chatty. Not as morose as some men can be . . . just the opposite, he could really be quite agreeable – is that a word?'

Eva Backman nodded.

'Yes, agreeable. But evasive at the same time. He was always smart and polite and considerate, but . . . well, there was something missing. I gradually worked out that he was depressed. Or I decided that was the diagnosis anyway. And then there was all that sex, our meetings; it was . . . it was like reading a book and never getting beyond the first chapter, reading it over and over again. Do you understand what I mean?'

'I understand exactly what you mean,' Eva Backman assured her, thinking how long it was since she had read even a first chapter. 'And did you ever find out what lay behind it: his depression, if that was what it was?'

'Depression doesn't always necessarily have an obvious cause,' said Marianne, 'but in his case I think there was some kind of trauma at the root of it. He said he'd lost his partner many years before, but he never told me how it came about. It was really only once that I felt I was getting under his skin

519

. . . if I can put it like that. It was that last time we met, in fact. Would you like me to tell you about it?'

'Please do,' said Eva Backman.

Marianne cleared her throat and drank a bit more water. 'Well, it was like this, and I've been thinking back to it for a couple of days now, trying to remember the details. We were spending the weekend at a hotel in Simrishamn. We got there on the Friday evening, and left on the Sunday. The second night, Saturday, he had some kind of nightmare. I was woken by him sitting up in bed and gabbling a string of words. At that point I wasn't sure if he was asleep or awake, so I asked him if he was all right. Then he said, in a loud, clear voice . . . and slightly accusingly, almost: "I killed my parents and my sister, can you write that in your books?"'

'What?' said Eva Backman.

'Exactly that. "I killed my parents and my sister, can you write that in your books?" He said it twice. I didn't mishear him, and I haven't been able to forget it since. After he'd said it the second time, he lay down again and carried on sleeping. Naturally I thought it was most likely some kind of dream that had run off the rails, and it struck me that he sounded as if he was up in front of some kind of judge . . . as if he was addressing a courtroom or something. I mean, dreams can be very strange, but when we woke up the next morning I told him what had happened and he reacted very weirdly.'

'In what way?'

'He seemed dumbstruck. From shock, I suppose, or something like it. We didn't even have breakfast together. We'd driven there separately, in our own cars, and he took a shower and left the hotel before nine without a word of explanation.

I got the feeling . . . Well, my immediate thought was that it was actually true.'

'That he . . .?'

'Yes, that he really had killed his parents and sister.'

Eva Backman sat in silence. Marianne drank more water and said hello to a nurse who was going past.

'And that was the last time you met, you said?'

'Yes. I rang him a few weeks later. He said it would be just as well if we didn't meet any more. I wasn't even going to suggest it, but I said that in principle I agreed with him.'

'And you didn't see each other again after that?'

'No.'

'Any phone calls or emails?'

'No.'

'When was this?'

'August 2005. It was about a year before I met Gunnar.'

Eva Backman nodded. 'Had the two of you ever talked about his parents before that time in Simrishamn?'

'I knew they'd died when he was quite young. But I had the idea it was a car accident; I think he must have said as much at some point.'

'But that night he claimed to have killed them?'

'Yes. But like I said, he wasn't awake.'

Eva Backman considered the matter. 'What do you think about it now?' she asked. 'Looking back?'

'I don't think anything,' said Marianne, shaking her head and looking troubled. 'Perhaps I came to the view that he felt the need to reproach himself in some way. And that he'd been doing it ever since the accident, whenever that was. Children do that sort of thing sometimes, don't they, although they've no reason to? They hold themselves responsible for things that can only be laid at their parents' door, for example . . . divorce and that kind of thing.'

'Yes, that's pretty common,' said Eva Backman. 'And even if it was only something in his imagination, it could have stayed with him all through his life – is that what you think?'

Marianne shrugged. 'It's a possibility, certainly.'

'You thought it could have been his unfounded imaginings underlying his depression?'

'If it really was depression. The other possibility is pretty appalling to contemplate, isn't it?'

'You mean . . .'

'That he might actually have done it.'

After she came out of the hospital, Backman took her statutory extended Sunday walk. But this afternoon it wasn't a question of the transition from the family home and her flat that was uppermost in her mind. It was Germund Grooth she couldn't get out of her head.

Again.

So where has that got me? she was thinking. Had that chat with Marianne clarified anything?

Or just further complicated the strange picture of Germund Grooth?

Kristin Pedersen's and Marianne's accounts of Grooth's character essentially tallied pretty well. But what about Marianne's disclosure right at the end there? Did it have any real significance?

I killed my parents and my sister, can you write that in your books?

It seemed extremely odd. Why would you say something like that, even in a dream? If she had understood correctly, his parents and little sister had died in a car accident when Germund was only ten or eleven. Sorrysen had tracked down the information. The car went off the road into a wide river and they drowned, didn't they?

She was pretty certain that was how it had happened, but she would check it with Sorrysen, of course. And anyway how on earth would a kid of that age set about killing three people? He wasn't even in the car with them, was he?

No, decided Eva Backman once she had crossed Barins allé and was making her way through Pampas. If his statement signified anything at all, it was surely just as one of those projections Marianne had talked about? The ten-year-old boy suffering some kind of survivor's guilt, and no one had registered how vital it was to free him from that sense of being responsible. So it had stayed with him – at least in his dreams – all his life.

A life that – for some reason as yet unknown – had ended at Gåsaklinten, ten kilometres south of Kymlinge, on 25 September 2010. That was one thing they knew, thought Eva Backman grimly.

But they'd known that much for quite a long time now.

63

She liked it in Gothenburg.

I spent twenty years of my life in Karlstad, five in Uppsala, she thought to herself that first wet and blustery winter there. And this is the city where I shall spend the rest of it.

She didn't care about the bad weather. Tomas had wangled them a flat in Aschebergsgatan – a decent-sized one on the fourth floor with a view over leaden skies and down onto the Vasastaden district. He'd got it through the bank, or so she understood, and she spent a lot of time fitting it out and decorating; she wouldn't be able to get a proper job until April, so she had all the time in the world.

It didn't really matter to them financially that she wasn't working. Tomas had an amazingly good starting salary at Handelsbanken, and she enjoyed just being at home, at least in these early stages. But it wasn't only working on the flat that made it easy to settle in. It was the Gothenburgers, too. Their outlook, their sense of humour – she had thought it was just one of those myths, but soon discovered people treated each other differently in this city. In shops, in the street, everywhere. A little joke, a smile; she had never found people in Uppsala particularly cool or disagreeable, but when she compared them with the locals here, the contrast was striking. A simple shopping trip became a pleasure.

This first Gothenburg winter felt altogether like the start of something new and good. The incident in Timişoara was more than two years ago. Her time at Ulleråker and the lost babies felt even more distant. They saw in the new year at a restaurant with Sirkka and Martin, a couple they'd just got to know. Martin worked with Tomas at the bank, and when Gunilla and Tomas got home around two in the morning they made love on the new hall carpet; they didn't get any further, the foreplay had started as soon as they left the restaurant.

This is the way to start the new year, remarked Tomas. Passionate lovemaking in the hall, when the year is but two hours old.

Gunilla laughed. It was like the old days, she thought. Like when we first met. I'm ready to get pregnant again now.

She didn't, though, and it would have been rather odd anyway, as she was still on the pill. But she came off it in January, without telling Tomas. Time does heal all wounds, she thought. It's an actual fact, not just a cliché.

Tomas was working long hours; he regularly had to go and see clients in the evenings, but that didn't worry her, either. Their love life was getting better and better, and she knew it was thanks to her. She was as receptive as she had been in their first year together. She felt more turned on, to put it simply, and found herself craving him even though it was still only morning and she knew he wouldn't be home until late at night, and wondered if it was because she wanted to get pregnant again. To think it could be that biological, and the clock of life had suddenly started working again.

But she didn't get pregnant. Her period arrived month after

month on the twenty-eighth day, and she decided she'd try to stop thinking about it. Not force it. Just in case it was her own desire that was proving an obstacle.

She started work on 1 April. It was for a translation agency that had some vacancies to fill, and even though she hadn't really completed her degree in Uppsala, she had been studying languages for quite a few years. She'd got the good marks to show for it in her English, German and Spanish courses; her translation work mainly consisted of business correspondence and contracts, hardly her speciality, but there were dictionaries and people to ask, and it was easy enough to learn. The agency had offices up at Guldheden, twenty minutes' walk from Aschebergsgatan. She was only working three days a week, but there was a good chance she could increase her hours, come the autumn.

She had got in from work one Thursday in early April to find the telephone ringing. She could hear it out on the landing and thought she wouldn't get into the flat in time to answer.

But it went on ringing. Someone was clearly keen to get hold of her. She threw her bag on the basket chair, picked up the phone and answered.

'It's Maria here. I want to talk to you about Timişoara.'

She had the sensation of something catching up with her.

64

Chief Inspector Asunander didn't normally laugh on Mondays and this morning was no exception. Eva Backman thought he looked hungover; she knew he was in the habit of sitting at home drinking grog on his own, but he wouldn't normally over-indulge on a Sunday evening.

Assuming it was a hangover. But perhaps he was just feeling tired and gloomy.

He was due to retire in two years' time. Then he'd be free to drink grog every night of the week and nobody would bat an eyelid, she thought. Asunander was unquestionably one of that happy band who prefer their own company.

'We've got to impose some order on this, and look sharp about it,' he said. 'It just won't do.'

'What are you referring to?' Gunnar Barbarotti ventured to ask. As a matter of fact he wasn't looking all that perky, either, noted Backman. Maybe he'd been sitting up with Marianne all night? He certainly hadn't shaved.

Asunander scowled at him. 'I'm referring to this Gåsaklinten shambles,' he said. 'I'm referring to a dead academic from Lund who's still in limbo. Over two weeks have gone by. It may come as a surprise to you, Inspector, but we do have a few other matters needing attention.'

Backman cast her mind back to the situation three or four

years before, when Asunander still had problems with his false teeth. He certainly hadn't been as eloquent then. He'd expressed himself more like an old-fashioned telegram, because his teeth were in danger of coming loose if he talked too much. Things were better back then, she and Barbarotti were in total agreement on that.

'It's a strange case,' she said.

'That may well be,' said Asunander. 'But I want to take this chance to talk to you both without that fusspot Månsson in attendance. Cards on the table. I want a proper idea from you of whether we should close this case or not. Go ahead. I'm all ears. Tell me what the hell you think.'

'Hrrm, what I would . . .' said Barbarotti.

'Backman first,' said Asunander. 'I know you're not really with it, after what happened to your wife. Nor should we expect you to be. How is she?'

'Getting better and better,' said Barbarotti. 'She probably won't be left with any after-effects at all. But it's going to take time.'

'Well, she's definitely worth waiting for,' said Asunander. 'So, Backman, what have you got to say about the Germund Grooth case?'

'You've read my summary, I assume?' queried Backman.

'I have. Read it last night. Well written, I must say, and really only missing one detail.'

Backman nodded. She had written the summary on Saturday morning and emailed it to him, as he had asked her to. It contained nothing about her conversation with Marianne and, on reflection, she felt it was just as well. She was pretty sure Barbarotti shared her opinion. But it was still conceivably the detail that the chief inspector was looking for.

'What detail is that?' she asked.

Asunander leant back and briefly looked rather pleased with himself. He likes being fed lines like that, she thought. He likes leaving people on tenterhooks. Childish. And whatever he says, he's not interested in hearing my view of the case. No, we'll be the ones having to listen to *his*.

'It's whether a crime has been committed or not,' he said, stressing basically every syllable. 'That's the little question we must try to answer. That's why I've called you in here. It's not obvious from your report whether anybody helped Germund Grooth over the edge or not. We're not going to waste resources investigating accidents and suicides; the taxpayers don't like it.'

'We don't know,' said Backman. 'It's impossible to tell at this point.'

'I had noticed that, thank you,' said Asunander. 'After two weeks of intensive investigation, we still don't know if he was murdered or not? Fusspot Månsson was making more than his usual fuss about it after our meeting on Thursday, I can reveal.'

Eva Backman sighed and looked at Barbarotti. Barbarotti sighed and looked out of the window.

'So the thing is,' said Asunander, 'we have to make up our minds. Are we going to carry on looking into this or not?'

'Perhaps the boss might be able to offer us a little tip?' suggested Barbarotti.

'It's lucky for you that my irony radar hasn't switched itself on yet,' said Asunander, raising a warning forefinger. 'But you may have noticed that I haven't in fact asked you to shelve Grooth. I've read Sandlin's folders from back in 1975 and I've been keeping an eye on you throughout. And it really is . . . well, a damn strange business. It's aggravating me.'

'Same here,' said Backman.

'One of the strangest we've had in a long time,' said Barbarotti.

Asunander cleared his throat. 'Now listen. Seven people go out into a forest. One of them dies. Thirty-five years later another of them dies in exactly the same location. Does either of you go in for sudoku?'

'Sudoku?' said Backman. 'Not me, anyway.'

'I tried a few when it first came out,' said Barbarotti. 'But I didn't get the bug.'

'I did,' said Asunander. 'But then I'm really a mathematician at heart, so it's not that surprising. I probably solve about twenty a week. Only the most difficult level, of course. Well, sometimes you get a problem that's insoluble – that is to say, it has two or more answers. Because the compiler wasn't thorough enough. The Grooth case reminds me of one of those, a badly constructed sudoku.'

'But surely it can't have two solutions?' objected Barbarotti. 'Either he was murdered or—'

'That's the difference,' Asunander broke in. 'We have to content ourselves with *one* solution. But sometimes, when you're solving sudoku, you reach a point where you have to take a step in the dark. Decide, even though it isn't really possible to make a decision. Without any foundation, otherwise you simply won't make any progress, if you understand what I mean, Inspectors.'

'Almost thirty per cent,' said Gunnar Barbarotti. 'But that taking a step in the dark thing is rather a speciality of mine, actually.'

Asunander raised his finger again and then slowly lowered it.

'So, what do you reckon?' he said in conclusion. 'That's all

I want to know. Was he murdered or not? Think carefully before you answer.'

Five minutes of silence followed. Asunander took off his tie.

'Yes,' said Eva Backman. 'That's my judgement. But I've nothing to base it on.'

'Agreed,' said Barbarotti. 'He was murdered. Baseless step in the dark.'

'All right,' said Asunander. 'I think the same, in fact. I wouldn't be sitting here wasting my youthful years otherwise. What about Maria Winckler then?'

Five more silent seconds passed. Asunander shoved his tie into the top drawer of his desk.

'You can't just answer yes or no, without imagining some kind of scenario at the same time,' said Backman. 'That would be pointless. Or that's normally the case, anyway. The problem is that I think Maria Winckler was murdered, too, but I haven't the first notion of any plausible scenario.'

'And you?' said Asunander, indicating Barbarotti with his pen.

'Not without reservations,' said Barbarotti.

'We don't take reservations in this bar,' said Asunander. 'Do you think she was pushed or not?'

Barbarotti thought hard.

'Count me in,' he said.

'Good,' said Asunander. 'I think the same. But it was past two in the morning last night by the time I made up my mind.'

And not without a few grogs, either, Eva Backman observed to herself. I suspected as much. The chief inspector paused to hunt through the papers littering his desk and excavated the one he wanted. He studied it for a second. To Backman, it looked like a page from an ordinary student notepad after an unusually unstructured lecture.

'My final question,' he said. 'One or two murderers?'

Backman eyed Barbarotti. Barbarotti eyed Backman.

'One,' said Backman.

'One,' said Barbarotti.

'Exactly right,' said Asunander. 'If we add together both your answers.'

'He gets more and more peculiar,' said Backman as they sat in the canteen fifteen minutes later. 'You have to admit it.'

'Yes,' said Barbarotti. 'Perhaps it's just as well he's only got two years to go. But he has that special way of seeing. God knows how he goes about it.'

'He solved that Mousterlin case for us,' recalled Backman. 'Do you know how he worked it out?'

'No,' said Barbarotti. 'He never told me.'

'Even though you spent a whole night on the grog together?'

'Only a few hours,' Barbarotti corrected her. 'But yesterday he was definitely there on his own. I almost feel a bit sorry for him really.'

'Me, too,' said Backman. 'What do you make of what he just said?'

'The bit about needing to look for two murderers? Damned if I know.'

'If we find one each, then the case is solved.'

'You make it sound so simple,' said Gunnar Barbarotti. 'Have you got a plan?'

'I'm thinking of a little trip to Lindås,' said Backman. 'I suggest you—'

'No need for you to suggest anything,' said Barbarotti. 'I know exactly what I'm going to do.'

FOUR

65

'A party at the vicarage?' said Rickard Berglund. 'Do you really think that's a good idea?'

'Why not?' said Anna. 'What else would you have a vicarage for?'

It was a Thursday at the start of August. They were sitting out in the arbour with its green garden furniture. Bumblebees were buzzing in the mignonette. They were into their second week of high pressure and he had just started writing his sermon for Sunday. The tenth after Trinity: *Spiritual gifts.*

'Well, maybe. But you didn't go right ahead and suggest it?'

'Of course not. I had to talk to you first, didn't I? It was just an idea I had, and I thought it could be interesting. I mean, it's been quite a while since we last saw them. And now Maria and Germund are moving here as well.'

'Did she tell you that?'

'Yes. In fact I'm pretty sure they're already here. They're going to be teaching at a school somewhere in town. They were both able to get temporary contracts there, apparently. And it would only take Gunilla and Tomas an hour to drive up here – an hour and a half at the most. They could stay over.'

Perhaps it wasn't such a bad idea? he thought. Perhaps the time had come for them to meet again? And why put a dampener on things, now that Anna actually seemed enthusiastic about something, for once?

'All right,' he said. 'Let's think about it.'

Seven months. More than half a year had passed since they moved into Rödåkra vicarage, and he still sometimes woke up in the morning and didn't immediately know where he was. When the hand-painted nineteenth-century wallpaper swam into focus. The mullioned windows and the shrubbery of lilacs outside.

It was like some idyllic storybook scene. Or an old Swedish film. The main house, with landscape timbers, dated from the eighteenth century, and two side buildings in the same style had been added fifty years later. There was a parish hall just across the road.

He had one of the side buildings for work and the other was furnished as a guest room, because there were only four rooms in the main house. But they were generously proportioned, and they never felt short of space. Rickard remembered that back in their Uppsala days he had imagined their children growing up here, and there would certainly be plenty of room for two of them beneath the solid, whitewashed roof beams. Not to mention the garden where they were sitting, in which ten children could easily run around and play; it sloped down to a muddy river and was home to a profusion of gnarled old fruit trees and tangles of raspberry canes, currant and gooseberry bushes. They had tentatively broached the baby question a few times, but there was still something in Anna that made her hesitant. He couldn't work out what it was, and maybe it was that little fly in the ointment that sometimes kept him awake at nights.

Why could she never be truly content? The thought kept

recurring to him. What was she lacking? Was it something in *him*? Or were they back at that old distinction between happiness and meaning? Though in reverse: was Anna so preoccupied with finding meaning that she couldn't feel happy? Was it anything to do with her upbringing? With those lugubrious parents and sullen brothers in Salabackar?

But they didn't discuss it, and he never found an answer to his questions – that is, he came up with a whole series of possible explanations, all of which he quickly dismissed. And even though he rarely, if ever, troubled her with his thoughts, she could see he was intermittently afflicted by them. Naturally she understood the score, at least when it came to the topic of having children.

What was the point of having a vicarage if you never threw a party? she said. But what was the point of having one if you didn't populate it with children? Rickard thought that was the better question.

And when she saw him looking sad, she would sometimes succumb to the same emotion. You've got to give me time, Rickard, she would say. A bit more time. Let's not talk about this for the time being.

He supposed that counted as some kind of understanding between them.

But he certainly filled his clerical role. His predecessor may have been in post for over thirty years, but Rickard soon came to realize that he hadn't really been all that popular. The Reverend Tömlin had preached too much fire and brimstone, especially as he grew older and became a martyr to his poor digestion, day and night. Mr Holmgren the verger had initiated Rickard into everything he needed to know in the first few weeks of February. Tömlin had died back in August, aged sixty-five and weighing twice that figure in kilos; the clergy of nearby parishes had obligingly kept things on the boil.

That was Holmgren's expression. Kept things on the boil. Which was something of an exaggeration, considering the sparse numbers in the pews at Sunday morning service.

But anyway the young vicar and his wife were warmly welcomed, and not only by the verger. Miss Bengtsson and Mrs Lavander, who were the registrars as well as dealing with other administrative tasks in the parish office, also expressed their appreciation from the very start, saying it was quite a relief. Then they laughed at their way of phrasing it.

'Do you need to get on with your sermon?' asked Anna, waving away a bee.

'Yes, I suppose it's about time.'

She had brought her typewriter outside, too, and he assumed she was going to start work on her report from the trip she had just made to the ancient grave sites on the west-coast islands of Tjörn and Orust. She had returned last night from her three-day trip.

'I won't disturb you if I tap away here?'

'No, of course not.'

He thought about how he loved her. Today she was having one of her gentle, contented days. Perhaps they would even make love later on.

He felt ashamed of the thought. Here we are in Paradise, he thought, the vicar and the vicar's wife. He's scribbling away at his sermon and she's writing an article for the *Swedish Church Times*. But the vicar's mind is on screwing.

Though there was no harm in that. He could laugh to

himself about it, and he assumed Our Lord could as well. Desiring your wife wasn't a sin. And if there were ever to be any babies at Rödåkra vicarage, it was the only way.

Things turned out the way he hoped. Afterwards they lay there in the huge double bed, feeling the warm night air filter into the bedroom. The high pressure seemed really stable; August nights weren't generally this warm.

'What do you think about them?' he asked.

'Who?'

'Maria and Germund. Tomas and Gunilla. How are they doing?'

She lay there in silence for a moment. 'Do you often think about them?' she asked. 'And about . . . that?'

'From time to time I do,' he said. 'It's not the sort of thing you can forget, and we used to spend a lot of time with them. Tomas was the very first person I met in Uppsala. It's strange that we drifted apart the way we have.'

Anna nodded.

'Maybe,' she said. 'But that's the way it goes, isn't it? She was a bit worried about Maria.'

'Gunilla?'

'Yes.'

'Why?'

'She's rung Gunilla a few times and she seemed weird. Yes, that was how she put it.'

'Weird in what way?'

'I don't know. We didn't really go into it. She was down in Spain for quite a long time. Maria, that is. She only got back in May, I think.'

'She's never been an easy one to understand.'

'No, but this seemed like something more than that.'

'Was Germund with her in Spain?'

Anna turned over and switched off the light. 'I think so. Let's get to sleep now. We can discuss the party idea tomorrow.'

There were times when he missed Uppsala, and tonight he lay awake for a while, doing just that. Not the town itself, or the period when they spent such a lot of time with their four friends – who might conceivably be coming to visit them at the vicarage – no, he sometimes longed to be back with his other companions. Rufus and Matti and Sivert. The smoky corner of Ofvandahls cafe and the never-ending discussions of faith, meaning and ethics. And all those other vital issues of life. Matti Kolmikoski and Rufus Svensson had both been ordained at the same time as he had, but Sivert Grahn had decided to go abroad and work at mission stations first. Rickard had received a couple of letters, from Uganda and Tanzania, and it really was a world away from the parish of Rödåkra–Hemleby. But he thought it was typical of Sivert, in a sense. No compromising; he followed his inner voice, and if it told him to go to Africa, then he did. Rickard couldn't help feeling it was admirable.

The discussions of faith and the Word that he had experienced since leaving Uppsala had been limited to three diocesan study days in Härlanda, and even they had proved disappointing. It had largely been about all the practical stuff attached to the ministry, and he had been the youngest and least experienced participant. No, it hadn't been about the Christian faith in any deeper sense.

Mr Holmgren the verger couldn't stop talking, but it was the same with him – he rarely touched on spiritual matters. That was to say, never.

But then that wasn't the important thing in the long run, Rickard would think to himself. Talking to other people about God. The central point of it all was your own dialogue with God.

Which didn't always run without a hitch, either.

I'm twenty-six, he thought suddenly. Will I be the vicar of this parish in thirty years' time, like Tömlin? What will life look like by then, in the year 2005? What thoughts will I be thinking when I'm fifty-six? Or sixty? What does the world look like? How many children have we got? Grandchildren? Will I have discovered the meaning behind it all?

Meaning? Spiritual gifts? He sighed. Rolled over onto his side and thought it would actually be rather interesting to see their old friends again. Tomas and Gunilla. Maria and Germund. We're all mature people now, he thought. Adults.

Reunion at Rödåkra vicarage. Earlyish in September, perhaps. See what had become of them all.

Yes, why not?

66

Sparrow. Before I started my degree in Uppsala, I honestly thought it was le Piaf in French. Or *la* Piaf. But it isn't, I've already been into that.

These are the dog days and the year is 1975. In all known languages. Spain – Uppsala – Kymlinge: that's the journey I've made in the past few months. Germund and I arrived here a week ago and the autumn term starts in four days' time. It feels very strange, indisputably, but we decided when we came home in May that we would leave academic life, and Germund said what the hell, they always need teachers.

So he found us these two posts at the same school; that was in mid-June. He called and spoke to their director of studies, and got a semi-promise. They firmed it up a week later; there was something about them not wanting qualified teachers because they could never get rid of them later. If I understood Germund correctly, that is, and if Germund didn't misinterpret the director of studies. His name is Flemingsson, incidentally, and he's almost two metres tall and used to be a top-flight basketball player. I met him a couple of days ago and liked him, and there was absolutely no doubting that he liked me, too.

I assume I'm on the right track, then. I can function among people again, or as well as I ever did anyway. But the most important thing is for me to function for myself.

I am Sparrow, I fell and there was no special providence in my fall. But I came back.

And I'm not scared of teenagers, not in the slightest. I shall teach them English and French as well as anybody can. Flemingsson asked if I spoke Spanish, too – they might be setting up a little trial group in due course, whatever that means – and I said it was no problem. *Niemos problemos*. Brilliant, said Flemingsson.

She is brilliant, Germund said. What have you got for me?

Germund will be doing maths and physics of course. I find it rather hard to imagine him in front of a class, but then he says he thinks the same about me. So we'll both be coming from the same starting point, as it were.

But there's nothing to it, really, says Germund. Think of a good teacher you had and do more or less the same. There's no need to complicate things.

I was lucky that he came down to Spain. I honestly think I would have gone round the bend if I'd stayed on my own for much longer. That bar and that strange girl and the overwhelming loneliness. No, there was no sane way it could have carried on. We left Torremolinos after just a week and found a couple of rooms in the centre of Malaga instead, in the heart of the old town, right by the cathedral, and we stayed there from then on, right until we came home at the end of May. We rented from an old lady who was the widow of a bullfighter, or so she told us; I don't know, maybe all Andalusian widows say the same thing.

Germund had enough money for us not to need to work. I stopped smoking hash. We began taking long walks, through the old Jewish and Moorish quarters, up round the fortress and along by the sea, and suddenly it was a different sea. Not like in Mamaia, or like over the winter in Torremolinos and Fuengirola; it was Germund being there that made the difference of course, and I told him so. You're a bloody vital organ for me, Germund, I said. I simply can't exist without you.

It wasn't a declaration of love but simply a statement of fact, and he understood it as such.

I have some problems with my breathing when you're not there, too, he said.

It was on the beach that we managed to make love for the first time. I'm very deliberately exchanging 'fuck' for 'make love' here, because that was what it was this time. It was night, and moonlit, and I can still call to mind the sighing of the waves, if I want to.

You know that thing about pure maths and physical love, I said afterwards. Do you still believe in it?

There could be a third component, said Germund.

Beauty? I asked.

A fourth then, said Germund.

He met my parents, too, for the first time in fact. It was at their house in Fuengirola, and Mum had made a huge paella and invited a few neighbours round, to be on the safe side. We sat on the roof terrace and it all went pretty smoothly. But Dad, at least, was relieved when we left, I know he was. He's a bit scared of me and that's just fine. It was partly his fault that I fell off the swing when I was eight, and my very presence is enough to remind him of it. I think Mum occasionally does as well.

Remind him, that is.

★

But now here we are in Kymlinge. It turns out Rickard and Anna live not far from here, in a vicarage in the country, about half an hour away. Rickard rang yesterday and invited us over. In a month or so, he said; he was just sounding people out about dates. Trying to find a sermon-free Sunday, maybe. He talked about going out to pick mushrooms as well. The idea is for Tomas and Gunilla to come, too, driving up from Gothenburg, I assume. I felt an instinctive aversion to the scheme, and when I told Germund he felt the same way.

What the hell would be the point? he wondered.

I wondered the same thing. That time is behind us now.

But there again, I don't suppose it can do any harm. We both came round to that view after a while. The instinctive aversion seemed to run off us like water off a pair of ducks' backs, and an hour later we'd decided to accept the invitation. A dinner party with some nice wine at a country vicarage would be endurable, surely?

I'm sitting here on our little balcony, looking out over the river flowing by, only thirty metres below the flat we've just started renting. In their infinite wisdom, they call it the River Kymlinge. Where do they get all their bright ideas? I'm waiting for Germund, who is out buying paint. We're going to paint the bathroom and we've decided on yellow.

I don't think about Bernard Grimaux any longer.

And Gunilla, what can one say?

67

Eva Backman left the detached property in Lindås, drove 500 metres and pulled into a parking place. She switched off the engine and engaged in some brainwork. Two murderers? she thought. Sudoku?

Well, I'm damned. Chief Inspector Asunander, you're a dark horse.

She had really been hoping to speak to Tomas Winckler, but he wasn't in. She wondered how much time he actually spent in that expensive house in Hägervägen, as he seemed to be out most of the time. But to be fair, it was a Monday, an ordinary working day. That travel company needed a bit of attention occasionally, she assumed.

And she deliberately opted to arrive unannounced. As she happened to be passing and there was one little detail she wanted to clear up.

That was how she presented it to Mrs Winckler-Rysth, too, but it would have been more interesting to have done so to her husband. Distinctly more interesting.

She checked the time. It was half past two. She had no children to cook dinner for, this being Ville's week. No restaurant meal booked with some intriguing new man. No obligations.

She took the map out of the glove compartment. How far was it up to Strömstad?

Gunnar Barbarotti pressed the doorbell and waited.

No reaction.

He tried again. Took four steps back and tried to peer through the kitchen window, but the slats of the blinds were angled in such a way that all he could see were confusing narrow strips. As far as he could make out, there was no light on in there. It was the same with the living room; it was to the left of the front door, he remembered. That was where they'd sat last time he came. Both times, to be precise.

If he was at home, he would have switched on a light or two, Inspector Barbarotti decided. The rain was hanging in the air and the twilight had deepened over Kymlinge to the shade of overripe plums, even though it was only five.

Surely he wasn't sitting in the dark just because he didn't feel like receiving visitors? Or was he?

It was his third attempt. He had rung on the doorbell at 1 p.m. and again at 3 p.m. He had checked with Linderholm's funeral directors too, but Linderholm said he hadn't seen Berglund since the funeral.

Barbarotti gave a shrug and went back to the car. I'll have to try again in the morning, he said. He won't be leaving the country.

'Can I talk to you?'

He was at the kitchen table, leafing through the recipe file. He hadn't been home more than five minutes. Jenny was in

547

the doorway through to the sitting room and he could hear from her voice that she'd planned this. She'd clearly had something on her mind. Jenny was indisputably the quietest of the children, the one who always thought before she spoke. She was sixteen and at her first year in upper secondary, where she was taking the social-sciences programme with the language specialism, which meant some subjects were taught in English or French. Barbarotti had tried to imagine what it would be like to have your maths taught in French, but the only image that presented itself to him was of being drawn into a black hole.

He really admired her for it, though. Naturally. Plus, she was very much like Marianne, in both appearance and manner. That was no less admirable.

'Of course,' he said. 'Come and sit down.'

She pulled out a chair and sat down opposite him. Then she seemed unsure of herself and looked down at the table.

'You've been thinking about Mum,' he said.

'Yes,' said Jenny. 'I've been thinking about Mum.'

'We all have,' said Barbarotti. 'Ever since it happened. But she's going to be fine.'

Jenny nodded. 'Yes. Everybody's saying that. But what if it happens again?'

Barbarotti swallowed. 'There's nothing to point to it happening again.'

'I know they say that.' She gave him a quick glance as if seeking some sort of mutual understanding. Something that meant both he and she knew what was really going on. That those sorts of things were said as a comfort. By doctors and other know-alls.

'What is it you want to say, Jenny?'

She gave a deep, shaky sigh and he realized she wasn't far from tears.

'If she'd died, what would have happened to us then?'

'Us?'

'Johan and me.'

'I don't understand what you mean?'

Well, perhaps he did, but he thought it would be better to let her put it into her own words.

'I talked to Dad last night.'

'Oh yes?'

'And he said if Mum dies, we're to go and live with him. He . . .'

'Yes?'

'He didn't ask if we wanted to. He just said that was how it would be.'

Barbarotti shook his head. In his considered opinion, Marianne's ex was a bastard, but it probably wasn't the time to be pointing that out to his daughter.

'She's alive, Jenny. Your mum's alive and she's going to live for thirty years more. Fifty!'

'Yes, but if? I want to know, don't you see that?'

He thought about it and suddenly he did. He realized what it was she was asking him.

'Sorry, Jenny, I'm a bit slow. This is your home. You know that, don't you?'

She didn't answer. She was waiting for him to say more. Give her some kind of assurance.

'You don't want to live with your dad, do you?'

'No.'

'Nor does Johan?'

'No.'

'Well then. Come here.'

He stood up and held out his arms. She hesitated for a moment, but then folded herself into his embrace.

'I love you, Jenny. You can live in this house until you draw your pension, if you want. I promise. We can have a family grave in the garden when the time comes. Over by the compost heap, do you think?'

That made her laugh.

'Thank you.'

'Why on earth did you imagine anything else?'

She didn't reply. She rested her head on his chest and took a few unsteady breaths. He was aware of the tears prickling his throat, too; the good sort of tears, but he still bit his cheek and fought them back.

'She's alive,' he said. 'We're all alive. We've got to learn to be grateful. To value life rather than being scared of death.'

'I know,' said Jenny. 'But it's no fun, not liking your dad.'

'I haven't got a dad.'

'No, you told us.'

'He disappeared before I was born. That's no fun, either. But there are some things we can't do anything about.'

'Your parents, for example?'

'Yes, them. And a fair amount of other stuff, too. But things we *can* put right, it's our duty to put right. We've talked about that before. But let's put that to one side for now. Do you want to help with dinner? I'm looking for that recipe for mushroom risotto, what do you reckon?'

'OK,' said Jenny, letting go of him and blowing her nose. 'She'll be coming home soon then?'

'In a few days' time.'

'I'm grateful that she found you, anyway.'

The good tears threatened to well up again, and a warm feeling spread right to his marrow. Sometimes you get more than you deserve, he thought. Is that what they mean by a *state of grace*?

68

'How are you?' asked Tomas. 'Everything hunky-dory?'

Gunilla nodded. 'Everything hunky-dory.'

'Sure?'

She couldn't help laughing at his solicitude. 'Tomas, I'm in the fourth month and I'm doing fine. We're not even halfway yet, you can't go on like this for the whole pregnancy.'

Tomas smiled and opened the car door for her. 'Sorry. Right, let's go and see the vicar then. What do you reckon?'

'How do you mean?'

'What do you think? How will it be? Like before?'

He started the car and pulled out of the parking place, tapping his fingers lightly on the steering wheel.

'I don't know what you mean by "before",' she said. 'Like the early days at Sibyllegatan, or later on?'

'It would be great if it could be like the early days,' said Tomas. 'Wouldn't it? I'm glad we can stay the night, though. It wouldn't be much fun chomping your way through a long dinner and then having to drive back. And I assume there's plenty of room in a vicarage.'

'I expect so,' said Gunilla. 'I don't suppose it's Rickard and Anna we need to worry about. If we're assuming it won't all be like the early days, that is.'

Tomas frowned and glanced over at her.

'You're referring to my little sister?'

'I'm referring to your little sister.'

'You surely don't think she'll bring that up, do you?'

'You never know. She did on the phone, after all.'

'That was in April. She was really going to pieces just then.'

'But in May, too. I just don't get what she wanted. I mean there's nothing anyone can do about it now. Good grief, it's been over three years now.'

'Perhaps she just needed to talk.'

'I tried to talk to her for a whole year afterwards. I didn't get a word out of her.'

'You're uneasy, though. Would you prefer us to pull out of this?'

Gunilla shook her head. She tried to laugh but could hear how unnatural it sounded. 'Of course we're damn well going,' she said. 'After they've gone to all the trouble, how would it look if we rang now and said we weren't coming?'

'Better to take the bull by the horns?' said Tomas.

'That's right,' said Gunilla. 'And who knows, we might really enjoy ourselves. It's just that slight worry . . . you know?'

Tomas sighed. 'Germund and Maria, yes. Christ, what a pair! Maybe it's just as well they've got each other.'

'Definitely,' said Gunilla. 'She sounded normal when you last spoke to her, though?'

'As normal as she ever does,' said Tomas. 'We'll be in plenty of time for four o'clock, anyway. Why do they want us there so early, did Anna say?'

'We're starting with an aperitif and some kind of treasure trail, apparently.'

'Treasure trail?'

'Yes. Don't ask me. But if we make it through the evening,

it'll be nice to get out into the forest tomorrow and look for mushrooms. There's no better way to spend an autumn Sunday.'

'Don't forget you sometimes get tired quite early,' said Tomas. 'Pregnancies can be a good excuse for all sorts of things.'

'I wasn't born yesterday,' said Gunilla, putting a hand on his thigh.

Sparrow.

I'm having doubts, but then I knew I would. Germund suggested we each knock back a shot of vodka before we go. Idiot, I said, we can't turn up with alcohol on our breath.

We've decided to take a taxi back, at any rate, so we don't have to sit through it sober. The bus on the way there, of course; there's a rural yellow one that goes at half past three. Its stop is only a hundred metres from us; Germund checked. But there's no night service, not in these parts.

They want us there at four. We're going to have a drink in the garden first, I think, and take a stroll around. And why not? I'm sure it's infernally idyllic and all that, out there in the sticks. But I'm feeling nervous, though I don't usually. Germund seems on edge as well; the fact is we're both regretting that we said yes to this lark. I don't want to see those people again, and Germund would much rather stay at home and get on with painting the walls – I can see it in him. We're half done already.

But he won't admit it. Pack it in, Maria, he says. They're even providing the wine. We can stoke up on a good meal and drink ourselves pleasantly woozy, and then we can have a nice walk in the forest tomorrow. I'm a real wizard at finding chanterelles, didn't I tell you?

You'd rather stay at home and paint the walls, stop pretending, I thought. And we could find our own way to the forest. But I don't say anything. I tell myself anyone who deals with hundreds of teenagers every day can surely cope just fine with a vicarage dinner party with a few old friends.

It's a quarter to three. Germund is telling me I need to start doing my make-up now, so we don't miss the bus.

Damn, we ought to have bought some flowers, too.

But I bet the vicarage garden's full of flowers. I ask Germund if we've got anything we could take. He shakes his head, but then he remembers we've got an unopened box of chocolates somewhere.

'These questions on the treasure trail,' said Rickard. 'Have you been round to check them out?'

'No,' said Anna. 'I know they're meant for the young people who come to confirmation camp. But that doesn't matter, does it? We're not really taking this seriously. And I didn't want to look at them in advance – that would be cheating.'

Rickard laughed. 'Well, they'll just have to take them as they find them. All I've seen is the sign at the start of the trail. *In the garden of Our Lord. Twenty questions about animals, nature and Christian life.* I think I'll put a bit of extra vodka in the punch, we might well need it.'

'You don't think it's a problem, do you?'

'No, not really,' Rickard assured her.

'The weather's nice. What can be wrong with taking a little walk with a drink in your hand? They'll like it. It'll stimulate their ironic side.'

'Three teams?' asked Rickard.

'Three teams. You and Gunilla in number one. Tomas and

Maria in number two; you never know, brother and sister might appreciate the chance to have a word with each other. Germund and I are number three. I've got the pens and the answer sheets ready. What time is it?'

'Quarter to four. They could be here any minute now. Anna?'

'Yes?'

'I love you. We're going to make sure it's a really lovely evening, aren't we?'

'Of course. But we'd better finish getting these potatoes ready for the oven, hadn't we? So we're not still messing about with it all when they arrive?'

He wondered for an instant whether to kiss her on the neck, but he decided not to. She didn't seem to be in that sort of mood.

He went on peeling potatoes instead. Every purpose under Heaven . . . and so on.

69

'Good morning,' said Gunnar Barbarotti. 'I hope I'm not disturbing you.'

'It's becoming a habit,' said Rickard Berglund, holding the door open to let him in.

'Thanks. I could do with a few more minutes. Have you got time?'

'I'm made of time,' said Rickard Berglund. 'It's all I've got. I assume you'd like some coffee?'

'It might be just as well,' said Barbarotti.

'Horrible wet weather we're having.'

'Yes.'

Five minutes later they were sitting in their respective armchairs. Berglund was wearing the same jeans and polo-neck sweater as last time, or it looked like it anyway. The almond biscuits on the plate had been replaced by a slew of ginger snaps.

'Your wife's gone to her grave now,' said Barbarotti.

'Yes,' said Berglund. 'How's yours?'

'Much better. She'll probably be coming home this week.'

He took a ginger snap and thought what a bizarre opening to an interview this was.

'Why do you want to talk to me this time?' asked Berglund.

'I've nothing against it, but I'm sure you understand I'm curious.'

'Same agenda as always,' said Barbarotti. 'We can't make any real sense of this case. Though we do feel we've got a little further.'

'Oh?' said Berglund with interest. 'In what way, if you don't mind my asking?'

Barbarotti cleared his throat and played his false ace. 'We're pretty much convinced Germund Grooth was murdered. And that his murderer is to be found among a very small circle.'

Rickard Berglund clasped his hands over his knee and regarded him at some length over the top of his glasses. He looked about as relaxed as you would while trying to decide which newspaper to buy. Or not bother with one at all.

'What is it you want from me then?' he said finally.

'First of all, I want to know exactly what it was that happened at that dinner party the evening before Maria Winckler's death,' said Barbarotti. 'In detail, if you wouldn't mind.'

'It was thirty-five years ago,' said Berglund.

'Something tells me you still remember,' said Barbarotti.

Berglund didn't answer. He leant forward and picked up a knight from the chessboard in front of him, which was still set up for a game. He weighed it in his hand for a few seconds and then replaced it. Barbarotti waited. Last time it was a pawn, he thought.

That same Tuesday morning, 12 October in the year of grace 2010, DI Eva Backman overslept. Instead of getting up at 6.30 when the alarm clock was supposed to go off – and conceivably had done – she woke up two and a half hours later, and when she saw 09.01 on the digital display, she assumed it was a Saturday or Sunday and dozed off for another quarter of an hour.

There were reasons for it, and she worked flexitime, so it was nothing to worry about, she thought, when she was finally standing under the shower. Might just as well stay away from police HQ until the afternoon, now the day had started as it had. She realized she could do with listening through the tapes from her two interviews the day before, and she could just as easily do that in her attractive living room in Grimsgatan as perched in the drab surroundings of her little office over in Norra Långgatan.

The most plausible reason for her oversleeping was the fact that she hadn't got back from Strömstad until after midnight, and had then taken another two hours to get to sleep. There were reasons for the latter, too, or she liked to imagine there were.

She prepared a breakfast tray with eight healthy ingredients and about the same number of unhealthy ones, sat down in the armchair with the view over the park and woodland and switched on her tape recorder. She spooled it to and fro a few times before she found the right place.

EB: So the two of you set off for that dinner at Rödåkra vicarage on the Saturday with rather mixed feelings?

GW: Yes, you could say that.

EB: Because your own relationship with Maria Winckler – that is, your sister-in-law – was rather strained?

GW: Yes, but I didn't know. We'd had very little contact over the preceding year.

EB: And why was that?

GW: Why was what?

EB: Why had there been so little contact between you?

GW: I can't go into that.

EB: Why can't you go into it?

[*A long hesitation*]

GW: We agreed on it.

EB: Which 'we'? And what did you agree on?

GW: The rest of us. We agreed to keep quiet about it. It had nothing to do with the accident anyway.

EB: And what was it you were to keep quiet about?

GW: That's what I can't tell you.

EB: We're talking about an agreement made thirty-five years ago. Two people are dead, possibly murdered. Anna Berglund has passed away as well. How many of you made this agreement?

GW: Five.

EB: Not Elisabeth Martinsson?

GW: No.

EB: You, your husband and Rickard Berglund. You're the only three left now, aren't you?

GW: Yes.

EB: Then I urge you to tell me what it was about. If you don't do it here and now, I shall have to take you to Kymlinge police station.

She switched off the tape recorder. This was the point where Gunilla Winckler-Rysth had burst into tears. They had flowed unchecked for several minutes and, once they ebbed away, she told Backman what had happened. Or her version of it.

A gang rape.

In Romania.

In the summer of 1972. The perpetrators had been four unknown soldiers, or guards of some kind, or possibly policemen.

The victim had been Maria Winckler.

But the intended victim had been Gunilla. Maria had taken her place.

Sacrificed herself.

It had taken a long time to extract the facts. More pauses. More tears. Backman had left the tape running, but there was no need for it now. She could remember it word for word.

Why? she had asked.

Why on earth had Maria sacrificed herself?

Gunilla didn't know.

So she voluntarily allowed herself to be raped by four soldiers?

Yes. But it was meant to be me. We drew lots and I lost.

You drew lots?

Yes. It had to be one of us. Those were their conditions.

She couldn't explain Maria's sacrifice. Not then, or thirty-eight years later. But Maria hadn't been the same afterwards. She'd been strange even before it happened, but afterwards she was unfathomable. Unfathomable and unpleasant.

According to Gunilla Winckler-Rysth.

Was she so unfathomable and unpleasant that you pushed her off Gåsastupan?

No, no, no, and more tears.

Do you think anyone else did?

No, no, no.

Was it because of this that you all stopped seeing each other? Backman had eventually asked. After the summer of 1972?

I think so.

And why did you all decide to keep quiet on the subject?

Because Maria didn't want to talk about it. Nor did any of us; we never referred to it between us. And it had nothing to do with 1975, so it would only have dragged things up needlessly. We'd agreed to keep quiet about it forever, basically. It became a sort of taboo.

Taboo?

Yes.

How can you know it didn't have anything to do with the accident?

Gunilla Winckler-Rysth made no reply. She just shook her head.

As did DI Backman, replaying the scene in her head a day later. She poured herself another cup of coffee and changed the tape in the recorder.

70

He gradually felt a strange sensation suffusing him.

Perhaps it was God, he thought. It was some kind of presence, anyway.

Something that lent weight to this moment, this hour. Six people out on a treasure trail round Rödåkra vicarage. On a Saturday afternoon in September, with a big blue sky and air that was crystal-clear. Not a hint of a breeze to rustle the yellow leaves of the aspens.

'It's beautiful,' said Gunilla.

'Yes,' he said. 'It's beautiful.'

They chatted as they strolled along. It was a quiet and undemanding conversation. They pondered the quiz questions as they came to them, talked them over, laughed a little and filled in their answer sheet. Perhaps she was suffused with that same presence, Rickard thought. With this moment, this hour in which they found themselves. It didn't feel at all awkward or uncomfortable being in her company after all this time, that was one thing.

He remembered how he had admired her when he first got to know her. How he had envied Tomas; that was before he met Anna. Before he had properly been with a girl, even. It was only six years ago, but to him it felt like a lifetime. Will the next six years change me as much? he wondered. And the six after that? In that case, I shall be an entirely different person by the time we get to the year 2000.

Assuming he got to live that long. Maybe there was another world war in the offing? Or some other sort of catastrophe. One could hardly demand to live in peace and harmony for another quarter of a century.

And such thoughts made the hour and the moment seem even more portentous.

'Imagine living here,' said Gunilla. 'It's just delightful.'

'Yes,' said Rickard. 'It really is delightful. I hope we shall have the good sense to appreciate it, too.'

'I'm sure you will,' said Gunilla. 'You and Anna have an eye for what's important in life.'

'Do you think so?' said Rickard, and she nodded.

Ahead of them they had the two siblings. Tomas and Maria. They were walking rather more briskly and seemed to be deeper in discussion, too, but maybe that was only to be expected. He caught occasional glimpses of them between the juniper and blackthorn bushes; they didn't look as though they were drawing full benefit from the hour, or from that mysterious presence. The trail took them along a path through the rolling landscape just south of the vicarage. It was a kilometre and a half in length, or so they had been informed by the wooden board at the start, and it was Miss Bengtsson who had devised the questions and gone out to put them up for the confirmation class, sometime at the start of the summer. In the Garden of Our Lord, as she'd chosen to call it.

Animals, nature and Christian life. There was more about animals and nature than about matters of faith, thank goodness. So far, at least.

Germund and Anna were a few hundred metres behind

them. Are they enjoying the moment, being filled with that benign feeling? For some reason he doubted it, at least where Germund was concerned. But Anna wasn't entirely content, either, or so it had felt to him today.

As he chatted to Gunilla he let his thoughts flow on, and neither activity impinged on the other.

We're six people walking together as part of our allotted span on this earth, he thought. Nothing more and nothing less. We've come to know each other through a series of chance events, and we could just as well have been six other people walking here on this glorious autumn day.

But it happens to be us. It just happens to be the six of us, and in a hundred years we'll all be dead. We've got to . . . we've simply got to appreciate this hour and this moment. Fully register that we're alive, here and now. Autumn days like this exist to remind us of it.

He wondered whether he ought to say anything about it whcn they sat down at the table. Something about the warm, intense feeling that had washed through him during the treasure trail. Give voice to it, interpret it. Assuming the others had felt the same way, that is. Or could do with reminding.

Maybe, maybe not. It was important to put things into words. But if you didn't find the right words, you could easily end up with the opposite. Obscurity instead of clarity. Fools drivelling on about the divine – and there were plenty of them – gave God a bad name.

He had learnt a few things in his first eight months as a clergyman, and this was one of them. And he could detect that sermonizing tone in his thoughts.

'Four months gone then?' he asked.

'Four months, yes,' said Gunilla.

'It doesn't really show yet. But this time it's going to be fine, I know it.'

'You can't possibly know,' said Gunilla with a little smile. 'But I know it too, actually.'

They stopped in front of question no. 8. It was a Latin flower name that neither of them had a clue about. They read the alternatives and ticked one of the boxes. Common tansy – how on earth could your average confirmation candidate be expected to know that? he wondered. Miss Bengtsson had high ambitions, there was no mistaking the fact.

They feigned a toast as best they could. Gunilla was drinking an alcohol-free alternative, in view of her condition, and their glasses were plastic cups, but Rickard's had plenty of alcohol in it.

'It's been a long time since we saw each other,' he said. 'It's a bit of a shame.'

She nodded and they continued along the path.

'It's because of the whole Maria thing, I guess.'

'Do you know how she is?'

She shrugged.

'Don't know. Better, I think. But it looks as if Tomas has got his hands full.'

He pointed out across the field. Brother and sister had stopped about fifty metres ahead of them and seemed engrossed in their discussion. Tomas was gesticulating, but Maria stood motionless, hands at her sides.

'Well, it doesn't look very much like brotherly and sisterly love,' said Gunilla.

And Rickard suddenly felt a chill little breeze catch him in the back of the neck. No, he thought, I shan't bother with my homily.

*

There's something wrong, thought Gunilla. And not simply the usual.

They were just finishing their main course. Tenderloin of pork with rosemary sauce and potatoes au gratin. Nice, but nothing that special. The others were onto the third bottle of red wine, but she stuck to water. They were seated round a large oak table of quite some vintage. They'd really fallen on their feet, Anna and Rickard, she thought; it was so cosy and attractive here and they had so much space. They hadn't had to buy very much furniture, only things to replace what they didn't want to keep, Rickard had told her. When you took over a vicarage, a lot of other things came with it, undoubtedly.

Not the widow of the previous incumbent, I hope? she had asked.

No, thank heavens, he had laughed.

Lit candles on the table. Simon and Garfunkel on the stereo, which had not been part of the inventory, she was sure. She was seated next to Germund. Maria was opposite and the hosts sat at the two ends of the table. Tomas was holding forth. About interest – short rates and long rates – and about the government, and about a tennis player no one had heard of, whom he tipped for global stardom. Rickard said a bit about what it was like to be a vicar in a rural parish, and she put in a word here and there about how they liked living in Gothenburg. The other three round the table didn't say much. But maybe that was how it had always been, she thought. Back then. It was certainly nothing unusual for Tomas to do all the talking, and just at the moment she was grateful for it. Six people round a table and no one saying anything would have been excruciating.

So she backed him up as best she could. Places she was getting to know in Gothenburg: Guldheden, Majorna, the shops and cafes along Avenyn, Haga.

As long as no one says anything about Romania, she thought. I shall be straight off to bed if they do.

But no one said anything about Romania. Their tacit agreement held. They had dessert, just ice cream, but with redcurrants and blackcurrants from the garden that had been in the freezer and were served with a sprinkling of sugar; Rickard said next summer they would all be very welcome to come and pick as much fruit as they wanted; this summer they'd only had time to deal with a fraction of what was on the bushes.

Then coffee with a little cognac and Swedish punch. They left the table and sat round the open hearth. Germund and Maria went out for a cigarette, as they had done after the main course; they were the only ones who still smoked. The others talked about it for a minute or two. In Uppsala they had all puffed away, and Gunilla could still remember the smell of smoke in the Sibyllegatan flat the day after.

Tomas went on talking. She and Rickard, too, though not to the same extent.

And something was wrong.

Was Anna normally that quiet? Were Maria and Germund?

She tried to watch them surreptitiously, slouching there in the wicker chairs. She attempted to fathom what was going on inside each person's head. There was a clear advantage to being sober, in actual fact; they were sitting there; in their slightly grumpy mood, they didn't seem particularly observant. She could watch them unnoticed.

Had Anna and Rickard fallen out? Or Maria and Germund? Or were explanations like that just too readily to hand? Had Maria really recovered?

Gunilla realized she was scared of her. And that she had been scared of her five years ago, too. The phone calls in the spring hadn't helped.

When 11.30 came, she decided it was time. If you were pregnant, you needed a proper amount of sleep. And tomorrow they had the mushroom hunt. Sufficient unto the day, and all that.

Sparrow.

Fifteen minutes, the girl on the switchboard promised. Twenty minutes max. I know, because I was the one who made the call.

Where's that damn taxi got to? said Germund. Did you really tell them where we are?

I asked him what was up.

He asked me what I meant by that.

We were cooling our heels by the roadside. A little way along from the gate, so we couldn't be seen from the vicarage. It was cold, not below zero but close to it.

You'd think Gunilla could have driven us home, said Germund. She didn't have anything to drink.

I don't think Gunilla would be very keen on driving you and me, I said.

You're right there, said Germund.

I asked him again what the matter was – while we were still standing there, stamping our feet to keep warm – and he again pretended not to get what I was driving at.

All right, I said. You needn't talk about it, if you don't want to.

Then the taxi finally turned up. It was a young female driver and she apologized for being a bit late. She said she'd taken a wrong turn and it was only her second night in the job.

Germund told her where we were going and we sat in silence all the way home. I wondered if that old nightmare of his had started recurring; I haven't seen him so miserable for a long time. Not the whole time we were in Spain, or since we got back.

But I found it heavy going this evening, as well. As soon as my shit brother starts, I clam up; I don't remember it being like that before. It's a sign of weakness and I don't like being weak.

I'm sorry, said Germund when we got home. I just find them very hard to be with – I don't know what it is.

I said it was OK and asked him if we ought to skip the mushroom hunt after all.

Germund shook his head.

No, we might as well tag along.

'Why?' I asked.

Trust me, said Germund, and I had no idea what he was talking about.

I've been lying here awake for ages since he fell asleep. There's a sense of anxiety pulsing through me and I don't know what it is. Everything feels so fragile again; I'm aware of how dependent I've grown on Germund. When he falters, I falter. It shouldn't be like that. If two people are going to be together, one has to carry the other. You can exchange roles, but one of you always has to keep their head above water.

In the best of worlds.

Dear Almighty, if you exist. Grant me a little sleep. It will all be different in the morning.

Sparrow, over and out.

71

'Yes, I think you still remember,' repeated Barbarotti.

Rickard Berglund wasn't looking at him. He was staring down at his folded hands instead. Several seconds of silence drifted by on their way to eternity, and Barbarotti reflected that it was these wordless phases of an interview that were the most interesting. The pauses while thoughts were seeking direction and decision. Or something along those lines, and he noticed to his surprise that his heart was racing.

'That dinner party,' Berglund said finally. 'You're right. I do remember it, and I remember it was a happy day. Or *I* was happy, perhaps I should say; I was aware of God's presence, somehow. And I don't know if everything would have been different if we hadn't organized that reunion . . . Well, it would, of course.'

Barbarotti waited in silence. It was Berglund's thoughts seeking direction, not his. The wrong question at this point could close the door rather than unlock it. Not that he had any clear perception of where that door might lead, but something was happening, that much was clear. He could feel that familiar little whirring sensation in his temples as clearly as anything.

'The fact is,' went on Berglund, unclasping his hands, 'the fact is, there's closure now. Worldly misery shall give way, as

Archbishop Wallin put it. I've nothing more to say to you, but I've enjoyed our little chats.'

'Me, too,' said Barbarotti. 'But I'm not sure you're making the right decision.'

'Decision?' queried Berglund.

'I have the distinct impression there are things you're not telling me. I could see it just now when you were looking down at your hands. I thought you might be praying.'

Rickard Berglund looked at him in surprise. 'No, I wasn't praying,' he said. 'But I have been talking to God a lot these past few days, it's true. Since she died, that is, this week. You have some sort of religious faith, too, I think you said. Or was that just a pose you thought you ought to adopt when you were talking to someone ordained into the priesthood?'

'No,' said Barbarotti, shaking his head. 'It wasn't just a pose. Don't underestimate me.'

'Sorry,' said Berglund.

'But is it just you talking to God, or do you let Him get a word in sometimes?'

Rickard Berglund's face broke into a smile. 'Good question,' he conceded. 'And unusual words to be coming from a representative of law and order, I dare say. But perhaps that's not the role you want to see yourself in?'

'One often ends up wearing several hats,' said Barbarotti. 'Well then?'

'Well then, what?'

'Where have your conversations with God led you? Assuming you let him speak, I mean.'

Berglund didn't answer.

'I assume someone who was a vicar for as long as you were

can distinguish between the voices,' ventured Barbarotti. 'Between your own and Our Lord's? And I find it hard to imagine that he told you to hold your tongue.'

But Rickard Berglund did just that. He said nothing. More seconds went marching by, their eyes met momentarily over the table, and Barbarotti finally made up his mind. The time for patience and postponement was past. He had always been a fan of the slow approach, but there were limits.

'As I see it,' he said, 'there are two alternatives. Either you tell me everything, here and now. With dignity. Or dignity will have to go out of the window. I shall be obliged to drag you off to the police station and put you in an interview room. I'm sorry, but I really can't see any other solution. There is no third way.'

I've blown it now, he thought. Glad I didn't start recording this, otherwise someone would have had to listen to this and hear me messing up.

Berglund cleared his throat. Barbarotti looked at him and found himself held there, pinioned. It was impossible to read anything in his eyes, other than a great sense of calm.

'I hope you'll choose the first alternative,' added Barbarotti. 'The here and now.'

Berglund raised his right hand in a gesture that seemed to lose itself halfway. He was left sitting there with his palm raised to the ceiling and his fingers spread out as if he was expecting to receive something from above. And perhaps that was precisely what happened.

'Very well, since you insist,' he said finally, putting his hand down. 'But I'll get us another cup of coffee first, all right?'

'Fine by me,' said Gunnar Barbarotti. 'And I'll just switch on my tape recorder.'

Blind chicken about to find a grain of corn, he thought. It was a recurring and rather irritating image, but he supposed it could be seen as a step in the right direction. The blindness was questionable. He had found quite a few grains of corn over the years.

'You started by asking me about that dinner party,' began Berglund. 'I didn't know anything then. I hadn't a clue what was going on. Not a clue. Only those involved did.'

Barbarotti nodded. He wondered what was meant by *those involved*, but kept his mouth shut.

'It took thirty-five years, in fact. Can you imagine it, almost thirty-five years before she told me? To think you can live so long and be so oblivious. And to think you can live a lie for so long. Though her torment was greater than mine, we have to remember that. If a man and a woman stay together for a lifetime, they achieve a kind of balance over time. It can be hard for outsiders to comprehend, but inside, you notice it's that way. You understand it.'

He paused and looked Barbarotti in the eye as if seeking some kind of confirmation. Barbarotti considered whether there was really any truth in a balance theory like that, found no answer and made do with nodding again.

'In a way, she was grateful to get ill,' Berglund went on. 'She took it as a well-deserved punishment. Our lives had been wasted, it was her fault and the cancer was her punishment . . . yes, that was roughly how she saw it. I have a slightly different picture of it, of course. But there's room for her picture within mine, if you see what I mean. It was only in the face of death that we became really close to each other, which is naturally not the way it's supposed to be, but that was how it went with us, and it's a kind of comfort, in spite of everything.'

'I think you'd better explain from the beginning,' said Barbarotti.

'Sorry,' said Rickard Berglund. 'I'm getting ahead of myself.'

'We've got all the time in the world,' said Barbarotti, checking that the tape was turning in his recorder.

Rickard Berglund collected his thoughts for a moment and seemed to be looking for the right way in. 'There was something demonic about him,' he said finally, leaning back in his seat. 'Yes, that's how I would put it. Demonic.'

'Who?' said Barbarotti.

'Germund Grooth,' said Berglund. 'It's Germund Grooth who is the crux of all this, but maybe I don't need to inform you of that.'

'On the contrary,' said Barbarotti. 'Please inform me.'

'Of course. Sorry.' Berglund coughed a couple of times into his closed fist and launched in. 'I never understood him and I really have been trying to, these past few years, more recently. I know Ekelöf writes in his poem that what is bedrock for you is also bedrock for other people, but that really didn't apply where Grooth was concerned. He is – was – an alien being, to put it simply.'

He sighed and lapsed into silence again. Barbarotti waited.

'Christ, it's awful being old and knowing your life has been totally screwed up,' observed Berglund, and now there was a touch of anger in his voice. It was also, Barbarotti couldn't help noticing, the first expletive he had allowed to pass his lips.

'You go on building and building,' he continued, 'bringing your damn twigs to life's nest, year in and year out, and you think you're learning something along the way . . . You think the balance is busy establishing itself. You so much want to imagine *that*, at least. Don't you?'

'We like to think the journey is taking us forward,' said Barbarotti.

'Quite right. Only in my case, it wasn't. I deserted my calling as a preacher of the Word, I didn't have any children and, throughout our entire marriage, my wife loved another man. One wonders what the point was, really.'

'She loved Germund Grooth?'

'Germund Grooth,' answered Berglund, running his hand over his mouth and chin. 'They had an affair that lasted twenty-five years. More than twenty-five. From the very day . . .'

His voice broke. He shook his head and took a deep, unsteady breath. Barbarotti wondered momentarily if he was about to witness a breakdown, but that didn't seem to be the case. Berglund needed frequent pauses before he moved on to what lay ahead, but he held it together.

'From the very day we moved in together . . . Imagine the melodrama. Germund was helping us shift the furniture and they had sex when I was called away for a couple of hours. I went to visit a friend who'd had an accident . . . he'd been admitted to the Akademiska hospital in Uppsala. While she was being unfaithful to me in our first home. October 1971.'

He checked himself, looked at his hands and let his shoulders droop.

'It went on way into the 1990s. Until she got cancer the first time, I think. Yes, that's right. She was . . . obsessed with him. She didn't want him, but she could never say no, he was . . . it's a strong word, but I think he was evil. Demonic, as I said. I've tried to understand him, his motivation and everything, but I just can't. I mean, he had other women as well, the entire time.'

'How did you know that?' asked Barbarotti, suppressing an impulse to touch the man opposite him. Where do impulses like that come from? he thought. He realized, too, that there must have been ten years between Anna Berglund and Marianne, and it was an insight that seemed about to open a route to wholly undesirable regions – *demonic?* – but Berglund's continuing narrative dispelled his private mist of misgivings.

'She told me,' Berglund was explaining. 'When the cancer came back, she told me everything. She wanted to kill herself as well, but I managed to stop her. She was grateful for that; she didn't see Grooth again after the millennium, not even once. These last years have been devoted to atonement. The remarkable thing is . . .'

'Yes?' said Barbarotti. 'The remarkable thing is . . .?'

Berglund gave a short, doubtful-sounding laugh. 'The remarkable thing is,' he said, 'that she came to hate him . . . Or maybe it isn't remarkable at all. The pendulum swung to the other extreme, you might say. Sometimes I found myself all but defending him. Reminding her that it takes two, but she found it hard to see that. He was the drug and she was the victim – that was how she used to describe it. But however you look at it, Germund Grooth destroyed our lives; of course he's *my* scapegoat, but for Anna he was even more so. Is it possible for any of this to make sense to an outsider?'

'Perhaps that's not the important thing,' said Barbarotti. 'I mean, reason and emotion don't always get on with each other. What was it that happened at Gåsaklinten in 1975 then?'

Rickard Berglund frowned for a moment, still apparently

pondering the comment about reason and emotion. Then he drank some coffee and straightened his back.

'My wife pushed Maria off the cliff,' he said.

Barbarotti let this sink in for a few moments. He checked the tape recorder was still running.

'Why?' he asked.

'Because she knew Germund would always put Maria before her,' said Berglund. 'Maria and Germund, it was almost as if they were of the same blood. That much had been made clear at the vicarage the evening before; he said it straight out to Anna, and that was when she made her mind up. She murdered Maria so she could have Germund, it was as simple as that.'

'Simple?'

'Yes. Things can be analysed this way and that, of course, but I don't think it makes a scrap of difference. It was precisely as simple as that.'

'I see,' said Barbarotti. 'And nobody suspected anything?'

'Nobody suspected a single thing,' asserted Berglund. 'Especially not Germund. Until a fortnight ago he still thought Maria slipped over the edge of Gåsaklinten on that outing. He thought it was a fatal accident. But Anna miscalculated. It didn't turn out the way she expected. Germund didn't want her, even though Maria was gone. Not properly, only as an illicit bit on the side for another twenty years. And she made do with that . . . She was obsessed, there's no other word for it.'

'And when,' asked Barbarotti, 'did you find this out?'

'Five years ago,' said Berglund. 'Five and a half, to be exact. When she got really ill. I hung up my cassock for good a couple of months later; the two are connected, but I can't cope with going into the exact details right now. It proved impossible for me to go on – you'll have to make do with that as an explanation. Do you understand what I mean when I say my life's screwed up?'

'I think so,' said Barbarotti. 'But just for the sake of clarity, I want you to tell me about Germund Grooth's death as well.'

'Gladly,' said Berglund, and Barbarotti could hear that he genuinely meant it. It would give him a bitter sort of satisfaction to describe how his wife's lover had ended his days.

And who could really begrudge him that? thought Barbarotti, pushing away the picture of Marianne and Germund Grooth that was trying to resurface in his mind. He stamped it down into oblivion before it had a chance to come into focus.

'You could say she drove me to it,' said Rickard Berglund. 'But that isn't really true.'

Barbarotti nodded.

'If she hadn't forced it to that point, I would have done it of my own volition. I certainly hope so. At any rate, she didn't want to die herself until she knew I'd got rid of him. Punished him, and that was all that kept her alive these last few weeks. Are you following?'

'I'm following,' said Barbarotti. 'And I'm not an idiot.'

'Good,' said Berglund. 'I've noticed that you're not an idiot. So, we devised the plan together, and we had such a feeling of togetherness while we were doing it. She was weak and in pain, but what we were doing had to . . . well, in a way it had to compensate for the entire failure of our marriage, of our lives. And I followed the plan. I got in the car and drove down to Lund in the middle of the night. I rang him from a mobile – a pay-as-you-go, like a proper criminal. It was early in the morning and I was standing outside his block of flats. I asked if I could come up; he was surprised, of course, but I said Anna was dying and it was important. He asked me to wait a couple of minutes, then he let me in, and naturally I could . . .'

'Yes?'

Rickard Berglund stood up. He went over to the bookshelves and pulled out a drawer. He took out various papers and files, standing with his back to Barbarotti, and when he turned round he had a heavy revolver in his hands. He held it between his two cupped hands as if it was something delicate and precious – the image of a communion chalice flashed into Barbarotti's mind – and carried it almost ceremoniously back to his armchair. He sat down and laid the gun in his lap. As far as Barbarotti could see, it was a Berenger – or possibly a Spanish Baluga. Resting on Berglund's knees, it looked as out of place as a Bible in an aquarium.

'Put that away,' said Barbarotti.

Berglund shook his head.

'I can't continue this conversation at gunpoint.'

'I'm not sure you have any choice,' said Berglund.

Gunnar Barbarotti thought about it for about five seconds. Then he nodded. He felt oddly grateful he wasn't armed himself. It would have altered the situation if he had had access to his police weapon. It would have forced him to act, in one way or the other. He didn't want to act, only to listen.

'I could have killed him straight away, of course,' said Berglund, continuing where he had left off. 'With this. But that wasn't the plan.'

Barbarotti folded his hands.

'And what was the plan, exactly?'

'But you already know that,' said Berglund. 'Get him back there and unite him with Maria. Close the circle. Anna was fond of saying that in those last days. 'We must close the circle, Rickard,' she would tell me. 'Trap the evil inside.'

He fell silent and ran his fingertips thoughtfully over the revolver.

'Go on,' said Barbarotti. 'I must say I'm a little surprised by that . . . object.'

'Me, too,' admitted Berglund. 'Vicars and firearms don't really go together, do they? Not even ex-vicars. I came across it a couple of years ago. I'm not sure why I appropriated it; it was just a strange impulse, and now I've put it to good use . . .'

'Came across it?'

'An estate inventory,' said Berglund. 'I was going through the estate of a deceased person; that's been my area of work at the funeral directors' these past few years, and I saw this in a box down in a basement storage area. Ammunition and everything, and I simply popped it into my briefcase; I didn't say anything to Linderholm, who was upstairs going through the actual flat . . . When I say I've put it to good use, I don't mean I've fired it, of course.'

'Oh?' said Barbarotti.

Berglund cleared his throat and prepared to continue his story. 'I had it in my coat pocket when Germund opened the door that morning, but he came with me voluntarily, as it happened. I got the impression he suspected what was coming, but perhaps it was my imagination. I asked him to drive the car and we didn't exchange many words. I told him Anna wanted to see him before she died, and that was enough. He could have made a big song and dance and objected that he didn't see why, but he refrained from that. He just shrugged his shoulders and came with me. He got into the driving seat and started the car. I climbed into the back, telling him I had to take a nap and it would be more comfortable there. He didn't want to talk; I recognized the old Germund from years before as we sped north on the E6. Quiet and self-sufficient, in a way. Defensive. He only asked once how she was, and I said she was in a bad way, and it could only be a question of days. We were just twenty kilometres or so from Kymlinge when I pulled this out.'

He nodded at the revolver and pulled up the corners of his mouth in a fleeting, crooked smile. 'He saw it in the rear-view mirror and all he did was give a little shake of his head. I don't know if he was even surprised. I told him to drive to Gåsaklinten and he nodded, said he couldn't remember the way. I gave him directions, and we got there and parked in the same place as thirty-five years ago. We got out of the car, first me and then him; I kept the gun trained on him and walked three metres behind him and, well, within fifteen or twenty minutes we were there. We were standing up there on the rock and had reached the end of the road. "What happened?" he asked. "Perhaps you could tell me how Maria died, before you kill me?" I asked him if Anna had never mentioned it during any of their assignations through the years . . . I knew she hadn't, of course, and he shook his head. So I told him. Told him Anna had killed her.'

Rickard Berglund paused and raised the revolver. He looked at it as if hoping to extract some kind of answer from it. Then he stuck out his lower lip and nodded to himself.

'And?' said Barbarotti.

Berglund gave a shrug. 'Hmm, how can I put it? I got the impression he had known about it, somehow, but perhaps I was just imagining that. I thought he blanched and . . . well, all the air went out of him and he kind of subsided. But all at once, with us finally up there and everything so close to consummation, it didn't seem important. It was as if all the world's emptiness and desolation were suckering onto me, taking me in their grip. Life and death were nothing more than two husks in eternity. It felt as if God had turned his back on us, which I hadn't expected Him to. I asked Germund if he would jump of his own accord or would prefer me to shoot him. Do you know what he did?'

'No,' said Barbarotti.

A shudder ran through Berglund. 'He . . . he looked straight at me and there was nothing to read in his eyes. No fear. No regret. No distress. Not a damn thing. It was only for a couple of seconds, then he turned round, stood right on the edge for a moment and then took a step forward. Straight out into the void, and all I heard was a faint, dull thud when he hit the ground. I felt something give way inside me and I thought I was going to throw up, but I pulled myself together somehow. I went back to the car and drove straight to the hospital. Anna was asleep and I had to wait an hour for her to wake up, and then I told her. That's . . . well, that's all there is to tell.'

'All there is to tell?'

'Yes.'

Barbarotti reflected and looked out of the window. It had started to rain and a tree branch was scraping against the window. The wind seemed to be coming in squally gusts. He shifted his gaze to the tape recorder, where the tape was still turning. Where Rickard Berglund's woeful testimony was secured and documented for as long as anyone wanted it. It felt utterly irrelevant.

'You didn't push him?' he still had to ask.

Berglund shook his head. Barbarotti indicated the tape recorder.

'No,' said Berglund. 'I didn't push him.'

'Did you threaten him with the pistol?'

'No. I didn't need to.'

'And if he hadn't jumped of his own volition, what would you have done?'

Berglund hesitated, for a heartbeat at most. 'I would have shot him. I preferred not having to, of course, but let there be no misunderstanding about this. I accept full responsibility for Germund Grooth's death. It's the most moral act of my entire life, so don't try to take it away from me. Do you understand?'

'I understand,' said Barbarotti. 'It's just that with a view to the impending . . .'

'There is no impending,' said Rickard Berglund. 'One more thing before we're done. We never had any children, Anna and I.'

'I know,' said Barbarotti. 'Would you like—'

'She had an abortion,' Berglund interrupted. 'In the spring of 1975. The same year, you see, but I didn't know about it until thirty years later. After that abortion, she never got pregnant again.'

He stopped talking and looked at Barbarotti across the table. His eyes wouldn't settle and one leg had started to shake. I have no control over this, thought Barbarotti. And neither has he.

'You mean . . .' he said. 'You mean it was his baby, Germund Grooth's, and he didn't want—'

He broke off. Berglund had raised his gun, with just one

585

hand this time; it suddenly looked entirely natural and Barbarotti noticed a note had started ringing in his head.

'Just the opposite,' said Rickard Berglund with immense weariness in his voice. 'It was my baby, and that was why she didn't want it. It's Tuesday today.'

In one unexpectedly swift movement he put the muzzle of the revolver in his right ear and pressed the trigger.

72

The sky was an impenetrable greyish white. A cold wind from the north-west was sweeping in over the open, ploughed fields, and the low stone wall running round Rödåkra churchyard afforded scant protection. Barbarotti was freezing cold and he felt relieved that Marianne had decided not to come. There was no reason for her to stand in a windy churchyard to accompany a former vicar to his last resting place.

No reason at all. It was enough for him and Backman to be there. A few others, too, of course: the current vicar and Linderholm; two elderly women who had worked with Berglund in the parish office for over twenty years; and a stooped little old man of sixty or so. Barbarotti had no idea who he was. He had shaken hands in the church, but Barbarotti hadn't caught his quietly mumbled name.

The ceremony was mercifully brief. The vicar, who was called Silvergren and had a limp, declared that the two people who had lived their lives together were now reunited. Death proved powerless to divide them for more than a few weeks. The rest had already been said in the church. Forever and ever, amen.

That was basically it. Barbarotti knew that the vicar knew that Rickard Berglund had shot himself in the head, and an apostate priest who had committed suicide was of course not worthy of many words. Perhaps the cathedral chapter had issued instructions to keep it short.

Linderholm and Silvergren nodded to the others and left the graveside. The parish-office ladies followed them; Barbarotti, Backman and the stooped gentleman were left standing there, the man a little apart from them and looking slightly unsure of his next move.

'So we've got two murderers lying here,' said Eva Backman with a shiver. 'As it happens.'

'As it happens,' echoed Barbarotti, 'although his contribution is a bit debatable. He didn't even touch his victim.'

'All amounts to the same thing,' said Backman. 'It feels as if it might start snowing.'

'Not impossible,' said Barbarotti. 'What are you thinking about?'

Backman shivered again. 'I'm thinking about everything,' she said. 'All those dead people. But most of all I'm thinking about Germund Grooth.'

'And to be more precise?' queried Barbarotti.

'To be more precise, those notes Ribbing came across in his storage area. The part about Grooth's parents.'

'It's playing on my mind, too,' said Barbarotti. 'To think it could all have started with that.'

'He claims he killed them,' said Backman. 'Do you believe him?'

Barbarotti thought for a moment.

'I don't know. How did he do it, if so? He doesn't explain a thing.'

'Maybe he's just lying?'

'Why should he lie?'

'No idea. But it does tally with what Marianne told me. My

sense is that there's some kind of underlying truth to it. But don't ask me how he did it. They drowned in a river, for goodness' sake. Trapped inside their car.'

'Tough to be left alone like that, though,' said Barbarotti. 'When you're only ten. And if he had some kind of hand in it, that would only make him feel worse, of course. Maybe it's not so odd that he turned out the way he did.'

'Not odd at all,' said Backman.

She thrust her hands into her coat pockets and hunched her shoulders against the cold. 'That Uppsala sextet,' she said, 'there aren't many of them left now.'

'Only the Wincklers,' concurred Barbarotti. 'They didn't come to the funeral. Neither hers, nor his. But perhaps that would have been expecting too much.'

'Shall we go?' suggested Eva Backman. 'It's time to draw a line under this now.'

'I suppose it is,' said Gunnar Barbarotti, but before they could move off, the stooped man approached them. He gave a nervous cough and raised his black hat.

'Excuse me. Would you have time for a quick word?'

Barbarotti looked at Backman and nodded.

'My name is Helge Markström. I knew Rickard once. We were on military service together. And yes, I met Anna, too . . .'

'It's a sad story,' said Barbarotti. 'Both of them dead now.'

'I heard that he shot himself,' said Helge Markström. Was it because . . .?'

Barbarotti glanced at Eva Backman again and decided not to answer.

'It's so long since I saw either of them. He couldn't carry on living without her, was that it?'

'I don't know if . . .' said Barbarotti.

'Yes,' said Backman. 'That was exactly it.'

Helge Markström nodded. 'I realize they were deeply devoted to each other. Rickard and I exchanged a few letters over the years. Not that many, but we wrote now and then. I was actually there when they met for the first time . . .'

A smile flitted across his face and vanished.

'She was on a march, a demonstration. It was in 1970. She missed her footing and fell sideways . . . straight into Rickard's arms. We were standing on the pavement and he caught her. And then they became a couple. I've always thought how lovely that was. The way fate intervened, I mean. I never got married, myself.'

He fell silent. Barbarotti felt something suddenly constricting inside him and he hoped Backman would find something sensible to say, but there was no comment from that quarter, either.

'Well, I'd better be getting on my way,' finished Helge Markström. 'Thank you for that little chat, I'm glad to know that Rickard had good friends, anyway.'

He shook their hands again, nodded goodbye and set off towards the parking area. Backman and Barbarotti stood there watching him until he had climbed into his car, a white Saab that looked at least twenty years old.

'Don't say anything,' said Eva Backman. 'I don't think I can take any more.'

Barbarotti gave a shiver and thought he felt pretty much the same way himself.

And he would make sure to have a serious conversation with Our Lord at the earliest opportunity.

*

Marianne was asleep. They were both lying on their side facing the same way and she was snuggled up against him. She felt as light as a feather in his arms.

And as heavy as a life. As heavy as a feather and as light as life. It was long past midnight and the first snowfall of the year was whirling outside the bedroom window. They hadn't made love, but nearly. It wasn't quite the right time yet.

Now was the time to hope and trust. The deaths out at Gåsaklinten had been filed away. The Grooth case had been *set aside*. It felt satisfying to reach the final full stop. Like when you got to the end of a book, say. Or the end of a life. Like Rickard Berglund.

Satisfying, but not always right. Whatever one meant by *right*?

My beloved is lying naked and feather-light in my arms, he thought. She's alive. She survived and all our children are alive as well. Here we all are, under the same roof in the first snow-storm of the year. All of us, Sara too. Safe and sound.

But I shall dream of the Berglunds. Anna and Rickard. Set aside or not.

I shall dream of Germund Grooth and Maria Winckler, too. Especially of her, whoever she was, the girl who sacrificed herself one night in a Romanian town and died in the bloom of her youth.

Set aside?

Yes, this and more would accompany him through the night, he was sure. Those words of Philip Larkin's, for example. *Most things may never happen: this one will.*

But that's the way it is, he thought, pressing himself still closer to Marianne. The winding path to the province of trust.

Epilogue, September 1958

He sat there at the kitchen table. The little box of pastilles nestled in the right-hand pocket of his cardigan. The decision lay in his head, still feeling like a warm ball. He was alone at the table.

But within a minute or two the others would be sitting here. Father and Mother and Vivianne. Mother was busy laying the table. Father's place was already set, and the two pills were sitting there on the plate beside his teacup. There was no time to spare. If it was going to happen, it had to be now.

He felt the excitement ticking in his temples. Making his arms and fingers tingle. Now, he thought, I've got to do it now.

The sun sent a few piercing morning rays between two slats of the blinds on the window facing the street. They stabbed at his eyes. It was like a summons – hurry up! He put his hand in his pocket and curled his index finger round the box. He checked his mother had her back turned and then! It was done in a second.

Swapped the pills for the pastilles. Father's were in the box, and there were two others on his plate. And no one in the world could tell the difference.

It was done. The easiest thing in the world. Vengeance is mine, he thought. That was the title of one of the cowboy-and-Indian books he had borrowed from Benke. *Vengeance is mine.*

★

They were setting off sometime that morning. When he got home from school, Auntie Hjordis would be there. Father and Mother and Vivianne would already be by the lake at Rödtjärn. They were staying for four days. Father would have something to work on, as usual; Mother and Vivianne would be with the dogs, go out in the boat, play board games in front of the fire with the cousins.

He would be at home with Auntie Hjordis. Vivianne was allowed to go with them because she was only little. She didn't have the responsibility of school. She was just a little kid, and that meant she was allowed to go with them to Rödtjärn.

Mother had sat on the side of his bed last night and told him. That was how it was going to be. He was ten and a half and he had school to think of. You couldn't just take three days off in the middle of term – that went without saying. He was a big boy now, nearly grown up. And they would be home on Sunday, maybe even on Saturday evening. It depended on the weather.

He hated Auntie Hjordis. He hated Father and Mother. He hated Vivianne, for only being a snotty-nosed brat who was allowed to go with them to Rödtjärn and didn't have the responsibility of school.

But vengeance was his. If Father noticed he'd swapped the pills, he was in for a thrashing. No doubt about it. But he didn't think Father would see any difference. He'd been thinking about this for a long time. At least six months. The pastille-shaped pills his father washed down with a swig of gooseberry cordial each morning looked exactly the same as the Ziggy sweets. If he chewed them, he would notice the difference, but Father never chewed his pills. He tossed them straight into his mouth and chased them with a big gulp of home-made cordial; it was the same every morning, and he needed them for some illness he suffered from. Some kind of dizziness.

It served them right if he was sick at Rödtjärn. Or if they didn't even get that far. He would never own up to having swapped the pills. He wouldn't tell a living soul, not even Benke.

And he would throw away the box of lozenges that had now been joined by Father's two pills. He would bury them under a rock in the forest, if the going got tricky. If his father was really ill or anything. And nobody would suspect a thing; a sort of giggle started inside him at the thought of it, but the giggle died away because now they were here. Father and Vivianne, and suddenly all four of them were sitting at the table. Father was joking about something Loony Holger had said or done, and Mother laughed. Vivianne poured too much milk on her cereal as usual, and then Father tossed his pills into his mouth and washed them down with a mouthful of gooseberry cordial.

He pulled a slight face, but then he generally did. The deed was done. A shiver ran down his backbone, and when Father asked if he was sorry not to be coming with them to Rödtjärn, all he said was that he had to think of school. You couldn't just miss three days in the middle of term.

And Father said that was how a real man talked, and all was sweetness and light in the sunny kitchen of the Holy Family.